INSANE

Hollie Thubron

*For my sister Becca, who has always been there for me
and supported me through everything*

PROLOGUE

Today was going to be a good day. I couldn't predict the future, but I knew that no matter what the wind blew my way, I could face it with my head held high.

Walking into the local café in this area of Southhurst, I made an effort to wear a beaming grin. I read somewhere that simply smiling releases hormones to make you happy. You could literally fake your way to being happy. And that was what I planned to do.

I asked Heidi for my regular and I took the steaming mug over to a corner table, sitting in the chair placed neatly under it.

Flicking through the Sunday paper, I soaked up all the happenings of Southhurst. I wanted to be involved in every aspect of the city. I was getting back on track again, it was time to be involved in my community.

I meant what I said – that today was going to be a good day. I really did. I meant it when I said that I was turning over a new leaf. That I would no longer be a hermit, isolated from society. I meant it.

But then I saw her. Sitting on the opposite side of the café, intently tapping away on her keyboard, the table she occupied covered in scraps of paper. It had been so long since I'd laid my eyes upon her. So long since I had been close enough to touch her. I couldn't even remember the last thing that I'd said to her. That time was such a blur.

Even though the years had come and gone and we had both changed with them, there wasn't a doubt in my mind that it was her.

I really did want to be a better person. I wanted to make a difference, do something good. Move on from her.

But as I sat there, unable to take my gaze off her, all the rage came flooding back.

CHAPTER 1 - AVERY

The blood smeared across my face somewhat ruins my makeup – I was going for a more *au natural* look today, but man, do I look good in red.

I stare at my elusive reflection in the one-way mirror of the interrogation room and I listen to the tedious tick of the clock that is undoubtedly broken as it has not been 12:32 for the full twenty-three minutes.

I wonder if they are on the other side of the glass right now. Watching me. Analysing me. Discussing how they are going to crack me.

Or maybe they're doing rock-paper-scissors to decide who has to talk to me because none of them want to listen to another whiny, pathetic girl and her sob story.

Eventually a large, rounded man with the shadow of a forgotten beard creeping across his face approaches the chair opposite me. *Those pigs really need to lay off the donuts.*

I examine him and his mannerism. He definitely went with rock. I shake my head. Everyone knows that rock is too obvious, you never go with rock.

I cringe as the detective drags the metal chair along the floor and it shricks in protest. He shuffles around in his seat for a good seventy-three seconds.

That's fine, I have nowhere to be. You take your time. Get yourself comfy. I think to myself as I roll my eyes.

He clasps his hands on the table in a very let's-get-to-business manner and stares me down for an entire forty-three seconds. I bet he thought I was going to break. He obviously doesn't know who he's dealing with. I don't break.

Instead, I maintain the doe-eyed gaze and quivering lower lip of a woman who has just experienced that traumatising event.

At last, the oaf actually speaks; "Miss, can you please tell me exactly what happened before we found you early this morning at half past two?"

I glance down at my hands and twiddle my thumbs. I want to drag out my pause for as long as possible. You know, to really build up the suspense.

The interrogation room is cold, standing the hairs on my arms up on end. It doesn't unsettle me, though. In fact, I feel at home in the hostile, hollow room.

I gulp down a deep breath.

Show time.

CHAPTER 2 - AVERY

5 months, 1 week, 6 days, 5 hours and 32 minutes earlier…

I scan my eyes across the eerie, chilled streets and I glance up at the morbid sky that set the scene for tonight's earlier event.

I click the door shut as I slide the old rucksack off my shoulder and kick off my tatty shoes – dropping them into a plastic bag. I look at my wrist – 4:15am.

"Not bad, well done me." I applaud my time efficiency and make my way into the living room.

I strip down to my delicately woven lace underwear, leaving all my clothes folded with the rubber gloves placed on the top in the hallway and I pluck up my comfy old trackies and hoody.

Newly clothed, I aim straight for the oak desk in the corner and settle myself in the chair behind it. The chair's leather cushioning moulds to my body shape, the soft leather clinging to my perfectly sculpted legs, as I relax into it.

Pulling the chain draped around my neck, I take hold of the small key at the end and unlock one of the drawers. There is only one item that resides in this drawer. As I slide it open, it catches on the rusted metal rollers. I pick out the little brown book, placing it in front of me.

Only the corner where I am located is lit by a small, cream side lamp to avoid suspicion because, let's be honest, who the hell is mad enough to be up at such a stupid time?

I breathe in the rich and addictive smell of the nappa leather and run my fingertips over the intricate handstitched design, feeling every curl and twist etched into its cover, before flattening the notebook out on the first page.

I stretch out my mouth and let out a shriek as I yawn. *The quicker I get this done, the quicker I can get some damn sleep.*

I close my eyes, take myself deep within my mind and recall everything. Every smell, every sight, every expression, every scream…

And I begin to write.

Poor little mermaid. She was sound asleep, dreaming about her prince. Her prince with another woman. The woman he chose over her.

Silly little mermaid. Thinking that she would have her happy ever after. Believing her prince really did love her. Dreaming that one day they would ride off into the sunset to the echo of wedding bells and the cheers of the whole kingdom. That they would share true love's kiss and have six children and she could tell them about their parents' inspiring love story. That everything she sacrificed paled in comparison to what she had now.

What an idiot.

The foul stench of her fuzzy flea bag came to settle in my throat and left my tongue scarred by the taste. I scrunched up my nose in disgust at the wretched thing resting there – completely ignorant of my unwelcomed presence. It was a rather pointless creature if it hadn't even woken up to me sliding through the window. Is that not the only reason to keep such a being?

It's safe to say that the little mermaid hadn't been the most fortunate of fish; looking at her…place of residence. The entire contents of the space were squished into a single area, with every room represented by a single corner. The place looked as though it hadn't seen a hoover since it was built and the amount of insects that had taken up residence were enough to create an entire ecosystem.

Thank goodness this was all only poorly illuminated by a tacky, sea blue night light which I could only imagine the little mermaid acquired from a hobo selling junk out the back of his car. I don't think my eyes would have survived seeing this carnage in full light. For the life of me I don't understand how anyone could allow themselves to reside in such a sad location.

But, then again, who am I to judge? After all, I only had to stand the place for another forty-six minutes. Then again, I suppose the same went for her.

She lay there with her silk auburn hair sprawled across her peaceful face. I could have almost pitied the girl being so unfortunate in her life choices that she ended up where she was now. Almost.

Perhaps it was due to my lack of bloody sleep; perhaps it was due to my wooziness from all the fumes in this godawful place, but I observed her for just a moment too long and before I had the chance to prepare myself properly, her 2:15am alarm sounded and the mutt's eyes sprang open. Directly aimed at me.

Within the next three seconds it began to snarl and this turned into a bark which quickly alerted the fish to my presence.

As I had suspected, the little mermaid abruptly sat up and pressed her back against the wall behind her, hiding behind the mongrel and hoping it would protect her. Fat chance.

It didn't take her long to go through the motions of acknowledging my presence, realising I was not on a friendly visit and for the adrenaline to start pumping through her body. This was the fun part, when the warrior gene was enacted. I always made bets; were they fight or flight? She stuttered with the beginnings of questions, only managing one or two words before freezing.

Her incessant whining pierced my eardrums, I just couldn't listen to it anymore, so I briefly explained to her why I was there.

She acted completely oblivious. As if she was sweet and innocent. But I knew better.

I drew my attention back to the snarling pest. It hadn't moved from the bed and was trembling even more than the fish. Some guard dog. I kneeled down, unzipped my bag and plucked out my pointed-tip friend. I approached the animal and swiftly injected the fluid into the scruff of the beast's neck before it had the time to realise I was near and then it slumped back onto the bed and laid as it had just a few minutes before.

Oh it was such a disgusting specimen, I was so glad to no longer have its filthily suffocating breath on me.

The little mermaid looked horrified and immediately leant forward to cradle the animal, staring at me and fearing the worst. I have to say, I was taken back by her calm and composed reactions, I had her pegged for a more skittish fish.

I put her mind at ease by assuring her that I had merely injected a sedative so that the rodent (a dog is a rodent, right?) would not cause an obstruction.

Immediately after this, I slid the needle of the other syringe I had been concealing into her neck, the fluid coursed through her veins and her eyes rolled back into her head.

I leant forward, trying to adjust my position on the knock-off coffee table so that I didn't get a numb arse. I played with the sharp metal in my hand and dragged the shrieking edge along the surface – engraving a figure as it went.

Amidst my moaning and shuffling, the little mermaid came to. It took her four seconds, though still nauseous, to gather her memories from before she entered the dark.

When she had, she began pulling at her limbs, willing them to come together and obey her commands – but they were no longer under her control. She eventually stopped when her right wrist began to bleed from the cutting edge of the hard plastic restraints.

Heavily breathing and heart racing, she stared at me. She started to become progressively more demanding, asking me questions like she was in control. Clearly she hadn't properly gauged the situation.

She wasn't the shiniest pearl of the oyster, so I decided I would cut her a bit of slack. After all, this must have been a pretty stressful time for her.

I decide to take a quick sabbatical from my entry. I sit there for a moment trying to put my finger on what I am feeling whilst writing all this down. Then it comes to me.

I am so frikkin' hungry. I haven't eaten since ten past eight last night, how did I completely forget to eat? That wasn't like me at all. I shuffle over to my kitchen and swing the fridge door open. I grab the milk, boil the kettle and make myself a good old English cuppa tea – white, no sugar, of course. I then select an apple and walk back to the desk.

Before reaching the desk, I dart right and crouch down in front of the fire with lighter in hand. After poking at the pulsing golden coals for two minutes, the flames hurl towards my face and I make an escape back to the safety of my chair.

I take my first sip and the steaming liquid warms my throat as it flows past my trachea. My first bite counteracts the heat and returns my mouth to its core temperature. I hum in pleasure before getting back to business.

I laid it out for her. I told her that I was there because I was going to make her understand the pain she had caused herself. The stupid fish had everything. Her father ruled the ocean and she was heir to his empire. She had friends, she had fame, she had a family. And now? Now, she had nothing. All because she wanted to be human. All because she loved her silly little Prince Eric.

As I approached her, I saw the water beads trail down her cheek and her beautiful fiery locks fall flat from the moisture radiating from her pores.

I played with my shining companion, dancing the tip across my fingers. A waltz we'd danced so many times before. I stroked away the stray hairs from her face with the chilling touch of the metal.

I grinned inside at the fear that was blazing in her eyes. The fear of the unknown, the fear of the pain, the fear of me.

The little mermaid sacrificed so much when she left the sea. She made a deal with the witch and was made to walk on knives with every step. She did this to herself. I only made her feel it.

Now this is the part when she really irritated me. I clarified with the little fish beforehand that she was not to scream and she told me she understood. But what did she do? Scream.

I can't tolerate foolish people. I just don't have the patience.

But anyway, she evidently didn't have a clear mind, so I gave up on expecting her to withhold her scream and shoved a pair of moist, mud-soaked socks in her mouth instead.

As I continued, the beautifully sweet and metallic fragrance reached my nostrils and I revelled in the reminder of all my past endeavours, but the stale malodour of the little mermaid's flat returned me to the task at hand. I had been in her jail cell for thirty-two minutes; surely I should have been used to the smell by then?

No matter, the little mermaid grew frail so very quickly, I didn't have to bear my surroundings for too much longer. I was unimpressed by her lack of strength; I thought she was a more determined little fish.

Once I felt that she better understood the pain she had put herself through, I used the gag from her mouth to wipe the tears and sweat from her face, preparing her for the pain I was about to put her through.

A small shimmer of relief hid inside her eyes. Poor little mermaid, she thought I was finished?

I'd barely begun.

CHAPTER 3 - HARRY

Half four. Have to be up in three hours. Fucking great. Harry lies staring into the cracks of his ceiling, counting them as if they are sheep to no avail.

His body is not willing to sleep. He groans lightly, sits up and plants his feet on the cold wooden floor. Cupping his face in his hands, he strokes the bristles on his cheeks and neck before throwing himself up and stumbling down to the kitchen.

He tries to stop his body from shivering by throwing his arms around himself in a pathetic attempt at comfort.

We've got to fix the bloody heating in this hell-hole, he complains to the draught brushing through his leg hairs, knowing that the chances of this being accomplished are slim.

"Lighter…lighter…" he mumbles to himself as he snatches the pack from the counter. Harry rustles through all the drawers and pats down the kitchen sides in an urgent attempt.

Why is there no fucking lighter anywhere? he grumbles, but he quickly gives up his search and bends down over the cooker with the fag in his mouth as the gas fills his nostrils and the embers blaze.

Stepping outside into their overgrown garden, Harry breathes in the musky chemicals that his lungs want to resist, but eventually give in to and he closes his eyes as he enjoys the gratifying feeling. Although his hands will not remain steady, he sighs in satisfaction. A small part of his emptiness has been filled.

Harry wants to think. He wants to feel. He wants a sense of pleasure that lasts longer than the life of a cigarette. He stares at the vacant, black sky. If you were to see him, you'd assume he is deep in thought, worlds away. But his mind is blank and all he feels is the crisp wintry air of March hitting his unprepared skin.

When the wind slams the door shut behind him making his way back inside, he winces and hesitates, listening to see if the echoing has woken Martha. Thinking the coast is clear, he begins making his way across the kitchen and through the hall.

Harry's toe suddenly catches behind him, taking him off balance. His head plummets and suddenly his vision is at an angle and his cheek is flattened by the stone cold tiles. Everything fades to black.

A ringing thrashing through his head brings him back to consciousness and he sways, uneasy, as he tries to hoist himself into a seated position.

His vision will not focus and the furniture is dancing around the room. With the urgent need to vomit, Harry determines that he perhaps isn't as sober as he thought.

Cradling his head, Harry scans for what caught him and there on the floor, the corner of the rug curls upwards, proud of its trickery. Some of Martha's ornaments have fallen off the mantelpiece. *Not broken, thank God.* And a picture frame lies cracked in front of him.

Harry stares, emotionless, at the beaming couple clinging onto each other with the sun burning their cheeks and their golden beagle pulling them along the pier.

At first, it is as if he hardly recognised his parents, but gradually the corners of his mouth twitch as he becomes a child again and is taken back to that afternoon.

Dad had just got a promotion at work, so we went to Brighton for a day by the sea. I was only nine and had only been to the beach a couple times that I could remember. I was so excited to splash across the seashore and make sandcastles and play fetch with Lucy.

The sun was shedding golden dust, the sky was as clear as the sea. Both Mum and Dad's faces were lit up with elation; they spoilt me all day. They bought me ice creams and toys and an "I Heart Brighton" fridge magnet. We went on the Ferris wheel, to the museum, to the park…

We bought a disposable camera and Mum let me take photos of everything. We were so happy.

Little Lucy was going crazy. It was the first time she'd ever seen the sea and she wouldn't stop jumping around in it, splashing her paws into the waves and lapping up the white horses as they came charging into shore. Every time she came out, she ran up to us and jumped on me because I was small and covered me in sand, water and smelly bits of seaweed.

As the sun began to lower in the sky, we walked back along the pier and headed home. Lucy and I were so tired that we slept the entire journey home.

Poor Lucy. At least she had a fun last day.

Harry is jolted back into the present by Martha bellowing down to him. Once he regains his bearings, he dabs the tear from his eye with the knuckle of his thumb.

"I'll be up in a couple of minutes, babe," Harry replies as he grabs the picture frame, placing it on the mantelpiece and shoving the memory to the back of his mind again.

He hastens into the kitchen and fills up a glass half-empty. Tiptoeing back upstairs, Harry punches the landing light switch and crawls back into bed.

"What were you doing?" Martha slurs her words, half-asleep.

He plants a soft kiss on her forehead and replies, "was just getting some water, go back to sleep." Martha has already settled back to sleep, a wave of calm washing over her face.

Harry strokes the hair from Martha's face and looks down upon her. He wills himself to feel. He wills himself to see her and get a sparkle in his eye. To see her as his whole world and all he needs and will ever need.

No such luck. Harry's stomach sinks and he sighs with the discovery. Perhaps he has felt too much too soon. Perhaps he has become numb to love.

He pictures her. He fixates on her. He examines every curve of her body, every crease in her smile, every line on her hands. With her image in his mind, Harry finally finds peace in his subconscious.

CHAPTER 4 - AVERY

She stopped screaming once she had taken her vow of silence.

I think she understood then why I was there. She no longer denied her transgressions; instead she accepted her fate.

I could see it in her eyes as the memories of her mistakes flashed past. She should have never left the ocean. She should have never sacrificed her tail. She should have never fallen in love. There were always consequences of decisions made in love.

I grew tired and she grew faint. The little fish had already put herself through enough; there was no need to drag this out. She'd felt the pain and I'd had my fun. It was time for our discussion to come to an end.

She was barely conscious and her little fish heart was beating so dimly that she was unaware of what was happening.

I went into my bag and hoisted out the tub of clear liquid.

I prodded her pet with the tips of my toes so that it was further away from the bed on which the little mermaid lay so lightly. Regardless of my disgust for the slobbering animal, it was nothing to do with this tale, so I saw no reason that it should suffer because of its owner's poor decisions.

I then stood 0.85 metres from the bed myself and pulled the plastic goggles down, covering the middle of my face. I gave my eyes over to her with one last glance.

Her once radiant auburn hair was now dampened by sweat and dulled by a darker shade of red. Her face, as soft as silk, was now sticky from the salted water that ran down from her eyes and nose. Her mouth that just a moment ago smiled with hopeful dreams of love and happiness, now hung low and only showed the slightest expression through its turned down corners. What was once such a beautiful creature was now a worn out ragdoll.

I sighed and shook my head as I brought my gaze away from her and unscrewed the cap before watching the liquid fall out.

I shook the last few drops from the container and then I shoved it back in my bag. Before sliding back out of the window through which I had entered, I finished off my routines and had one final scan around the flat to make certain I had not left anything unattended to.

As I pulled the glass shut behind me, I blew a kiss to the little mermaid and grinned at my work.

I exhale heavily, calming my heart rate after reliving tonight's events. As much as I enjoy the rush of recalling them, I always forget that this part takes a fair amount of time and that I can't just come home and curl up in my warm, cosy duvet and satin sheets. I guess everything has its drawbacks.

I skim read my words a few times over so as to imprint them on my brain and so that I will never forget a single detail. Then I grab the lot in one hand and rip them out at the seam.

I tear them in half and pace over to the fireplace, sitting cross-legged in front of the burning heat.

One by one, I drop the sheets into the flames and watch as they turn black and disappear into nothing. Just like the little fish.

Once I have seen the last of my words dissolve, I rearrange the logs on the fire so that the blaze will begin to die out.

CHAPTER 5 - AVERY

There is something different about waking up this morning. I wake up with a swirl of adrenaline coursing through me that makes my stomach tickle. I wake up with a beaming smile on my face.

For a moment, I forget why. Then I remember the happenings of last night (or this morning rather) and my smile extends to my ears. It had been so long, I had forgotten the thrill of it all.

I leap out of bed in a manner that most people would deem inappropriate for 6.27am on a Monday.

I'm ready and downstairs in just thirty-two minutes. I think that's a record.

Today I feel daring, so I put on my silk white blouse with a slight plunging neckline, which clings to my carefully crafted body and a tight black leather skirt, cutting off right on my knees.

My Louboutin heels click and clack on the kitchen tiles as I hasten around the room making my morning coffee and fixing myself something to eat.

As I swallow my last mouthful of granola, my alarm clock sounds telling me it's time to get the hell to work.

I snatch up my bag and jacket before heading out to face the day.

The sky is as clear as the Caribbean Sea, with only a few swollen clouds splashing the ground with spots of shade. Before you step outside, you can almost believe that you are in the height of summer. Yet, the cold winter breeze hits me, exploding over my entire body, covering me in goose bumps and the sharp air suffocating me with every breath.

Oh I completely forgot to introduce myself.

My name is Avery Blake. I will be the hero for the next 300 pages. Well, in *my* opinion I will be anyway. After all, this is *my* story.

Let me tell you a little bit about myself. Let's see… I'm thirty-one years old, I haven't found any grey hairs…*yet*. I'm starting to get wrinkles but they are only faint and I am using every anti-wrinkle product I can get my hands on so they won't be there for very long.

I have thick, luscious, deep chocolate brown hair that any woman would kill for. All natural of course - I would never murder my gorgeous locks by using those chemicals.

I'm a Leo, but I most certainly don't believe in any of that horoscope crap.

High school was a waste of time; I was far more intelligent than any of those state teachers. I got straight A's of course and a first in my master's degree.

My primary occupation is as a pharmaceutical rep. I have to say I do love the sales and I definitely love the cash… but it doesn't send adrenaline shooting through my body and make me bounce up and down like a kid in a sweet shop whose parents fed them way too much sugar.

No, the things that really get me going include painting, volunteer work, killing, tap dancing and golfing.

Yes you read that correctly. Like how I slipped that in there? Okay, if I'm being completely honest, I hate painting…and golfing…and tap dancing… and I mean I wouldn't say my volunteering record is of an extremely impressive length…so I guess it's just the one then.

Before you go and get all judgemental and shut off your tiny little minds to anything I have to say because *killing is so awful* and *killing is so wrong,* just turn your noses back down for a minute.

I'm sure you're thinking right now that I can redeem myself in your eyes by selling you with a sob story about how *daddy was mean to mummy and I was raised by wolves so I don't know any better.* Blah, blah, blah.

Well, I'm sorry to disappoint, but that is not what happened in my case. Between you and me, I think anyone who tells you that little tale to 'justify' what they do is simply spinning you lies.

I was raised by two, happily married parents and we had a wonderful little, perfectly picturesque life. It was all rainbows and butterflies and we even baked flippin' cupcakes.

I hate to burst your naïve, ignorant bubble but I can say nothing in 'defence' of my passion except for it feels good. I enjoy doing it. And why should I feel bad about something I get pleasure out of? Just because you can't understand it doesn't mean your right is right and my right is wrong. Who gets to decide these social norms, anyway?

Now that you know my little secret, I suppose what happened last night with the Little Mermaid makes more sense to you. Once again, before you get all judgemental, if you ever took the time to read the original *Little Mermaid*, the poor fish is supposed to turn back into sea foam because her Prince married another. So, I was merely finishing off her tale. Is that so wrong?

Please don't try to psychoanalyse me. I am actually a functioning member of society (I know I can hardly believe it either). I have friends, I have a stable – and very well-paying – job, and as difficult as it may be to comprehend, I do, in fact, have the capability to feel.

But anyway, I'm bored with talking about this so I'm going to get back to telling you wonderful strangers my story.

CHAPTER 6 - HARRY

There isn't a fibre in Harry's body that wants to get out of bed today. He would love nothing more than to stay in bed cuddling a bottle of whisky in one hand and a pack of fags in the other, watching mind-numbing TV and laughing at reality shows where he feels like their lives might actually be more pathetic than his.

But Harry can't do that. He has to go to work. He has to stand his simple colleagues for a further eight agonizing hours, because today might actually be the day that he takes them down. Today might be the day he has been waiting for, for fifteen years.

After all, that's the reason Harry went into the police force in the first place.

Harry hears Martha switch the shower off. He waits until he thinks she has finished drying herself down and is about to come out of the bathroom before he shoots up from the bed and opens the door for her.

Martha, startled by his abrupt appearance in the doorway, jumps back slightly and lets out a soft gasp.

"Good morning, darling," she greets him with a warm smile and a peach glow in her cheeks from the humidity of the small room.

Harry pecks her on the cheek and hurries a response; "morning, babe. I've just got to jump in the shower quick otherwise I'll be late to the station."

"Okay, well I'll be gone by the time you're out then so…I suppose I'll see you when you get back tonight?" Martha asks with a hopeful sparkle in her eye, although the delight in her tone has dulled as she was hoping to spend time with Harry this morning. At least for a short while.

But that's exactly what Harry wants to avoid. He wants to avoid having to play the part of *the perfect husband* for any longer than he has to.

It isn't like Harry is a monster. Of course he *cares* for Martha and wants to spend time with his wife, but he wants to avoid Martha's prying questions. Martha always believes she is helping and being supportive by talking to him about what happened. She is so empathetic, it's as if she experienced it with him.

She didn't, though. She can never fully understand what happened.

"Of course," Harry reassures her, "but I'll be a bit late tonight. I've got some things to take care of at the station." When he sees her expression drop again, he adds, "I won't be that much later. And I promise, this will be the last time I am late this week."

Pushing her shoulder against his as she paces past him, she sighs, "That's what you said yesterday *and* last week."

Harry knows he should go after her and make a few more false promises to reassure her that he's trying and yet he shrugs it off and slides across the floor tiles into the shower.

The station's appearance would make you think it was designed in the 1800s, without a single modification. The only feature that seems as though it is from the 21st century is the one glass window in the top right-hand corner that allows just the smallest amount of natural light to shine through it. All the other windows are made of thick, clouded glass which have become completely immersed in mould, ensuring no sunlight would even attempt to pass through. The frames are broad and painted a common white which is peeling off on every edge.

The dulled red bricks can barely hold the place up, every corner is chipped and the cement would surely crumble if there was the slightest change to the pressure it frailly supports.

As you walk towards it, the building looks like some kind of slaughterhouse or some old, broken down hotel that is undoubtedly haunted and that no one in their right mind would ever want to enter. Despite this, the building is supposed to be a place of refuge and safety.

Harry stops and stares at the station for a moment to gather enough energy to go in and start the day with his…*lovely* colleagues.

Grant is the first to catch sight of him.

"Hey, hey, hey, look who it is!" Grant marches up to him, "it's the little rugrat." He stares at Harry and pouts, "why so glum? Did Mum pour too much milk on your cereal and it went all soggy?" His mocking tone makes Harry's skin itch, but he shrugs it off and laughs at Grant's 'funny joke'.

"Little rugrat."

"Hey, rugrat."

"Whatsup, lil' ruggy?"

As Harry walks through the station more and more of his colleagues chime in. They all wink, click and smirk as he passes.

Harry smiles back and brushes it off. He thinks to himself that one day they'll accept him.

He reaches the locker room and finally he sees a friendly face and calls, "What's up, man?"

Walking over to the locker where Harry's standing, James returns the greeting.

James was out of the station all of yesterday, so they catch up on each other's current events. Harry asks James about his kids and James tells him all about the weekend from hell, where the kids wouldn't stop tantruming and his wife was being all uptight with him because he hadn't washed the dishes on Friday night and it was his turn. James asks Harry about Martha and how she's doing and he replies with *well you know, just the same old Martha*.

"Oh, mate, did you watch that Knicks-Lakers game yesterday? That was a great game."

Harry is quick to respond, "ah yeah, of course I did! I watched it live actually, man, that was intense."

Puzzled, James hesitates; "it was on at one in the morning. What were you doing up so early?"

Harry's heart skips and he moans, "Oh Martha is obsessed with one of the shows out there – *America's Got Talent* is it? She made me stay up with her so she wouldn't fall asleep, and I couldn't stomach that crap so I watched the game instead."

They share a long, awkward stare before James shrugs and complains, "Wives, 'eh? Got to keep 'em happy."

Just as they are finishing the 'weekend' talk, another detective walks past, scruffs up Harry's hair and yells *Rugrat!*

"You've only been in the CID for nine months. They'll stop treating you like a kid eventually," James assures him.

Harry chuckles a sigh in response as if to agree, although they both know that that isn't going to be happening anytime soon.

"We've got a briefing now and a new crime scene from the Grimm Reaper."

The two start walking towards the meeting room. A sharp jolt shoots through Harry's body.

"Really? How do we know it's them?"

James shrugs, "well we don't exactly. I guess that's what we're going to be told now."

"But," he continues, "From what I read in the notes when I snagged a quick peek earlier, it fits his MO. Not many others out there who do it like him."

CHAPTER 7 - HARRY

"Take your bloody time, why don't you," the Chief complains as the squad pile into the briefing. He starts speaking in spite of people still strolling down the hallway.

Clearing his throat, the Chief calls, "Grant and White—" he pauses to ensure he has their attention, "you take the stabbing victims. Seems like a bar fight gone too far but the superintendent thinks it's got something to do with this drug case so I want you two down at the ICU taking statements and seeing if and how they link in.

"Marks, Foster and Baker, you're going to be on the rape case from last week. Catch up with Grant before he heads off to see where we're at with that.

"We've got a murder victim on South Street in one of the apartment blocks. From what the local PD described it's looking like another GR case so I want you two," Chief points at where Harry and James are standing, "down there in twenty."

"Everyone else carry on with your daily duties." He glances down and moves pieces of paper around as an indication that the briefing is over and everyone should leave now.

Harry walks out with James and nudges his shoulder. "You can drive."

When they arrive at the crime scene it is difficult to determine what smells worse; the Jane Doe or the apartment itself.

The place looks forgotten. There isn't a spot of floor that isn't covered in clothes, food or mould. The robust fragrance of an uncleaned dog floats around in the air and makes it too thick to breathe. The kitchen corner is barely distinguishable, with both dirty dishes and soaking pieces of clothing thrown in the sink.

The crisp aroma of death radiates through the surroundings, so strong it would stand the hairs upright on your arms and send spiders scuttling up your spine. The atmosphere is hard and cold like slabs in a mortuary, and the mangy green walls are smeared with sticky, scarlet blood smeared in the form of words.

You can practically see the waves of odour emanating from the body. The scent comes to rest in Harry's mouth and removes all the moisture from it, leaving his tongue like cotton wool. Still, the Jane Doe only just overpowers the other pungent stenches of the flat – well, what's left of her.

Suddenly, Harry is taken away from the scene entirely.

The lady sitting across from me has a warm face. It's comforting. I suppose that's why she chose this profession.

She sees the nerves surfacing in my eyes and reassures me, "it's going to be okay. I know it hurts now, but you'll get through this. I'm going to help you get through this."

"Mate." James jolts Harry back to the present and directs him to the police constables who had taken the call, so they could get filled in on the scene.

"Morning, gentlemen," Harry greets them. "What's the situation here, then?"

The less timid of the two replies, "we got a call about a noise complaint from the neighbour upstairs. He's called the council several times over the past month about a dog howling, so they handed it over to us. We came here expecting to have a short, easy discussion with the owner of the dog," the PC pauses and gestures to their surroundings, "but we came here to find this."

Both detectives nod and James announces, "We can take it from here."

The forensic team have gotten there before them and are swiping for prints and any possible remnants of DNA. Harry knows that they won't find any, though. He has seen this crime scene time and time again and they never do.

"Bad luck, DC," one of the forensic team directs at Harry, "no prints, no hairs, no skin cells. Nothing." The man adds, "If there ever was any, they made damn sure that we wouldn't find it."

The man speaking to Harry holds himself in a manner that makes it clear he is very sure of himself. There is no way this forensic scientist is missing a single detail. He has black, slicked back hair and a completely clean-shaven face, indicating his organisational and hygienic traits. Although, this is barely visible beneath the all-in-one protective suit he is wearing. Regardless of the eyesore, every time the man makes the slightest movement, the papery fabric makes a high-pitched scratching sound, making the suit rather distracting and irritating.

"That's alright," Harry responds. He already knows who did it. He's always known who did it. "Any chance of an ID on the Jane Doe?"

The man shakes his head firmly and without any hesitation says, "not any time soon. In the state she's in, we'll have to use dental records. There's no way someone is ID-ing *that* face."

Harry walks over to the body and studies her.

He determines from the way she is positioned that her hands and feet were bound to the bed posts with cable ties which are still fully intact.

There's visible muscle damage on her feet and there are slight indents on the bones. Harry knows this would suggest multiple knife wounds.

Harry crouches down and examines the wooden board at the end of the bed where there is further writing; *'every step you take it will feel as if you were treading upon sharp knives'*

He captures the writing with his camera and continues to document the scene. No matter how many times he witnesses their work, it never gets any easier. He's always taken back to that night.

Jane Doe's expression hangs low and the remnants of sheets she rests on are now a muddy red. Harry scans her upper body to identify what the source of the blood could have been. After he reads the characters above the headboard, he realises which feature is missing.

'then she cut off the mermaid's tongue, so that she became dumb, and would never again speak or sing'

"This is definitely him," James murmurs over Harry's shoulder.

"Well, we can't officially say that. We've got to look into any other potentials first, but yes," Harry agrees, "we've got the blood writings mimetic of the state of the victim. Not a trace of fingerprints or DNA. I haven't seen the marking yet—"

"No, we've got that too," James interrupts, "that's over here on the table. Carved with a knife from Jane Doe's drawer. The knife was dumped over on the side covered in blood which we'll need to check but I'm guessing it's Jane Doe's, so that must be the one he used."

"Of course. They'd never use their own weapons."

On the dark wooden table is a figure scratched into the surface, with the etchings curved, meeting at a point and then parting ways again, representing a fish.

Once Harry has recorded the marking, he points to one of the walls. "Well, at least we know why they decided to end it how they did."

On this particular wall, the blood is painted to form the words: *'you will become foam on the crest of the waves'*

Reading it, James scrunches up his nose in disgust. "God, this guy is sick, isn't he?"

Harry doesn't reply. He doesn't have to.

"Well, none of these other quotes are making sense right now, so why don't we head back to the station, wait for an ID and start piecing it together?" James suggests.

They agree and just as they are about to leave, the constable that they spoke to earlier rushes after them.

"Detective Constable!" he calls.

"The woman has—" he corrects himself, "—had a dog. Since we don't know who she is or who her relatives are…"

"Well, why not give it to a neighbour? Or dog's rescue?" Harry queries, his face puzzled.

The PC hesitates. "We tried that. The couple downstairs is out of town and the neighbour upstairs is the one who called us about it barking in the first place. We could give it to a rescue service, but when we called them to enquire, they told us there would be a twenty-four-hour period before the dog would be euthanized."

Harry and James stare at each other. No words are needed to know what they are communicating.

I've got two kids who cry all day and a wife who never stops moaning. I cannot have a dog.

Well I can't have it. Martha would kill me, and besides she's allergic to the hair.

Why doesn't it just go to a rescue shelter then?

What if the relatives want it? We can't buy a replacement dog.

They stare at each other for a while longer before James cracks.

He lets out a groan and sighs. "Fine. I'll take it until we get an ID on her and give it to a relative."

The constable smiles thinly and speeds off in the other direction, clearly very pleased he didn't end up with it.

A few moments later he returns, holding tightly onto a torn up, crimson lead with a sturdy, fiery red bloodhound attached to the other end of it.

The dog seems timid and walks with his head low, but when he sees James smile gingerly at him, he slowly starts to whip his coarse tail.

James puts on a more high-pitched voice and raises his eyebrows as he addresses him. "Okay, little pup, I guess you're coming to stay with me for a while."

"I don't think you can call that animal little, mate," Harry mumbles, failing to hold back his amusement. "This will be a good laugh for the guys back at the station."

James shoves him lightly.

"Aw come on. It'll give the kids something to play with."

Rolling his eyes, James says, "Maybe, but I can tell you one thing's for sure; I'm gonna be the one in the dog house tonight."

CHAPTER 8 - AVERY

"Look, Chris…can I call you Chris?" I don't wait for his approval. "You and I both know that you're going to keep acting uncertain and doubtful and I'm going to keep telling you how much more amazing Invega's antipsychotics are than Stemetil's.

"Then I'm going to read you all the benefits of Invega which you know since you have already researched it yourself because you would never trust a rep to speak the absolute truth. Thus, you have already made up your mind on whether you are going to purchase these and you are merely sending me on a wild goose chase.

"Of course, I am completely aware of this. Yet I will play along and I'll tell you how Stemetil's meds have worse side effects and that they are less effective and that you should really be looking to become more modern and try new drugs to give to your patients if you want to evolve along with the rest of the world.

"And you'll inquire about the price and I know you'll be wanting to haggle so initially I'll quote you a price a whole lot higher than it actually is, you'll say that there is absolutely no way you can pay that, so I'll drop the price right down to just above the actual retail value and you'll think you've won because you've got *such a bargain,* so you definitely won't pass up the deal.

"Then I'll be on my merry way with my hefty commission and you'll be on yours with your new drugs."

The doctor sitting opposite gawks at me, speechless and still processing my proposal.

"Trouble is," I persist, "this whole scene will take up a good thirty-two to thirty-seven minutes of both your time and mine and I'm sure that your time is highly precious. So, why don't we skip all of that nonsense and just strike a deal and go our separate ways?"

Once I have finally finished my speech, the room echoes silence. The air is so stiff and uncomfortable I can practically hear the fan flying above me, cooling the tension in the room.

The doctor avoids eye contact with me and fiddles with his heavy silver pen, clicking the top on and off.

After I have aged three years, he opens his mouth to form a sentence. "So, tell me, Miss Blake," he begins, "in what quantities will you be selling these?"

The corners of my mouth twitch slightly, but I withhold my smirk.

Fish meet bait.

"Thank you for meeting with me."

"My pleasure, Miss Blake. I expect I will be seeing you soon."

We shake hands to seal the deal and he holds the door open for me.

As I approach my car I sigh in relief, knowing that he was the last one of the day. Now I can go home and relax.

I know that my sales approach may be a little…abrasive, but I have been playing this game for a long time now and I've tried every trick in the book. Truth be told, a decent dose of upfront honesty is the most effective way of getting a sale in my experience. Of course, it isn't successful a hundred per cent of the time, but really, what is? If that doesn't get them hooked, a healthy bribe or blackmail will work just fine.

You may be wondering why I don't incorporate the drugs I sell into my extra-curricular activity. Well, in my opinion it is a cop out. It makes it too easy and takes the excitement out of the whole process. It also creates a link between us that there absolutely cannot be.

My most important rule is to never have the slightest connection to the victim.

It has been eight days now since my meeting with the Little Mermaid, and they are no closer to identifying the fish.

After I have visited a victim, I tend to move on rather quickly to marking the next, but I still keep tabs on the previous. Just to ensure everything plays out as it should.

By that, I mean the police will eventually identify the body, they will interrogate – sorry, *interview* – the relatives and friend, crossing their names off a list one by one until they officially conclude that the killer is, in fact, who they know it to be. Then, they will put the details of the case in my file because they think that there absolutely has to be a pattern to the tales. Therefore, one day the detectives on the case will have a great epiphany, find the missing link, realise who I am and take me down.

It's a sweet dream.

Naturally, I have access to all the CCTV, so my surveillance of their progress is always very thorough.

Tonight's episode of *CSI: Grimm Reaper* presents the detectives who are working my case and they just cannot catch a break. I grab a beer from the fridge, pull on my comfy clothes and watch the show.

This is the first time I have ended my victim in the way I did, so the poor sods have a stifling first obstacle to overcome.

The old and beer-bellied detective just received a phone call from the landlord of the Little Mermaid's apartment to find out that she had rented the place under a fake name. They really were going to be taken for a spin trying to put a name to her wrecked face.

Only about ten minutes later does the short, bearded one walk into other's office.

"Just spoke to Ned from downstairs." He sounds low-spirited. *Why so glum? Don't worry you'll catch me, I'm rooting for you,* I mock to myself.

"The dental records aren't going to be enough to ID her. She hasn't had any work done and unsurprisingly there are no matches in our current records."

The old one shoves his hands against the desk, pushing his chair back against the wall. He stares blindly and says nothing for a moment.

"Well, I guess that's it then. We'll just need to wait until someone reports a missing person who fits the profile." With more grit in his voice he adds, "even though we have hardly a profile for it to fit with."

This seems like it's going to be long episode. Perhaps I should bring out the popcorn.

CHAPTER 9 - AVERY

With the cops being in a bit of a rut, I begin to focus on my next victim.

I keep a list of potential victims buried in my subconscious, bringing it forth when the time is right. I bring out my little brown book once again and scribble down names, the stories, the tales. So many I've done, so many left to do. How to choose the right one for the right person for the right time. Some tales are yet to play out. Some tales are just ending. Some tales will never begin.

My heart and mind are racing so rapidly my hand is struggling to keep up, the blood coursing through my veins causing them to tremble.

I settle. My choice decided. *Now, to find the right person,* I think to myself as I watch the pages catch alight and shrivel into ashes.

It is noon on Saturday. The sun is welcoming the people of Southhurst with a warm smile and a soft kiss. She is more affectionate to some, I notice as I pass strangers with a rosier hue to their shoulders than I observe on others. This attitude of hers is unexpected due to her timing, but nonetheless it is greeted with open arms by everyone.

I make my way to the coffee shop in the centre of town, scuttling across the road and dodging old, speeding British taxi drivers as I go.

The Cosy Coffee is discreetly located between two competing estate agents, yet its buoyant, candyfloss pink colour theme and large, goofy letterings make it unmissable.

As I enter I'm greeted by a beaming grin attached to the soft face of a tiny little girl with lopsided pigtails messily tied up above each ear. She has on a '*my little pony*' t-shirt, reminding me of my oh-so-distant youth, and a bright pink tutu which has so many ruffles it almost engulfs her entirely.

"Hi there, cutie," I smile back as I'm scooting past her.

I catch sight of Heidi and wave, "hiya, how are you?"

"Well I'm just peachy, dear. How are you? Not working too hard I hope." She raises her eyebrow in a motherly manner as if she holds wisdom far beyond her years.

I breathe a faint laugh and assure her, "no, of course not. Can I just get the usual ple—"

My sentence is cut short by a tugging on my jacket. I look down to find the little girl again.

"Oh, Maya, will you stop that!" Heidi exclaims. The little girl quickly releases me.

"Sorry, sweetie. She's going through a phase, she just has to hold on to everything she sees." She shakes her head and sighs, as if she has given this speech to countless customers before me. "I swear you just can't find a good babysitter in this town. They'll just cancel on you last minute and leave you stranded, having to take your five-year-old to work!"

I sympathize with her and assure her it is not a problem. We chat for a few more minutes until my skimmed coconut cappuccino and lemon and poppy seed muffin are ready.

Irritatingly, my usual table is being occupied by a middle-aged man scratching his head and rubbing his face vigorously with his clammy hands. I assume he is fretting about the bald patch on the top of his head spreading towards his hairline. I feel as though he has enough taxing issues to worry about, so I let this one slide.

Luckily, there is a vacant corner table on the other side of the room and so I set myself up over there. When I visit here on the order of business that I am on today, I always have to take a table situated in the corner as these give the best field of vision to observe from.

I open up my laptop and tap away at it, pretending to be engrossed in some serious documents and emails. While my fingers are typing, my eyes are watching.

Cosy Coffee, I found, is the best place to find new people and new tales, because it is a place where people come not for a quick fix on-the-go or for a serious but supposedly unofficial business meeting, like they do in a commercial café like Starbucks. No, here is where people come to catch up with old friends or family. Here is where people come to have a killing-them-softly talk with a significant other if they want to 'still be friends'. Here is where people come to take a step back from the hustle and the bustle of the town and their lives and to be in their own company.

Which is great for me.

So many different kinds of people with so many different tales come into this café and I get to witness it all. I've found nearly all my victims in here.

I can never know exactly how long I will have to sit here before the right person comes along. Sometimes it's a matter of minutes. Sometimes it's a matter of hours. Today, I have been residing in this corner for eighty-seven minutes before a potential comes through the door.

About time, I grumble, *a girl can only handle so many coffees without a toilet break.*

CHAPTER 10 - AVERY

She strides towards the counter where Heidi eagerly awaits and begins to address her quickly, saying, "can I please have a black coffee?" Quickly, she adds, "to go."

Her loose curls glisten in the sunlight as she brushes them over her shoulder, revealing her softly bronzed cheeks. The sheer cobalt blouse hugs her hourglass figure. She twists her neck to view the entrance, allowing me to see her eyes. At first glance they appear a deep hazel shade, but the longer I study them, they become a rich hunter green splashed with golden specs of dust that reflect the light shining through the shop window as if they are a mirror.

The warm glow to her gaze lowers as she catches sight of him shuffling in after her, only a few moments later. He reaches her and grabs her wrist as she tries to turn away. Heidi witnesses this and shoots her with a concerned look, but she smiles politely and dips her head, giving reassurance.

They are a young couple, barely out of their teen years (or maybe they're just blessed with good genes). Yet, their expressions mirror those of two adults with the weight of life's worries placed heavily upon their shoulders. Young people nowadays really do worry far too much. Then again, who am I to judge?

She sighs and glances down, avoiding direct eye contact as he pleads. They hum under their breaths to prevent their words from being overheard. Though, their efforts are in vain since this café is only small and I am seated close by.

"We've been through this so many times," she declares to him, "I'm not going to tell you again."

He hangs his head low, resembling a puppy being scolded by its owner. "I'm not going to give up. You know I'm not going to give up."

She is handed a coffee and she hastily pushes past him, aiming for the door. She is a strong character, I can tell that much, but he is strong too. His persistence stops her from leaving and she puts her cup down on the table next to mine.

I turn back to my computer and pull up a few more files, clicking them open and closed. The burning need to let my eyes fall so that I can stare at them is intolerable, and it takes all of my will power to only observe them with my ears.

He is rambling continuously and at the speed of a rocket, whilst she avoids saying anything at all and gives only one- or two-word answers.

With my peripheral vision, I see him reach out and caress her hand. Though he has attempted this multiple times, this is the first time she does not retreat back into a folded position.

"Please," he begs, "what do I have to do? Just tell me what I have to do and I'll do it. I would do anything for you, you must know that."

This time she takes his hand in both of hers, surprising both him and me equally and gazes straight into his eyes. For the first time in twenty-eight minutes, he is completely silent, and so is she.

One agonizing minute later she shrivels back, sitting upright in her chair and a good two feet away from him. With her eyes returning to staring at her jeans, she murmurs, "I just don't think it can work. I don't think I can risk everything for this."

"You mean for me." His tone is no longer desperate and insecure. Suddenly, it grows cold and harsh. As if he had just had a complete character-reboot.

I purse my lips and suck in a quick breath. *Oh that's got to sting*, I think, kicking myself for not bringing some snacks to this show.

She dabs a finger to her eye and shoves the chair back as she hoists herself out of it, scuffling her way onto the street.

Unfortunately, the evolution of his character doesn't stick since when he sees this he immediately hurries after her, apologising copiously.

This guy is such a wuss, I mutter as I follow not far behind them. I mouth to Heidi as I'm leaving, *two minutes*, since I just abandoned my possessions. I place the phone to my ear and pretend to start speaking into it.

When I have tailed them out of the view of the café I throw my phone into my jeans' back pocket.

Having caught up with her, he leads her round the corner of a building where a slim passageway has been created between two office blocks.

He continues to beg and she continues to turn him down and it seems like this never-ending cycle might actually prove to be exactly what I am looking for.

"We've tried already. It didn't work. He found out and just look where we are now."

I'm unsure about what I'm hearing, but I continue to listen, thinking perhaps it won't pose a problem.

"Yes I know, I know," he admits, "but we can be really discreet. Why can't it work? He can't be keeping a close eye on you twenty-four-seven. We can lay low for a while so he loses the scent and eases off. Then we can try telling him again, and this time we can be the one to tell him instead of one of your sisters."

She sighs. Even I know that he is most definitely not going to get what he's after from the way she's acting. I'll give it to him though; he really is a determined little dude.

"Didn't you listen to me when I told you what he threatened? He'll cut me off. I'll have no funding for uni, no funding to eat. I won't be able to pay rent. If I want to be a doctor I can't afford to have this setback, I'll never be able to compete with everyone else.

"My father may be a controlling asshole who is way too involved, but I need him—" she hesitates "—and he doesn't want you in my life. It was too risky to begin with, we're lucky we got even six months together." I can hear the tears in her voice as she whispers, "I'm sorry."

I have to stop myself from eavesdropping. Even though this story seems mighty interesting, it isn't the right one. They aren't the right ones.

Disappointed, I go solemnly back to Cosy Coffee and return to my table.

Entertaining myself with only the work I am pretending to complete, I remain there until the sun begins to lower in the sky and a peach glow paints the horizon.

A few other potentials pass by throughout the afternoon but none of them are right. None fit this tale.

Heidi begins to close up for the night and though she is sweet and polite, I get the hint that it is time for me to leave.

The walk from the café home is not a long one. Fifteen minutes tops. From the sky having only dimmed somewhat when I set off, the darkness now conquers the light at a frightful pace and still at least eight minutes from my house, the heavens have gone into hibernation and my vision is obscured, causing me to squint, although this does little to improve the clarity.

Saturday evening in Southhurst is as typical as any big town's party night. For the most part, it is desperate girls dressed in smaller amounts of clothing each weekend, just hoping they will meet a guy drunk enough to take them home and take it off. It is herds of 'lads' making peculiar noises resembling wild animals and laughing at their inside jokes which aren't half as funny as they make them out to be. There is always that group of mums stumbling over to the nearest club acting far more tipsy than they actually are, who started drinking at noon because this week-end the kids are with their dad so they want to make the most of freedom while it's theirs.

Of course, this is all taking place in the town centre. The street along which I am now walking is as silent as the house of a married couple who just announced their plans for divorce.

The road is barely lit by ominous streetlights, so faint and trembling that my shadow is scarcely distinguishable and it bleeds into the pool of black ahead of me.

In this moment, if you were to ask me why my stomach flipped and my heart began to dance in my chest, I would not be able to give you any logical explanation. If you were to ask me why I thought that I was not alone walking down the street, I would not be able to tell you.

In the month of March the breeze becomes angry in the evenings and this road is lined with trees. They are whipped by the gales and their arms often thrash about trying to regain balance.

Though it's a town, vast amounts of wildlife roam the streets at night. From rodents to foxes, from rabbits to deer. They wander through the darkness, mostly staying a great deal away from human residence, but occasionally they will happen upon the estates and the pathways and linger there for a while.

I know all this. I am completely and confidently aware of the many possible reasons why a shadow would scamper behind me and why I would believe I am hearing breathing. But tonight, I feel the hairs on the back of my neck spark up. I feel a cold wind pass through me like ice. I notice the softest movement of the leaves on the bushes, and abruptly jerk my attention towards it, as if I were a gazelle grazing and paranoid about a lion lurking, stalking me from the high strands of Sahara grassland.

As I pull myself up the steps, fumble my key into the door and slam it shut behind me, I am certain I have been followed.

I watched her tonight. She didn't see me, but she knew
I was there.

CHAPTER 11 - HARRY

Martha is shouting at him. Martha is always shouting at him. Harry has no idea what she is saying. He knows that it doesn't matter – he'll do what he always does. He'll apologise, he'll ask how he can make it up to her and he'll wait for her to forget the whole ordeal. That's how their marriage has held together for six years.

When she finally finishes her rant (and her second rant) Harry responds as he always does, pressing *play* on his autopilot.

"Just be here!" Martha implores, "You were late home from work four times last week and for the past two days as well! Am I really being that unreasonable, wanting to spend time with my husband?

"How are we supposed to raise a child together when we hardly spend any time together? Actually forget that, how are we supposed to even *have* a baby?" She regrets it as soon as she says it. It hits Harry like a full-frontal collision in a smart car with a juggernaut. They stare directly at one another and both their eyes begin to swell.

Harry says nothing. He simply picks up his fags and jacket from the foot of the stairs and takes off.

She is jolted by the slamming of the door vibrating through the living room. Martha is stunned for a few minutes. She doesn't move one inch, unsure of what to feel, of what to think. Then, her knees buckle, she falls down to the ground and she weeps. Her howls resonate through her throat and flood through the house and the street. Her eyes sting from the salt being rubbed into them by her fists and her stomach sinks so low it makes her want to throw up.

Harry makes his way through all eighteen cigarettes that he has on hand in under an hour. He knows this is killing Martha more than it is him, but he's angry. Angry at her maybe, or angry at himself. He blames himself. Secretly he thinks she blames him too.

Finding out a year ago is what sent him into a spiral. All he wanted was to bring some good into the world and being told he couldn't do that brought his whole world crashing down. Harry wanted to honour them, in some way. He wanted them to live on through something other than just him. He didn't want to be where they ended.

The doctors said that about twenty per cent of men are like him. Harry supposed that the doctor thought this would make him feel better since he was not alone. It didn't. Now, all Harry thinks about is why he couldn't be like the eighty per cent.

They were given some other options to discuss. He and Martha argued about every single one of those options a thousand times over. They didn't want an alternative.

As Harry sucks down the end of his last cigarette, he receives a text responding to the one he sent as soon as he left home.

I'll meet you in the usual place

Picking himself up off the crumbled brick wall he had stumbled across, he quickly deletes the message and begins to make his way to the warehouse.

Harry is not naturally a paranoid character, he is always sure of who and what is in his surroundings – that's why he makes a decent detective. But whenever he goes to meet her, it's as if all his skill and reason are washed from his body and are replaced by stupidity and suspicion. He checks behind him every ten seconds, he's shaken by every sound and he conceals himself as if he is on his way to seal a high-profile drug deal.

The warehouse isn't really a warehouse – it's too small to be one. Harry came across it about a year ago when he met her. It has been out of use since he and Martha moved to this neighbourhood four years ago and no one tends to it, yet the foundations are still strong and the water mains still run so it became the perfect hideout for them.

It is situated a few yards further back from the road than the other buildings and is well disguised by overgrown thorn and holly bushes which no one would ever attempt to fight their way through or be able to see through, so they are never spotted by evening dog walkers or London commuters coming back far too late from work.

Harry trudges down the pathway he had made to the back entrance, yelping silently every time a thorn jabs into the back of his legs.

He reaches the moulded, rotten door and cringes at the sound of its groaning that seems to echo through the entire building. He whispers her name and a few moments later she tiptoes out of the shadows and runs to him.

It is only a brief visit tonight. Harry knows he can only be away from Martha for so long and still make it seem convincing that he had only stormed out to 'cool off'.

He tells her that they have to be more careful. He tells her that Martha is getting suspicious and is noticing him being late from work so often. He tells her that they cannot see one another for a while until Martha loses the scent.

Processing this, she is reluctant and angry at first; eventually understanding that it is the only way if they want this to work.

Harry swiftly leaves her there and hastens back home to Martha. A wave of guilt flushes over him as he thinks of her and shame mocks him silently. He shrugs it off but its claws sink deep into his shoulders and hang off his back.

Clicking the door shut carefully, he slinks into the living room to find Martha slouched down on the floor, head hung low and hair slapped across her face – stuck to her cheeks by tears. Harry gazes at her for a long while and a tickle forms in his throat which he hastily swallows back down.

Lowering himself onto the floor behind her, he engulfs her entire body with his limbs and holds her tight.

At first, she offers nothing in response, she is as cold and still as the ornaments on the mantelpiece. But she soon gives in and melts into him, gripping on to his arms as her tears drop onto his skin.

Their two bodies fall together.

Harry fervently presses his quivering lips against her neck and squeezes her closer into him, never wanting to let go.

"We'll keep trying," he whispers into the hollow of her shoulder, "there's still a chance." His words are barely comprehensible, muffled by the sobs of them both.

Martha nods her head precariously and he rocks her gently in his arms.

For the time that they sit there, entwined in one another, Harry feels something that he has not felt in such a long time he had forgotten what it was. Happiness. There, with Martha, he feels as though he needs nothing more than her in his life, he feels safe. He feels peaceful.

It doesn't last. Harry's mind flashes to her face and he quickly realises that it is not so. He cannot be happy with just Martha. He needs more.

CHAPTER 12 - HARRY

Wiping the water beads from his panicked forehead, Harry jogs through the doors of the station.

He throws his belongings into his locker with little care, his mind only mulling over the bollocking he is about to receive from the Chief. This is the first time since he joined the department that he had even been five minutes late – let alone forty.

He and Martha reconnected last night and this morning was the first time in a year that they both truly and mutually enjoyed each other's company – neither of them wanted to leave their bed. Though it puts Harry in physical pain being late for work, he doesn't regret a moment of it. He just wishes the dark cloud of secrets would stop lurking over his every move and making it nearly impossible to enjoy any time with his wife.

The briefing is just finishing up as he lurks in the doorway, heart thumping and mind racing.

Chief catches sight of Harry but ignores him while James shoots him a *good luck mate* look and Harry swallows with an audible gulp.

Fiddling with his 'important documents' as he always does following the morning briefing without even looking up, Chief remarks, "so nice of you to join us, Ellis."

Like a puppy being scolded for taking the turkey leg off the kitchen counter, Harry whimpers, "I know, Chief, I'm so sorry. There was an accident along the main road I take from home and the entire thing was blocked up—"

"Don't feed me bullshit, Ellis," he cuts Harry's ramblings short. "I honestly don't give a flying rat's arse why you weren't here when this briefing started. All I care about is the fact that you were not here."

He pauses briefly to see if Harry is going to spin him any more lies. Luckily, Harry is smart and knows when to keep his mouth shut. Marriage has taught him some things after all.

"Just make damn sure it does not happen again, or there will be hell to pay. You may still be new here but don't think for a second that that gives you some sort of free pass. Don't be late again. Got it?" When Harry doesn't reply immediately, Chief promptly repeats with a razor-sharp tone, "Got it?"

Clearing his throat, Harry murmurs, "Yes, Chief. Sorry, yes."

Chief inhales heavily and breathes his turkey bacon sandwich onto Harry. "Right, well get out of here and start doing some bloody work for Christ's sake."

As if he was just dismissed by Miss Trunchbull herself, Harry is out of that meeting room before Chief finishes.

"Why have you brought that damn dog in again?" Harry complains as his eyes are drawn to the slobbering lump that sits under the desk at his friend's feet.

James rolls his eyes, frustrated by the question. "Mate, we both have full time jobs and the kids are at school. There is no way in a million years the wife's work is gonna let her take him in and I can just about get away with it here."

Harry chuckles at him, "why not just leave him at home?"

"Oh shit, you must be a bloody genius. Why did I never think of that! That is such a good idea and just on the spot like that? Man, you shouldn't be a detective you should be the 21st century Einstein!" James's mocking tone shifts into an unamused glare. "We tried leaving him at home, he ain't having none of it. We're out the house from eight until five and seriously—" his voice lowers "—this thing pisses and shits everywhere! It has some serious anxiety issues."

"Anxiety issues? A dog with anxiety. Really?" Harry tries to remain sincere and serious but he cannot control the beaming grin that forms at the corners of his mouth.

James death-stares him for a long couple of seconds before breaking into a laugh himself, slapping his belly and sending waves of sound across the room as the beer in his gut knocks around.

"Okay, man. Just keep that thing away from me then, yeah? That is one stinky dog."

Shaking his head back to his job, James suggests, "Shall we try getting back to this case now?

"Oh hey, I just remembered," he interrupts himself, "completely random but my wife was raving about how much better *America's Got Talent* is than *BGT* and I remembered you said Martha kept you up a couple weeks ago to watch it?" Harry nods confidently and James adds, "She mentioned it doesn't start this year until May." Though a statement, James presents this fact as a question, waiting for Harry to answer it.

The temperature of Harry's cheeks start to rise at a staggering pace and he is unconsciously tapping his foot to the beat of his hummingbird heart. He brushes it off lightly and appears surprised by what he just heard.

"Oh really? Huh." He pauses and tilts his head, as if deep in thought. "That's strange. I must have got the show wrong."

James agrees and they briskly drop the subject.

James doesn't join Harry for lunch today, as he normally does. He claims he has a *ton* of documents to file so he works through until the afternoon.

As Harry gets back into the station he catches James just as he comes out of Chief's office with an expression on his face darker and heavier than usual.

Harry jokes, "Looks like I'm not the only one in the pigs' pen today, eh?"

James huffs in response, more reserved than normal. He doesn't play along as usual. Harry looks at him concerned and queries, "are you alright, mate?"

Saying nothing, James drags his coarse hand from his temple down his neck and ruffles his uncut head of grey wires. Harry repeats himself, a more intense element to his voice now.

As if he had just been awoken from sleepwalking, he springs back into life and back into his normal ways. "Oh yeah, yeah, everything is fine,

I'm fine." He gestures with his hands frantically. "My mind is just scrambled at the moment, you know? Got so much on my plate."

Before Harry has the chance to say anything in the form of a response, James bounces away from the topic, announcing, "Guess what? Whilst you were at lunch, I got a call from the missing persons department and a woman has reported her sister missing. She says she's a redhead, recently moved to a flat and she wouldn't tell anyone the address." James's expression lifts significantly more with the next detail; "*and* she says that she has a red bloodhound."

James rests his hands on his belly in classic *PC Plod* fashion with a wide smirk on his face. Harry thinks he's more pleased about getting rid of the dog than he is about possibly having a lead.

Scratching the head of said dog as they go into James's office, he adds, "I've asked her to come in so we can speak with her and figure out if it's the same person. I think we've got a pretty good chance that her sister's the Jane Doe."

Harry inhales the thick, dog-scented air of the room. "Well, let's hope that we've had a change in luck."

He and James discuss how they are going to handle the woman in the interview room and go over some details of the crime scene that they still haven't quite figured out.

When they are in the midst of taking a break, Karen from the front desk taps the wood of the door and feebly squeaks "um, 'scuse me… detectives?" She waits for them to take notice of her. Due to the decibel level she spoke in, this takes far longer than it should have. "There is a Miss Lewis here to see you, sir."

James twitches his eyebrows, shooting Harry a look before replying, "Great, thanks, Karen. I'll be there in two ticks."

With her fingernails between her teeth, Karen bows her head and dashes out of the doorway.

Harry heads to the interview room whilst James collects the woman.

Those rooms are the coldest of the entire station. Since they are not used on a day-to-day basis, the station saw no reason in making them luxurious – or modern for that matter – in any respect.

They each have an old rusty radiator which leaks oil so are never turned on, and one air-conditioning unit that merely moves around the musky air of the room rather than do anything in the way of cooling it down.

The ghosts of lies told and confessions made pierce your skin as you enter, and asphyxiate your lungs as the shards of the spirits of sin that were once within these treacherous walls scrape down your throat, sending the hand of a demon trailing the curve of your spine and caressing your neck.

The old window on the wall opposite to the one-way mirror is the only feature of the space that fails in an attempt to lighten the atmosphere just a fraction. In fact, it seems to have the opposite effect since the iron bars in front of it block the minimal light that is able to penetrate the mossed-over glass from ever reaching you. Instead, they create a faint shadow of lines resembling that of a jail cell, reminding you that your right to freedom is a fight whilst you sit in the cold steel chair of the interview room.

Every tap of his shoe or drum of his finger is amplified by the concrete walls bouncing the echo about the room, creating a ringing in his ear that ceases to fade.

Even Harry feels impatient and uncomfortable sitting in the interview room alone – though he has been in them so many times he should be used to it by now.

Not too long after Harry takes up residence in the room, James follows, leading a large woman in with him.

"Miss Lewis." Harry stands up with his hand outstretched to greet her; "thank you for agreeing to meet with us."

She, also disorientated by the abrupt change of atmosphere, hesitantly takes his hand. "It's *Mrs* Lewis," she corrects him before adding, "and I'm happy to."

Harry glances at her with an apologetic expression on his face and offers her the seat opposite him and James. She squeezes herself into the chair and makes a few attempts to haul it closer to the table.

"Please accept my sincere apologies for the disappearance of your sister," James begins, "I can't imagine how surreal this must be for you.

"The woman we found was renting an apartment on South Street. Is that where your sister was living?"

Impatient and uptight, Mrs Lewis murmurs, "I'm sorry, I wouldn't know. She up and moved without telling any of us two months ago."

CHAPTER 13 - HARRY

Of course she did, Harry moans inside. *Of course we can't have a single breakthrough in this case.*

Only briefly glancing up towards his friend is enough to let him know that James is thinking the exact same thing. Regardless, they both withhold their frustration and listen to the woman sitting in front of them intently.

"I went to her place one day to find it completely empty. Thank God, she hadn't changed her phone number – I got so worried I called her straight away to ask what was going on and to make sure she was alright.

"She said that she needed to be away for a while and have some alone time." Looking them directly in the eyes as if to reassure them, she adds, "of course, I begged her to tell me where she was so that I could come and visit her and be there for her but she just wouldn't give it up. For the life of me, I couldn't understand why. I'm her *sister,* shouldn't she want me there?"

She pauses to get a reassuring nod from the detectives, but the words are falling from her mouth at such a pace, it is as confusing for their minds to follow as it is keeping your eyes on just one horse at the races. Fixating on the movement of her mouth, Harry is sure that she has not yet taken a breath.

With no response, she hastens on. "I suppose I should be grateful that she kept in contact at all really. I made her promise to call me every single week. That's why I got so worried when I didn't hear from her, you see. Knowing she wasn't keen on the daily updates, I initially left it alone thinking that I had pushed too much and she just wanted her space. But then the days turned into weeks and I was kept up at night praying for her to call me," she clutches the cross hanging around her neck, "and she never did, not even a text.

"I mean, I know she was ashamed about the whole scandal and how it was exposed and perhaps I was one of the most unaccepting – but she is my sister and I would always have forgiven her. Besides, it's not even my forgiveness that truly matters, and—"

The cogs in his head turning at a far slower pace than her mouth, Harry suddenly processes what she said and raises his hand as a signal to stop her. "Sorry, what was that you just said?"

Stunned by the interjection, she frowns and repeats, "It's not my forgiveness that truly matters?" Her voice trails off on a high note, showing the uncertainty in her response.

"No, the other part," James reiterates, now up to speed with Harry's thoughts, "did you say she was part of a scandal?"

Gazing up to the heavens, Mrs Lewis gasps, now having the bulb light up about their query. "Sorry, yes she was. You see, our father owns Lewis & Co Enterprises and both my sister and I worked under him with the hopes of taking over the company in partnership when our father retired…"

Harry sits there, listening and now actually comprehending what this woman is saying. She tells them all about how her sister was never happy working at the company and always wanted more.

"She met the Chief Editor of Bennet and Roy Publishing House and my goodness she fell head over heels for him – completely smitten."

Mrs Lewis rambles on that her sister did everything she could to get a job as a receptionist at the publisher's – "cutting her pay straight in half. Can you believe it? Everyone in our family told her she was being an idiot to leave a well-paying, promising job for some little girl crush, but by God she just would not listen. It was outright career suicide!"

As Mrs Lewis says this, a quote from the crime scene blurs Harry's vision as the words dance across his mind: '*for when once your shape has become like a human being, you can no more be a mermaid*'

The man had his eye on her and seduced her. He wined and dined her, taking her to plays and concerts for a few weeks.

"And then the little sleezeball tells her that he has a fiancée! Of course, she and I are close and she called me up to break the news almost the second that she found out. We had some Ben & Jerry's and ranted about how awful men are – as girls do – and she promised me there was absolutely no way she would ever see him outside of work again. She told me that unfortunately she had signed a contract so she had to work there for the entire year.

"In truth, she had continued to see him in secret. The only condition being he made her swear she would not speak a word of it to a soul and they had to tread very carefully around each other at work to avoid suspicion."

Another line of blood writing flashes through Harry's thoughts: '*she had given up her beautiful voice, and suffered unheard-of pain daily for him*'

Shaking her head, she recalls, "He told her that he would leave his fiancée for her. She couldn't understand why he was holding off but whenever she asked him, he just promised that he would." She glances down. "Silly girl. She should've been smarter than to believe him. Love truly does make you blind."

Mrs Lewis goes on to tell them that his fiancée caught the two of them and everything went into chaos.

"When the fiancée found out, she told absolutely everyone at the company. My poor sister was shamed wherever she went. The only thing that got her through it was knowing that she had done it because of love and that she had found her true love – which made all of it worth it. Little did she know."

His high reputation was rapidly deteriorating and so he turned on her sister and made out as if she had forced him into the affair.

"That little weasel told everyone that he was merely being a kind friend to her and she threw herself on him and he was so *helpless* and *victimized*. Then what does he do? Marries his fiancée that same week."

The constant public shaming she received, along with a broken heart sent her spiralling and she became depressed and obsessive. She stalked the newlyweds day and night until they filed for a restraining order against her and she was not allowed within a hundred yards of them or their home.

Recalling the memories brings tears to Mrs Lewis's eyes, "She had completely lost it. She quit her job, refused to speak with any of us, then she up and left. Without even a word of warning."

Both Harry and James scribble down notes on this new information as Mrs Lewis collects herself again.

The steel table echoes their hollow breaths.

The sound of James clearing his throat vibrates throughout the uncomfortable silence of the ice cold interview room.

"Thank you so much for your cooperation; it will really help our investigation. We just have a few more questions for you." James glances down at his notes before asking, "the woman in question signed a lease to the apartment that we found her in, under the name of Murphy Carter. We also believe she owned a red bloodhound. Do either of these sound familiar to you?"

Mrs Lewis has a certain frailness to her voice now, as if at any moment tears would flood from her eyes.

"Murphy was the name of our first family dog. Carter is our mother's maiden name." Her tone and face lower. "Yes she has a red bloodhound."

"Finally," James starts, "can you tell us where you were after eleven pm on Sunday 12th and between one and three of the following morning?"

Her once fast-speaking mouth now slows and stumbles over its words. "Um yes, yes." She thinks long and hard before answering, "I was at home asleep. I go to bed at around ten on a Sunday night and I am up for work at seven."

"Is there anyone who can verify that for you?"

"My husband came back late that night. He didn't tell me what time but he had been to the pub with his friends so I'm assuming it was on the later side. He would have seen me when he came to bed."

Harry thanks her again and leads the way out of the interview room. Mrs Lewis seems less put together now than she was when she arrived. James guides her towards the reception.

Before she leaves the station, she turns to James and with a desperate look in her eye, asks, "So do you think it's her?"

She doesn't really want to know, but she can't help herself. Even though she is pretty sure of what the answer will be, for some unidentified reason, she feels that she needs confirmation. Even if it is what she is afraid to hear.

James knows this. Yet, he has to answer her. He stares into her chest-nut eyes, filled with lost hope and desperation, and tells her the one thing that she is praying to God he will not tell her. "We have strong reason to believe that the Jane Doe we found on South Street is your sister. I'm so sorry."

As the words fall from his mouth, the tears fall towards hers.

Having seen Mrs Lewis out of the station, James returns to his office to find Harry in a bonding session with the dog sitting under his desk.

"I thought you said he stunk?"

Harry laughs insincerely and smiles, "oh he does. But since she wouldn't take him and you aren't getting rid of him any time soon, I feel like we should get to know each other a little better."

The walls vibrate as the door slams shut and James sighs.

"Well, on the bright side, I think we've found our girl."

CHAPTER 14 - AVERY

This week has been a strange one I have been looking over my shoulder everywhere I go. I am certain I'm not alone. Yet, I have seen no one.

I try to put my newfound paranoia to the back of my mind and stay focused on what I need to do. I haven't yet found the right potentials. That's why I am returning to the coffee shop this weekend as well.

When I get there, I partake in small talk with Heidi as I always do and then sit at my corner table and my day begins.

This process may seem rather tedious to some and perhaps pointless. I disagree. I find this step the most intriguing – well, besides the end game. Observing the people who cross my path and understanding their tale fascinates me. For example, the man over by the door looks as though he is having a lovely morning coffee with his wife – on the surface. But why is there merely the ghost of a wedding band on her ring finger and why do his eyes continue to shift between the door and her?

Unusual for a Saturday, business is slow this morning and few people come into the coffee shop. Those who do enter are not very telling people at all and are most definitely wrong for the tale I am searching for. It's a shame, really. Waking up today I felt as though this was going to be a productive day. Nevertheless, I wait patiently and observe. I know that the right one will come in eventually.

Early afternoon, the clouds have blanketed the sky and I am close to calling it quits for the day and joining the sun in her slumber, when a young woman comes into the café with a girlfriend on one arm and a hot pink Marc Jacobs clutch bag on the other.

"Honestly, it was the weirdest thing ever!" Her irritatingly screechy voice is so loud that I need not eavesdrop – she is hanging her dirty laundry very much in public. "He went completely *notebook* style. He was hanging there I was like *what are you doing?* Like completely freaking out obvs, then basically he was like *agree to go out with me or I jump* and I was just thinking OMG what if he actually does? Like he wasn't going to die or anything but he might have broken something and I don't wanna carry that on my shoulders!"

Her voice resembles nails on a chalk board and I wince with every word. *I want to kill her just so she'll shut the hell up.*

"So anyways, I was like *yeah fine okay I'll do it* and he actually made me keep to what I said but I was just thinking like one date and then that's it, you know?" Her friend acts like a Beverly Hills Chihuahua, grinning and laughing along with everything she says. "But anyways, I like so wanted to not like him, like at all, and I kept saying throughout that I didn't. Like he is such a loser! But I couldn't help it, I just did, you know? Like, you can't control who you like, even if you really, really don't want to."

Through the ringing in my ear caused by her intolerable high-pitched squealing, I can just about concentrate on her story. The corners of my mouth twitch as I breathe into my steaming cup.

I think I've found my Beauty.

CHAPTER 15 - AVERY

The two of them only buy drinks to go and before I know it, they're flicking their overly-bleached blonde hair and clacking their wildly inappropriate stiletto heels back out the door.

I pull my phone out to take my usual fake call and casually amble out after them.

I don't have to put in much of an effort to make it look as though I am not following them since Beauty is too wrapped up in herself and her little Chihuahua is so intent on lapping up every word that comes out of her cherry red lips, they wouldn't see me anyway.

Beauty sighs, exhaustion in her eyes with an expression reading *oh why is my oh-so-popular life just so much work.*

"So, now as much as I don't want to admit it – like to anyone – I think I kinda like him. I can't believe those words are coming out of my mouth, I mean him? So not cool."

"Yeah, he's such a loser," the Chihuahua snorts with an overly-exaggerated laugh. Beauty death-stares her, clearly thinking *and you are talking because…?*

She quickly realises and shrivels back up, handing the limelight back to Beauty. "So, have you told him yet?"

"God no, are you kidding? If I told him, he would think that he had me and if he thought that, this would have to end right now. I can't have him thinking he's good enough for me then he wouldn't try anymore."

Oh Jesus, this Beauty is far more pretentious than I'd read about. Isn't she meant to be humble and kind? *Ah well, can't have it all.*

By this point I have been tailing them for a good fifteen minutes – completely unnoticed, I might add.

Having made the decision that she is the right one, I have to track her to her final destination, so that I can start gathering the details. And find out about Beast, of course. As much of a shock as this might be to Beauty, she isn't the only one this tale concerns.

So far, the roads they've gone down have been relatively crowded so I didn't stick out like a sore thumb. However, the next turning they make as a shortcut takes them down an alleyway, and I think even *they* would notice me then.

I decide to wait a few moments until they have reached the other end before going through myself. The two *White Chicks* won't exactly be difficult to find again.

When I reckon the coast is clear, I begin to trace their footsteps. Since the sun buggered off already, the alleyway is dimly lit by the greyness of the clouds. It isn't a very long stretch; it should take thirty seconds to walk through – if that. Yet, for some reason it feels as though I am pacing through the eerie tunnel for minutes and never reaching the end.

The breeze suddenly picks up and the cruel cold air whispers in my ear, gripping my neck. Strands of hair are thrown across my face, impairing my vision of what's ahead, and the screaming of the wind prevents me from hearing what's behind me.

Something hits the back of my neck. I slap my hand on the point of pain to find it bare. I jerk my head back, changing my window of view. No one's there.

Footsteps. Footsteps patter to the side of me. I'm sure of it. I see a glimpse of a shadow in my peripheral vision. The skips I pass rustle. I do a three-sixty view, but still I see nothing.

What's wrong with me? Am I going mad?

I've got to pull myself together. I need to pull myself together.

I have been walking through for five minutes now, surely. But I am only halfway through.

The walls surrounding me seem to mute the comforting murmurings of busy civilians either end of the alleyway. It feels silent. Too silent. Dead silent.

I'm sure I'm going mad. I'm convinced I'm going mad.

Something hits me again. This time bigger, this time harder, this time in the back of my knees. They buckle. My unprepared hands fail to soften the blow, remaining firmly at my sides. My head smashes against the ground and I taste a bitterness on my tongue. A scent all too familiar.

I wasn't being paranoid. I wasn't going mad. I can now feel the shadow that's been lurking all week towering over me.

My brain is expanding in my skull at such a rapid pace that the sharp sting is almost unbearable. I cough red into my elbow – a colour I am far less used to seeing when it comes from my own mouth.

I slowly turn around and prop myself up on my elbows to face the silhouette. At first, it's only an outline – I can't make out who it is.

"Nice to see you again." A voice. A sweet voice. A sweet voice trying to appear menacing.

Slowly, the pieces start to fall in place and my vision becomes clear.

My racing heart calms and the ringing in my ear silences.

My voice is not shaky or frail as my mind was only a split second ago. "Likewise," I reply with a thin smile growing, "Cinderella."

Sorry, Beauty, your time will have to wait. Looks like another princess has taken your place.

CHAPTER 16 - AVERY

It's been so long I almost don't recognise her. She's changed in the year and five months since our paths last crossed.

The sweet, naïve little girl I once knew so well, who hid her rosy cheeks beneath worn out rags and cowered at the hand of her wicked stepsisters, is buried deep within the woman standing before me. Now, she stands confident and tall with a fire roaring in her eyes which had never before been lit. I almost feel proud of whom she has become, knowing I had a part to play in it.

I begin to pull myself off the ground steadily, still rather shaky from the fall. "Sweet Cinderella, look at you. You've grown."

"That's it? After all this time, after all you have done, you see me now and that's what you have to say?" She sounds disappointed in me, as if I was meant to see her and break down with tears streaming down my cheeks – realising the horror I had committed.

I laugh under my breath. "Were you hoping for a sorry?"

She doesn't respond. Now perhaps realising that her expectations have been held at a different standard than what I can offer.

Although only moments ago, I was the vulnerable mouse underneath her feline shadow, the roles are now reversed and Cinderella has lost her train of thought and her ability to command the situation.

I can tell from the expression on her face that she has an absolute purpose in standing in front of me, so I give her the benefit of the doubt and take the steering wheel for a minute, until she figures out what bone she has to pick.

"I would love to catch up with you, little princess. We can go grab a coffee, have a little girl-bonding session and hell, I'll even let you braid my hair." Her expression remains poker-straight, unmoved by my attempt to lighten the mood. I switch to a more serious approach. "But I have a feeling that's not the reason you're here."

Though her silhouette appears solid, her outline is blurred slightly, shaken by the adrenaline shooting up her spine either because of anger or because of fear. I am about to find out which one.

"Why?" she finally builds up the courage to ask, "Why did you do it? What had they ever done to you? You didn't even know them."

I stare at her, trying to hold back the pity from seeping through my eyes. I take a step towards her. "Oh no, it's not what they did to *me*. It's what they did to *you*. Surely I made that clear back then?"

Her young face becomes confused and slow to process this new information. "Then, what was in it for you? Why did you do it?"

We are close together now. So close that I can feel her breath against my skin, our body heat is interchangeable.

Her eyes meet mine, the fire roaring loudly inside.

My grimace widens and I whisper, "It's what I do."

Her breath catches on my words and her eyes glisten with the tears she's holding in. She grits her teeth and her jaw locks so tightly it vibrates under the pressure.

There is now a sharp sensation pressing into my stomach. I glance down and catch sight of the blade reflecting the white of the clouds.

I have to take my hat off to her – that was done very smoothly.

I raise an eyebrow in disbelief and I fail to suppress my mocking smirk. "And what do you think you're going to do with that?"

Cinderella death-stares me and offers no response. The chilling aura that radiates from her stands the hairs on my neck upright.

When the silence becomes so uncomfortable it makes my skin itch, I continue to taunt her. "You think you're going to kill me? Is that how you saw this playing out?" An involuntary laugh bursts out, "Oh please, you don't have it in you. You're sweet, innocent little Cinderella. You could never even hurt a fly, could you?"

She tries with all of her pretend strength to stay expressionless, but I can see the angel and devil screaming at each other from either side of her collarbone. I am watching intently, eager to find out which will win.

"I've changed," she finally decides to speak. "I'm not the same person that you remember. You did this to me."

"Oh come now, I don't want to take all the credit."

The emotion fuelling the blaze in her eyes surfaces through the brittleness in her roar. "You killed them. They were my sisters and you killed them!"

Her aura now burns red and I feel the knife press harder against my skin. This angers me and I decide now that play time is over.

Before she has time to react I push all my weight through my hands onto her shoulders and it creates a space between us.

Regaining her balance, Cinderella appears wide-eyed. She didn't expect me to fight back. Her vision of how this was going to go was clearly very, very optimistic.

She strides towards me like some crazed psychopath. Reflecting the white of the clouds, the blade shines as she frantically cuts the air.

I sidestep as she lunges at me and hugs the air. I drive my elbow into her jawline as she passes and she lets out a wail. Her grip loosens on the knife and it whines as it plummets onto the ground.

I still think she has keeled over when her hands wrap around my neck and jerk me backwards. I hit the ground.

She stands over me thinking she has victory. However, while she is distracted, I snake my foot around her ankles and pull her off balance.

I scramble on the ground and clamber on top of her. Centring my weight on her chest, I slam her wrists against the gravelled concrete, pinning her down.

Without me noticing, the sky has dimmed to the point that I can't make out her face anymore. I can only see her dampened blonde hair – as dirty as it was the first time I ever laid eyes on her – and the blood seeping from her nose, dimly lit by a flickering light.

There's something about the combination of a flickering streetlamp and an alleyway. A flickering light on its own is profusely irritating. An alleyway never fails to carry the stale words of the winds with you as you wrap up tighter, suddenly as cold as walking through a ghost. But the two together, well, the two together I have come to realise are a bad omen.

The incessant flickering is no longer irksome, but bloodcurdling. The alleyway's breath no longer makes you shiver, but makes you weak at the knees. The two make a perfect pair for something Wicca this way comes.

Out of breath, I gasp, "Stop this, princess. Stop it now and we can forget it ever happened."

The blood across her face now mixes with tears. She clamps her eyes shut and nods faintly, apparently kicking herself for failing. I'm relieved by this since I haven't been to the gym in an embarrassing amount of time and I think I'm starting to realise just how unfit I am.

I ease the pressure I'm placing on her wrists and begin to de-straddle her. When my body is no longer restraining her knee, she drives it into my gut and I gasp, winded and debilitated.

Before I know it the tables have turned and she is straddling me and crushing my ribcage. The only difference being she has the blade in her grip and holds it pressed against my jugular.

I gulp under the knife's edge and my heart's thumping is audible now.

"Why are you doing this?" I reason with her, "You hated your step-sisters."

"They were my sisters!" She breathes a pungent combination of food onto me.

My expression becomes confused. "They were awful to you."

With more grit in her voice, she repeats, "they were still my sisters." With her free hand she plunges a fist square into my jaw.

A loud thunder resonates throughout my skull. Pain explodes along my jawline and travels up my cheek. *Oh that's going to leave a mark.* Now I'm pissed.

My anger makes me ignorant of the knife pressed against my throat and I try a different tactic.

"Oh what so you think you can kill me?" Now that she is in the position of power, I begin to fuel the screaming match between the angel and devil again. "You may have changed, princess, but that doesn't mean you're a killer. You're sweet little Cinders. Would fairy godmother be too happy if she saw you now? What about your Prince?"

I can see that I'm getting to her. Her eyes are flickering uncontrollably, showing her scattered train of thought and uncertainty of what to do.

"You look for the good in everybody. Can you not see the good in me? How could you ever harm another person, let alone *kill?*"

For a split second, the blade presses deeper into my neck and I fear the devil has won, but almost immediately the cold metal is gone from my skin completely.

"I thought I could do it," Cinderella murmurs through her weeping. "I thought I had the strength. But I can't."

She removes herself from me, and air can reach my lungs again.

"It's okay, Cinders. You're good and pure – that's nothing to be ashamed of."

She drops the knife to her side and sobs, "I just wanted to get justice for them. I just wanted to get closure."

"I know, I know. But hey, it's not for everyone."

I take a step back for a moment and appreciate how fucked up it is that I am comforting the woman whose stepsisters I have been less than kind to, and who was holding a knife to my throat literally twenty-seven seconds ago.

"Look, now you can have closure, okay? It's the taking part that counts, yeah? You tried your best and you couldn't go through with it. Now, unfortunately for you—" I press my lips to her ear. My sympathetic tone switches to a low, ominous whisper. "I can."

CHAPTER 17 - AVERY

I act quicker than she can say Happy Ever After.

Her eyes widen in disbelief and denial. I stare straight into them with no expression except the toothy grimace smeared across my face.

I sit idly by as she falls down and grows fainter.

"I just have one quick question for you, my sweetness," I declare, "how did you find me? I wore a wig and contact lenses when I last paid a visit, how did you find out who I was?"

With the pain and the life slowly leaving her body, she muffles through wine-stained lips, "I'm not the only one with a grudge."

I let her cold words roll off my back as I lean down and press my lips against her earlobe. "The clock's struck midnight, Cinderella. Time for you to turn back into a pumpkin."

This goes against all of my rules. It's during the day…in a very public area…with no exit strategy…no disguise…I don't even have gloves on. My fingerprints are going to be all over the little princess and amongst all the commotion there are bound to be some strands of my hair either on her or close by.

Then again, what was I meant to do? She ambushed me, I had no idea she was going to do that. Most people who are seeking vengeance break into your house and sit creepily in the corner until you get home, don't they?

With my hair slicked back into a bun and my sleeves pulled over my hands, I attempt to wipe some of the evidence off her and the knife – even though I know it will make little difference.

She couldn't have chosen a more clichéd place to attack me than an alleyway. It makes it difficult for me to get creative when I try to conceal her sleeping body.

I scan the surrounding area in hope of a Cinderella-shaped hole that just happens to be here and is just about to get covered in cement the very same day. Unfortunately, I have no such luck.

Against my better judgement, I resort to laying her to rest in the skip on a soft bed of waste. I feel like I'm the inexperienced kid killer in some crappy crime movie.

Before throwing her in to join the trash, I take out the top layer of bin bags and cover her with them. I chuck the knife in with her – there's no way I'm keeping hold of that thing.

Luckily, it is only my jacket that is stained with blood so at least there is something good going for me. That would have been a little more difficult to clean up.

It is obvious that my half-arsed clean up won't keep her hidden for long, mainly since the stench of her bodily fluids greeting the rest of the skip is radiating waves that are pretty much visible – and it hasn't even been ten minutes.

I catch my breath after all the heavy lifting and fling my bag back over my shoulder. Taking one last glance around before I head back the way I came and re-enter civilisation.

I check my phone for the time – though it felt as though time had stopped, I have only been in the alley for twenty minutes, thank goodness. That makes it less odd that I up and left my things in the Cosy Coffee for so long.

I have both mine and Cinderella's blood splattered on my clothes, face and hands. Like that isn't at all suspicious.

Keeping my head low to avoid the nosey stare of others, I pace into the coffee shop and head straight to the toilets.

I strip off my jacket, roll up my shirt sleeves and blast the water. I scrub my hands so vigorously, I'm pretty sure I remove several layers of skin in doing so. It takes a good couple of minutes for my hands to turn from a deep crimson to a mere rose hue and I know that's as good as it's going to get. You'd be surprised how tricky that stuff is to wash off.

I repeat the process with my face, with a slightly lighter touch, inhaling sharply every time I go over a bruised area. The side of my jaw is only a little red at the moment, but that is going to be a pain to cover up. *That little brat.*

I don't even look at my jacket. It was leather and pretty pricey, I might add. There is no way that stain is coming out and I'm not about to put my neck on the line for a jacket, no matter how pretty it is. I shove it in my bag with the mind-set to burn it when I get home. Even thinking about it brings tears to my eyes.

I admire myself in the mirror, combing fingers through my tatty hair and touching up faint blemishes to make myself more presentable.

I recall what Cinderella said with her last breath. *I'm not the only one with a grudge...*

Who on earth could she have meant? None of my friends know about my extracurricular activities and I make damn sure none of my victims are able to ID me or find anything out about me. Besides, Cinderella was in the only tale in which I left someone who witnessed it alive, wasn't she

I'm completely stumped and I feel myself losing brain cells by over-thinking it, so I shove it to the back of my mind for the moment. At least until I get back home.

Somehow the day has sped on and it is late in the afternoon now and peak time for the Cosy Coffee.

Aiming to grab my stuff and split, I sit back in my corner and begin to pack away my computer and random documents which are just there to look pretty.

I'm just about to get up and go when a large, rough hand appears on the table. My eyes follow a thick black trail of hairs on tanned skin to find its owner and are greeted by a tall brown-eyed man staring back at me.

Puzzled, I frown and wait for him to inform me as to why his hand is on my table.

The corners of his mouth slowly turn up, revealing his impeccably white teeth which the light so smoothly bounces off. In a deep, husky voice he says, "Hi."

I saw the whole thing. She did it. She finally did it. She messed up. Now she was going to get what she deserved.

CHAPTER 18 - AVERY

"Hi," I reply sitting to the back of the chair with my arms folded.

He glances down and rubs the back of his neck; as he does this I can see the muscles, lying dormant under his tanned skin until now, flex. I can't help the smile creeping across my face. I hope he doesn't notice.

"Sorry," he starts, "you're probably wondering why some strange bloke has come up to you out of the blue and…" He trails off. His eyes are intensely staring at me, and he begins to lean in, getting so close that I can pick out hints of gold in the hypnotic dark shade.

"Then again," he restarts," Lots of strange men must come and talk to you," he declares, whilst rolling his eyes over me.

I mean, I'm flattered but I really do have other things to attend to right now, my leather jacket (*RIP*) is burning a hole in my bag and I can't risk him getting too close to see what is left of Cinderella on my top.

He seems so nervous. I throw him a bone and extend my hand. "I'm Avery." My reason sighs at me as I do this. *What are you doing? You had the perfect out, you're just making this harder for yourself.*

His shoulders drop and he eases slightly, leaning back in the chair he had invited himself into. "It's a pleasure to meet you."

"So, was there a reason you came over here, or was it just because you were bored?" I try to sound relaxed and nonchalant but the frustration of wanting to leave seeps through into my tone. His gentle, strong features screw up slightly. I shouldn't care about his reaction; however I can't help but be intrigued.

"Oh, Avery, I really didn't mean to bother you." *Whoops*, he's offended.

I should just let him go, I really need to get home to sort myself out and deal with what has happened. But I find myself reaching for his arm, grabbing his hand, as he starts to make his way out of the old leather chair.

Those deep hazel eyes pierce mine as he turns to look at me. "You're not bothering me." *Do you want to sound any needier?* My reason is disappointed in me.

"What are you drinking? You seem like a regular here and I need a recommendation." His persona has changed somewhat, there is a newfound confidence in the way he holds himself.

"Coconut latte." I match his confidence.

He turns and heads towards Heidi, and I can't help but feel slightly disappointed that he merely wanted a drink. Suffice to say, my ego is severely wounded.

As I pick up my bag and attempt to pull myself out of the corner (the chairs are far too low in here, it does not make for an easy getaway), I hear his deep voice softly ask Heidi, "two, please." He glances over to me and I'm once again pinned down by those eyes. There's something about them. They appear to be as bright as the sun yet as dark as the moon. I just can't put my finger on what it is that I am fascinated by. And I really hate not understanding something.

"I was actually just about to head off…." I call softly to him but he disregards me and marches over with the two coffees.

"I'm going to take you out." His almost sheepish approach I witnessed only moments ago has now transformed into a commanding, self-assured character that appeals to me a little more than it should.

With a soft laugh, I ask, "Oh is that so? Do I not get a say?"

He returns the laugh but retains his assertive manner. "I'm afraid not. I'll have to take you hostage if you protest."

I'm slightly taken back. After a long day, a harmless bit of flirting is a nice way to calm myself down but extending it on to tomorrow? I'm not sure how comfortable I am with that.

A flush of repulsion spreads across his face as he takes a gulp of my favourite concoction.

"Don't you like it?" I tease with a flutter of my eyes and a glimpse of my killer smirk. I am taking pleasure in his dislike of the drink. I'm happy that it will still be mine and I won't have to share it.

"It's…interesting," he returns, the corner of his lip lifting in a side smile. I feel myself mirroring him. He takes an even bigger sip and makes a sound of joy for my entertainment.

Though I am having a back and forth debate with reason as to whether I should accept his offer, he seems to win every rebuttal. "I'll pick you up at seven tomorrow," he confirms, "From?"

"Lexin…No!" I catch myself as I go to respond. *You almost gave him your address? It's like you're a completely different person.* My reason scorns me – I can't disagree with her, but for some reason unknown to me, I go against her wishes of leaving and never looking back. I notice that he looks confused and slightly startled by my abrupt response and the silence that follows which lasts just a little too long.

I calm my voice and put on a casual mask as I scramble an excuse together, "Sorry, um…there are road works down my street, it's a mess. I can just meet you?"

"Okay, meet me in the town square."

"Great!" I exclaim. My eyes widen as I hear myself. *What is wrong with me?* I sound like a schoolgirl getting asked to the dance. I compose myself and add, "I've got to head off."

"I'll see you tomorrow," he states with no question in his voice. He takes my hand in his, his eyes fixating on mine. "It was lovely to meet you, Avery."

I brush past him, and feeling his warm body against mine even for a second sends energy pulsing through my body. I feel a sensation in my stomach that wants to make me sick and giggle at the same time.

I push through the doors of the Cosy Coffee and as the cold sweet air hits my face, I feel reality begin to set in. It's as though I have just stepped out of a dream.

My reason, muted by him, until now suddenly kicks back in and I take notice of her. *What the hell do you think you're doing? Now you've really gone and done it. This guy is only going to be trouble.*

I waltz home with an unfamiliar spring in my step. I feel a tingling in my stomach that I don't recognise and there is a subtle smile creeping its way across my face as I open my front door.

Although, it immediately falls and my heart stops as I catch sight of a handwritten envelope in front of me. The envelope is a dirty cream and it looks as though it has been crumpled up in someone's coat pocket for hours.

With fragile hands I lift the thin paper, although it feels the weight of a boulder. Once I open it, I am greeted by another cream sheet of paper with cut-out letters from magazines forming words.

"Whoopsy daisies, looks like the grimm reaper's made a little bit of a mess, have fun cleaning this one up."

CHAPTER 19 - HARRY

"The sister's alibi checks out," James announces as he crashes through the doors.

"Well that's what we expected, isn't it?" Harry goes over to the board with the red marker pen.

When you picture a board for a murder investigation, you'd imagine there to be loads of different faces and names, clues and pieces of evidence. You'd imagine a mess of chaotic drawings, question marks, scraps of paper, possible murder weapons. Those are how the boards of investigations going *well* look.

The board for this particular case has a total of three photos. Of which one now has a red cross over it. There is no display of evidence and the only clues from the crime scene are quotes from a fairy tale which make little to no sense and offer no leads on the one large question mark at the top of the board. The Grimm Reaper.

The two detectives remain hopeful but they have seen this case time and time again. The board always looks exactly the same, as the case goes on the leads die out, every alibi stands and they're stuck in the rut they will never claw their way out of.

The only thing keeping Harry going is that the walls of the pit, though slippery, have tiny ridges that he persists in using to clamber to the top, only to slide back down to the bottom with every quiver of his breath.

But one day he will reach the surface. One day he will catch them.

James joins him, mindlessly staring at the board.

"The restraining order against the victim and her stalking of the editor must be this one." Harry points to the photo displaying the words *'unseen she kissed the forehead of her bride'*.

"Yeah." James tilts down his jaw, drawing attention to his under-bite. "We've made sense of all the others, yet we're no further forward with the case than we were three flippin' weeks ago."

Putting a hand on James's shoulder, Harry assures him, "look, we've still got to bring in the chief editor bloke. He's got more motive than anyone. GR gets a lot of coverage in the news, you never know, maybe he killed her in that way to try get himself off the hook."

Neither of them truly believe his words, but it brings the two angry and frustrated detectives some form of comfort.

They have been fighting to get the editor to come in for an interview for almost a week now. His secretary has continued to insist that his schedule is just too booked up. Of course, they can always arrest him but they want to keep their interactions friendly so he will be more willing to cooperate in the interview room.

"Right," James snaps after a few minutes of silence with a newfound energy. "This is what we're going to do; I'm going to call that man's bimbo secretary again, you're going to get hold of the landlord and double check that the CCTV footage has been erased and there isn't any backups and then…I'm going to give in to my rumbling stomach and we're going to break for lunch. Sound good?"

CHAPTER 20 - HARRY

"So, how are things with Martha?" James asks while guzzling down his third burrito from just *this* lunch.

Harry sits upright in his chair, trying to steer clear of the spray of sauce coming from James's mouth. He can't mask his disgust at James's lack of table manners.

Swallowing down his snobbery, Harry sighs. "Well, it was great last week. For the first time since we stopped trying, we actually wanted to be around each other, rather than just smiling to make the other one happy." He sniffs audibly, brushing a hand against his nose. "But I don't know, this week she's back to being closed and distant. We got married straight out of high school – we were stupid and immature kids. Maybe just too much has happened now."

Whilst engulfing the last of his meal, James attempts a sympathetic face, but he and Harry both know that he is not the most comforting guy on the planet. "Well, I'm sorry, mate. I hope it works itself out. You've been together six years; it'd be a shame to give up on that."

I guess it's the thought that counts, Harry thinks, letting out a chuckle. James's words aren't exactly encouraging.

During a brief moment of silence, Harry's crappy old Samsung lights up and jumps around on the table, alerting him to a new text message.

We need to talk

And only a second later, another one pops up on the screen.

Meet me in the usual place tonight, normal time. I really need to see you.

Spotting the identity of the sender, he is quick to flip the phone so it is face down on the table. Harry realises he acted slightly too quickly when he glances back up to find James staring at him, one eyebrow raised.

"If I didn't know any better, I'd think you were keeping a secret from your partner," James declares with a sarcastic undertone.

Waving off James's suspicious expression with a flick of his hand, Harry assures him, "oh it's nothing. Honestly, don't worry about it."

James lets out a forced laugh and says with a glimmer in his eyes, "Yeah, it sure seems like nothing."

Suddenly Harry's look changes and his tone is now more serious as he demands, "Seriously, just let it go."

James changes his face to mimic Harry's and his eyes lock onto the checked tablecloth for a moment, as though his thoughts are venturing deep within his mind.

Finally, he speaks. "You said you're having problems with Martha." His brows furrow further towards his eyes. "You're not having an—"

"No! God, no, why would you think that?" Harry interrupts him before he can say what they both know he was about to say. "No, absolutely not."

Like being on a stomach-curdling rollercoaster, Harry's mood and aura went from light and sarcastic, plummeting straight down to serious and threatening, straight back up to normal. It makes the two of them feel a little nauseous.

"It's nearly one, maybe we should start heading back to the station." He is quick to change the subject and James goes along with it, not pushing who the texts were from any further, but James has known Harry for years. He knows when he is lying.

The door shakes the framework of James's office as Harry hurls it open with a toothy grin smeared across his face. He skips over to the desk behind which James is sitting, rubbing his dry, tired eyes with his even drier hands.

"Happy birthday!" Harry declares as he drops a disc inside a clear plastic wallet down in front of him.

James stares at it, very much less amused than Harry appears to be. "It's not my birthday."

Harry mockingly looks down, sad and replies, "Oh, well then I guess I should save this CCTV footage from March 12th for Christmas."

Harry raises his eyebrows waiting for James's brain to catch up.

With a newfound spark in his eye, James asks excitedly, "you found the footage?"

"I found the footage," Harry confirms with a smirk covering the rest of his face. "The landlord found a backup file and sent it over twenty minutes ago."

Having plucked the wallet back up off the desk, Harry throws it in the air a few times playfully. "So what do you think? Shall we find our Grimm Reaper?"

James jumps up and snatches the disc out of Harry's hands, placing it in the old-fashioned CD tray of his laptop. "I could kiss you right now."

"Please," Harry quickly responds with a grimace, "Don't. Just buy me a few pints and we'll call it even."

Rolling his eyes, James nudges him and hits play on the video.

The quality of the footage forms a picture which is barely distinguishable; it's difficult to tell what is the wall and what is the floor of the main entrance to the building currently on the screen.

In the top right-hand corner of the screen lies white, bold text reading: *08:00 12th March 2016, Camera 1*

The lack of activity on the screen urges James to fast-forward the footage and as the hours speed on, figures begin to scurry across the screen going in and out of the building. Each time someone appears, they pause it and cross-reference the face with the building residents who already have a line crossed through their name on the suspect list, which by this point is nearly everyone.

To add to their everlasting roll of misfortune, all the people who appear in the footage are accounted for. On the upside, they have hours and hours of footage to get through from over ten cameras.

James and Harry start out hopeful, thinking they finally have a breakthrough on this case, but as they go through camera after camera, their eyes grow heavy and their morale plummets back into the rut they fear they will never escape from.

"Hold on, let's not lose hope yet," James urges, "We've still got four cameras left to look at. We'll find something."

Harry isn't used to James being the optimist; usually he is the painful voice of reason that neither of them want to hear.

They have been having déjà vu of the same hallways through all the footage for the past couple of hours. Having to remain so focused on something that they both know in the back of their minds will most probably be a dead end like every other lead they've had.

They reach Camera 8 and they are both dozing off, practically prising their eyes open with their fingers. This is the first camera out of the three that shows the outside of the building and is outside the main entrance.

The screen shows an image of a road painted with potholes and a pavement, which is in a similar state to the road, opening up into a small driveway for the building. There is a selection of parking spaces, bordered with faded white paint. The area is scarcely lit by dim streetlights on either side of the street entrance.

The volume of traffic on the road begins to decrease as the light from the sun fades out of the sky and the limitless rocks a billion lightyears away overcome it.

"Stop!" Harry exclaims suddenly, jolting the both of them out of their daydreams. James does as he is commanded and Harry continues, "Go back a bit. There."

Pointing at the screen with his rough fingers, Harry nods to James, who now sees what Harry caught sight of.

The image is of a dark figure in a long black coat with sunglasses on and a baseball cap. In their hands they are carrying a slick, black bag which resembled a briefcase and a white container.

"Who wears blackout sunglasses at this time of night?" James taunts.

Harry throws it back to him and replies with, "And what's in that container?"

The two are interrupted mid-flow by the rattle of James's office phone.

Wincing at the ringing that scratches his eardrums, James presses the cheap plastic to his ear.

He says, "Yello," in a more cheery mood than he seemed to be in earlier. Harry can hear a squeak of a voice on the other line but cannot make out any words from the noise. James pauses for a moment and then nods. "Sure, okay, Karen, we'll be through in five." He thumps the phone back onto its hook.

Harry stares at him expectantly.

"Right, my friend." James gives his chair a dramatic shove, abruptly standing up and throwing his hands up in the air as he does so. "Let's go meet Mr Big Shot."

"He's here?" Harry's surprised expression reflects just how difficult it was to get hold of him. "Finally he's decided to grace us with his presence." Harry's eye roll mimics his poor attitude towards the Chief Editor.

"Now make sure you withhold your distaste towards him, we want him to like us." James sounds like a stern parent warning his child to behave.

"Okay," Harry agrees reluctantly. "I guess we'll have to wait to find out who the *Man in Black* is. Let's go grill the hell out of this guy."

CHAPTER 21 - HARRY

"You have the most beautiful eyes, you know that?" Leaning across the reception desk is a pristine, dark navy suit without even the slightest crease in the silk material. The deep, blood red tie matches the suit effortlessly. Occupying the impeccable attire is a clean-shaven, emerald-eyed figure. His golden locks are slicked back without a single strand out of place.

Karen collapses into herself and stares down with a shaky smile when she receives the compliment. "Oh, no…my eye…no, no…um," she stutters, unaware of how to handle such a comment.

Fortunately for her, it is obvious that this is not her admirer's first rodeo. He seems somewhat amused by her coyness and he only persists further.

"Oh, now, Karen, you can't tell me you haven't noticed how blue your eyes are?" The corners of his lips turn up. "My goodness, they are just mesmerising."

As if she were a deer caught in headlights, Karen freezes. When she finally manages to will the muscles of her face to reshape, she lets out a high-pitched giggle and slaps her hands over her face in an attempt to mask the blood rushing to her cheeks.

"Do you know what I think?" He reaches towards her face slowly and gently coaxes her palms back down to her sides. He then places his hands on either side of her spectacles and Karen is frozen again, completely hypnotised by his touch.

As he pulls the glasses from her face, he gazes into her eyes and remains silent for a moment.

"There," he finally declares with a smirk, "just as I thought. You shouldn't hide those pearls behind such thick lenses."

Harry coughs sarcastically to break Karen out of her trance. He and James have been standing next to the desk for a minute or two now.

"Detective Sergeant Flynn!" Karen spurts out. "Sorry, right." She fiddles with stationery on the desk and jerks her head and eyes in all directions, trying to bring herself back into the present. "This is Mr Erikson," she states with a far more aristocratic tone than she actually has.

"Please, call me Jack." He shoots her a smoulder and she forces herself to refrain from turning giddy again.

"Mr Erikson," James says as he extends his hand, unsettled by the interaction he is currently witnessing. Mr Erikson grasps it. "I'm Detective Sergeant—"

"Flynn," Mr Erikson interjects, "Great to meet you. Please, call me Jack."

"Okay, Jack," James responds and gestures towards Harry, "this is Detective Constable Ellis." Harry bows his head towards Jack. "We will be interviewing you this afternoon. If you wouldn't mind just coming with us and we'll get to it."

The two detectives lead Jack down the corridor and into the same interview room that Mrs Lewis was in just last week.

Although unlike her, Jack doesn't seem affected by the eerie nature of the room.

As they open the door, Jack marches past them and sits in the single chair tucked neatly under the table without instruction.

His posture is formal and upright, with both his feet planted level on the concrete. He tilts his chin to be at just more than a ninety-degree angle, and looks down his nose at his hands which are clasped together gently on the steel.

James and Harry sit in the two chairs before him and mimic his stance.

"Mr Erikson," James begins, notepad in hand, "I have in my notes that you are the chief editor of Bennet and Roy Publishing House, is that right?" Once Jack confirms this, James continues, "and you are newly married, correct?"

"Yes I am. Almost three months now." He seems proud of his newly contracted marriage.

Can't love it that much if you're flirting with the first woman you see, Harry thinks snidely whilst his face is steady, portraying a pleasant smile.

Shifting in his seat, James says, "Now I'm sure you are aware that we found your previous employee deceased in her apartment on March 12th."

"Yes, I do know. It's so awful I can't imagine who would do such a vulgar thing." Jack shakes his head. "So awful." Harry can't help but detect a lack of genuine grief in his tone.

"Yes, it truly is a tragedy," James agrees. "The reason we have brought you in today is because the victim's sister came in last week and explained to us that the victim was in fact having an affair with you. Is that correct?"

His head drops lower and Jack lets out a long breath before replying, "Yes it is true. You are the police and so I will not lie to you about this."

Oh how kind of you, Harry comments to himself as he chuckles silently.

"When it all came out, I was not entirely honest about my role in the affair. When I met her, I found her charming and beautiful." He takes a long pause, as if building himself up to continue. "I admit that I gave in to my corrupt desires and I did willingly partake in an affair with her."

Again, Harry fails to sense any real remorse from Jack. His answers feel almost robotic.

"But." Jack suddenly lifts his head to its previous superior position. "As time went on, I realised how terrible I was being. When she found out that I had a fiancée, I had an epiphany."

Harry shoots James a look. *Jesus, drama queen.*

"I immediately ended the affair with her and I thought that was the end of it." The tones in his voice are as if he is narrating a screenplay. "Obviously I couldn't fire her due to our indiscretions – no doubt it would bring the lawyers in. So, I saw her at work and tried to be polite but avoid conversation with her unless it was essential.

"Gradually, she started becoming obsessed. She texted me at least twenty times a day, filled up my emails entirely, I had missed calls from her…it truly freaked me out. Because of this behaviour, my fiancée was getting suspicious of why I had all these mysterious phone calls and messages. So one day, when I'd finally had enough, I arranged to meet with her to ask her to stop."

Both James and Harry know that this story wasn't aligning with the one Mrs Lewis gave them, but they want to let him finish before poking holes in his narrative, to see where he takes it.

Jack lets out a heavy sigh again. "Unfortunately, on that particular night, my fiancée decided to follow me and she jumped to the conclusion that we were having an affair. Before I could explain to her what had happened, she declared it to everyone we knew. Now, I could have told my fiancée that I did have an affair with her and ended it, but in the state she was in I highly doubted she would've believed me. So, I told her that when she came to work for us she took a liking to me and I only went to meet with her to ask her to stop harassing me.

"Since we had been through so much, we decided to stop waiting around and just get married the next day." Jack's pause this time is longer than his previous one, and James takes this as a sign he is finished.

After clearing his throat, James begins, "thank you for explaining that to us. I just have a few queries; I understand that you filed for a restraining order against the victim two months ago – after you got married – however, if she was harassing you for such a long period of time before this, why did you not contact the police sooner?"

"Well," Jack starts, "To be honest, I didn't want my fiancée finding out the reason she was harassing me. I thought that if I could handle it myself then there was no reason for her to ever find out. Clearly, it didn't quite unfold as I had hoped and when we did finally get married, she didn't relinquish her obsession and she began to watch the both of us at our home. It was no longer just me who was in danger and so I felt at that point it was necessary to take formal action against her."

The two detectives nod and glance at each other in silent conversation. *Well it's not the same as the sister's story,* Harry thought. *If he is lying he's pretty damn good,* James thought in response.

"That's great, Mr Erikson, thank you for your cooperation," Harry says. "Since you did engage in a relationship with the victim at one point, we would just like to ask you a few questions about her typical daily whereabouts as far as you are aware. For example if and where she went out for lunch on weekdays, if she was a member of any clubs and if she had a particular routine on the weekends?"

"Absolutely," Jack agrees willingly. "She typically brought salads into the office and wouldn't go into town on her lunch break. As far as I'm aware she wasn't a part of anything outside of work – she kept herself rather isolated. And…let's see." Jack rubs his forehead. "I believe she went to the gym in the mornings on weekends – oh yes, she was a member of the gym, I forgot that. She never did much on the weekends, just visited family and friends. Though, she did go to this little café every Sunday." Jack frowns as he recalls the memory. "She would go there to do work. Said she enjoyed the sound of *people*. I met her there once – I could never understand why she found it peaceful, to me it was raucous and claustrophobic. But anyway, that's all I can remember."

As James clicks the top of his pen, he smiles down at Jack. "Just one last thing, could you tell us where you and your wife were on March 12th from nine pm?"

Sighing, he responds, "oh goodness I really can't say for certain – I've never been very good at remembering the little things. I suppose I was in bed asleep. I go to sleep at ten pm sharp every night without failure, so there is no way I would have been roaming about at all. Now my wife, if I remember correctly, she went out for a girls' night with her two sisters. I don't know when she got back – I can sleep through pretty much anything. I'm really sorry I can't give you any more than that, sorry if it's not much help."

James excuses him and thanks him again for coming into the station. They all stand up in unison and make their way out of the room.

Reaching the reception, Jack slides his forearm across Karen's desk. "It was great to meet you," he says with a smoulder and a wink. Karen's mouth spreads across the entirety of her face and she giggles in response.

Just as Jack heads round the corner for the exit, Harry hurries after him. "Wait!"

Jack spins around with a stressed expression, tapping his impeccably polished Italian leather shoes.

"You said she went to a little café every Sunday, do you remember the name of it?"

"Look, I'm sorry, I have a meeting I really need to go. It was a small café in the town square. Something like Snuggles…Comfy Coffee…" Glancing down at his watch again he exclaims, "look, I really have to go, I cannot be late for this meeting. I can't remember the name of it.

Goodbye." And without a second look he pushes through the heavy metal-framed doors and disappears around the corner of the street.

Harry shrugs as he ambles back over to James. "He said Snuggles or Comfy Coffee. The only small coffee shop I know of in the town square that sounds like that is Cosy Coffee. That's what my money's on."

"Yeah, well at least we know a little more about her now. I have no doubt that he is the one lying about the extent of their relationship, but I don't think it's because he killed her – he just doesn't want his new wife finding out," James declares as the two of them re-enter his office.

"That's what I was thinking," Harry agrees, "but we won't rule him out completely. If this wasn't *youknowwho*, then he has the most motive."

"What about the wife? We haven't interviewed her yet. It seems wholly possible that she wanted revenge on her husband's mistress. Especially since the two of them got married so speedily, nearly the day after she found out he was having an affair. It could be a cover up," James suggests.

"You're right. Let's go round to their house for an informal interview this week to check out her alibi. But for now," Harry says as he slumps into one of the chairs behind James's desk, "Let's take another look at those tapes."

CHAPTER 22 - AVERY

Today is a good day.

It's been nine days, 1 hour and 41 minutes since my little run-in with Cinderella, nine days, 3 hours and 32 minutes since I received that peculiar message and nine days 2 hours and 14 minutes since I met Him.

I don't want to speak too soon, but I would say this is so far my best week this year – following what was probably my worst.

To start, I have formulated an airtight plan to correct my slip up last week and since I am the one who has created it there is very little chance of it going awry. I have also heard nothing more from whoever that creep was who put the letter through my door, and I have been going through all my previous indiscretions with a fine-tooth comb in order to identify who exactly Cinderella was referring to when she said *I'm not the only one with a grudge.*

Finally, I am seeing Him tonight. It's very unlike me to become excited over such a trivial thing as going on a date, but I've got to give it to him, He's proving to be an addiction.

With everything going on at the moment, my love life would serve me better by remaining dormant. As hard as I tried not to become involved with Him, there is just something about Him that I find elusive. And I am determined to uncover exactly what that thing is.

It seems to have had an abnormal effect on me though. Even the doctors that I have regular meetings with have noticed my out-of-character *chirpiness*. I can't decide if I like it or find it insufferably irritating.

I bang my forehead with the heel of my palm several times, trying to knock his image from my thoughts, and begin to focus on what is really important – Cinderella's Prince.

Now, I have of course done my research and it seems that Cinders and her little Prince weren't living as happily ever after as you'd think. In fact, having done a small amount of observation, I've discovered that she moved out of his place a few months ago and they haven't spoken in weeks.

Apparently, she was never quite the same after her family died.

This benefits me in two ways. One, he isn't concerned about her lack of contact and so it will take longer for the police to be notified of her body. Two, it means they were having issues. And who is responsible for thirty per cent of all female murders? The husband.

I settle into my six-month old Audi TT and breathe in the cream leather's aroma. One of my old friends dragged me to a car showing and there my baby was – spinning on the platform, perfectly lit by studio lights and finished off with a slick shine. It was an impulse buy, for sure, but it was love at first sight. And I don't regret the £53.5K dip in my bank balance for a second.

I tap the postcode of Cinder's fella's office into the built-in satnav and pull away from the entrance of Southhurst Medical Clinic.

The palace is just outside of town so my journey isn't too time-consuming. The time now is 1.37pm and if I have my facts right, the Prince began making his way back to his office seven minutes ago. He will be pushing the button for the elevator at 2.03pm, giving me just enough time to casually slide in next to him, I am sure we will be in close proximity when all the other businessmen pile into the elevator, hurrying to meetings they are already late for.

Why my sudden desire to be drenched in others' sweat in a claustrophobic cuboid of bacteria? That you'll have to wait for.

I enter his office block at exactly 2pm and immediately catch sight of the three lifts in the far corner of the reception. My heels echo into the high ceiling as they hit the marble tiles and I lower my head ever so slightly, ensuring I do not draw attention to myself, and no one asks my reason for being there.

I see him pacing over to the far corner just as the clock turns to two minutes past the hour, his fitted suit trying desperately to cling to the ghost of muscles that once were. His expression isn't as confident as I remember, there are a few new wrinkles above and between his eyebrows and his fiery locks are dull and flat, clearly abandoned to simply rest on his sweat-covered scalp without any kind of care. I suppose he hasn't been doing too well without Cinderella.

I attempt to subtly follow on behind him, though this attempt is hindered by the clicking and clacking of my thinly pointed heels meeting the ground. I should have worn my tailing shoes.

Just as I predicted, the crowd starts to formulate only a minute later and *ding*, everybody hurtles into the five by five foot space which we will be sharing for the next three minutes.

I am perfectly positioned slightly behind and to the right of the Prince and I prepare myself – trying to avoid thinking about all of the vile microbes these greasy men are exhaling into my air.

The Prince exits at level 15, so I have a suitable window of time to do what I need to. I don't want him to notice me. I can only act when the herd of suited figures exit, so that he's expecting to be pushed around a little bit.

Unfortunately, only one or two people leave at a time and the elevator continues to move up level by level, getting uncomfortably close to 15.

The doors open for level 8 and finally a mass of people leave the elevator and several more enter, creating just the kind of commotion I need.

As both the Prince and I are being knocked around by people shuffling, someone pushes me and I fall, grasping his jacket sleeve for balance. He glances back at me sternly and I whisper *sorry* and he returns to facing the bland steel doors.

I stare down and uncurl my closed, leather-covered hand and admire the small, dark grey fibres which lie in the centre of my palm. I smile briefly but then quickly clench my hand shut again and peel off the glove, making certain the fibres are securely sealed in the fabric, before placing it into my handbag.

Only one thing left.

A mere thirty seconds later, another herd awakes and I have my second shot. As I am reaching for the strawberry blonde strands at the nape of his neck, he is suddenly no longer in my grasp.

I don't understand why, for a long microsecond, and then I realise he is part of the herd. I stand, frozen, stunned by his figure growing smaller and smaller as the distance between us increases, until he disappears from my sight completely.

I never get things wrong. My calculations are always correct. This is level 10 he isn't supposed to be gone. This isn't right.

I make my way back down to the ground floor with a frown screwed onto my face.

A slideshow of last week speeds through my mind while I try to remember everything I did, everything I learnt about the Prince. I can't understand where I went wrong, it made no sense. I'm so careful when I am doing research, this has never happened before.

Did he get off on that level just by chance today, even though he has not done so every day last week and the different floors are completely separate companies? So why would he visit one?

As I advance back across the main hall I stop abruptly at reception and even though I have the overwhelming urge to hurt someone, I put on my best smile and quietly ask, "Excuse me, would you be able to tell me which floor Harrison and Taylor Solicitor's firm is on? I think I got some wrong information and I have a meeting with them in ten minutes."

The scruffy male who is sitting behind the desk beams back at me enthusiastically and replies, "Yes of course, it's on floors ten and eleven. Would you like me to call up there for you?"

I hold my breath as the odour emanating from his mouth invades my nostrils and I have to choke down a gag. God, has this guy ever heard of a breath mint? Looking at him – probably not. He looks as though he hasn't even hit puberty yet. I can see the one chin hair that he refuses to shave because he's so proud he's *finally becoming a man*. His face is covered with acne and my God, is his hair greasy. I struggle to mask my disgust but keep up the smile.

Persevering through the pain, I assure him, "No, no, that's okay. I need to wait for my business partner. Thank you though."

Once he nods a goodbye, I hurry away from the area he has infected and make my way back down the street to my car.

How did this happen? The firm was floors 15 and 16. I double-checked it. I triple-checked it.

As I unlock my car, I remember. I throw my bag on the passenger seat and thump down next to it, slamming the door hard behind me.

It was Him.

That flippin' bastard called me just as I was looking for the floor numbers. He must have distracted me.

This is why I never let people get that close to me – they will always ruin everything. I suppose I should be angry at myself, though. I knew this and yet I still went through with that first date and then did so again and again and…Oh shit. I'm fifteen minutes late to the restaurant where I'm meant to be meeting Him.

My blood boils at the thought of seeing the face that screwed up my plan and I linger in my car on the side of the street for at least seven minutes, deciding whether I should go to Him or go home.

Looking at how much my hand is twitching, it'll probably be safer for the both of us if I definitely do not see Him now, so I rev the engine, skid out onto the road and stick my middle finger out the window at the people behind the wheels of the cars that are beeping their horns at me.

As my fingers' shaking slows and my bearings are once again gathered, I can't help but twitch as I see a small van with all blacked-out windows three cars behind me. It's been going the same direction as me for a while, now. I didn't notice it when I left the Prince's workplace, so it can't have been following me, it's just a coincidence. Yes, a coincidence.

Then again, when I left the office block, I wasn't in a state to notice.

I cross the threshold of my house at 3:17pm, kick my patent black heels off and drop my bag to the hallway floor before heading straight to the kitchen and grabbing a beer fresh from the fridge.

Throwing my jacket on the stairs, I slump into the couch with a long sigh. My veins have now cooled down to a simmer but my fists are still clenched.

Having been in a fit of stupidity, I cancelled all my afternoon appointments in order to see Him, so now I have nothing to do except lie around and mull over my unnecessary slip up. There is no way I can go back and collect what I need from the Prince now since he will be in his office until

6:40pm when everyone else has left. Even I can't go unnoticed in such a desolate situation. I'll have to return tomorrow, what a bother.

I dangle the bottle in the air and lap up the last drop of its contents before sitting upright and examining the lounge.

The ground floor of my house is an open floor plan, so the hallway leads straight into the lounge which leads straight into the kitchen which leads straight into the dining room. As my eyes look over to the hallway, I can't help but grit my teeth at the sight of my belongings strewn across the ground.

I was in a less than optimal mood when I returned home and so I gave little thought to putting everything in its correct place, but now that I have calmed down, seeing the mess makes me squirm.

I immediately pace over and pick up my heels, placing them on the shoe rack to the right of the front door, next to my other pair of black business heels. Once I've removed my phone from my handbag, I hang it up on the empty hook on the wall and then hang my jacket up on the rack opposite.

Now having my hallway properly organised, my mind is put at ease and I unlock my phone.

Three missed calls and five text messages. All from Him.

Hey, where are you?

Are you running late? Just shoot me a text so I know you're alright.

You didn't answer my phone calls. I'm getting a little worried.

It's been an hour. I'm still here, just please tell me what's going on.

I've gone home. Call you when I'm back. I just want to know if you're okay.

It has now been two hours and thirty-three minutes since I was supposed to meet Him. Though I originally blamed Him, I have started to admit now that perhaps I should have been more focused and I suppose I can't really blame Him. I'm still annoyed with Him, even though he can't know why, but I didn't want Him to worry about me, so I text Him back.

I'm fine. Sorry I didn't answer, phone died.

I try to be as least blunt as I can manage, but I don't think it is very convincing. He messages me back almost instantly.

What happened? Why didn't you show? What's wrong?

Usually when you can tell that someone's upset, you try and ignore it and pretend like you didn't notice so that you don't have to deal with it unless they directly bring it up. Don't you? That's what I always thought, anyway. But with Him, it's not like that. If he thinks something's up he doesn't mess around, he wants to know straight away and he wants to know what he can do to help. It was a real shock at first and I wasn't quite sure how to handle it, but now I've realised that he won't stop so it's just easier to give in. Of course, I can't tell Him why I am really in a mood this afternoon for obvious reasons.

Just a bad day at work. I had a headache and I just wanted to go home.

I know I can lie my way out of it if he asks about any details, I've had so many bad days at work I merely have to choose which one I want to rant about.

Come to the park now, I've got a surprise for you.

I contemplate whether to take Him up on his offer or not, all things considered. But I come to the conclusion that I will go, if not to see Him then to find out what this surprise is. One of my only flaws? I'm very, very nosey.

CHAPTER 23 - AVERY

The park in the centre of town is a perfectly picturesque scene in the midst of the never-ending hustle and bustle of Southhurst.

It stretches across acres of land, so when you entered the park, you wouldn't believe you're still in an urban city. Rather, it harbours the scents and sounds of the New Forest with the alluring aroma of pine and oak trees, as well as the soothing sounds of nature.

There he is, just where he said he would be.

I am still a fair distance away from Him and he hasn't seen me yet. He shuffles around on the bench, tapping his foot anxiously and jerking his eyes around the green field.

A few moments later he catches sight of me. His foot rests, his eyes fix on mine and the corners of his lips turn up.

I stare at Him. *That's the man who screwed up my plan.* I try so hard to remain angry as I waltz up to Him, reciting this over and over in my head.

"Hi," I say once I am only a metre from Him, keeping a stern expression and tone.

He immediately stands up, takes my hand in his and presses his lips against my cheek before replying, "Hey," in a sweet and gentle voice.

I feel like I'm having an out of body experience. I watch myself and sigh. *I've got bigger problems to deal with than some stupid guy. My involve-*

ment with Him has already tripped me up once, why am I entertaining this idea any longer?

My reason screams at me, telling me to deal with what is really important and stop being so naïve, yet despite the headache she is giving me, I melt into his eyes and I can't help the smile taking over my face.

"So," he starts as we sit down on the unbearably uncomfortable bench. "Tell me what's up."

I let out a heavy breath, preparing for my role. "Oh, honestly like I said, it's really nothing. I've just had a bunch of meetings today and it's safe to say none of them went very well. The doctors were just being so flippin' stubborn. I swear they all have two metre long sticks up their arses. Oh and that annoying girl from the office, remember Kirsty?" I pause, waiting for his nod before continuing. "She is such a goody-two-shoes, she's got her head so far up our boss's behind that she's getting her spray tans for free. And the fact she had *such a good day* and sold *loads and loads of drugs* just really made me resent her. When I headed back to the office, her incessant high-pitched whining literally pierced my skull, I just had to go home and lie down to try and get the ringing out of my ears."

When I finally finish my rant, I study his face, expecting puppy-dog eyes or a pouting lower lip because he just *feels so bad for me* and *just wants to comfort me* and blah, blah, blah.

To my surprise, I look up to find Him with a grin smeared across his face and his eyes squinting whilst laughing silently.

"What?" I ask, slightly vexed by his lack of sympathy, but at the same time intrigued to know why he found this amusing.

"You know," he starts once he manages to withhold his laughter, "you're a really nice person. I've never realised just how lovely you are."

I frown. "Are you being sarcastic? Aren't you supposed to be comforting me, or whatever?"

"Oh come on, that's not that bad," he shrugs, "certainly not bad enough for you to blow me off." He chuckles.

"Hey!" I exclaim defensively. "It really pissed me off. I thought I would do you a favour."

He strokes my shoulder and moans quietly. "I'm sorry. You probably were doing me a favour. I get the sense that I wouldn't want to be on the wrong side of you."

I laugh, partly with Him and partly at the irony.

I nudge Him. "So come on then, you only got me down here by bribery. Where's this surprise, huh?"

He reaches down and picks up a tatty old rucksack which I only just notice is even there, and he pulls out a navy blue, peculiar looking soft toy with a beaming purple grin and tiny horns. I stare at it sideways before I realise what it is.

My eyes widen and my expression is that of a six-year-old. "You got me one!" I exclaim while bouncing in my seat subtly. I'm barely able to control my excitement.

I snatch it from his hands almost instantly – maybe a little too aggressively – I stare into its bright green eyes, running my fingers through its spikey, synthetic pink hair.

"Oh my God, I haven't seen one of these in forever!" I embrace the toy as childhood memories flash before my eyes. "Where did you find it?" I ask but before letting Him answer, my expression changes and my eyes narrow. "Wait. Did you buy this at a shop somewhere? Or did you win it? You know I can only accept it depending on your answer."

He rolls his eyes and smiles, "As easy as it would have been to just go to a shop and pick one up, I went through the agony of winning it on a claw machine, which was enormously difficult to find, by the way. Believe it or not, most claw machines don't stock popular toys from the eighties."

I switch my frown back to a smile and hug the toy again. "Okay, I accept it. I can't believe you did this. Where did you even find one that had it?"

He sighs, clearly preparing for a long story. "I researched all the fairs and arcades in Southhurst, but when they didn't have any I looked up the city next to us – Braxton, and I managed to find a little corner shop that sold old children toys and thank goodness they had a claw machine in there which was stacked full of these little guys." He gestures to the toy still tightly pressed into my shoulder. "And then I spent a hell of a long time in there trying to win it. Do you have any idea how difficult it is to beat one of those things?"

His tone is sarcastic, his eyes show that he is lit up by my excitement and I wrap my arm around his neck and kiss Him.

"I can't believe you did that."

He shrugs with pretend modesty. "Well, I'm an old romantic, me."

A laugh bursts from my mouth. "Oh you are, are you?" I raise my eyebrows in disbelief and he bows his head. "You took me to laser tag on our first date. I don't think that counts as very romantic."

His face is an oxymoron. His brows furrow and his lower lip sticks out in a defensive expression, but his hazel eyes are sprinkled with embers and the corners of his lips disobey Him, curling up ever so slightly and creating two faint indents just below the apples of his cheeks.

"Hey!" He reacts, fabricating his heated tone. "Laser tag is dark with small lights – that's romantic. There were other people there – just as there would be in a crowded restaurant. The only minor difference is we were running around a bit instead of sitting at a table."

I roll my eyes. "I don't think it was a *bit* of running. By the way you were smelling after it, you're lucky you got a second date."

He nudges me gently. "What can I say; I'm just a little competitive. Would you have preferred an overly-priced dinner at a fancy-shmancy restaurant?"

"Oh no," I insist. "Showing off your real-estate money to try to impress me with how much you can spend? That's just a little too clichéd for my taste. Are you kidding me? I crushed it at laser tag, I'm a real prodigy."

That's no fib, it really was my first time playing laser tag. Don't get me wrong, I love to be wined and dined every now and then. But nothing can beat a little game of cat and mouse.

Nestling my head into his shoulder I take my attention back to my new friend. "What shall I call him?" I ask, tilting my head up slightly.

"How about…" He contorts his face faintly. "Jeffrey."

"Jeffrey?" I exclaim in surprise. "You can't name a *my pet monster* Jeffrey. All the other my pet monsters would make fun of him."

He chuckles at me. "Okay, then how about Fluffy?"

"No," I say abruptly. "You're rubbish at choosing names. How about Dopey? You know, from the Snow White fairy tale?" Adrenaline shoots up my spine as the sweet memory flashes across my vision

"Hmm, yeah okay then." He agrees and wraps his arms around me when he notices my body shiver.

I admire Dopey, stroking his face. After a few moments of silence, I proclaim, "he's so ugly."

At first he doesn't respond, merely stares at the soft toy on my lap along with me. Then, he bursts into laughter and agrees.

We talk for hours, lying on the mouldy planks of wood that make up the bench. People come and go from the park, their visits becoming less frequent as the sky darkens. Once the moon has taken up its watch for the night and the burning rocks sparkle above us, it is only he and I who remain in the grassy area.

Neither one of us realise how late it's gotten until we have to squint to see each other's expressions. It is then that I realise my body has been shivering and my teeth have been involuntarily chattering because of the numbing molecules that have now overcome the air, no longer heated by the sun.

"I better be heading home, my bed will be wondering where I am," I announce as I begin to hoist myself off the bench and I shake my legs in an attempt to wake them up. *Ow, pins and needles.*

"Okay, well it's late and dark, I'll take you home. Did you hear that serial killer struck again? Bloody sick. It's not safe for you to walk home alone." There is no humour to his voice now, only concern.

Part of me wants to giggle at the comment and part of me is made uneasy by how close to home that is.

"I am a grown woman, you know. I can look after myself," *especially against myself...* "But mentioning a serial killer right before I'm about to walk home is definitely a sure way to make any girl drag you along for the ride, so sure."

The walk isn't too far from my street – I do it in eleven minutes and fifteen seconds, but the journey the two of us take spans over twenty-two minutes. This isn't because we are walking slowly; in fact it feels as though I am at a constant jog trying to keep up with his stride. No, the extra time is due to me instructing us to take a right at the second corner shop when my abode is left.

Nevertheless, we roam through the various streets that I am honestly picking at random, before I grind to a halt outside a plain-looking house with no name or number and a replica of all the other houses along the road.

"This is me," I declare as I turn to face Him.

"You know," he starts with a suspicious nature, "I've never actually been in your house before."

I'm taken back by his implication. "You can't just invite yourself into a lady's house," I state with a disbelieving smile. "Did your mother never teach you social etiquette?"

"Yeah, alright, just thought I would give it a go."

He brushes his hand over my neck, stroking my hair back over my shoulder. "I'll call you tomorrow, okay?" His voice is soft and quiet. I lean into his chest to feel his warm words.

Looking up at him, I respond, "Okay."

He wraps his arms around me and we say goodnight. I begin to lumber towards the front door of the house as he speeds back down the street. It isn't long until he is around the corner and out of sight. Still, I wait a few moments to ensure he will not return before I walk away from the door and make my way home.

I hate myself for doing it, but every four paces I check over my shoulder, certain there are not only the fox and badger's eyes on me. Certain there is an echo to my footsteps.

I slide the key into the lock at 9:12pm. *Click* and I gently coax the door open, but I don't make it past the threshold.

Lying on the floor in front of me is a cream envelope. *Another one.*

My heart flutters and I jerk my head in all directions, trying to catch a silhouette. There is no one in sight.

I snatch the letter up off the wooden flooring and I hurry to get myself into the house before double-locking the door.

Staring only at the envelope, I walk over to my desk and sit in the chair behind it. Just like the other one, the envelope contains a folded A4 piece of paper, with letters cut out from magazines that are barely clinging to the material with poor quality adhesive.

Throwing someone else under the bus? You didn't think it would be that easy, did you? Try again.

Now my paranoia of someone constantly watching me is confirmed. They know what I'm doing. They know where I am. They know where I'm going to be.

I suddenly feel unsettled and nervous, with a voice in my head saying they're in my house, or they're listening in on my phone.

Being in the place of less knowledge is not where I am meant to be. I do not like this.

My hands now shaking, I yank the drawer open and throw the letter and envelope inside, covering my little brown book before slamming it back shut.

Once I have calmed myself down, I begin to think logically. For all I know, this person could just be bored with their own life and is looking for something exciting to do. Perhaps they don't have anything against me. Perhaps they're just bluffing.

Yes, they know who I am and they know about my dealings with Cinderella, but what can they do with that information? My DNA and fingerprints will likely be found on her body, but they cannot do anything with that information unless I am a person of interest and I have no connection to her. Even if they tip off the police and point them in my direction, they have no grounds because in their eyes I have no motive and a tip-off isn't enough to charge me for murder – even if there is a forensic match. The probability of me even coming up on their suspect list is slim to say the least.

Then again, better safe than sorry.

I slap my hands together and a burst of energy flows through me.

"Right, it's time to make a plan," I say to myself and I go back into the drawer and grab my little brown book.

It was a close one tonight. I only just left before she came back. I mustn't let that happen again. But it was worth it. I've gotten under her skin.

CHAPTER 24 - HARRY

He jams the key into the rusty lock and jiggles the door until it gives and falls open.

Another late night, Harry thinks, *Martha isn't going to like this.*

He steps into the house and is greeted by the exaggerated bangs of saucepans and dishes. Martha is in the kitchen, fully aware he has entered but she refrains from paying him any attention.

After several moments of lurking in the kitchen doorway, watching her, Harry finally says, "Hey."

She stops immediately and shoots her scolding eyes in his direction. "Oh, hello. It's so nice of you to make an appearance. At half past ten."

"Babe, I'm sorry, it's just—"

"You know what I thought? I thought Harry must be having such a tough time at work. Wouldn't it be nice of me to make him a romantic dinner with all his favourites?" Martha's voice is shaky but Harry is not yet sure if it is from her withholding tears or withholding anger.

After she says this, Harry catches sight of the uneaten rib-eye resting on top of the rubbish in the open bin. Harry sighs and slaps his hand over his face.

"Darling, I'm sorry," he says, approaching her cautiously in order to analyse her response. He gets within a foot of her and reaches for her hands but Martha storms off in the other direction.

With his patience wearing thin, Harry goes after her in a similar manner. "Look, how was I supposed to know you were going to do all this?" he exclaims as he follows her into the lounge. "I don't focus how long I work for on the basis that you may or may not have made me dinner."

"You are supposed to be home at six! And you have the audacity to walk through the door three hours later? A one off – fine, I'm understanding. But near to every god-damn night? I have the right to get pissed off."

Harry's face is now flushed red. "In case you haven't noticed, there is a serial killer on the loose." With every word, his volume escalates. "This sick person has been terrorizing this town for fifteen years and I will stop at nothing to see them taken down!"

"You know what, I am sick to death of feeling sorry for you. You can't use that as an excuse every time you do something that upsets me." She turns from him and marches up the stairs but before she is out of sight, she adds, "oh and don't think I'm some ignorant, naïve little wife. I know that your Chief wouldn't keep you until dark every day for months on end. Maybe try coming up with a new lie."

Damn, Harry cusses himself, before wincing at the bellowing echo of the bedroom door.

Even though Martha was making a brass marching band when Harry came home only ten minutes ago, the kitchen is a mess. Harry is tired and cares little for cleaning up, but he knows that if he doesn't make a dent in the dirt then this argument will just continue until morning.

After making the ground floor of the house marginally more presentable, he steps outside for a fag before grabbing a blanket from the cupboard under the stairs and setting up camp on the sofa.

He and Martha have been together long enough for Harry to know that when she slams the door in that way it might as well be bolted shut.

His phone projects a flashing light onto the ceiling and Harry is quick to snatch it off the coffee table and switch it off. He doesn't need to see who it's from, he already knows.

My back's really gonna feel this tomorrow, Harry complains, before rolling over with his face compressed into the corner of the arm rest. He focuses on the tick of the clock. It starts off as a drumming in his ears, but as his heartrate steadies and his breathing slows to a pace that might make one wonder if there was any air coming from his lungs at all, the tick softens and a few seconds later it mutes completely.

All Harry wants tonight is just a few hours of decent rest. That's it. That's all he wants. He yells this over and over to the darkness that is hurtling towards him, with its hands outstretched, ready to take him.

He's woken up by a crashing that resonates up his arms and back down his spine. He throws himself upright in bed, with his heart thumping against his fragile ribs, while his stomach somersaults. He's unsure of the source, but he's certain it isn't a friendly one.

His eyes are so wide, they feel as though they will pop out of his head. The room is pitch black, but somehow he can see everything as clear as day. Suddenly the room begins to shrink and the pirates on his wall that used to smile sweetly at him, now seem to bear a menacing grin. His parrot clock which used to give a soothing rhythm for him to fall asleep, now makes him tense all his muscles with every tick. The ticks now sound like they are counting down, creeping closer and closer to zero.

He hears a deep groan. His teeth are chattering now and his breath is so loud, it bounces of the walls and lashes at his eardrums. He hugs the matted blue teddy tight, with his eyes now squeezed shut. He doesn't want to see the eyes on him anymore. All the eyes staring right at him.

Hearing light footsteps press on the old wooden planks of the hallway and making them creak, leads him to leap out of bed. He knows he can't stay there. He has to go somewhere.

He's about to crawl under the bed, but something inside tells him not to and instead to jump into his laundry basket. He's still only small so it's an easy fit. He pulls a handful of clothes over his head to cover his trembling hair and he stares through the mesh fabric at his open door.

He's sure his eyes are playing tricks on him. It's as if everything in his room is now against him. The toys that used to comfort him at night are now the cause of his fear, the hallway light that he always kept on to scare all the monsters away now dims and flickers.

And then the light is blocked out of his bedroom completely.

He can't make out who it is. All he sees is a black silhouette. A demon. A monster with flaring nostrils and glowing eyes. Holding a peculiar object in its hand.

Harry is jolted awake and gasps. Beads of sweat run down his face and his blood pumping through his wrists is visible.

His throat is constricted and he struggles to take in air, causing his body to waver and his head to grow faint.

Calm down, he says to himself. *Deep breaths. Inhale for three, exhale for five.* He repeats this process until his muscles relax and his lungs can expand again.

This is the third time this week he has been woken up in this way. He thought he had taken control of it. He thought he had beaten it. But every time Harry is taken back there, he knows that no doctor can help him. There is only one way he can move on. He has to find them.

CHAPTER 25 - AVERY

Plan 1: Fix Cinderella Mistake

1. *Get that damn hair sample. Note: His office is on LEVEL TEN. LEVEL TEN.*
2. *Find out his alibi for the time of her death. If not verifiable, luck is on my side. If solid, formulate a strategy to make it invalid.*
3. *Check in to see if police have been notified of her body.*
4. *Go to crime scene and place suit fibres and hair in skip/close to.*
5. *Play Station CCTV every other night to keep up to date with progress.*
6. *Hope to hell he's convicted or the case goes cold.*

Plan 2: Find the Bastard with a Grudge

1. *Make a list of each fairy tale I've ended.*
2. *Make a list of each fairy tale character involved but not terminated.*
3. *Narrow down suspect list by location – must be within a 10 mile radius of my house.*
4. *Look at each of the final suspects in extensive detail.*
5. *Simultaneously pay great detail to any more letters and use them for clues*
6. *Follow each lead until I have the Bastard with a Grudge.*

I take the notes from the little brown book in my mind palace and read over them repeatedly whilst I zip up the back of my peach linen dress. I admire myself in the mirror sunken into the back of my wardrobe, hanging lifelessly.

The hem of the dress skims my knees and the long sleeves sculpt my arms. The neckline plunges slightly, keeping the outfit modest but still stimulating subconscious intrigue.

I can't say I've ever been one of those women who is ashamed of her body. I have always taken care of my figure and I am proud to show off my hard work. Plus, it really sets up a warm atmosphere for my meetings with new doctors.

I only have two meetings this morning – although they are in Braxton so it's a bit of a trek. On the upside, it means I have a free afternoon to get on with Plan 1: Action 1.

On my way out the door I wink at the plant pot hanging outside the house entrance. No I haven't had a mental breakdown and started *talking to nature*. If you want to get specific, I am winking at the camera I installed within the plant pot late last night. If the Bastard with a Grudge plans on playing Postman Pat again, I am damn sure going to catch it.

Though they are far away, my meetings get me a sale. A great start to what I hope will be a great day.

I jump back in my car straight after the second meeting, make my way to the Prince's building and it's not long before I am back in the exact same parking space as I was yesterday, glaring up at the office block. On the bottom half, the construction is made up almost entirely of glass before transitioning into a traditional red brick setting, with two thin panels of windows further up. As I observe the building, I notice its thin glass eyes narrow and its smile grow wider, baring even more of its teeth, daring me to confront it and inevitably fail.

Any normal person would take the hallucination as their reason telling them to spin back around and retreat. Fortunately for me, I have learnt how to turn the dial on my reason to *low* every time she pops up inconveniently.

I haven't yet mastered this trick with my phone, though.

The default iPhone jingle, embodying a banshee, shrieks through my coat pocket and makes me jump, causing my heel to give way and a burn to spread through my ankle.

Damn phone. Damn shoes.

I yank my phone into my vision to discover who made me scuff my Louboutins. Before I am able to see the name, I blow the mess of hair that has shaded my face.

He really does have the worst timing ever. It's like he does it on purpose.

"Hey," I greet Him as I begin walking into the building.

"Hey, how's your morning been?"

"Oh you know, the norm—" I let out a gasp as I swerve out the way of the window cleaner's ladder which almost just became a part of my face. "I've had a couple meetings, how about you?"

I check my phone – 1.58pm. I've got five minutes, that's plenty of time. I relax slightly and pay more attention to Him.

"- and there was this really lovely couple – they just got married a few months ago but unfortunately they couldn't afford the house. I felt really bad, they were so sweet but I know the sellers won't go any lower than asking price."

I nod and say *right, oh okay* and *I see* on rotation until I am caught up with what he's talking about.

"But anyway," he finally abstains from his rambling, "I just wanted to call you and see how you were. Also, I wondered when I was next seeing you."

The butterflies giggle and I can feel the blood rushing into my cheeks. "Well." My calendar pops up in front of me. Although I have nothing set to do, my new plans of action are sure to occupy a lot of my time. Then again, I can't tell him why I am not available and if I give him some cryptic excuse, he'll think I'm blowing him off. The lies just never end. "I'm going out with some friends tonight and I've got stacks of work to do so maybe Saturday?"

"Yeah sure, what do you want to do?"

Pondering the thought, I take a quick look at my phone. 2.05pm. Shit.

I jerk my head around the corner so I have a view of the elevator and sure enough, the crowd has gathered and the Prince is beyond my vision.

"Anything would be great, I'm sorry, I've really got to go." I hang up the phone without waiting for a response and begin parading towards the far corner as the steel doors in front of the crowd open.

The distance is further than it looks as by the time I reach it, the elevator has begun to close.

I'm not giving up that easily.

I bite my tongue and jam my hand into the small gap between the doors and for an instant, I don't think they're going to stop. The metal presses into my hand and I feel the ligaments shift into unnatural positions in order to escape the compression. I suck in a sharp breath, trying to bear my screaming hand and finally the doors release me.

The doors open to faces staring at me, unamused by my, now throbbing, hand causing them to be late. No one is exactly jumping at the chance to make a space for me either.

It wouldn't kill people to be a bit nicer every once in a while.

Nevertheless, I squeeze myself between two men. The two of them alone consume so much space I'm surprised the other bodies in here fit.

I can hear my heart banging against my rib cage, demanding more room, and my lungs gasp for the little oxygen that my throat is allowing them to have.

Luckily for my respiratory system, the two men leave the elevator only a couple levels up from the reception. As soon as the oxygen deprivation ceases and the stars circling me disappear, I stand up on my tippy toes and scan for Cinderella's fella.

The advantage to him being a redhead is that they have a built in *I'm here sign*. Making my job a whole lot easier.

He is in the very back corner. I roll my eyes. *Of course he is.*

With every *ding* of the elevator and every switch between those leaving and those joining, I edge myself closer to him.

We reach level 9 and I am two people away from him. I'm not one to play things safe, but this is cutting it a bit fine – even for me.

The doors open for level 10 and I see him begin to shuffle out with the rest of the crowd. Bowing my head and covering my face with my hair, I wait for him to be just past me before snaking my fingers around a lock on his tightly curled head and I *stumble* backwards.

I don't fall very far before my back smashes into someone only half a foot behind me, but it is far enough to give me the force I need to pluck those hairs right from their roots. I sense them in my hand, almost amazed that I have managed to peel them from his scalp. You'd be surprised how difficult it is to yank someone's hair out.

He slaps the back of his neck where the strands resided only moments ago, but he doesn't look back. Instead, he merely scratches the sensitive area and pushes his way out of the elevator.

I let out a sigh of relief and rest my head back against the stiff fabric coating the wall.

Plan 1, Action 1 – check.

CHAPTER 26 - AVERY

"Grant and Flynn," the Chief calls and both Grant and James's heads perk up. "There's been another Jane Doe found in a skip in an alley off of the town square – go check it out. White—"

"But, Chief," James exclaims and the Chief cranks his neck towards him, unamused by the interjection. "I'm still working on the most recent GR case with Ellis."

"Oh is that what you call it – working? You've got no leads, no suspects, no motive and no tips. I'm not taking you off the case, I'm just giving you another. You're a sergeant, you should be able to cope with more than one task."

Chief then continues handing out the jobs for the day and James gulps and shrinks back into the wall.

After the briefing, Harry catches up with James and accompanies him to his office. "Hey, mate. I can't believe that – putting you on another case."

James just shrugs. "Yeah, but I mean he isn't wrong. We really haven't come up with anything. The closest we came to identifying a suspect was those CCTV tapes and surprise, surprise they didn't turn up anything."

Harry agrees. "I can't believe the tapes of the last two outside cameras were missing. We could've seen GR going through the girl's window." Having reached James's office, Harry crouches down and fusses over the slobbering bloodhound. "Hey, Bertie. But still," he adds, "this case is over a decade old. Even if we haven't got anything for this specific murder, surely it shouldn't be brushed over so soon."

"Well they've got guys going over the old cases all the time. We don't even know if this was actually him – it could easily be a copycat. So we've gotta treat this like any other case."

Harry's face expresses concern; he doesn't want this person to go un-identified. He feels as though it's been so long that people are beginning to care less and less with each death.

Sensing his worry, James reassures him, "don't worry, mate – we'll get him. But in the meantime, I've got to go find Grant. Any chance you want to do your work in my office today and keep an eye on Bertie?"

Harry moans about how he doesn't want to babysit the smelly mutt, but he reluctantly agrees. In truth, Harry has begun to grow quite fond of the animal. Although it does carry a less than pleasant aroma and it has some attachment issues, Bertie seems to always have a glint in his eye and he is always wagging his tail. Seeing something still so happy after losing his only partner, it gives Harry hope.

After his rough sleep last night, Harry is unenthusiastic about accomplishing anything too productive today. He's just glad he is able to take his mind off it for even a minute. It's gotten worse recently, Harry doesn't know what triggered it. Perhaps it is the rough patch he's having with Martha; however their problems aren't exactly a new occurrence, they've been disconnected for longer than the two of them care to admit. Perhaps Harry got his hopes up too high again of catching them after their reappearance.

Harry is pleased when his phone takes him away from the meaningless tasks he has been using to procrastinate. Since he and James will no longer be together every day, Harry feels less paranoid that James will become suspicious of his activities. So, he arranges to meet up with them for lunch. His phone lights up, notifying Harry of their confirmation and one o'clock approaches quickly. Harry is up and heading out the station within a second of the time change.

On his way out, Harry waves to Karen.

Since *Mr Christian Grey* paid a visit, Karen has been wearing contact lenses instead of her 60s style glasses, and she's started wearing her hair down in wavy locks that frame her face rather than the slicked-back ballerina bun she used to have every day. Harry notices the wobbly black line hugging her top lash line and the two circles of rouge plopped on the apples of her cheeks. She seems to have more confidence now.

This lunchtime, Harry doesn't go to the Cosy Coffee and order his standard black Americano, with a grilled cheese on the side. He fears if he goes there he will be seen.

Instead, the two of them lunch in a rundown corner shop that has only two tables and that cowers at the sight of new customers. The greasy owner of the joint is expressionless, showing no enthusiasm about their presence actually giving him business. He wears a t-shirt one size too small so it doesn't cover the bottom of his stomach, which is folded over his worn-out denim jeans.

Harry is almost certain that he will get food poisoning from his Coronation chicken, nevertheless he knows he is safe from being discovered.

They both emit a suspicious aura and are quick to scoff down their meals. They only saw each other yesterday, but they already have so much more to tell one another.

They are both unsure of whether this can carry on, if it is the smart thing to do. Perhaps they are being foolish.

Harry reassures them both, though. He has grown too attached, he couldn't end it even if he wanted to. They have dived in too deep now.

"There's my boy!" James calls, as he crouches down and Bertie jumps into his lap. "Were you a good doggy for Uncle Harry?"

"Yeah, he wasn't the worst company," Harry admits. "He definitely smells better than you."

James pouts defensively. "What do you mean? This," he gestures to his entire body, "is where the goods are."

Harry laughs sarcastically. "Nah, but seriously, I got a bunch of work done over lunch and we even had a little bonding session."

"Oh, you were here all lunch?" James frowns, Harry nods. "I just passed Chief and he said he wanted me to make sure you were back 'cos he saw you head out."

"Oh right, yeah, yeah. I just nipped out to my car to grab my salad. I've gotta eat sometime." Harry chuckles faintly, "he probably just missed me coming back in."

"Anyway," Harry says after a long pause. "What's the deal with the alley chick?"

James slumps down into his chair and the seat drops to half a foot above the ground. "Well, whoever did it was no expert. The clean-up was sloppy and forensics have found fingerprints and hair samples all over the place. It certainly doesn't look like it was planned and there was definitely a struggle. We'll get more info back with the autopsy report, I suppose."

"Oh okay, so it's looking like a pretty standard murder? Probably an argument gone too far? Do you know who she is yet?" The room vibrates with the speedy tapping of Harry's foot.

"Yeah, doesn't look like a mugging since none of her belongings were gone and no, we don't have an ID for her yet." James's eyebrows furrow. "What's got you so interested?"

Harry's face presents a defensive expression. "I'm a homicide detective. Aren't I supposed to be interested in homicides?" Harry jokes.

James shakes it off with a wave of his hand.

"What have you got to do this afternoon? Should we look into some tips from the public on the GR case?" Harry suggests.

James tenses and his face is now stiff. "Yeah sure, um, I've just got a meeting with Chief first. We have to go over some stuff. Just need to finish closing some cases. I'll give you a shout when I'm done."

His tone indicates that he wants Harry to leave. Harry's slightly thrown off by the cold undertone, but he doesn't think anything of it – putting it down to stress.

Giving Bertie's head a quick scratch, he heads back to his cubicle with the intention of getting some work done.

His intention falls short when the images from his dream last night claw at his memory and refuse to give him any peace.

I'd been camping outside her house for weeks, ever since Cinderella. It was a good thing there were hedges along her street. I'd been trying to analyse her schedule and predict when she would and wouldn't be home. It was proving a lot more difficult than I had expected. She didn't have a very regular pattern, which was strange considering her organisational tendencies.

She installed a camera last week. Smart girl. I'd have to be more careful the next time I ventured out of my cosy hedge and paid a visit to her door.

CHAPTER 27 - AVERY

Not an expert? Me, not an expert? I play the cop's harsh words on repeat. Being objective, I know that it's an advantage that they think Cinderella's killer didn't know what they were doing because it significantly reduces the possibility that they would ever think *they* and the *Grimm Reaper* are the same person.

But I can't always be impartial – I have feelings too. Quite frankly, this hurts them. And my ego. It almost makes me ashamed of myself. I, dubbed the Grimm Reaper, have fallen so far that they consider me *no expert*. As if I were just anybody off the street.

I sense a pressure on my shoulder and a distant voice calling me.

"Avery…Avery."

I turn to face Him, expressionless, as if I were sleepwalking. You know what they say – never wake a sleepwalker.

"I thought I'd lost you for a moment, there," he jokes, but I am still staring vacantly.

Not an expert…not an expert

His face begins to morph into the cop's and my jaw locks. *I really want to hurt him. I can't believe he belittled me like that.* My eyes narrow and my nostrils flare slightly.

He nudges me again, this time with a more serious tone.

I break out of my trance and rub my fists into my eyes several times. "Sorry. I'm so tired, I think I keep drifting off." Once I gather my bearings, I try and focus on our conversation. "What were we talking about?"

He laughs at me with a glimmer in his eye, finding me amusing.

My stomach does little somersaults and a tingling shoots up my spine as I watch Him. I'm unsure of what exactly this foreign sensation is, what it means and why I feel it. However, as much as my reason hates things she can't understand, some part of me likes this unknown feeling.

"Clearly nothing too interesting if you can't remember." He shuffles around on the sofa. "But anyway, what do you want to talk about?"

I sigh, unenthusiastic about his question. I glance around his lounge and my eye catches the window. "The weather?"

He chuckles again. "Do you want to be any more British?" I shove Him playfully and he says, "Tell me about yourself."

I'm thrown off by this. People don't really ask me anything personal. I usually engage in small talk about what job I do or what university I went to. My conversations with people rarely go beyond this, I'm in new territory.

How much am I comfortable with sharing? How much am I expected to share? Does he want to know my favourite colour or the ins and outs of my entire childhood?

You're probably thinking that I've never had a relationship before, since it's normal to have long-winded conversations about your insecurities and all that crap. You'd be wrong. Of course I've had relationships before, but they were all mostly physical. I've always preferred to keep the friendship aspect strictly with my girlfriends. Which I do have, by the way. I know you haven't been introduced to any of them but they aren't relevant to this tale and quite frankly, it's my story, I can choose what I do and don't show you.

I realise that I have remained inside my head for too long without responding to Him and he starts to notice. "Well," I finally begin, "my name is Avery Blake, I'm thirty-one years old but to the rest of the world I'm twenty-seven. Um…"

I kill people

"I work as a pharma rep."

I kill people

"I used to live in America with my parents when I was really young. And..."

I kill people

"I love animals...as long as they're behind ten-centimetre thick glass and..."

I kill people

"I can't think of anything else."

"You lived in America?" he asks, intrigued by the sliver of information I gave Him.

I nod. "Until I was five. We moved back for my father's job."

He raises his eyebrows, impressed, and sits back into the sofa. *As if I was doing it to impress Him...*

"Where are your parents now?" he asks as he brushes loose hair behind my ear. I've noticed Him do this more and more often. Every time he does I have the instinct to slap his hand away, but I have built up a tolerance to it. Now, it's almost comforting.

However, having processed his question I immediately go stiff, knowing now exactly where the line is and that I am not willing to cross it.

I shuffle and create more distance between us, suddenly feeling uneasy. I've been quiet for several seconds now, I know I must give Him an answer.

"Oh, my parents? I don't really see them anymore. I mean, I visit them sometimes but they don't live close so it's hard to make the time." After answering I relax a little, though I'm still cautious and uncomfortable with the conversation, so I try to flip the focus back onto Him.

"What about you? What was your wild childhood like?" I ask, attempting to lighten the aura I am emitting.

He slouches back into the stiff fabric of his new grey sofa. "Well, I wouldn't exactly say I lived a very *wild* childhood, as such. My family lived in Southhurst for generations and we never really went anywhere else. When I was older I decided I wanted to go out and actually see the world, so I took a couple years out after school." As he begins to speak of his travelling, a fire is lit behind his eyes and it illuminates the hazel flecks in his irises. "It was amazing, Avery. Seeing all the different cultures, being able to go and help people who are less fortunate than we are? It made me so happy."

It fascinates me that he gets so much pleasure from helping others, without getting anything in return. I wouldn't say I'm a selfish person, of course I help people, but there's usually something in it for me. Then again, I suppose he isn't that different. He's helping others because it gives Him pleasure which is why he does it, whereas for me it doesn't so I don't. Is it wrong of me to draw a comparison between *this* and *my* extra-curricular activities?

He continues to go on for twelve minutes about how his parents are his role models since they are such passionate and caring people and that one day he wishes to have a love like theirs. He tells me about his relationship with his siblings – one brother and one sister, both younger. He has a good relationship with both of them but gets on the best with his brother. He had an older sister, but she was killed sixteen years ago when she was just nineteen by a drunk driver.

"It was so hard to process and cope with," he says, "especially when we saw the guy who did it. He didn't seem like a bad guy – he was the one who called the ambulance for her. He was almost as broken as we were, ashamed of what he had done.

"It took a while, but eventually we all accepted it. We were all so angry at him, we couldn't believe what he'd done, but he was convicted, he felt awful and he took his sentence with no objections. We all managed to forgive him.

"Except for my little sister, I don't think she ever quite got over it. She looked up to Christie, she could never forgive the guy who did it." He pauses and glances down, fixing his eyes on the floor. "I still miss her."

I have no idea how to handle the situation. It's safe to say I'm not the most comforting person you'll ever be introduced to. I don't do well with this sort of stuff, it makes me uneasy.

I know that anything that comes from my mouth will be entirely inappropriate, so I keep it tightly shut and reach out for his hand. It seems like the safest route to take.

He remains quiet, but he squeezes my hand in response.

I stare at Him, drawn in by his willingness to share so much. It was as if once he began, he just couldn't stop. Is that normal? Was I supposed to share that much? Maybe he's just comfortable with his past.

After an unpleasantly long silence, I pull my hands from his grip and clap them together. "Right," I announce, "go make some popcorn, we're watching a movie."

He's taken back by my newfound energy, but doesn't argue.

Falling to my knees and shimmying across the floor, I clench my hands into a fist, grasping the soft fibres of his freshly steamed carpet in my fingers. The clean and tidy state in which he kept his living room makes me all the more attracted to Him. Don't even getting me started on the perfectly coordinated dark blue and grey colour scheme.

I crouch down in front of the TV and open the cabinet to be greeted by at least a hundred film cases – organised by genre. I think I'm in love with Him.

"What are you feeling like?" I call to the kitchen. "Thriller, drama or horror?"

Shortly afterwards he pops his head back round the newly-painted cream door. "I thought girls liked romance films?" He has a genuinely confused look on his face. I laugh silently at his naivety.

"Yeah because the only reason a girl would choose to watch a horror is to get scared and cuddle up with a guy…" I shoot Him a look with one eyebrow raised. "Clearly all your ex-girlfriends have been as clichéd as a Hollywood movie."

"Hey!" he exclaims defensively, masking a smile, before disappearing back into the kitchen.

I run my finger along the line of cases, reading the titles as I go before stopping on one that I know I like. I set it up so that the film menu is being displayed on the screen and then I jump back onto the sofa.

A few moments later he re-emerges, this time with a large bowl filled with popcorn. "Ooh, *The Shining*," he remarks whilst glancing at the screen. "Good choice."

He places the popcorn right in front of me and I spoon out a large amount and pluck them from my hand one by one while he presses *play* and the film starts.

There is no doubt in my mind that I will love the film – I've seen it so many times and it never gets old.

I've even snatched some ideas from Jack.

We only have small conversations while Jack is on screen. Every time we start talking for too long, I shush Him and turn my attention back to Jack.

Towards the end of the film he decides to squeeze my waist, causing me to jump as the jolt shoots through my body.

"Stop." I smack his hand away, but he perseveres. At first, I am finding it rather irritating. Especially since the action is starting to happen on screen. But as the time goes on and he keeps on squeezing my waist, I begin giggling when he does it, entertained by his will to continue.

Gradually, my giggle turns into uncontrollable laughter and we start play fighting. As if we were eight years old again.

My reason is screaming at me, asking; *what the hell are you doing?* I don't listen to her, instead my attention has been completely taken away from Jack and his axe, which is something that I thought would never happen.

It feels strange to be so goofy, when I'm normally so serious. Although, in some peculiar way, it feels good.

He pins me down, and the rough material of the sofa brushes against my arms. I can feel the weight of his body suspended over mine. His hands lift once again to brush a stray hair from my face and rests underneath my chin, lifting my eyes to meet his.

His eyes look on mine and there is something so genuine and loving in them. As he leans down and his warmth radiates onto my body, I snake my fingers around his neck.

I have no idea when the film ends, I'm too wrapped up in Him. I don't know what it is about Him that makes me go against my reason – she's the one who's got me through my entire life. There is just something.

I don't want to leave, I want to stay there with Him until the sun yawns over the horizon. Alas, duties call, and my duty is calling me to Cinderella's resting place.

CHAPTER 28 - AVERY

I had to park in a side road a mile from the alleyway, so that my car isn't linked to the scene. I've been walking for ten minutes and I still have a quarter of a mile left to go.

It's flippin' freezing. I wiggle my toes at the end of my worn-out trainers, but I receive no indication that I didn't lose them half a mile ago.

The moon stalks me as I soldier along the street, its eye following my every move. The night sky blankets the entire area. I normally see it as a protection and it comforts me. Tonight, it's trapping me.

As I approach the alleyway, I slow my pace and become more cautious, spinning around to confirm there is no one in sight – or out.

As I had expected, the slim passageway is taped off by iridescent yellow plastic with *"CRIME SCENE"* painted across it repeatedly.

I slink under the tape and spring myself back upright once I am clear of it. I must say, I'm rather proud of my elastic back – it must be why I always won those limbo contests.

There's something about going against the rules at night that makes the atmosphere all the more sinister. Every time the breeze whips past my ear I can almost hear it warning me, *careful now, don't get caught.* The paranoia does send spiders crawling up my back, but I shake them off and block out the wind. Listening only to my reason.

Although that seems like a rare occurrence nowadays, she reminds me.

I tread judiciously, making sure I leave no shoeprint. There isn't much chance of this since I'm wearing my trainers which have had their out-soles completely run down. Still, it's better safe than sorry. I can't afford to make any more mistakes.

I reach the area next to the skip and I see the events that unfolded only seventeen days ago as if they are happening right in front of me all over again.

I have mixed feelings when I travel back to that day. A part of me smiles, remembering the thrill as Cinderella faded away. Another part is resentful of her sudden need for vengeance and my ego taking over my reason. If it weren't for my one moment of weakness, I wouldn't be in this mess.

Then again, I wouldn't have met Him, either.

I pull out the plastic bag from my coat pocket with the fibres from the Prince's suit and I scatter them on the ground. Amid doing so, I do a a three-sixty, certain I felt someone's breath on my neck.

Come on, Avery, concentrate. My reason lectures me as I turn my attention away from the glowing eyes I am imagining lurking in my shadow, and back to the task at hand.

The placement of the fibres is very important. They must be randomly positioned and form no sort of pattern, but at the same time they must be situated in places that the forensics team are sure to find when they do their second sweep of the crime scene.

A few strands are scattered on the floor next to the skip, to show there was a struggle. Then, there must be some on the corner of the skip, where he caught his jacket as he threw her body in.

Next, I position the strands of hair I ripped from his scalp. It may have been more humane to just cut them off, but the forensic experts would analyse the hair and see that there was no root, making it very obvious they weren't pulled out due to a struggle. I focus the positioning of these on the ground, since this is where the fighting took place. I also place some further down the alleyway, just to create some diversity.

I was careful not to touch the suit fibres or his hair in the procuring and the transporting of them, and I am just as careful now – wearing leather gloves which are sure to create no impression.

I check over the scene again and once I am satisfied that no one has seen me or is walking the streets at this time of night – which is suspicious in itself since it's one o'clock on a Wednesday morning – I make the painful journey back to my car, unsure of whether I still have all ten piggies.

As I walk back to the car, I can't shake the image of a figure being in that alleyway. I know it's just my mind playing tricks on me, sometimes I feel cursed to have such a marvellous imagination. Even still, the image is there, cemented in my mind.

The police will have to go through all of Cinderella's friends and family…well just friends I suppose, before they consider it to be a random attack. This means I have plenty of time before there is even the possibility of me being a suspect. Still, with this creepy dude following my every move and doing nothing to indicate that he just wants a friendly little chat, I can't afford this case going past her friends…and Prince. Besides, they have found my DNA. Even if they have no match for it, it is already on their system. I need to make sure they find the culprit. Or the one I want them to find anyway.

Now all that is left is to ensure that Cinderella's Prince doesn't have a solid alibi. After a little bit of digging, I've discovered that the Prince was, very conveniently, out of the office on the afternoon that Cinderella met her end. Unfortunately, he left work for a doctor's appointment, which poses a bit of a dilemma. Doctors' offices keep records.

The drive home isn't too long – only six minutes. And it hadn't taken me long to walk to my car from the alley – only thirteen minutes.

So you can imagine my surprise when I return home, a mere nineteen minutes after leaving Cinderella's resting place, to find an envelope posted through my door.

The envelope matches the rustic cream colour of the other two. You don't need to be as smart as me to figure out who it is from.

I don't even open the envelope to discover its contents. I hurry straight to my desk, switch on my laptop and fast-forward through the footage of the camera until the date in the corner of the screen matches today's.

I'm searching through hours of footage until the time on the screen is 1:10am – only twelve minutes ago – and I see a figure walk up to the door.

If there was any light, even from the moon himself, it was swallowed whole by the shadow the figure created. They were dressed in all black.

They wore a long trench coat and a fedora hat, angled down to cover their eyes.

I can see nothing. There is not a single distinct feature I am able to pick out of the silhouette. I can't even tell if it's a man or a woman. So much for the camera idea.

How is this person one step ahead of me? No one's ever a step ahead.

Disappointed by my findings, I draw my attention back to the envelope and I rip it open. Just as I expected, the words are formed with letters cut out from magazine.

Stupid woman. I thought I told you not to frame someone else. We all have to face our judgement sometime. Your time is now.

My heart flutters inside my chest, no longer wanting to be a part of me. It wants to escape – just as I do.

This letter means that this person followed me to the alleyway, watching the entire time and was at my doorstep less than seventeen minutes ago. I thought I was careful when I went there tonight. I thought I made sure no one followed or saw me.

The fact that he knew exactly where I was and what I was doing shakes me to my core. This is the first time I've been outsmarted. This is the first time I feel like I might be out of my depth.

She'd been spending less and less time at home in the evenings. I was confused as to why she had suddenly changed her routine and where she was going. Even though she was irregular with her movement before, she would always come home at some point in the evening. Always.

Tonight she was especially late home. Although, I already knew the reason for this.

CHAPTER 29 - AVERY

Pinocchio – no one left alive

Rapunzel – no one left alive

Little Red Riding Hood – grandmother missed

Snow White – two dwarves missed

I rack my six o'clock brain, searching through all the different files I have stored in the corner of my mind dedicated to the fairy tales. I list all the different stories that almost began, that I ended and that are yet to complete, trying to pick out which fairy tale is the cause of my unwanted new postman.

I quickly rule out Red's grandmother since the last time I checked in on her, she was in a care home in Scotland.

Sneezy and Bashful are a bit of a nuisance – I really do hate loose ends. It wasn't my intention for them to go amiss, but you would be surprised how difficult it is to get the seven dwarfs and Snow White and the Wicked Queen all into one place. It isn't like I can return and finish the job later on – that's far too risky.

So, although it tugs at my mind every time I think of my failure of Snow White's tale, I decided many years ago that the wisest route I can take is to let them live out their little dwarf lives and I would make sure to keep an eye on them.

I have stayed true to my decision and as far as I am aware, the two of them have no idea that the death of their friends is even related to other murders, let alone who the culprit might be.

Even so, I must consider the unlikely case that they are smarter than they let on and they are scheming against me.

Apart from them, there really aren't many other suspects. I am never fond of leaving people out of the tale and if I do, I am extremely careful not to show them any of my features, lest they identify me.

Of course I would never tell anyone about my double life. I've never trusted someone enough to know for sure they wouldn't squeal. So there's no one there.

Well, I suppose there is *one* person who knows my secret – but he's still in prison and it doesn't look like he's getting out any time soon.

It has been fifteen days since I revisited the alley in which I screwed up royally. Yesterday, forensics finally did their second sweep of the murder scene – and to my delight, they picked up on the suit fibres and the hair follicles.

"Forensics found some more evidence," the arrogant, slender man on my screen announces. The audio from yesterday is slightly crackly, but I am able to just about make out what they are saying. "It is microscopic," he continues, "so it's really no surprise they missed it the first time."

The beer-bellied man seems unimpressed by the slender one's negative attitude, but he simply nods along. "How long will it be until we have the fibres and hair strands identified?"

The slender one groans. "Oh, I don't know, Flynn. It will take as long as it always does. It gives us time to bring in family and friends and get DNA samples off them."

I've been watching *CSI: Grimm Reaper* for years now, so although I get rather mixed up with the names, I know enough to know that the fat one is of a higher ranking than the other. I'm confused as to why he lets the annoying one speak to him like that. Oh well, it's not my place to tell them how to do their job. Even though I do it better than them.

"It looks like the victim and her husband have been living separately for several months now and they have been on bad terms. I think we need to bring him in first."

Perfect. That's just what I want to hear. The pigs are playing so easily into my plan, I might as well attach string to their heads.

If it weren't for the misfortune that led me into this situation, I would say that luck is on my side.

The timing so conveniently allows me to taint his alibi just before they call him in. They already have him as a person of interest, all they need is a little push in the right direction. Or is it the wrong direction?

Due to the company I have kept over the years, I have acquired some basic hacking skills – hence the personal TV show. All I have to do is bypass the firewall of Southhurst New Surgery, eliminate the records of the Prince's appointment and the police have no solid proof of his alibi. Him *faking* an appointment and being out of the office on the exact day his wife is killed is really just the icing on the cake. There is no way that the police will assume this is a mere coincidence.

I only have one meeting in the afternoon today. The rest of the day I spend at the office, having my ears pierced by Kirsty going on and on about her amazing deals to our boss. I swear, if I didn't know her, I would create a goddamn fairy tale *for* her.

I have the option to take my work home and most days during the winter I do – simply because the office is frikkin' freezing. I swear they have never heard of the invention *radiator*.

Today, however, I grin and bear the pain of my teeth bashing against one another and the burn on my arms I'm sure to find this evening because of the friction being caused between my cashmere jumper and arms by my hands.

It's worth it, though. I am borrowing my friend's computer today because mine *'crashed last week'* and by using company owned computers, it'll be more difficult to trace the IP address that hacks the doctor's records all the way back to me.

I won't bore you with the details of the hacking process, since I doubt many of you would even understand the technical language, but in simple terms? After a few minutes the firewall crumbles like the Berlin Wall in 1989.

A pulse of energy shoots up and down my spine as I admire the beautiful sight of information loading on the screen, right before my eyes. There's something about gaining information that I probably shouldn't have that makes me feel so superior to my fellow persons.

As I'm scrolling through the *long* list of names, I hear Kirsty's stilettos (which she really cannot walk in) echo on the wooden planks as she struts up to my desk. I immediately close down the screen and bring up a list of clients. In all honesty, I have no idea who half of these clients are or what they are doing on the system, but I pretend to concentrate intently on the words in front of me.

When Kirsty is next to me, she leans down – very much invading my bubble – and her ash blonde split ends fall onto my shoulder as she studies the document on my screen.

I grind my teeth together, trying to push my anger out through them instead of through Kirsty. I couldn't deal with a scene at the office, right now.

"Hi," she finally says. Her mouth is so close to my nose I can smell her breakfast. Raspberry jam on toast with a banana.

"Hey," I smile back, trying not to let my dislike of her shine through the mask.

"Ooh, what do we have here? Looks like we're going to be competing for clients," she says with a little too much enthusiasm. How typical of her, to immediately make it a competition.

Had she approached me two months ago in this way, I would have jumped at the opportunity to knock her down a few pegs. Yet, it takes all the self-restraint I can muster to simply smile and laugh softly, praying that she will hurry the hell up and remove herself from the particles which are surrounding me.

She finally struts off in the opposite direction. *By God, I don't like her.*

Once she is firmly out of sight, I reopen the website with the doctor's records and click on the Prince.

I have to say, my trait of snooping really could keep me poking through his entire medical history, if there weren't more pressing issues at hand.

I focus my eyes only on the appointment dated 2nd April.

CHAPTER 30 - AVERY

It's an eerie evening. Tonight, dusk is accompanied by his cool old friend Jack Frost. Jack skips alongside me as I pace from my car to my front door, keeping a firm grip on my hands and I am unable to break free. Dusk watches from a distance, gaining pleasure from his observation, but he is unwilling to join in with his friend's bidding. Dusk is a more subtle character. You never know when he's coming and by the time he's crept up on you, it's too late. Jack seems the greater threat in hindsight, but it's dusk who is the real villain.

I'm not fazed by the corner of a cream envelope poking out of the letterbox. I've learnt that I cannot think clearly if my mind is obscured by caution. Instead, I retain a steady pulse as I click the door shut behind me and peel open the envelope to uncover magazine letters stuck to a piece of crumpled cream paper.

Roses are red, violets are blue
You don't see me, but I see you
But don't be alarmed, I'll stop soon
Because the clock has struck twelve
This fairy tale's over for you

My stomach drops and my hands begin to tremble. My act of being calm and collected is thrown out the window and I am wide-eyed, staring frantically into the deserted street, in a desperate attempt to find the owl who will not cease his pursuit. I'm not used to being the hunted.

The part that I find most troubling is the fact that I have no idea who this person is. If I knew who they were – I would deal with them faster than Cinderella could run from the ball. Alas, I am being kept in the dark. It is a strange feeling, not liking the dark – that's usually when I'm at my best.

I study the individual letters. They have no distinct features. They are a rather bland font – some larger than and in different colours from others, but it isn't enough to go on. Unless I want the challenge of searching through every single magazine out there. That doesn't sound too appealing.

As I run my fingertips over the raised words, my nail catches on the edge of the 'F' of 'fairy tale'. I tease the corner and it resists at first, but eventually yields, bringing some of the paper it is clinging to along with it.

I flip it over and from the back, the piece of paper is just a rectangle. Whoever took the time to cut out each individual letter was clearly too lazy to cut around every corner of the 'F'. On the other side of the 'F' is the words "for sa" and the rest is cut off. Below this is a picture. I can't quite make out what the object is, since the middle of it is covered by the remnants of the white paper it was stuck to. It looks like an outdoor appliance of some sort. A lawnmower maybe? It may seem like little to go on, but most of the time the smallest details are the most important.

Then again, even if it is a lawnmower there is no way I can track down which magazine and which issue, so I suppose it isn't that much help.

Before setting the thin paper down on the desk, I raise it to my lips and drag my taste buds along it.

I'm about to begin removing the other words to examine the back, when the muscles in my hands are startled by a thud that resonates through the entire ground floor. The source is the door.

My legs protest the movement that my brains commands, but I force them forward and I approach the source.

It's as though the subtle *tick* of the clock has been muted. The noise of the fridge is absent. It's deafeningly quiet. All I can hear is the blood drumming into my ears.

With my heart lodged in my throat, I turn the lock and pull the door towards me.

There is no one there.

I am greeted by the streetlight and the car that parked in my space when I wasn't home. At first, I am relieved by this – though I am confused as to the source of the thud. Perhaps it was just my imagination being overactive.

But when I glance down I see them. On my doorstep. Staring back up at me, smiling.

Buttercups.

CHAPTER 31 - AVERY

November 2008

I shaded my newly trimmed fringe with my hand from the raindrops that were catapulting down from the clouds.

I hated London on crappy weather days. It was on days like this that I would notice how truly uneven the streets of the vibrant city were – since every single one was covered in two inches of murky water.

The rain made Londoners, who were already grumpy and slamming into me, the Grinches that stole Christmas. If you want to witness the true bad nature of humans, take a stroll down Oxford Street on a cold winter's day. You would have lost all faith in humanity by the time you reached the end.

I raised my hand, trying to signal the taxi with the yellow sign lit up like a beacon of warmth and comfort that was coming my way. For a moment, it looked as though he had seen me and he was going to pull up next to me, so I stepped one foot off the pavement and into the road.

I let out a high-pitched squeal as the taxi didn't stop next to me, but sped right past, sending the pool of water next to me spraying over me like I was the statue in the middle of the Trevi Fountain.

I was completely unimpressed. My suede boots were drenched – there was no question that they were ruined beyond repair. My beach waves that I had spent seventy-two minutes perfecting that morning were a distant memory and I could feel my makeup trickling down my face as if I was a sorority girl who had just watched *The Notebook* for the fifteenth time.

I took my anger out on my unlucky palms and dug my nails into them. It didn't go far to calm me down, but it did make my skin tougher. Literally.

I called over another taxi. This time I wasn't so quick to leap out and meet my showery doom. To my delight, the taxi slowed and pulled up next to me.

I lean into the rolled down passenger seat window and address the slender, grizzled man.

"Can I go to Finchley?"

The man confirmed, speaking with an imagined sense of authority and I went to slide into the back seat when the handle was snatched away by another hand.

I wasn't that crazy. The other hand definitely didn't belong to me. I traced the hand to its owner and I found a chiselled jawline accompanied by rich emerald eyes and a thick head of blonde hair swept perfectly to the side, with just the right amount of mess to it.

"Sorry, Buttercup, this is my taxi." He noticed my horrified expression and he simply shrugged. "You snooze, you lose."

He went to duck his head into the car, but I slammed the door back shut before he had the chance.

"I don't flippin' think so," I growled. He seemed shocked by my aggression, but at the same time impressed. I shoved him out the way and prepared to finish his actions for him. "Get your own goddamn taxi," I demanded, "and stay the hell out of mine."

His eyes went wide, as if he was the alpha in a wolf pack and he was being challenged.

"It's each man for himself out here, love. If you can't handle it, don't come to London," he declared and he tried to coax me out the way of the door. I wasn't budging.

After a stretched out minute of a staring match, I was satisfied that he was going to back off, so I turned to get in the back of the taxi. For the fifth time.

All of a sudden, I felt his warm breath on the nape of my neck and an unnerving chill pulsed up my spine. I was paralysed for a few moments.

"You've got a mouth on you, I like that," he whispered next to my ear. "Although, it's very difficult for me to take you seriously when your flaming red bra is showing through your rain-soaked blouse."

When I'd processed what he said, I gasped and threw my hands over my chest. He took this brief moment of me being distracted to slip past me and glide onto the now soaking seat

"Hey!" I yelled, having realised what had happened.

He simply raised his eyebrows and winked before calling out of the slightly opened window, "See ya, Buttercup."

CHAPTER 32 - AVERY

December 2008

I wouldn't say I was a scrooge, but walking down any given street and being blinded by flashing lights and greeted by a waving Santa and his reindeer really wasn't my idea was fun.

I thought that Christmas decorations could be tasteful and elegant – hell, I even had a Christmas tree with tinsel on it – but when a pub looked like an elf threw up all over it, it's simply too far.

This is what had become of Old Bernie's. I'd been going to this place since I moved back to Southhurst a year ago to do my master's. The rustic, rotted pub in need of some serious renovations, was now paying its rent by being sponsored by Santa.

It was a Thursday night and I just thought I would pop down for a quick beer, say *hi* to the locals and head home to get on with assignments. As I was throwing back the last few drops of my Carlsberg, I caught sight of a familiar face.

I stared at his reflection in the mirror, trying to be as discreet as possible since I just couldn't recall where I knew him from. When he caught me staring and glanced back, I remembered those emerald eyes.

He recognised me at the same time as I did him and after breaking away from the circle of guys he was with, he approached me.

"I know you," he declared. Not even a *hello*.

"Yes, you do," I confirmed. "You're the guy who stole my taxi."

It was quite obvious that I was *not* over the incident yet by my tone of voice. He laughed at my reaction and sat on the stool next to mine – uninvited.

"Oh come on," he began, "where's your Christmas spirit? Can't we just forgive and forget?"

I huffed, "Maybe *you* can." And then I turned to face the mirror behind the bar, avoiding his gaze.

"What if I told you that I just received a phone call saying my pregnant wife was going into labour and there were no other taxis?"

I raised one eyebrow, disbelieving of his claims. "I would say that's most definitely not true," I answered without hesitation.

"Oh really? How can you be so sure?"

"Because—" this time I took my eyes off his reflection and turned to focus on his face, which was intensely peering at me, awaiting my response, "—if that were true, you would be at home taking care of a screaming baby instead of here flirting with me."

He tilted his head back and let out a soft laugh. "You're pretty sure of yourself, aren't you, Buttercup?" I didn't disagree. "Do I at least get a name?"

I paused, contemplating whether or not to comply. "Avery."

"Avery. What a great name. I'm Julian."

CHAPTER 33 - AVERY

The screams echo throughout the house, shaking the walls and causing the photos to tilt.

I stumble down the stairs, my breaths quick and sharp. My brain is working too fast for my feet and I trip on the last step, sending a cold pain up my leg.

The dim lights flicker, telling me to hurry my pace.

I almost feel safe, as though I have made it out, when something clinging to my neck weighs me down and causes me to crash down onto the sofa.

"Stop!" I yell, trying to protect myself. "Stop!" But he doesn't listen to me. I squirm underneath Him and my restricted lungs release an involuntary giggle as he wiggles his fingers on my sides.

I'm blushing and laughing like an eight-year-old girl. He's throwing his head back and laughing, flashing a goofy smile. Together we might as well be two primary school children sharing an inside joke, exchanging coy looks.

It was four months ago today that he approached me in my coffee shop. A day that I thought was one of my worst turned out to be one of my best.

I've never been *all-in* when it comes to relationships, but with Him it's different. I miss Him as soon as I close the door to his house. I wait for his 'good morning' text and the butterflies, which I have become very familiar with over the past few months, dance around in my stomach.

My reason and I really haven't been getting on, though. She doesn't like him and she isn't afraid to make that *very clear*. It feels so wrong to go against her better judgement like this, but I can't help myself.

It's been two months and twenty-eight days since I found the buttercups on my doorstep. Still no sign of Julian.

He always did like to have a dramatic flair, but waiting this long before making an appearance is unlike him. And it is certainly unnerving.

Every time I unlock my door and step into my house, a wave of fear rushes over me, when I realise that maybe tonight is the night he pays me a visit. I'm not prepared for when that time comes.

He isn't supposed to be out for at least another three years. I can't understand how he managed to swing his release after only seven.

"Avery…Avery." He shakes me gently back into the present. I shake my head, glance up at Him and smile. "You've been zoning out a lot recently," he jokes, "are you okay?"

"Yeah, of course I am," I reassure Him. I shuffle up and rest my head on the back of the sofa. "Hey," I start, nervous and unsure of whether I should continue. "I was thinking that maybe tomorrow night—" I hesitate again as my reason calls me an idiot. "If tomorrow night you would want to come round to my place? I could cook us dinner…I mean it will probably be spaghetti but it will be damn good spaghetti."

He's completely taken aback by my suggestion. This is the first time I have even mentioned my home in the four months we've known each other, let alone asked Him over. We never spoke about why I was uncomfortable with Him coming round, but it was definitely obvious and so he knows how big this is.

"Yes, um." He stumbles on his words, unsure of how to react. It's cute. "I mean sure, it will be nice for you to cook us something for a change," he jokes. I'm relieved by his attempt to lighten the atmosphere, it was getting a little too serious for a moment there.

"Don't speak too soon," I warn Him, "there's a reason I always have takeout."

I nestle my head into his sturdy shoulder and I rest my eyes. He wraps his arms around me and I feel safe surrounded by Him, warmed by the soft kiss he places on the top of my head.

When I open my eyes again, the room is no longer lit by the natural sunlight, instead it is lit only by an old lamp in the corner. It takes me a moment to adjust to my surroundings. When I do, I look up to see Him peacefully asleep.

I don't need to check the time to know that I should have been home hours ago. At this time in summer, the sun doesn't go to sleep until well after ten. The fact that the streets are completely black, suggests we are in the early hours of Thursday morning.

I have half a mind to just stay here, and pretend that I never awoke. I can wake up in a few hours, panicked that I slept over and have to rush off to work. It would be so lovely to stay here in his arms.

But I can't do that. I must get home. I can't allow Him to make me irresponsible in every decision.

Reluctantly, I pull myself out of his grip and a few moments later he is awoken by the air he is now hugging.

With his eyes only marginally open, he smiles at me and says, "Hey."

His husky tone warms my body. I take his hand and play with his fingers. "I've got to get going," I tell Him. "We fell asleep – it's half one. I've got work early tomorrow and I need to be home."

He pouts, saddened by the news. He resembles a needy puppy. Something which is usually intolerable, seems so sweet to me.

"No," he moans. "Just stay here and call in sick tomorrow. I can call in for you," he suggests, still slightly unconscious, "I'll just talk really high-pitched and cough loads."

I laugh at his imitation of my voice. "As much as I would love to witness that, I'm gonna have to go home."

I lean towards Him and gently touch my lips on his. I could stay in this moment forever.

Driving home is a struggle. It's only a fifteen-minute journey, but I have to pin my eyes open the entire time.

I meander towards my door. If anyone saw me they'd think I'd had a little too many tequilas. Though, my blurred vision springs into high definition when I reach my door.

There they are. Buttercups.

This is the second time I have found a small bouquet of buttercups on my doorstep. My previous sensation of being tired is a distant memory. I am alert and shaking as I open my door.

Everything seems normal. Nothing in the hallway is out of place. I relax – just a little.

Suddenly, as I'm taking off my shoes, my radio starts screaming The Foundations.

Why do you build me up, Buttercup
Just to let me down, mess me around

I know all the words by heart. And I know that nothing good will come after them.

I charge into my lounge and the light on my desk flicks on, revealing the silhouette under it.

I take a deep breath and an audible gulp. The walls are closing in on me and I can hear the buzz of the light bulb as if it is a jack hammer in my ear.

I stare directly into his emerald eyes. "Julian."

He flashes his white teeth and winks. "Hey, Buttercup. Did you miss me?"

CHAPTER 34 - AVERY

October 2009

"The fuck are you doing every goddamn night?" I interrogated Julian as he tiptoed through the door at two o'clock in the morning.

My hearing was impaired by the drumming of blood coursing through my veins, and my vision was obscured by the red spots in front of my eyes.

"None of your business, Avery," he exclaimed, the volume of his voice increasing with every word. "I didn't realise that when I moved in I had to get permission from you to fucking leave!"

"Oh don't be so overdramatic. I've got every right to want to know why the hell you're walking through the door every day when the sun is coming up!"

"I don't have to listen to this." Julian disregarded me, storming up the stairs. I could hear a crack form in each step as his weight pressed down on the old wood.

My fists clenched at the sight of him walking away and I swear there was a faint wisp of smoke emitting from either my ears or my nose.

I snatched up the piece of paper from the coffee table and chased after him.

When I reached the bedroom I held up the paper and presented it to him with a question. "Why don't you explain this, then?"

He stopped dead and examined its content. Suddenly he wasn't so confident.

"Where did you find that?" he shakily demanded. The poor little thing looked like a deer in headlights.

"Well, since you're home so late every night, I have a lot of time on my hands. When I get bored I snoop. Man, did I hit the jackpot snooping through your drawers." I glanced down at the sheet, taunting him. "I guess now I know what use you have for all those flashy computer skills."

He laughed snidely. "You don't even know what you're looking at. For all you know, that could be a kid's online game." He really was scraping the bottom of the barrel. Even he knew what he was saying was just plain stupid.

"Let's not forget who got a first in her master's now," I reminded him, slightly defensively. "I may not have learnt all of your fancy computer codes and tricks, but I have enough common sense to work out that this is no kid's game. It's got Parliament's emblem. And is my eyesight starting to go or does this," I pointed to a word on the paper, "does this say *government security?*" I raised my eyebrows and shook my head. "Those two things combined with all these fancy codes and passwords that I really don't think an IBM tech geek should be knowing, it's not looking good for you."

His shoulders slumped and his eyes dropped to the floor. Bringing someone who thought they were so powerful under my control was almost a better feeling than the sensation my extra-curricular activities gave me. Almost.

"Okay," he finally yielded. "What do you want?"

I threw my hands over my mouth in offence. "But I'm your girlfriend. Why would I want anything but to protect you?"

Julian simply raised one eyebrow. I supposed he knew me too well.

"Well", I replied as I began pacing around the bedroom. "Firstly, I want you to teach me how to bypass simple firewalls and how to access someone's CCTV. Next, I get to choose the dates we go on without any complaints from you. Do you know what that means? That means if I want to go shopping and I want you to carry my bags, you'll eagerly turn yourself into a frikkin' pack mule." I paused, dragging out the moment of power. "And finally, I will be keeping evidence against you in case there ever comes a time that you need a gentle reminder of where your loyalty lies. Let's just say I've had a few run-ins with the law over the years myself."

He looked up at me, puzzled by my last demand. "What are you talking about?"

I rolled my eyes and sighed. "Nothing you need to worry your pretty little head about. It's nothing major so don't let your imagination run wild. It's simply a precaution."

Julian reluctantly bowed his head, agreeing to my terms.

I walked up to him and leant down since he was now sitting on the bed. I twirled my fingers in his golden locks and touched my lips a millimetre from his, waiting for him to close the gap completely. He refrained for three alarming seconds, before the electricity was too much for him to resist. He pressed his lips hard against mine and pulled me into him, our bodies fused in heat and I had to manually yank my atoms from his.

"Now," I announced, after regaining my breath, with a more chirpy tone. "I'm glad that's all out the way, I don't like when we argue."

He chuckled. "Really? Even though it's multiple times a day?"

I hummed, reconsidering my statement. "Okay, maybe I like it just a little bit," I admitted. "I'm not really tired now, so what do you want to do? Make-up sex or pizza?"

He thought about the decision probably a little longer than he should have. The choice was pretty obvious – in *my* opinion, anyway.

"How about," he finally replied, "we have make-up sex eating pizza?"

I beamed at him. We must be two of a kind. "Ooh, good plan. I'll stay up here and you go sort the food out."

"Oh?" He raised one eyebrow. "And why do you think I'm gonna be the one making the food?"

I let out a soft laugh. What a silly question, wasn't it obvious? I flicked my eyes briefly towards the sheet of paper. "Are you forgetting something? You're basically my bitch now."

CHAPTER 35 - HARRY

Harry propels his engine. It wheezes, trying desperately to regain its energy, which was drained by the lights being left on for the entire night.

Please, please, Harry begs the engine to turn over. He pictures the soothing sound of it waking up. It doesn't obey. He hears it yawn and fade back to sleep.

Flat battery. Great. He moans as he hurls himself from the car and starts the twenty-minute walk to the train station.

Fortunately, Martha is away for the week, visiting her mum and sister in Norfolk. This means Harry won't have to explain his late arrival home – again.

Harry knows Martha isn't stupid. He knows that she is choosing to turn a blind eye to his secret ventures. Harry also knows that she won't keep it up for much longer. Every morning he promises himself he'll stop. He promises he'll be better to Martha and better to himself. He'll stop being so self-destructive. But every night he says he'll start tomorrow.

Although it's summer, the nights in Southhurst are hostile all year round. As soon as the sun checks out for the day and the darkness rolls over the horizon, the wind chases after you, warning you to go back inside where it's safe. Where the night can't reach you.

Harry brushes his hands together and exhales sharply into them. He even adds a spring to his step to try and get the blood pumping around his body faster. His ears are completely numb, yet at the same time they burn.

The exhausted train station is finally in sight. Harry subtly skips towards it, excited to reach the poorly heated waiting room. At least it will be marginally warmer than the cruel night air.

It's not long until the rusty early bird train pulls up. Harry steps onto a carriage and the entire body creaks towards him, unable to take the unbalanced weight.

Harry found himself on the other side of town tonight, so it's going to be a good forty-minute train journey to get home.

After scanning the carriage for the best seat, he positions himself on one of the three-seat rows, kicks his feet up onto the farthest seat and rests his head on the uncomfortable, make-do glass pillow.

There's one other person on the carriage. He continuously flicks his eyes onto Harry, unsettled by his presence. He is dressed in torn-up, navy tracksuit bottoms, a khaki pea coat and an old woollen hat that bears the ghost of a grey tint.

Making an educated snap judgement, Harry guesses that he is the tramp of the train and that he is so cautious of Harry's presence because he doesn't think anyone should be on *his* train at such a peculiar hour.

After examining him mindlessly for a few minutes, Harry turns his attention to the ceiling, fearing he is making the poor guy nervous.

The grimy ceiling is covered with graffiti and scribblings engraved into the metal work. Harry studies them.

The most of them are some derivation of *I wuz 'ere,* and *R+L 4eva.* But some have more to them. Some of them are poems, some of them are suicide notes and some of them are genuinely impressive sketches.

There is only one that catches Harry's eye, though.

The letters GR followed by the silhouette of a scythe and below this are the words *not so happily ever after.*

The headline flashes across Harry's vision. *COUPLE BRUTALLY MURDERD BY KILLER - DUBBED THE GRIMM REAPER. The couple who lived not so happily ever after.*

He smashes the image from his eyes with his hand and shakes any remnants of it throughout the carriage.

Harry's head is thrown back and forth onto the glass window by the train's un-serviced wheels meeting the bumpy metal tracks, shaking the foundations of the carriage with every cycle of the wheels.

The train's chuffing irritates Harry at first, but as time chugs on, it becomes soothing. He feels like he is in his mother's arms being rocked to sleep.

Within the confines of the carriage, Harry almost feels safe. He almost feels at peace. He takes advantage of this and gives in to his heavy eyelids.

His head jerks from side to side and his eyelids flutter as the images flash through his mind. Although he's asleep, his consciousness knows that these are not welcome images. He wants to wake up, he wants to escape the nightmare before it overcomes him.

But he is paralysed by his sleeping limbs and he is dragged, kicking and screaming back into that room.

The demon creeps around the room with a wide grimace. He squeezes his eyes shut, begging the nightmare to go away. Begging to wake up.

His wish isn't granted. The silhouette prowls closer to the laundry basket. He's scared it might be able to pick up his scent. His lashes are now clumping together and a salty fluid sticks his mop hair to his cheeks. The demon is close now. He realises that as his heartbeat quickens his breath grows louder, so he blows air into his cheeks and prevents his lungs from sucking in any more.

The figure twirls the object in its fingers, using it to look through the clothes in his wardrobe. He hears it growl, frustrated that it fails to seek out his hiding place. His entire body crumbles with the growl. He lets out a soft whimper, unable to contain the sobs.

He immediately freezes, petrified his location has been given away. But, slowly, it creeps past him and approaches the exit.

Thinking that he is now safe, Harry lets out the air he was holding hostage and draws in new molecules to keep his heart from halting in fear.

The figure stops abruptly as he does this. Turning its shadowed face back towards the room, it paces towards him. Harry thinks that this is it, he's been found. His heart no longer races, in fact, it is alarmingly calm. Perhaps it's because he knows there is no hope now.

Just before the demon reaches the laundry basket and he prepares for what is to come, it spins away from him, falls to the ground and shoves its head under the bed.

Harry's breath is fragile, but it is no longer as loud as before and he is no longer scared it will give him away.

When the figure is greeted by some old trainers, odd socks and tatty soft toys, it huffs and flings itself back upright before marching back out of the room.

Harry doesn't move for hours. Even when he hears the door slam shut, and silence echo throughout the bungalow, he stays cradling his bear – frozen.

It is not until the birds sing outside his window and the warm sun welcomes him, that he stiffly stands himself up.

Being in that laundry basket for hours and refusing to sleep has left Harry's mind to wander – imagining every scenario – the best through to the worst.

But nothing prepared him for this.

CHAPTER 36 - AVERY

He stares at me, smug. Ravishing in my wide-eyed expression. He ruffs up his ash blonde hair and taunts me. "Well, Avery are you going to just stand there gawking at this gorgeous face? Or are you going to say something?"

My jaw locks and I grind my teeth together. I'm not sure if my reaction is due to fear or rage.

"You've still got another thirteen years on your sentence," I finally say. "How'd you swing getting out so early?"

"Technically three years," he corrects me, "until I would be eligible for parole. But," he lifts himself out of *my* chair, "I was just such a good inmate that they let me out early for good behaviour. After all, it's not like I am any *real* threat to society. Unlike you."

Julian creeps towards me, so dauntingly that he makes the floorboards groan in a way that they never have before. As he approaches, the blood flees from my brain and the spiders are going frantically up and down my arms and spine.

I roll my eyes and relax my posture, trying to keep up my pretence of confidence. "What do you want, Julian? Do you want me to say I'm sorry? Do you want me to tell you how much I've missed you? Because I'm not and I haven't." I tilt my head up so that my eyes meet his as he comes closer to me. "Truth be told, I haven't given you a second of my time in seven years."

He clasps both hands to his chest and contorts his face. "Oh Avery. That hurts, truly it does."

His body is so close to mine that I feel the heat radiating off his skin. I take in a deep breath and his aftershave fills my nostrils. As it does, a sea of memories flood through my mind. He still wears the same earthy fragrance he did when we first met. It's a subtle scent, you have to be up close to notice it, but it has a true grit that is impossible to resist.

"But I don't want your apology." He breathes into my ear. My heart skips with every word, his breath makes me catch mine and I feel paralysed by his presence. Even the flickering streetlamp right outside my house is jarred by him.

He hovers there, only for a few seconds but it seems eternal. The electricity between us vibrates through the room, causing the lights to short-circuit. Every time he inhales, our bodies touch briefly and each time it shocks me. Everything around us fades out into darkness and I am unable to turn away. In fact, my body doesn't want to turn away, caught in the spell of his emerald eyes.

Suddenly the connection cuts off and reality seeps back in. He strolls around the room again and I clear my throat, glancing down at my trembling floor. I wish it would stop hyperventilating, it's making it very difficult to keep my balance.

"So, tell me, Buttercup, what's been going on with Avery? I've noticed your alter ego has been up to no good as always, but I want to know what's been going on with *you*."

I know Julian well enough to know that he's just stalling – he doesn't care for small talk. I just need to figure out what he's really doing here.

"Well, after I finished my master's, I got a job as a pharma rep. I'm great at it, obviously –"

He muffles a laugh into his hand, interrupting me. "Now, now, are you really going to take me for a ride? Come on, Buttercup, haven't we been through enough to be honest with each other?" I play dumb, unwilling to swim up and place myself on his hook. "You don't think I've been sitting around playing video games in my half-way house, do you? No, I've been learning your new routine – it's quite different from seven years ago."

After gesturing a *one minute* with his hand, Julian marches into the kitchen. I'm blown off my feet slightly by a sudden gust of wind as the air rushes after him. I don't follow; as much as my body wants to join the air, my head knows better. I hear clashing of glasses, opening and closing of cupboards, before he returns with a beer bottle in his hand.

He curls his lips around its top and twists. The sight makes me cringe and sets my teeth on edge. He then spits the lid onto my floor. I take a deep breath, trying to prevent my anger levels from rising.

Once Julian catches my stiff expression, he says, "Ooh sorry, you don't like it when I do that, do you?" The corners of his lips turn up. "Would you look at that? I've only been back ten minutes and it's back to the glory days of me making a mess and you cleaning it up. Who'd have thought we'd end up back here?"

"Certainly not me," I murmur to myself, my jaw locked and an unmasked hostility in my tone.

He ignores it. "Me neither, Buttercup, me neither." He slumps down onto my sofa and takes a swig from the bottle. "So, how's the new beau?"

I'm taken back slightly by his knowledge, but then the more I think about it, it isn't that surprising. Julian always did have a jealous streak.

"*He* is none of your business," I snap back at him. I can't mask the defensive tone in my voice.

He holds his hands up to surrender. "Steady on there, love, didn't mean to step on your toes. I think we should be able to talk about these things. We've been over for a long time now. What happened to forgive and forget?"

He is talking sweet, but I know that 'forgive and forget' is definitely *not* his style.

"He seems cute. I didn't think dark skin, dark eyes and shaved head was your type but hey, who am I to judge?"

"How was prison?" I am eager to change the subject, although my question isn't sincere – I really couldn't care less. "I bet you made friends pretty quick in there. What with all your…charm." The smirk on my face gives away my insincerity.

"I'll have you know that I was quite the celebrity. Everybody loved me." His voice and smug expression mimics that of a little boy who just proved his elder wrong.

"I find that hard to believe," I remark under my breath. My posture is far more relaxed than it was when I first laid eyes on him, but I must remain cautious, I won't allow myself to fall into his trap.

Julian now ambles back to my desk at which I had found him only twenty minutes ago. He taps on the keypad of my laptop and I hear the hum of recorded footage.

"I see you're putting my lessons to good use." He glances up at me. I know he is looking at the CCTV of the police station. "Just keeping up to date with your case, are we? Who needs TV when you've got your own custom detective show right at the end of your fingertips?"

"Okay," I blurt, my heart punching its cage, "this is ridiculous. Just tell me why the hell you're here. Have you come to torture me, is that it? To exact your revenge? Quit the bullshit and tell me what the hell you want."

Julian's sneering expression is lit by the blue light from the laptop. He chuckles, shaking his head and approaching me again.

It's now that I realise I haven't moved a muscle since I walked through the door.

His temperament is different to how it used to be. Less...hot-headed. It worries me, it makes him impossible to predict.

"Oh, Avery, you have no idea what I'm planning. The word *revenge* doesn't even begin to cover what it is that I want." He throws the now empty beer bottle onto the sofa as he closes the distance between us again. His tone is dark and menacing. Spiders scurry up my spine to escape it. "But I won't have you knowing exactly what that is. Not just yet, anyway." He trails his thumb gently along my thigh and my atoms instinctively want to latch on, after being reminded of our glory days and although they are put forward a very convincing argument, my reason tells me not to react. "You have been in control of every aspect of your life for as long as you can remember, but that's all going to change. I know things. Things that are dangerous for you."

We are now only a foot apart. I take a stride towards him and close the distance completely – accepting his daring expression. I crank my neck so that my eyes are tilted up and I challenge him. "So what the hell are you waiting for? What's stopping you from spilling them?"

He places the tips of his fingers gently on my cheek and trails them down my face and along my collarbone. My stomach leaps at the sensation and my skin tingles from his touch.

"I'm not one for rash decisions. Maybe I was before, but I've had a lot of time to re-evaluate. I'm going to make you sweat a little bit first,

Buttercup. You're going to drive yourself mad trying to figure out exactly what it is that I've got planned. That paranoia that creeps into your mind every day, that someone is following you, lurking in the shadows?"

I gulp, unsettled by the fact that he knows so much.

"Well, that's just the beginning of it, Buttercup." A wide grin grows from ear to ear. "You're going to be looking over your shoulder with every step, you'll be checking every room of the house each time you come home, you'll be suspicious of every single person you meet. And when you feel safe, even for a second, I'll be right there to plant another seed of doubt in your mind. You're not going to know what I've got planned until it smothers you in your slumber."

I disguise the effect his words have had on me with piercing eyes and a stiff scowl. After staying quiet for a minute, I lay my whole body weight on just the balls of my feet, giving me a couple more inches in height. I then put my mouth to his ear and whisper, "bring it on."

Julian doesn't seem affected by anything I have to say – apart from amusement. He's too sure of himself and his knowledge. If I were him, I think I would act the same. He knows damn well that I have no more ammunition. I'm a sitting duck.

But I will see to it that I don't remain that way.

I've been caught up talking to myself for the last couple of minutes so I don't realise until now that Julian is no longer within my breathing radius. Instead, he is next to the door with his coat in hand.

"Sleep well, Buttercup," he says as he unlocks the door and allows the cold night air to invade the hallway. "I'll be seeing you very soon." He winks and before I know it the door is shut again and I feel a discomforting gust of emptiness wash over me.

My first re-encounter with Julian went smoother than I had expected – I was sure it wasn't going to end up so pretty – but that fact doesn't make me feel at ease. If anything it scares me a hell of a lot more. The Julian I knew was controlled by short bursts of rage, he never stopped to look at the bigger picture.

The fact that he is doing so now, well, it scares the living crap out of me.

It was cold – bone-chilling. I don't think it was the weather, though. It was my guilt. I kept telling myself it was the right thing to do, that I had to do it. If I hadn't, more people would get hurt.

But that didn't stop the projections of them showing up like cardboard popups in a haunted house, making me jumping at every corner.

They didn't stop when I got home. I could triple-lock my door but I couldn't lock them out of my mind. Every time I closed my eyes there they were. Staring at me.

I tried to comfort myself.

I had no choice. This is not my fault. It wouldn't have happened if it weren't for her.

She's to blame.

CHAPTER 37 - AVERY

The sun is angry today. She has no intention of being kind to anyone as she throws her flames, hurling towards Southhurst. I lather up with 35 SPF, but I have no doubt that she will have slapped me a few times before I return home.

Regardless of her bad temper, I don't feel I can justify driving to the town centre at this time of year, since it's only a fifteen-minute walk.

I wouldn't say that I prefer the winter months, but I definitely prefer the attire that they require. There's something about dressing in a thick, faux fur jacket with cashmere-lined leather gloves and high-knee boots that makes me feel so…expensive.

As opposed to the short-sleeved tee and cream bodycon skirt I am currently wearing with an old pair of flip-flops.

Of course I have on a brown-tinted pair of shades worth as much as your car, so at least I've got a little bit of a price tag on me.

"Hey, Maya." I scruff up the little girl's hair and she lets out an ear-piercing giggle.

"I like the hair," I tell Heidi as I approach the counter. The last time I was in here she was sporting split ends, tatty dreadlocks and a wonky fringe. She has since then chopped the entire lot off into a pixie cut with pink streaks painted through it. "It suits you."

As she smiles, her chin folds in two and blood rushes to her plump cheeks. "Oh, thank you, dear. I got it done on Thursday. Fancied a bit of a change."

"Well I *don't* like it," a grumpy voice declares, coming from the doe-eyed face of her daughter.

Heidi scowls at her and Maya storms off into the back of the café. She then turns to me, rolls her eyes and laughs. "She used to hang – and I mean literally hang – from my hair almost every night. She hasn't quite got over the fact she can't do that anymore."

After sprinkling chocolate powder onto my latte, she hands it to me and asks, "So, what's the deal with this new guy then?"

I laugh at her shameless nosiness. Usually, if someone asks me a question as direct as this I would shut them down almost immediately, but I've known Heidi since I moved back here ten years ago, so I've got used to her intrusive ways.

"Well, I've been seeing him for a while now," I start. Heidi is leaning over the counter with her eyes wide like she's her daughter being read a bedtime story. "I mean, it's going good – I like him."

Suddenly her facial expression takes a turn. "Oh come on," she exclaims, "You like him? You've *got* to give me more than that. What's he like? Is he good looking, is he funny, does he tend to your…needs?" She gives me a sideways glance. Poor woman, her needs probably tend to sex since Maya was born. That's what kids will do to you.

"Of course he's funny. I don't know he's just…safe. He's reliable and affectionate, but at the same time he isn't afraid to knock me down a few pegs when I need it. He makes me feel like normal."

"Oh, sweetie, I'm so happy for you." Heidi has such a warmth to her voice. "I have to be honest, I get so worried about you, always coming in here at the weekends and working, then you go back to the office and work some more. I'm so glad that you are getting some male attention."

I've had just about enough of this conversation now. I thank her, grab the mug from the counter and sit in my corner.

I've only just managed to get Julian out of my head. Oh wait, there he is again. That slimy bastard really does know how to get under my skin. He always has. He hasn't popped his head up since early Thursday morning, but I have no doubt that he will come out to play very soon.

I hate not knowing what his end game is. Truly it is eating away at my brain. I know that is exactly what he wants and I would love nothing more than to screw up his plans, but I can't stop my stupid brain from trying to figure out what he is up to. One thing that the years have taught me about Julian is that you have to stay three steps ahead of him to survive.

There are some crumbs on my seat and today's newspaper left from the previous occupant. I brush off the crumbs and open up the newspaper, to entertain myself until he arrives.

I can't stop the smile as I read one of the headlines *Grimm Reaper, read more on page 5.*

When the media first dubbed me the Grimm Reaper, I have to say I was not the biggest fan of the name. I mean, I suppose it's a clever play on words with the Brothers Grimm, but I was hoping for something so much more daunting. However, as the name popped up more often in newspapers and on the news, I started to warm to it. And now? I'm quite fond of the idea of being the incarnation of death.

I suck in a large amount of coconut-y goodness as I read the headline about me for today.

Immediately, I spit it out.

The Grimm Reaper strikes again: Four women found brutally murdered last night

I read the article with frantic eyes. Unless I have a literal alter ego who is murdering people in my sleep, the Grimm Reaper is definitely *not* to blame for this. So why do they think I am?

Four women found dead…Grimm Brothers' quotes on the walls…etching of a spinning wheel…police say the signs point to the Grimm Reaper

I can't believe my eyes. I can't believe what I am seeing.

Why would they do this? What are they planning?

Up until now I have merely received less than pleasant letters and a few daunting threats, but this? This is a whole new level. This isn't the work of some teenager who is bored with their own life so wants to mess with mine. This is the work of someone who is out of their mind crazy and dead-set on revenge.

And I am the one who pissed them off.

CHAPTER 38 - AVERY

December 2009

"Stop it," I moaned as Julian persisted in tickling my sides. I couldn't hold back the faint giggles. "Stop!" I exclaimed with a beaming grin, grabbing his hands and pulling them all the way round my waist. Twisting my neck round to face him, I kissed him gently. "You're supposed to be teaching me how to bypass a firewall…"

He laughed into my hair. "Well, that's not as fun as other things I had in mind." He leant over the back of the chair I was sitting in and began trailing his lips down my neck.

I took a deep breath, soaking in his addictive aftershave and forced myself to push him back. "This first. Then that."

Julian rolled his eyes and let out a rather overdramatic sigh. "Fine, you downloaded the program I told you about?"

"Yep," I confirmed confidently, ready to be the perfect little student I always was in school.

"Okay," he started, taking my hand and placing it onto the keyboard. "So, first you want to drop malware into the RDP server—"

"And, how do you do that?" I interrupted, a frown painted on my face.

He sighed again and nudged me. "Well, if you give me a sec I'll tell you. God, I pity the teachers who had you for a student."

I gasped and hit him lightly. "Hey! I was amazing, thank you very much."

"I don't doubt that…" he agreed with a sideways smile, planting a kiss on my forehead. "Probably thought you were better than all of 'em."

"I didn't think I was," I mumbled, "I knew I was."

Deciding to bite his tongue, Julian pulled my hands back hovering over the keyboard. He then guided my fingers so that they pushed several different buttons. "So do that, then drop this encoded payload…" he instructed, pointing at the computer screen. "Perfect. So that creates the macrocode and the macro writes the binary."

"I feel like you're going slowly with me. I pick things up pretty quickly, don't treat me like a teenager." I tried to hide my bruised ego, but Julian saw right through it.

"Okay then, Miss Smarty-pants, I'll go fast." He said this and pushed my chair aside, leant down and began tapping on the keyboard, commentating as he did so. "So you bypass this by changing its policies, elevate to the admin privileges, type in this code and you're in."

I death-stared him. Unimpressed by his actions and attempt to challenge me – and dare I say win.

Julian, catching my stare, simply shrugged. "What? You said you wanted me to go quick, I went quick…"

I squinted my eyes even more. "You know, seeing you like this is really turning me on."

"Oh thank God," Julian abruptly replied. He threw the laptop off the desk, lifted me onto it and pressed his lips against mine.

I gave in to him. We could finish the lesson later.

CHAPTER 39 - HARRY

It never gets easier. Every time Harry goes to a new one of their crime scenes the memories leap across the room like gazelles in the Sahara. But he grins and bears it, because he knows that with every scene he witnesses, he is one step closer to finding them. He will find them.

Harry and James have been working on different cases for the last few months – after the tips from the public all hit dead ends and new information on the previous case didn't surface. But they're back together for this one.

As Harry enters the house, he is hit by the bricks of death. You'd think that, being a homicide detective, Harry would be immune to the stench by now. Still, every time he is greeted by the familiar scent, it invades his lungs, suffocating him and rendering him paralysed for a few moments before the oxygen can fight it off and he can function again.

The first feature apart from the limp bodies that catches Harry's eye is the spinning wheel carved into the dining table.

As he creeps down the hall, cuddling his soft toy close to his chest, the first thing he sees is the silhouette of a bear carved into the wooden post.

He then draws his attention to the surroundings and the Grimm quotes on the walls.

His eyes are blurred by tears, but he can just about make out the words written on the blinding white walls in thick dark blood.

And finally, he sees them. Lying almost peacefully. Their eyes are all shut and they are in delicate positions. Although the condition of their bodies tells something different, the expressions on their faces make Harry think that they went softly. That they felt little pain.

His knees buckle when he lays his eyes upon them. He's scared by them. He doesn't want to go to them. They don't look like the loving people he knew. He doesn't want to confirm what he already knows to be true. He doesn't want them to be gone.

"Harry," James calls him out of his trance and shakes his shoulder. "Mate, what are you thinking?"

"Oh I was just, um," Harry scrambles for a response, "I was just examining the patterns and drawing parallels between their other cases."

"Oh right, good shout." James applauds Harry's train of thought. "Good news, forensics found fingerprints."

Harry's face lights up with James's words. "Are you kidding?" he asks in disbelief.

"This is definitely *not* something I would joke about." James's tone is serious now.

This has never happened before. GR is always so careful, there has never been a shred of evidence in fifteen years. It makes Harry wonder, though, *why now?*

"Hey," James jolts him back into the present again. "Be happy. We've finally got a break!" he exclaims through gritted teeth. "Tonight, we're going out and celebrating, okay? Drinks are on you." He then trots off in the other direction before Harry can object.

"I'll meet you back at the station," Harry calls to James, who is gathering another lot of statements from the neighbours, so that they can cross-reference them with his. James waves his hand in Harry's direction as acknowledgement, and Harry exits.

Harry hops in his car and at the T-junction where the station is to the left, Harry turns right.

He didn't lie, exactly, Harry is going back to the police station and will meet James there – he's just taking a little detour first. He's got someone to see.

CHAPTER 40 - HARRY

"It looks like a match," James announces as he and Harry stare at the different Grimm Reaper cases.

"Yeah, it's got all the same features. We've got Pinocchio...Red Riding Hood...Rapunzel...Snow White...Little Mermaid and now Sleeping Beauty," Harry confirms. "They're all the same MO."

"Oh, don't forget Goldilocks." James points to the photo of the deceased couple. Harry nods and quickly glances down. "We can't forget the one that made him famous in the first place."

James paces his office with one hand placed on his belly and the other stroking the bristles on his chin. "So why has he left DNA now? After all these cases, why now?"

Harry shrugs his response. "Maybe he's getting cocky so he was sloppy. He thinks that he's too smart for us. Maybe he's bored of not being caught and wants to spice things up a little more. At the end of the day, we can never know why on this particular case he left fingerprints."

James groans in agreement, still deep in thought. "Or, maybe he's never actually been that careful but forensics have just missed the evidence."

Harry doesn't agree or disagree, he just lets James do his brainstorming.

James stares blankly at the board of GR victims for a few minutes. The cogs churning in his brain can be heard throughout the room. "I think we should get forensics to have another sweep of the Little Mermaid crime scene. It's still off limits and the only people who have been permitted to enter are her relatives, and we have prints and hair samples for all of them so we can rule them out. Maybe we'll turn up lucky."

"Yeah, good idea," Harry agrees. "I'll call down to them now and see when we can get that done."

Harry leaves James's office and goes to his cubicle. He dials down to forensics, "Hey, Jim, Flynn and I need another sweep on the GR case from March. When do you think that can be done?"

As he is answering, Harry gets distracted by his vibrating pocket. He pulls his phone out to quickly check what the alert is for. When he sees who it is, he clears the message from his lock screen and shoves the Samsung back in his trouser pocket.

Although his attention was diverted for only a few seconds, he misses the key information – a time period.

"Sorry, Jim, can you say that last bit again, how long until you guys can do that?"

Jim's tone is unamused by his need to repeat himself. "Three weeks."

"Any chance it can be done earlier?" Harry asks, hiding the desperation in his voice.

Harry hears Jim's sigh through the phone. "Look, rugrat, we're completely swamped at the moment and another sweep of a crime scene we ruled off months ago is not at the top of our list. I'm sorry, that's the earliest we can do." He then hangs up the phone.

Despite his manner when talking with Harry, Harry knows Jim is not a rude guy. He's just like all the others – he has no respect for Harry, since he's so young to be a detective and no one likes being told what to do by someone who has been in the job for half the time that they have.

When Harry arrives back at James's office he finds it empty. He doesn't think much of it – perhaps James just nipped to the john. So, he sits behind the desk and goes over the details of the case. There are only two Grimm phrases at the crime scene.

The one gave her virtue, the second one beauty, the third one wealth

These words are written above three of the women. And the last has written above her:

In the princess's fifteenth year she shall prick herself with a spindle and fall over dead

As Harry studies the last girl's face so full of youth, it is clear that every word of this rings true. Suddenly the image of a different woman, sprawled peacefully on the ground, shoots across his vision. He quickly shakes her from his head. He can't let those memories seep back in. Not now.

"Oh hey," James greets him as he comes back into the room. "How long have you been waiting for?"

"Only about ten minutes or so," Harry answers and raises an uncertain eyebrow. "Did you have a curry last night by any chance?"

James stares at him confused for a few moments, but he quickly catches on to what Harry is insinuating. He chuckles, "oh no, I just had to speak with Chief quickly that's all."

Harry nods and changes the subject. "Jim says they'll get another sweep done in three weeks. It's not ideal, but I suppose it gives us enough time to try and put the pieces together."

James agrees and snatches a glance at his watch. "What do you say we take the rest of the afternoon off and head to the pub?"

After Harry agrees, they grab their coats and head out of the station.

He can't quite put his finger on it, but something seems off with James. He was acting normal just this morning and when he came back from the Chief's office his voice became hollower and his whole body seemed to stiffen. It's been like that every time James comes out of a talk with Chief, recently. Slowly, it's been eating away at Harry's mind. What could they be talking about, to make James act so uneasy?

CHAPTER 41 - HARRY

Old Bernie's isn't exactly the shining jewel of Southhurst. Its foundations are on the verge of disintegrating, its windows are covered in mould and it has had hardly any modifications done to its Victorian setting. Even in the summer months, the pub has a cold draught wafting through it. Harry always makes sure to wear a warm coat when he pays a visit to Old Bernie's.

Once they have cheers-ed, Harry asks, "So, how's the old mutt?"

"Oh you know, she's the same old same old, doesn't stop nagging me as always—" James stops abruptly and smiles, "oh you mean the *dog*? Oh yeah, he's good too. The kids love him and the wife is warming to him."

"I haven't seen him round the office lately, I thought maybe he'd found a new home."

"Oh no, no. I don't think the kids would let him leave even if we wanted him to. No, the Mrs has been at home for the summer holidays."

For some reason, the atmosphere between them seems tense today. Harry thought it was just a bad conversation with the Chief, but now he's not so sure. James isn't the kind to brood – and it seems like that's all he's done this afternoon.

"Listen, mate," James suddenly speaks up after a couple minutes of silence. There's a shakiness to his voice that isn't there normally. "I've got something to tell you." His words are slow and hesitant.

Harry assures him, "of course, you can tell me anything. What's up?" He is eager to know what is on his friend's mind, mainly because he hopes whatever it is, it's the reason he is acting so strange.

"I've decided to retire."

Harry certainly wasn't expecting him to say that. "Shit, really? Why?"

James sighs and drops his shoulders. "I've been at this job for forty years. I joined when I was your age." He pauses to guzzle down some more of his beer. "I love it, of course I do, but I'm exhausted. I don't think I quite realised how tired of this I was until that GR case popped up in March. I realised that I have been in this job since before he even started. That makes me feel so...*old*. I don't know, I just want to try something new.

"I never see my kids," he declares. "I mean, when I get home in the evenings they're already in bed and sure I see them on the weekends, but look at today for example. Today I am meant to be at my boy's football game but because I'm the highest ranking detective who has been on the case for the longest, I had to come in on my day off to work on the GR case. I went and told Chief this afternoon."

Harry is sure this explains his strange behaviour. "So, you're leaving soon, then?"

"No," he assures him, "I didn't hand my notice in to Chief, I just notified him that I am definitely retiring and it is definitely soon. I think I'm aiming for the end of this year, so I can be home for the Christmas holidays."

Harry grabs his friend's shoulder and stares him straight in the eye. "Well, I'm sure going to miss having you around. I'll have to tolerate some other sergeant watching over my every move."

James shoves him playfully. "Who knows, maybe we'll have this case solved before I leave. That'll sure be a nice going away present."

CHAPTER 42 - HARRY

"I'm bored, Harry," Martha's soft voice calls from the kitchen as Harry pushes the front door shut. She seems calm – too calm.

Harry turns round the corner and finds Martha sitting at the breakfast bar with a wine glass filled to the brim with red and a bottle placed beside it – empty. She has a dangerous flare in her eye, Harry hasn't seen her like this in a long time.

"I'm bored," she reiterates. "I'm bored of waiting here like an idiot for my sweet, devoted husband to come home. From his whore."

"Martha, you have no idea what you're talking about."

"Don't!" Martha slams her hand down onto the counter and the sea of wine floods over the top of the glass and bleeds onto her hand. She very calmly lifts her fingers to her lips and licks the droplets off her cracked skin. "Don't patronise me, Harry. I am *not* some stupid little twit. I am *not* oblivious to your indiscretions. I have turned a blind eye because I know that the news we cannot conceive was a hard blow for the both of us and I am not an inconsiderate woman. I understand you have needs and I was not willing to meet those needs." She takes in a shaky breath, smoking with rage. "But it is enough now."

"Martha, you're being ridiculous. You're letting your imagination run wild, just calm down, go to bed and we can talk about this tomorrow."

"Don't tell me to calm down!" she screams as she hurls the empty wine bottle into the cream wall. Harry's skin jumps as the crimson fluid splatters and bleeds down towards Harry's feet. He has to shake the memory from his eyes.

Martha marches towards him, her eyes wide and burning with a new kind of fire that he hasn't seen before, and it forms goose bumps underneath Harry's jacket. "All I wanted was to be there for you. I've known you since it happened and all I wanted was to be there! But what did you do? You shut me out. And I can appreciate that when you were nine years old, but for Christ's sake it's been fifteen years, Harry. And we're married! I don't think I am asking too much for my *husband* to actually talk to me honestly for once. You have been chasing them for over a decade and it is time for it to stop. Do you hear me? It needs to stop."

"No it doesn't," Harry throws back at her. He has remained composed up until now but she has pushed him too far. "They were my parents and they are gone. I have every goddamn right to chase the son of a bitch who did it until my last breath and I will not let *you* tell me otherwise. I never asked you to care, I never asked you to comfort me—"

"Oh so this is my fault because I wanted to be there for my *husband*?" Martha cuts him off. Their faces are so close that Harry can feel her spit as it hits his cheeks with every word. "For fuck sake, Harry, you can't blame your screwed up head on everyone else. This is about you. Why the hell do I deserve a husband who cheats on me, simply because he doesn't have the balls to deal with his real issues?"

"For the last time I'm not having an affair!"

Without any warning Martha's palm hits Harry's cheek and pain bursts through his jaw. Shocked by her sudden aggression, Harry stumbles backwards and cringes as the broken glass catch his heel. Once the stars have cleared from his vision, he now sees the smoke coming from Martha's ears. "Don't you dare stand there and lie to me. I will not have it. I'm not going to leave you, Harry, because let's be honest there is no woman out there who would come within a hundred metres of you if she knew all the shit that's going on up there." She gestures to his head. "But I deserve to hear the truth from you. I want you to admit it – right now. I swear to God I don't want to hear another word from your mouth that isn't the truth."

"Fine!" Harry roars. "You want me to say it? Fine, I'll say it. I had an affair. I had an affair when we found out that I couldn't give you a baby because I felt like it was my fault. I felt like everything in my pathetic excuse for an existence was my fault. I thought what happened to them was my fault. And I couldn't bear coming to you about it because I didn't want you to see me as a broken toy. And then do you know what I realised? I realised that I am not like this by choice – this was done to me. It isn't my fault, it's theirs. So yes I had an affair but I am not having a flippin' one now! It ended months ago, my God, woman, what else do you want me to say?"

Martha's stance is now less aggressive. She wasn't expecting Harry to say any of that – she thought he would merely spin her another lie, as he always has. She's unsure of how to respond. Wounded by the truth and yet freed by it. After a few painful seconds of silence, Martha calmly asks, "So where were you tonight then?"

"I was out having a beer with James. What, do you want me to have a tracker implanted into my fucking shoulder? Call him up if you want, I don't give a shit. I am done explaining myself to you, Martha." Harry lets out a groan of frustration and then spins round and storms off in the opposite direction, paying no attention to the micro shards and wine droplets he is now treading across the hallway.

"Hey," Martha calls after him in a softer voice than she had been speaking with since he returned home.

"What?" He sighs as he glances back at her.

The corners of her lips curl and she bows her head. "Thank you."

CHAPTER 43 - AVERY

Now you know that I'm serious. Better watch your back.

The words of the most recent letter play over and over in my head.

The police have concluded that this latest case matches all the others, so it's the same person – aka *me*. Stupid pigs, they have no idea what they're dealing with.

Although, I have to say I am slightly saddened that the fat one is retiring. I mean, he's been there since the beginning, along for the whole ride. I wonder what *CSI: Grimm Reaper* will be like after his departure.

But anyway, sentimentality over, it also looks like there was a fingerprint found and having gotten to know my new pen pal over the last few months, my guess is that that fingerprint is *not* just them being sloppy. Which worries me.

I never like admitting that I'm in over my head, but just this once, I'll say it – I'm in over my head. I have very little to go on to find this bastard and at the moment, every move I make is just playing right into his hands. Or is it *her* hands?

One thing I noticed about the glue used to stick down the letters is that it contains TMDD (I would give you its scientific name, but I doubt you'd be able to pronounce it), which is one of the most dangerous adhesive ingredients and from my very handy pharmaceutical knowledge and paying a visit to one of my pals down in the lab, I know that there are only a handful of companies that sell glue using this ingredient. So I guess that gets me somewhere.

"Bugger!" I exclaim and I quickly cradle my burnt hand. I forgot that the metal handle of a saucepan is hot. After grabbing a kitchen towel, I wrap it around the handle and reattempt lifting the saucepan.

The steam clouds my vision and I stumble blindly, aiming for the sink. Pouring the contents into the colander, I cough as the vapour flares up even more, pushing the oxygen aside and invading my lungs.

Once the air has cleared, I pluck out one strand of spaghetti, stick out my tongue and drop it coiled into my mouth.

I almost choke on it, startled by the knock at the door.

As of late, I am usually rather cautious when opening my home to anyone, but tonight I bounce into the hallway and unlock the door without hesitation.

To my disappointment and unhealthy paranoia, no one is there. Now I start to get wary again and I reluctantly poke my head into the hostile street and jerk my eyes around the area. When I am sure there is no one in sight, I retreat back inside and go to close the door, my legs shaking a little more with every breath.

"Boo!"

My heart leaps from my chest and my lungs scream all the air from them. The blood drains from my face and my eyes are clouded by red spots.

"Jesus, don't do that!" I screech as I get to grips with my surroundings again and see Him flash his white teeth. "I almost had a bloody heart attack."

He pouts and enters my house with his arms open.

I fall into his bear hug and he cradles me, comforting me with a gentle kiss on my head. "I'm sorry, baby, I only meant to scare you a little bit."

Once my heartrate has steadied, I tilt my head up so that I am looking into his deep eyes and I stretch up onto my tiptoes to kiss Him.

"This isn't the house I dropped you off at when we first started dating," he comments, furrowing his eyebrows.

I shrug within his grip. "I had only just met you. You could've been a murderer, or a perv wanting to *have your way with me.*"

He laughs into my messy cooking bun and smirks, "Well, I did *have my way with you*, didn't I?"

I mimic his sideways smile and I stare up into the mischievous sparkle in his eye, shaking my head before stealing a quick kiss and pulling myself free.

"Shut the door, it's freezing," I demand as I make my way back to the kitchen to tend to my gourmet meal.

I stir the bolognaise sauce and lift the wooden spoon to my taste buds. I wouldn't say it's up to Gordon Ramsay's standard – but it'll do.

I feel his warm, coarse hands slide onto my hips and wrap around my waist. As I lower the spoon back into the mixture he nudges me.

"Let me have a taste. I can see what I'm in for."

I do as he asks and his lips curl around the end of the spoon. His expression is stern and serious while he lets his brain process the taste. He then nods in content, "not bad."

"Shut up," I joke and I go back to stirring my concoction. He nestles his head into my neck and then begins trailing his lips up to my chin. "Stop," I tell Him. My tone is not very convincing, even my reason is being quiet for once. "You're distracting me, this cooking thing is really tough."

He doesn't listen to me and continues to press his soft lips against my neck. I let out a little girl giggle and repeat, "stop," but I don't even believe myself. He then squeezes me tighter and I squeal, dropping the wooden spoon and spinning round to face Him.

As he bends down our lips touch. "You're in an especially good mood today. Any reason?" I say with our bodies so close I can only see those gorgeous eyes.

"Yes I am. Does there always have to be a reason? Can't I just be happy to see you?"

I contort my face, contemplating whether to let it slide or not. "Hmm, no," I finally answer. "There's got to be a reason."

Rolling his eyes, he sighs, "fine. I'm just realising how lucky I am to have you."

"Aw," I reply and shortly after add, "That's fine, you don't have to tell me."

We sit down on the sofa and as I turn the TV on, out of the corner of his eye he spots the cupboard placed to the side of the room with the door ajar.

He disregards his meal and walks over to the cupboard, gawking. "You have Battleship." He sounds like a little boy seeing a toy racing track he wants to play with. "Oh my God, screw *Friends*, we're playing it."

He doesn't even give me a chance to protest before he pulls out the box, pushing the centre table towards the sofa and begins setting up the game.

"Okay I guess we're playing Battleship then," I murmur under my breath, hurling myself from the sofa and onto the floor.

"I'm just warning you," I say as I strategically place my ships, "I'm amazing at this game."

"We'll see about that."

CHAPTER 44 - AVERY

"They say seeing a person's bedroom is like looking into their soul," he declares as I lead Him up the stairs.

"Oh do they?" I ask with a disbelieving tone.

"No, but I say that," he admits and makes an impressed expression as we enter my abode. "Very fancy. I can't see a hidden pile of dirty clothes anywhere."

I laugh a little harder than I should. "Trust me, you won't be finding that, I keep everything extremely ordered."

"So I've noticed," he comments while pointing to the rail of black trench coats in my walk-in wardrobe. "Does one really need fifteen of the same coat?"

"You never know, what if something were to happen to one of them." *Like someone's blood spills onto it and you have to burn it.* I lean back on the bed with my hands propped up behind me, watching Him snoop around my room.

"You're looking after Dopey, I see." He gestures to the purple soft toy propped up against the far wall in the wardrobe. "I would have thought you'd cuddle him every night because he reminds you of me," he jokes with a grin.

"Well, I would but…with all the people I bring in here, they might think I'm a bit weird if I've got a kid's toy on my bed."

He mouths *ha ha* sarcastically and approaches me. Leaning forward, he slides his hands over mine and softly kisses me. I lean back onto the bed and give in to Him. I wrap my fingers around his neck, pulling him closer and he pushes me into the bed. The sheer force with which he does this makes the butterflies somersault, there may have even been a hint of aggression – even better. The warmth of his body sends tingles up my spine. My reason is enjoying herself too – even though she'd never admit it.

A few minutes later he lifts his head up, brushes hair from my face and tucks it behind my ear before whispering, "I'm just going to pop downstairs. I'll be back in two minutes."

"Okay," I agree, hypnotized by his smile and I unravel my legs from his waist.

Once I hear his feet hit the staircase I shuffle off the bed and skid into my bathroom. I stare at myself in the mirror, fixing any makeup smudges and fluffing my messed up beach waves.

I then peel off my skin-tight patterned top and skinny jeans as well as my everyday lace underwear and switch them for another lace set – only this set is blood red. My favourite colour.

After surveying the area and seeing he has not returned, I hurry onto the bed and lie there, waiting.

There's nothing more difficult than choosing the awkward pose you want to be holding when they walk back through the door.

He's taking longer than he should be, if he's retrieving what I think he is, and I can't detect any noise coming from downstairs.

Just when I think he has decided to do a runner, I hear Him slowly trudging back up the stairs.

I get back into position and smile seductively as he opens the door. His reaction is far from unsatisfactory – it's abysmal.

It's as if his eyes don't even stray from my face – not even one glance down. I would be lying if I said I wasn't the tiniest bit offended. His face is serious. A complete change from the playful expression he was wearing when he left the room.

And then I see what has him so sombre. In his hand are several crumpled pieces of paper. With letters cut out from a magazine.

"Where did you get those?" I ask. My voice is husky and my eyes wide.

"What the hell are these?" he demands, disregarding my question.

I throw myself upright. "They're none of your business, that's what they are."

He comes closer to me and closes the door. "Avery, this is serious. Who is sending you these? Have you told the police?"

I snatch them quickly from his hand. "It doesn't matter. It's just dumb, bored kids. Just drop it." I'm silent for a moment, glancing down at my mauve carpet. "How did you get them?" I ask again.

"I saw one on your desk, and then there was a corner of the same paper poking out of your drawer so I opened it and saw the others. Avery, I want to protect you. Who is threatening you?"

My eyes flick up to his and the flame alight within them burns a hole through him. "I don't need you to protect me," I snap. "You don't even know half of what there is to me. I can handle some pathetic loser with an old magazine, a pair of scissors and no life. Back off," I demand as I walk into my wardrobe to retrieve my lilac silk robe, sliding it over my goose bumps. I have only just realised I am still semi-naked.

"Yeah, you're right," he agrees. "I don't know all there is to know about you. But that isn't my doing, that's *yours*. I have been completely patient and I have never pushed you into telling me anything you don't want to, but we've been dating for four months, Avery. And now I find these threatening letters? You've got to give me something!"

I can feel my heart pumping the blood around my body in double-time and red spots are beginning to float across my eyes. "Fine, you want to know what I'm hiding. You want to know my deep and dark secrets. Is that it?"

Avery, no, my reason whispers to me calmly.

"Yes I do," he answers, matching the decibel of my question.

What are you doing? I can hear the panic in her voice.

"You really think you can handle the truth, huh?"

He nods his head violently. "How bad can it be?"

Think about this. You're being stupid.

I can hear the words surge up my throat like a tidal wave about to break. I'm actually about to do it. I'm about to tell him.

"You want to know what it is?" The butterflies are no longer dancing but are hurling themselves against my stomach. My palms twitch and his face is just a blurred figure. I don't even hear my own words, all I hear is a ringing.

Stop, you idiot!

"I—" I choke on my words. It's as if everything has frozen and I'm seeing myself from the outside.

My reason is holding my hand and dragging me down to inspect the two of us. I can practically see the saliva being hurled from my mouth by the force of my words. My pupils are dilated so much that the colour of my iris is undetectable. My lips are curled up, baring my canines.

I don't even recognise myself. I clasp both hands over my mouth, disbelieving of what I am about to do. I stare at my reason's angry face and she smacks the back of my head, sending me back into my body and into the present.

He is waiting there for my big reveal.

"I'm into gambling," I finally spit out.

His shoulders drop and his expression is confused. "Huh?" The glint in his eyes dulls, as if he's disappointed.

"I'm a gambler," I reiterate. "A few months ago I bit off more than I could chew and now I owe some people some money. I told you it's nothing that serious. These guys are all talk." My voice is softer now and I feel my breath slow.

"Oh." He glances down and twiddles his thumbs. His voice is no longer gritty, but is instead frail from the screaming.

"Yeah. So there you go. Now you know my big secret. Are you happy? Was it all you were hoping for?"

He reaches out for me. "Avery…"

I quickly move out of his reach. "I would like you to leave," I say, in as calm a voice as I can muster.

He doesn't even fight it. He knows it isn't worth it. The lack of anger in my voice tells him that I'm serious. He simply lowers his head and whispers, "okay."

And then he's gone.

My body shakes with the slamming of the front door. Suddenly the house feels enormous, empty and lonely.

I cradle myself and as my eyes blur, I quickly wipe away the salt water sticking to my cheeks.

I don't move. I have no idea how long I am standing by my bedroom door. I'm completely paralysed by the shock. Though, it's not the shock of our argument that has me so rattled, but the fact I feel hollow now that he's gone.

CHAPTER 45 - AVERY

We haven't spoken in three days. I'm in agony.

Lately, I don't know who the hell I am. I've never been the kind of woman to pine over some guy. To be checking my phone every five minutes. With us not talking I can't concentrate. All my mind wants to think about is Him. It's rather inconvenient when I should be focusing on finding this bastard who's trying to take me down.

Even Kirsty's noticed I'm not myself and that I'm distracted. And she doesn't see anyone other than her own reflection and our boss.

My mind is so far away from the real world, that I am not even fazed when I return home tonight and the lamp on my desk flicks on, as if by magic.

"Hey, Buttercup."

I give Julian a sideways glance and then continue undoing the straps on my work heels.

He seems disappointed by my lack of enthusiasm. "Aw, why so glum?" He pouts and tilts his head to the side. "Aren't you happy to see me?"

This time I pull my eyes into his direction, manually forcing my heartrate to steady. "Once was enough for me. Thanks for looking after my house while I was at work but as you can see I'm home now, so you can see yourself out."

I then knock my shoulder against his as I push past him to get to the kitchen, maintaining my confident aura as I do so. When I return to the lounge with a beer in hand, I am sad to see him still standing there.

"Is there trouble in paradise?" he asks with a sarcastic, almost amused tone.

I glare at him and answer with another question; "don't you have anything better to do than break into my house and take my beer?"

He grins and with a firm shake of his head replies, "Nope. Let's not forget I was in jail for computer hacking. It's not like places are jumping at the chance for me to work on their tills." He shrugs and adds, "So I'm all yours."

I slump down onto the sofa. "If you don't leave in the next three minutes, I'll call the police and they can remove you." I then flick on the TV and try my hardest not to let my eyes stray from the screen.

"No you won't," he says almost immediately. His voice is deeper now, more sensual. It makes the memories flood in and I quickly swallow them back down.

"Do you want to call my bluff? Would you like to serve the rest of your sentence?"

Julian tilts his head back and forces a laugh before coming down to my level on the sofa, caressing my tatty hair with the back of his hand. As he does so, his fingertips lightly touch my cheek and I let out a heavy, involuntarily breath. "You know the deal, Buttercup. If I go down, you go down. It's how we stayed together all those years ago."

We aren't touching, but I can feel his lips hovering there as if they were pressed right against mine. I have to lock my jaw, trying my hardest not to show my weaknesses that he knows all too well. With my best poker face, I huff and smirk at him. "And look how well that turned out for you."

This comment has him unamused, his expression is no longer playful and he snaps, "One phone call and you're behind bars for life." The hairs on the back of my neck stand up as his eyes pierce through me. I'm reminded of the power he has over me, even without holding evidence above my head. Those magnetic emerald eyes. "One phone call."

"Yeah, right," I remark, slightly rattled by the threat and my evil desires, but giving no reaction to his empty words. "If you had anything on me you would've used it the day they locked you up. You know it and I know it. Now kindly remove yourself from my sofa and fuck off before I kill you."

Julian shrugs, not arguing with my logic. "Come on, Avery, you couldn't do that." He bends down, touches his lips to my cheek and whispers, "you'd miss me too much."

My lips quiver and my breath catches on his words. He's doing it on purpose. It's all just play. I can't let him know he's affecting me. I look him straight in the eye with no expression and say, "your breath stinks."

The smouldering grin on his face falls and it is replaced with a locked jaw and emotionless eyes. He stares me down, his face millimetres from mine. My heart begins to race ever so slightly, unsure of what I can expect him to do.

After forty seconds of this, he suddenly jerks his head back and walks into the hallway. It's not long after he has yanked the door open that the English summer winds gush into the lounge and make my teeth chatter.

Just before he leaves he turns back and looks at me. Those eyes latch deep onto mine and refuse to let me turn away. There are so many expressions behind them, I'm not sure which is dominant. Is he feeling playful, is he feeling nostalgic? Perhaps he's just feeling rage and anger. And is looking forward to his sweet revenge.

"Be careful, Buttercup. I may not have enough on you yet, but karma's a bitch. And she's coming after you."

There was some guy who kept going into her house when she wasn't home. I didn't recognise him. I couldn't tell if he was helping her or against her. I was hoping for the latter, but I couldn't be sure. I'd have to look into him and find out what I was dealing with.

CHAPTER 46 - AVERY

January 2010

I clicked the door shut as gently as possible, so that I didn't wake Julian at that hour. After I had taken off my shoes and placed my black trench coat on its allocated hanger, ready to go back upstairs in the wardrobe, I caught sight of him sitting on the sofa, rocking back and forth with his head in his hands.

I was thrown by his presence but I tried to act normal. "What are you doing up so late?"

He didn't answer me. He merely continued to rock. The door to the outside was shut but suddenly the air in the room was sharp and unsettling.

Finally, with a fragile, shaky voice he asked, "Who are you?"

I approached him and as I did his eyes widened and he shuffled to the other side of the sofa. "What's wrong, babe? You're acting weird."

He wouldn't look me in the eye, instead they were fixed on my collarbone and didn't stray. "I followed you," he declared. "I knew you were hiding something and I was getting suspicious. I thought maybe you were cheating, so I followed you."

"Babe," I said again, shaking my grown-out fringe from my eyes and grabbing his hand before he could pull away, now understanding what had him so rattled. "It's okay. Calm down, you just need to get some rest and we can talk about this in the morning." Although my voice was calm, my heart certainly wasn't. I couldn't believe I had been so stupid and sloppy. How did I not notice him following me? I'd never been in this situation before and I had no idea what he was going to do. I thought that maybe if I acted like it was normal, he would take it better.

It didn't work. "No it's not okay!" he exclaimed, staring at me as though he didn't even recognise me. "I saw you kill people, Avery! What about that is okay?" He then paused and stared down at the carpet. When he finally lifted his head back up he asked, "Were there others?"

I sighed and opened my mouth but he stole my words.

"You have, haven't you?" Julian was frightened by his own words. "Have there been a lot? Gosh, the way you did it…"

I decided to keep my mouth sealed shut and let him process what he had just seen before I said anything – so that I could gauge the situation I had on my hands.

Julian went back to staring at the floor. His emerald eyes were no longer the vibrant ones I was hypnotised by, but a dulled murky pigment. I could see him recalling his memories from tonight as horror flashed across his face.

Suddenly he gasped and backed up further into the sofa. "You're them. You're the Grimm Reaper."

There was no need for me to confirm it, he had already drawn his conclusion. Now all I could do was try and minimalize the damage.

"Look," I finally began after staying silent for so long. "I understand that you're in shock and I understand why you're frightened, but nothing has to change. I'm still me. Let's just forget about this, okay?"

"Forget about this? Are you kidding?"

I knew it was a long shot but I had to try.

"I've got to call the police," he declared as he reached for his phone. I grabbed his wrist and held it tightly in my grasp.

My eyes were now harsh and I tightened my jaw. I'd tried the nice route and it didn't work, so it was time to resort to my natural instinct.

"You're not going to call anyone," I told him with a low, husky voice. "Let's not forget your own illegal activities. Is it really worth going to prison for? Come on, don't pretend you're a good guy. Don't pretend you care about those people. If you did you wouldn't be stealing from some new stranger every week, would you?" I loosened my grip and moved towards him. "You care about *me*. You don't want to ruin what we have, do you? It's not like I'm some entirely new person, you've always known I've had a dark side."

I cupped his chin and stroked the bristles there. "You don't have to be scared of me." I smiled, like I was some sweet little child. "How about we go upstairs and get some rest. I'll tell you whatever you want to know tomorrow, okay?"

Julian was hesitant and cautious, but after gulping down his distress, he nodded and relaxed his posture. I pulled him towards me and touched my lips to his. He was still reluctant and he didn't move his mouth to fit mine, but I wasn't too worried.

I knew he'd come around. It's something I noticed about him from the first day he stole my taxi. Even if he didn't want to admit it, he was just as bad as me.

CHAPTER 47 - AVERY

"Her husband's doctor just got back to us," the beer-belly announces. "He and his wife had won a surprise trip to a desert island and he took all his holiday and sick days off to go. That's why he was unavailable to confirm the appointment."

"And?" the skinny one replies.

"And now he's back, he's confirmed it. The alibi checks out. He was at the appointment at the time she was killed. Her husband wasn't responsible. Suppose there was just a fault with the records."

Dammit, I think to myself. Why couldn't he have just stayed stranded on that island, it would have been so convenient for me.

I glance down at my phone and spin it around in my hands, debating whether to call.

I've come home for lunch today. Partly because I wanted to catch up on *all three* of my cases, but mostly to check that Julian isn't poking his head where it doesn't belong like he was yesterday.

"Well that's the relatives eliminated for the person of interests. What next sarge?"

The beer-bellied detective isn't amused by the nickname. "We'll look into her phone records. Why don't you get on that, Grant, and I'll go back to the forensics team?"

"Okay, I'll do that tomorrow."

I close the laptop as the skinny one exits. The Little Mermaid's case no longer has much attention because of my apparent resurgence, so that's gone pretty cold, apart from them doing another sweep of her apartment. This just shows their desperation. They really do have no leads.

As for Sleeping Beauty, the detectives on the case are still going over the fine details of the scene and trying to find a match for the fingerprint. How they got it I have no idea, but I know that those fingerprints are mine.

It's a pretty close match to my own work, I'll give them that. Whoever is responsible for this must have studied each and every one of my murder scenes – right down to the fact that I always use the property of the victim as a weapon. I don't even think that was released to the public.

I drum my fingers on the desk, impatient and trying to keep myself distracted. I need something to do, something to turn my mind to, something other than his number.

Keeping my home tidy at all times has its advantages, but one of the drawbacks is that there are very few household chores to do when I want to avoid things.

But I am stubborn and determined, so I make my way into the kitchen and wipe down the counters and wash up the mug and spoon I used for my morning tea. I even give the oven a good polishing.

My phone flashes up and moves along the counter.

"Ow," I moan when in a frantic rush to reach my phone, my head collides with the top of the harsh metal oven.

It's my boss, asking me to go to a meeting tomorrow in Braxton. I feel like an idiot. He's not going to call or text. He knows better than to do that. He's going to wait until I'm ready to speak with Him.

I don't want to, though, because I'm still mad at Him. I'm mad he went through my desk and I'm mad he confronted me about it. If you're going to snoop, at least do it right.

Then again, he seemed concerned for me. Perhaps I shouldn't be angry at Him. Perhaps it's okay for someone to want to protect me every now and then.

No, Avery. Be reasonable. It's a good thing this happened, it means you can concentrate on what's really important. Oh, her irritatingly familiar voice pops up in my head again. And of course, I can't exactly disagree with her logic.

I go back into the lounge, bounce onto the sofa and switch on crappy TV. There's never anything decent on at this time in the afternoon.

Even if there was I couldn't concentrate on it anyway. I know my reason told me this is a good thing because I can focus on the real issues, but all my mind goes to is Him. I need to get Him out of my head if I want to be at the top of my game and the only way I can do that is by calling Him.

I procrastinate for another thirty-three minutes, and while beating my foot against the floor at a quicker rate than my heartbeat, I snatch up my phone from the coffee table.

"Screw it." And the phone starts ringing.

I don't know why but I have an itch in my chest, making it hard for my lungs to function and causing my breath to shake.

"McKenzie's Southhurst Estate Agent, how may I help?" the chirpy voice of the receptionist sings down the phone.

"Hi." My voice is husky and I pause to clear my throat. Let's try that again. I ask in my politest voice if he is available and if I am able to speak with Him.

"Of course, ma'am. May I ask who is calling?"

I'm hesitant but eventually comply. "Avery Blake."

I hear a dulled tone play at a repeated rhythm, as if it is speaking to me in Morse code, telling me to back out and hang up the phone before he picks up. *If* he picks up.

"Avery."

My heart leaps at the sound of his voice. Although I am the one who called *Him*, it's as if I'm not expecting Him at all.

"Hi," I reply with a higher pitch than I have ever spoken in before.

"Are you okay? I feel so awful about the other night…"

I cut Him off. "It's okay. I've had some time to think over it. I want to meet and sort things out. I want to get back to before."

I hear Him sigh through the phone. "I'm so glad to hear you say that. I would love nothing more. I've got a house viewing this afternoon but…" He pauses and I can hear Him murmur something to one of his colleagues. "But I can get someone else to take it for me. Are you home? I can come over now."

"No!" I stutter. "No, um, yes I am at home but I've got work this afternoon."

"But, it's Thursday. I thought you had Thursday afternoons off?" he asks in a suspicious tone.

I grit my teeth and slap my head into my hands, ashamed at myself. "Yeah, I normally do but um …" I'm struggling to give him an answer. I'm usually great at being put on the spot like this, but right now my mind is blank. "I, um, my friend Kirsty is sick and she wants me to cover for her."

He laughs softly. "You hate Kirsty, why would you do that?"

Yes, I do hate Kirsty. Why would I do that?

"Yeah, yeah, I know." I mimic his laugh, trying to sound less stiff. "But she promised to give me one of her top clients if I did, so I couldn't really say no. I mean, it gives me the chance to poach a few more from her." It's not my best work, but it'll do. I add quickly, "I'm around to-night, though?"

"Sure, sounds great. I'll come round about seven-thirty?" he asks and I agree. He then adds, "I've missed you, Avery."

"I've missed you too. I'll see you tonight."

It feels like I'm missing three words. They're so easy to say and they are on the tip of my tongue.

But I hang up the call. I can't say them. If I do it becomes real. I'm not ready for it to be real.

If you're wondering, yes I was lying to Him – there is nothing Kirsty could offer me that would make me do anything for her. No, I have prior engagements.

Over the past couple of months I have been researching the glue used on the letters and after pulling a few strings, I've found two companies that use the exact ingredients that match what I am looking for.

One of the companies is in the Midlands and the other is situated in none other than Braxton.

Unlike Southhurst, Braxton is a small town and it tends to house local shops and companies that don't tend to do business too far from them. So, I'm paying a visit to the company today and I am praying to my lucky stars that one of their customer records gives me a clue as to who I'm up against.

CHAPTER 48 - HARRY

They've been distant the last few days. Harry hasn't had any calls returned and only half-word answers to his texts. But today they seem back to normal. Harry is relieved, he was worried that they might be starting to get a guilty conscience.

Harry just met them for lunch and now he's doing the walk of shame back to the station, looking over his shoulder at every corner.

The air is thick today. It's heavy to inhale, especially with Harry's tar-clogged lungs. The clouds are blanketing Southhurst, keeping it from the sun's warmth. The atmosphere is as stale as Harry's breath, when he exhales the addictive toxins of the cigarette he squeezes between his fingers.

As the nicotine rush hits him, his hands begin to shake and he struggles to take in any more. Having little control, he sucks in a sharp breath. Too sharp. It causes him to curl over and cough up the smoke. The smoke is supposed to be his only place of refuge, yet it too is turning against him.

Harry remembers his first time in a police station as if it was yesterday. Every time he puts the badge in his trouser pocket and enters Southhurst PD, the memory floods back in.

"You're gonna be okay, son." The woman who leads Harry into the station says, "You don't have to be afraid. We'll find someone to look after you."

She crouches down to Harry's height and rests her hands on his dainty shoulders. Harry pulls away and cradles the soft toy that he has not let go of since he fell asleep last night.

"Hi there," another policeman greets Harry. He is a lot bigger than the female officer. He has a wiry beard and a large beer-belly that Harry can hardly see his face over. "My name is Detective Constable Flynn. Do you mind coming with me and we can have a little conversation?"

Harry nods at him reluctantly and squeezes the teddy tighter. The large man softens his expression and gives Harry a warm smile. "He can come too, if you want?" He gestures to the teddy. Harry curls his lips up slightly and reaches up for the detective's hand.

The man leads him into a cold, dark room. Harry's pyjamas don't prevent the goose bumps from forming on his arms and legs.

He is told to sit in the metal chair, but when he is unable to see over the table, they fetch him a cushion to prop him up.

"Now, how about you tell me your name."

Harry is shy and doesn't answer immediately. After the detective gives him another warm smile, he whispers, "James."

The detective's smile grows and he says, "Funny, mine too."

"Harry," James calls when he catches sight of him in the station entrance. He then approaches. "I've just got some new info from forensics. Come into my office and we'll take a look over it."

Harry agrees and follows him down the corridor.

"So," James starts, "you know I was assigned to look into that alley girl case with Grant? Well, the fingerprints found there match the ones we found at the GR crime scene."

"Are you serious?" Harry's face is in awe.

Rubbing his beer-belly, James grins and dips his head. "Yep. Looks like the two are connected. Isn't this just our lucky day?"

Harry shrugs and replies, "Maybe, but the fact they are connected just confuses the case even more, don't you think? I mean, when has the Grimm Reaper ever killed without their signature? Does this mean that GR might be responsible for unsolved murders that don't fit the MO? Every pattern, every lead, every connection we've made with their cases since the beginning are just shattered."

James doesn't disagree. He simply sits back in his swivel chair and stares up at the ceiling. "We can't make any assumptions yet. The alley kill didn't look at all planned and it was sloppy. From the beginning, Grant and I have said that the killer can't have been experienced. It's an alley, so plenty of people go down it every single day. Maybe it's just a coincidence."

Pacing the room, Harry shakes his head. "I don't believe in coincidences." He stays silent for a few minutes, furrowing his eyebrows and stroking his unshaven chin. "Maybe," he finally says, "Maybe the alley girl was connected to one of the cases. Maybe GR was finishing one of the tales off."

"That's not actually a bad thought," James agrees. "I'll look further into the girl's background. Her step-family are all dead but I'm not sure how they went. I'll find out – maybe they were one of GR's kills."

CHAPTER 49 - AVERY

The atmosphere within a mile radius of the factory is thick, foggy and heavily polluted. I can feel the fumes attacking my cells with every breath – I might as well take up smoking.

Once I have found a suitable space for my car, I pull the rear-view mirror towards me and apply my Barbie pink lipstick. Whenever I am in my favourite blonde wig and blue contact lenses, I can't help but take advantage of wearing a colour that doesn't normally suit me.

I unbutton my blouse a little, just to let the girls breathe, and then make my way into the Industrial Revolution style building.

The building is small and dull, completely made up of concrete and steel. I'm not expecting the interior to be any better, either.

To my surprise, I am greeted by polished wooden floors, perfectly painted cream walls and a cheery smile behind the glass top.

"Hi, how can I help you, ma'am?" the frail man squeals in a Californian accent. I'm slightly taken back by his eyes ogling me, as they are double the size of mine due to his magnified glasses.

I lay my forearms on the counter and lean forward slightly, subtly displaying my cleavage. "Oh hi," I greet him. I then pause for a few seconds, studying him. Making a snap-judgement based on his chirpiness and high-pitched voice may be a little too stereotypical, I mean all Americans are like that. However, since he is dressed in the latest Ralph Lauren summer suit and a perfectly ironed, light pink shirt with just enough of his chest showing that I can tell it has been recently waxed, I think it's safe to say that he drives on the other side of the road.

I come to this conclusion due to his appearance, but also due to his lack of enthusiasm at my exposed chest. There's only ever *one* explanation for that.

So, I pull myself back upright and stare him straight in the eye. "Hi. My name is Susan Harris and I'm here to run a health and safety check on the premises. You should be expecting me." I try to remain polite but I lower my voice slightly, giving a sense of authority so that he will be less inclined to argue.

He frowns briefly but does not remove the grin from his cheeks. "Oh, I'm sorry I wasn't made aware of any inspections today. Let me just go and check the diary."

Gesturing to me *one minute*, he spins around and taps on the keypad which keeps the door behind the desk locked. I keep my head down but my eyes up and on him.

He returns a few moments later and says, "It doesn't look like we've got anything written down here."

I peer over at the diary, confused. "Oh, how strange. My secretary definitely said two o'clock on Thursday 10th. Is there perhaps anyone who can confirm the appointment?"

He drums his fingers on the counter for a while and moans in thought. I wish he would hurry up, these contacts are really starting to itch.

Finally, he replies, "If you can just bear with me one moment, I'll call my supervisor down to speak with you."

I bow my head and he begins tapping on the number pad. "Hey, Wanda, could you transfer me through to Mr Jackson, please?" There is then a long pause and some murmuring on the other line. "Okie dokie, thanks for letting me know, I'll be up there in just two ticks."

He then turns his attention back to me and with an even wider smile – if that is even possible – says, "sorry, ma'am, my supervisor is in a meeting and won't be out for another half an hour. Do you mind waiting?"

"I understand but I have two other inspections to do this afternoon and I'm already running late. Is there any way you could just run up and get him to confirm that he is expecting me and then I can be on my way?"

"Um." He seems hesitant and unsure of how to respond. My reason tells me he's new here. "I suppose that should be okay. Give me two minutes and I'll be right back."

He then scuttles off towards the elevator and once he is out of sight, I scurry round the desk.

Squeezing my eyes shut, I recall him unlocking the door.

1, 9, 5, 3, X, A, 6

Biting my lip, I turn the handle and let out a breath of relief when the latch releases and the door flies open.

I jerk my head from side to side, scanning the room for the cabinets. They are in the far corner. I head towards them.

I go through each drawer, scanning for the delivery records.

"Come on, come on," I murmur to myself while flicking through all the NOPs and H&S documents.

I start looking through the last cabinet and I can feel myself getting warmer. The first cabinet contains insurance information, the second contains employee information and I can only hope that the final contains customer information.

The first drawer is a disappointment – merely hundreds of sheets on stock.

And the second is locked. Typical.

I yank it a couple times but it won't budge.

My breath starts getting quicker as I realise it has been four minutes now. The chirpy man will be back soon.

I slide the hair grip keeping the wig in place, bend it so that it is more or less a straight, thin piece of metal and I begin to twist and turn it in the key hole.

I can hear a lot of metal-on-metal and it sounds like something might be moving due to the clicking noises, but I slump down to the ground and throw the grip across the floor.

I don't know how to pick a goddamn lock – what am I thinking. You think I'd have learnt that by now.

Running out of ideas and running out of time, I try the only think that seems logical — brute force.

I grip the handle of the drawer, place both feet on the cabinet, lean back and pull with every ounce of strength I have.

At first it seems to do absolutely nothing and all I can think is how stupid I am being. But then after a minute of an agonizing muscle workout, I feel the hinges give slightly. I push my feet harder against the cabinet and after another forty seconds, I am thrown backwards as it gives in.

Once I regain my breath I crawl back over to the now separated drawer and hurry through the folders.

This better be in here. Otherwise I'm suing this place for dislocating my shoulder.

"Yes!" I whisper as I spot a folder labelled *customer transactions.*

I begin flicking through it, but I am interrupted by footsteps echoing down the corridor.

"Shit," I growl to myself. I grab the first two sheets from the folder and pray to my lucky stars that they have on them what I need.

I shove the drawer back in place and skid out of the room.

"What are you doing?"

I am startled by the bug-eyed American's tapping foot and hands on his hips. He has caught me just turning away from locking the door.

My first reaction is pretty much *I'm doing something I'm not supposed to.* But I take in a deep breath, compose myself and mimic his overly enthusiastic expression from before.

"Oh, I'm so sorry, I don't mean to be rude." I make my way back to the other side of the desk. "I just have awful cramps and I was just having a quick peek to see if you had any painkillers behind there. I know I shouldn't snoop, I'm so sorry."

He looks at me through narrowed eyes and a pout. I'm not sure if he's bought it. But then he returns to a welcoming face and says, "Oh that's fine, I understand. I don't have any unfortunately. That time of the month, is it?"

"Huh?" I stare at him sideways. "Oh," I quickly say after I have caught up to his implication. "Yeah, yeah, it's a killer."

This time he pouts sympathetically rather than suspiciously. "Aw, well I spoke to my supervisor and he says that the inspection isn't booked for another two weeks."

Slapping my hand to my forehead I reply, "Oh my gosh, I'm such a numpty. I'll go to my office and go back over my schedule. It's been a hectic few weeks and I've just had to hire a new secretary. I suppose she isn't that good then, is she?" I joke and he returns with a squeaky laugh.

I wave him goodbye and march out of the factory, clutching the two pieces of paper I managed to snag to my chest.

Once I am back in my car, I examine the documents. They appear to be a list of transactions from the last three months.

I scan through the various company names on the list. Some I've heard of, some I haven't. But there's only one name that catches my eye.

McKenzie's Southhurst Estate Agent.

CHAPTER 50 - AVERY

A million thoughts fly around in my head as I drive home.

There are certain things about Him that I am now suspicious of. Things I had previously just put down to coincidence or convenient timing. But tonight I am going to find out exactly who he is.

When I unlock my door, I step over several buttercups on my doorstep. *At least he is giving me some warning now.*

"You know," I hear Julian's voice from the lounge, "I was planning to leave the buttercups and go. But as I was laying them down, I saw an envelope poking out of the letter box."

I burst the door open, now worried about his findings. I see him sitting behind my desk, waving the letter through the air. My jaw locks as my eyes gauge its content.

"You've really made some enemies, haven't you, Buttercup?"

I march towards him and snatch the letter from his hand, maintaining a cold expression even though I'm trembling inside, fearing this could be the ammunition he's been looking for.

"Now, now," he says defensively, "there's no need to get testy with me, love."

Come to the corner of Old Oak Street at midnight. I have a little present for you. And remember, no returns.

"Come on, Avery, spill the beans. Who have you pissed off this time?" Julian has a smirk on his face that I just want to rip right off.

"Don't give me that crap. For all I know you could be the one sending this."

"Oh you don't have to worry about me, Buttercup." He leans back in the chair and clasps his hands together. "When I take you down it'll be on my terms, it'll be forever." His grimace widens and he lowers his head. "And you'll never see me coming."

The both of us jump at the banging on the door and my eyes widen. "You've got to leave," I demand, my voice hurried and nervous.

Julian isn't fazed by the knock or by my change in temperament. "Oh I'm sorry, are you expecting someone?" He gives me a sideways smile. "Is it your new boy toy?"

I sigh and yank him out of the chair. "Oh shut up. Will you get out of here? Now."

"What's with the rush?" His tone tells me he is enjoying this situation far too much. "We're in a good place now, right? Surely it's time for the new beau to meet the ex." Julian then begins to approach the front door.

I grab his sleeve and spin him around, pulling him into me. I stumble off balance from the force of his body against mine and instinctively latch on tighter to him.

His face is so close to mine, I feel the warmth in his breath brushing against my lips as they tingle from the forgotten sensation. He presses into me so that the ridges of his abs caress my tensed stomach. The butterflies swoon.

Putting his lips close to my ear, he whispers, "Oh, Avery, it's not that I wouldn't love to break the bed again – you know, for old time's sake. But unfortunately …" Julian presses in even closer to me, wrapping one arm around my waist and relieving my feet of carrying my weight. My arms want to throw themselves around him, my lips want to give into the temptation that is only a millimetre away, my vision wants to fade away so it cannot be held responsible for what happens next. "You are a colossal bitch and even my best pal down there can't look past that." As his words form his tone grows harsh and strong. He immediately drops me back to the ground and I kick myself for almost giving in. Almost.

I shove him away, every fibre suddenly repelling him. "Don't be disgusting, I would never touch you again. Just get the hell out of here. And *not*," I quickly add, "through the front door."

Julian lifts his hands up in surrender and makes his way into the kitchen. "Fine, we'll have to be introduced another time then."

There is another knock at the door and I hurry Julian along. As he skips into the garden he turns to me with his smug expression and says, "Happy hunting."

Once he's gone, I quiet the butterflies and my reason tuts me for being so weak. Removing him from my mind, I shuffle over to my desk, throw the letter in the top drawer with the others and hurry to the door.

I compose myself and fix my hair, then I put on a smile and unlock it.

"Hey," I greet Him.

"Hi," he returns as he crosses the threshold. "I was worried you were going to leave me out there all night. Was there someone in here? I thought I heard talking."

I waved the question off. "Oh no, I was just watching some crappy telly." I usher him into the lounge. "Do you want something to drink?"

"Sure, a beer would be great."

I stare at him and hum. "Hmm, no, I think we should have some wine. Red or white?"

He chuckles softly. "Okay then, um, how about red?"

I agree and head into the kitchen to fix us a glass each.

When I return he has made himself comfy on the sofa.

"Thanks," he says as I hand him one of the glasses. He doesn't take a sip from it though, he immediately places it on the table and then takes the one from my hand and does the same. "Look." He stares into my eyes and takes my hands in his. "I feel so awful about the other night. I know you like your privacy and I absolutely should not have pushed you into telling me anything. I should respect your boundaries and I'm so sorry, it was completely my fault."

I squeeze his hands and assure Him, "honestly it's fine. You have every right to want to know more about me and I think I just overreacted a little. Let's just put it behind us, okay?" He nods and I change the subject. "Now, tell me more about you."

He laughs again. "Haven't we had this conversation before? Like on our first date?"

I nudge Him. "Shut up. I know we've talked about it before but I want to know everything. Like, how long have you been working at McKenzie's?"

"Well, it must have been about four or five years now. I went straight there from my old estate agent in—"

"Mhmm, and what's it like working there? Like are they strict on certain things like, I don't know, their supplies? Are you allowed to snatch a few notepads and pens here and there, or are they pretty tight on that kind of stuff?"

He's confused by my question, trying to mask his hesitance and curiosity. Nevertheless, he answers me in as confident a tone as he can muster. "Well, I suppose they're pretty relaxed. There's a few things that they won't let you use because it's expensive and has specific purposes like making the 'for sale' signs, but apart from that no, not really. Why the sudden interest?"

I shrug. "Oh I just want to get to know your work place a little better. I feel like I only ever see you at my place or yours. I would really love to meet your friends and colleagues."

A golden spec glimmers in his eye at my suggestion, but he tries to stay relaxed, probably afraid hiI shrug. "Oh I just want to get to know your workplace a little better. I feel like I only ever see you at my place or yours. I would really love to meet your friends and colleagues."

A golden speck glimmers in his eye at my suggestion, but he tries to stay relaxed, probably afraid his enthusiasm will make me change my mind. "Yeah, sure I would love that. Maybe sometime next week?"

I agree, "Sounds great. Also, I mean would you say you have a big family…small? Are you guys close?"

"Well, I suppose we're quite close. Especially after my sister died we really had to lean on each other. I have a few cousins as well but I wouldn't say we're close with them. We only see them at the holidays."

"Oh yeah, that was the same with me and my cousins growing up. Are you gonna have some of your wine?"

"Oh, sure," he says, clearly thrown by the rate at which I am burning through topics. I realise I might be going a little too fast so I calm myself down.

He reaches for one of the glasses but I stop Him. "Oh that's my one. Sorry, I had a few sips of it back in the kitchen and I think I'm coming down with a cold. Wouldn't want you to catch it."

Picking up the other glass, he gives me a subtle grin along with an eye roll. "Well, I'm sure there are more definite ways of me catching it."

I frown. "You're right. We should stay far apart and not touch at all the entire night."

He shakes his head and pulls me closer, causing a few drops of wine to escape the glass. "Come here."

I snuggle his shoulder and he kisses the top of my head. "I've missed you," he whispers.

I hold Him tighter, but my eyes remain cold and my face remains expressionless. I sip the warm liquid and my jaw locks. The butterflies are dormant this evening and the fire roaring within me isn't one of passion, but of rage.

CHAPTER 51 - AVERY

"Wake up," I whisper into his ear while stroking the back of my hand against his cheek.

After three seconds, his eyes begin to flutter until they open fully and he stares at me in a sleepy haze. "What..." he struggles to form his words. "What happened?"

I continue to trail my fingers along his jawline. "You fell asleep. Missed the entire film – and the Chinese food. I left a little bit for you, though."

Slowly, he eases himself upright and cradles his head. "Jeez, my head is killing me. I feel so lightheaded. I don't remember watching a film or ordering takeaway."

"Well, you were pretty out of it from start to finish so I'm not surprised. The film was good, by the way. If you were wondering."

He inhales a deep breath and shakes his head. "That's good, then."

I grip his hand and lean in to kiss his cheek. "Come on, I only woke you up so you didn't have to sleep on the sofa. Believe me, that is never a pleasant night."

As I start to pick myself up, he grabs my hand and stops me. "Wait," he demands. I do as he says. "I want to tell you something."

I look at Him, confused and hesitant to comply. "Okay..."

He takes another deep breath and looks down at the floor. "I don't remember my dream from just now, but there's one thing I took away from it." He lifts my hand to his lips and kisses them softly, and looking at me directly in the eye he says, "I love you, Avery."

My heart skips and the butterflies awake. I'm taken back by his words.

"When I saw you in the coffee shop, I was completely blown away by your presence, but I wasn't at all expecting to feel the way I feel. You're the most mesmerising woman I've ever met. You keep me on my toes, I never know what to expect. You're affectionate but you aren't too sensitive. And even though you haven't opened up to me completely, I know that I can love every part of you. I mean it. There is nothing you could say to me that would change how I feel. I love you."

I stare at Him, speechless. Frozen by his words. I can feel the adrenaline tingling up from arms and making my hands shake. Can he really mean that? Can he really love me no matter what? Despite my dark side?

"I…" I clear my throat and swallow the tears threatening to surge into my eyes. "I don't know what to say. No one's ever said that to me before."

He wraps one hand around my neck, pulls me into Him and presses his lips against mine. I fall into the kiss and throw my arms around Him, squeezing him so tight and I never want to let go. For this one moment, the rest of the world is gone. All my problems are gone. For this one moment, I am an ordinary girl, with an ordinary boy who loves me, who accepts me. I want to be here forever.

But forever has to end.

CHAPTER 52 - AVERY

I stare at the ceiling. I don't think I've blinked in over five minutes. I can't blink. I can't sleep. All I can do is watch the clock as it creeps closer and closer to twelve.

I check the clock. *11:47pm*. Time to get up.

As I slide out of bed, I'm careful not to wake Him. He looks so peaceful. I want to kiss faint freckles on the apples of his cheeks that are barely visible in the darkness, but I know exactly where they are. All of them. I refrain. There are more pressing matters to deal with.

I tiptoe over to my wardrobe, gently open the door and slide inside. I have to jump around a bit to get my jeans on – they shrank in the wash and I don't have any others close by. Once I have them hoisted up to my waist I peek around the door and see Him still sleeping. I then throw on a baggy jumper, chuck my hair up into a bun and creep back out into the bedroom.

As I open the door I hear Him change position and I flip my head around. He stretches out his arms and coughs quietly before dozing back off.

I suppose he caught my cold.

One may underestimate the amount of skill and patience it takes to be as quiet as I am being. It is ridiculous how many things make noise.

Like taking my coat of the hook for example. You'd think that would produce little sound, but no, the buckles on the coat hit the metal and the zips chime as they swing about. Putting shoes on is even worse. When noise doesn't matter they glide on without a problem. But, when you're trying to be quiet, the shoe screeches along the floor, and then you lose balance getting them on – which you never normally do since you've been putting shoes on since you were a toddler. Then they suddenly decide not to stay on your foot as you make your first step and you cringe as they fall and the sound of the heel hitting the wooden floor echoes throughout the house.

And don't even get me started on unlocking the door. You can be in the newest house in the world with the smoothest locks that glide like melted butter, but as soon as you need to leave in secret, they become fifty-year-old doors with hinges that have rusted from the English weather constantly lashing them with rain, and a stiff lock that refuses to comply.

When I finally make it outside, my hair is blown across my eyes by the summer night winds. My vision being obscured makes me more on edge, and more nervous that someone is lurking in my trembling shadow.

With every step I quicken my pace just a little, as I am sure that the wind is whispering in my ear, telling me to watch my back.

The moon is staring down at me, laughing. He's laughing at my obvious fear of the night, baring his teeth with a smile like the Cheshire Cat. I am usually the one lurking in the shadows, but now I am the one afraid of them.

I reach the corner of Old Oak Street at 11:58pm. I look around the area frantically, but I can see nothing. There is no one in sight. I don't even hear the nocturnal animals scurrying through the bushes. Southhurst has gone radio silent.

12:01pm – still nothing. I'm getting anxious now – as if I wasn't before.

The letter said there would be a present waiting for me here, but I can't find anything. Perhaps they were merely trying to get me rattled. Maybe they wanted me out of the house.

As the thought crosses my mind, my heart begins to gallop. It makes so much sense, and I've fallen for their tricks. I'm playing right into their hands.

I am about to begin sprinting home, fearing what I may find, when suddenly I'm startled by the grass on the corner of the street. There is something moving in it.

I approach the area cautiously and my legs beg me to flee. The movement becomes more vigorous as I draw near. I scream.

The shrew zips off, over my feet and onto the other side of the road.

My reason smacks both hands over my face, shaking my head. *Come on, Avery, you're being ridiculous.*

I take in a deep breath, compose myself and lift my head back up. I'm no more comforted by what I see.

Lying on the grassy corner from which the shrew had emerged, neatly folded, is a black trench coat. *My* black trench coat.

I don't want to approach it. I don't want to see it in any more detail than I am right now. I know that it can mean nothing good.

But, despite my childish response to run for the hills, I have to pick it up. This is my mess and I have to clean it up.

The thick material almost slips from my loose grip. I can't will my hands to hold onto it with anymore strength than that of a two-year-old.

I don't need any light shining on the material to know that the colour disfiguration is not just because of the coat's age. There is no doubt in my mind of what the dark, sticky substance soaked into the material is.

Whether the person who put this here meant for me to be freaked out by it and run, or for it to incriminate me, this is now my problem. Regardless of whose blood it is, my fingerprints are now on it. I certainly can't afford for any more of my DNA to be found on anything suspicious.

While before my ears refused to process any sound, they now refuse to give me peace. Not even the blood pumping through my eardrums drowns out the noise. Every blade of grass waving in the wind, every bug flying into the streetlight. Everything is magnified. And everything is watching me.

I've lost all sense of composure. I sprint through the abandoned streets, with the coat clutched to my chest, so fast that I can't feel my legs. They are working too quickly for my brain to process.

I don't care about the noise I am making, either. I run into the house, close all three locks on the front door and head straight into the lounge and to the fireplace.

My hands are shaking too much and it takes me more than a few attempts to light a match. When I do, I spark up the wood and once the flame is large enough to blind me, I throw the coat onto it. I don't need to know any more about the origins of that coat than I have already assumed.

AAs I watch it burn, my lungs are able to take longer breaths again and my heart rate slows. I look down and see the crimson-soaked dirt stains that have seeped onto my shirt.

I don't even give it a second thought. I immediately rip off the shirt, peel off my jeans and once the coat has shrivelled up enough for there to be room on the fire for them too, I throw them in.

I sit there, my arms wrapped around my bare legs, rocking. I don't know how long I am there for. Time is nothing but an abstract concept at this point. All I can process are the flames eating away at the fabric, tearing it apart thread by thread.

"Avery, what are you doing?"

I am nowhere near as conscious when I returned home – I must have woken Him.

I throw my head round to find Him standing at the bottom of the stairs, rubbing his sleepy eyes. I completely forgot he was still here.

I glance at the fire – the clothes are nearly gone. They have maybe another ten minutes left.

"Hey," I say as I stand up. "I just came down to get a glass of water. I was cold so I thought I would put the fire on for a little bit."

He approaches me. I reposition myself so that my body is blocking his view of the fireplace. "Okay," he replies. Confused and hazy. "Are you going to come back up soon? It's late, we've both got to be up early."

I nod with a grin. "I know. I'll be up in a few minutes."

"Do you want me to stay down here with you?"

"No, no." I hasten to stop him. "I'm fine, really. Don't worry about me, just go back to sleep. I promise I'm right behind you."

He sighs and waddles closer to me with his arms wide. "Okay, night, night." I accept his hug and my body shivers as he kisses my forehead. He then turns around and stumbles back up the stairs.

Once he is gone, I turn my attention back to the flames. Right now they are destroying my clothes, next, they'll be destroying me.

I rest my head on my knees and close my eyes, trying and failing to shut the thought out.

I can't sleep, though. Even if I wanted to I couldn't. All I can do is replay tonight over and over in my head. How did the trench coat get there? Why didn't I see anyone? How didn't I hear them? I don't really want the answers to my questions, though. Because it means someone really is watching my every move. The person who wants to tear me down was no more than three feet away from me. And I had no idea.

She hadn't changed at all over the years. She still acted like she was invincible, like nothing could ever frighten her.

But I stared at her face as she saw the trench coat. Her expression was undeniable. Pure fear.

CHAPTER 53 - AVERY

"Avery, I've got something to tell you."

I glance over to him from the dining table, munching on a large bite of toast.

He leans over the counter with his eyes staring intensely into mine, lifts up his spoon and says, "I'm a cereal killer." And then swallows a large gulp of Cheerios.

I laugh at him, shaking my head. If anyone had said that kind of thing to me at the beginning of this year, I would judge them and roll my eyes. But when he did it, I can't help but think how flippin' adorable he is.

My reason is shaking her head and making gagging sounds at me.

"Hey, I never knew you wore glasses," I announce as he joins me at the table, giving me a peck on the cheek as he slumps into the empty chair.

He beams at me, wiggles his ears and causing his soft-grey glasses to bounce up and down on his nose. "Well, I tend to wear contact lenses, but I forgot to bring over an extra pair. Why? Do you not like my glasses?"

Leaning slowly towards his face, I put my lips to his and with him otherwise occupied, I snatch the glasses from his face and slide them over my ears.

"Hey!" he protests.

"Yes, I do like your glasses. But personally, I think they look better on me." I playfully strike a pose. "What do you think?"

He squeezes my hand and replies, "They do look pretty sexy on you."

"Well," I remove the lenses and squint my eyes as they readjust, "as much as I would like to play out one of your teenage fantasies, I can't keep them on for more than a minute, my God is that prescription strong."

"Yeah well, we can't all be perfect, can we?" he asks with a sideways glance.

I simply scrunch up my nose at his remark and go back to flicking through the newspaper, pretending to be interested in the happenings of today, but really I am just thinking about last night.

Of course my mind is very much focusing on the bad parts of last night, but it keeps flicking between that and what he said. I can't decide which one had a greater effect on me.

He leans forward, tucks hair behind my ear and strokes my cheek. "You look absolutely knackered. What time did you come to bed after I found you downstairs?"

I shrug and swallow down some more of my toast. "Oh only about ten minutes later. Don't worry, I always look like this. You just don't usually see me without makeup on," I joke, trying to change the subject.

He chuckles softly. "Very funny." He then looks at me with a sincere frown and says, "There isn't a product in the world that could make you any more beautiful than you already are."

I lean forward and kiss Him. When our lips separate I only move a few inches from his face before murmuring, "Where did you get that one from? Some teen magazine?"

He nudges me playfully and digs back into his bowl of cereal.

Several minutes later, his phone dances along the table. He quickly snatches it up and pushes his chair back. "I didn't realise what the time was, I've got to go."

He leans down and kisses me goodbye.

"Bye," I reply with a mouthful.

I admire Him as he puts on his shoes and grabs his jacket. He loves me. He accepts me for me.

CHAPTER 54 - HARRY

"Hey, big boy!" Harry calls Bertie as he crouches down to the floor and the dog leaps onto him.

"Stop messing around, will you?" James rolls his eyes at Harry and gives him a sideways smile. "We've got actual work to do."

After Harry has brushed the hairs from his jacket, he joins James at the whiteboard. "Let's have a look," he starts, while stroking his chin and staring intently at the board. "The four women killed at the most recent GR scene. We've got a girl in her early twenties, her adoptive mother and the mother's sisters. Looking at the etching of a spinning wheel and the quotes, I think it's safe to say that we're looking at the Sleeping Beauty tale."

James agrees. "Yep. And from our interview yesterday with Sleeping Beauty's biological mother, whom she was reunited with two years ago, we know that she went to a regular coffee shop. None other than the Cosy Coffee."

"The Little Mermaid went there too…" Harry trails off, waiting for James to finish the sentence.

He does. "And the alley girl was found in a skip only a two-minute walk from the coffee shop." James then raises his eyebrow at Harry, simultaneously with his lip. "Am I right in saying we have a link here?"

Harry grins back at James. "We have a link."

Without exchanging another word, they both silently grab their coats and headed out of the station. They know where they're going.

The Cosy Coffee is only a ten-minute walk from the station. They are in front of the goofy, candyfloss-pink themed café in no time.

Being that Harry is also a regular, the owner of the café spots him immediately.

"Harry! How are you, my dear?" The lady comes round the counter to suffocate him in her arms.

"I'm good, thanks. How about you, Heidi?"

Heidi plays with her pixie cut hairdo and nods. "I'm good, I'm good. You know, just doing the same old." She springs up with new energy and shuffles back to the other side of the counter. "What can I get you two?"

James and Harry look at each other. "We're actually here on business," James declares in a deep, serious tone.

Heidi's chirpy face transforms into a concerned frown. "Oh, really? What's this about? I can promise you I don't partake in anything illegal – I'm much too exhausted to handle the stress of that."

Harry reassures her. "Don't worry, Heidi, we aren't here about anything you have done. Detective Sergeant Flynn and I are working the Grimm Reaper case and we have found that there is a link between the recent victims and this coffee shop. We just wanted to ask you a few questions."

She holds both hands to her chest. "Oh, absolutely. Let's go take a seat down here." She ushers them to an empty table.

"We just want to know if anyone has particularly caught your attention over the past few months," James begins, with his notepad at the ready.

Heidi drums her fingers against her jaw and frowns. "Oh, I don't think so. There isn't really anyone who comes to mind. It's usually just the regulars who I've known forever." She gasps suddenly with widened eyes. "Well, there is this one man. He's tall, quite attractive, amazingly bright green eyes. He's been coming in once or twice a week recently. He's always…looking around. Not in a casual way, more in an observing way – if that makes any sense at all? Like he's looking for someone or something."

James scribbles her description down. "Yes I understand. Any chance you know his name?"

Heidi glances down and sighs. "No, I'm sorry I don't. I'm pretty sure he's an ex-con. I briefly remember overhearing a conversation between him and what I think was his parole officer." She quickly widens her eyes defensively. "Not that I make a habit of eavesdropping. No, it's just sometimes very difficult to turn your ears off to certain conversations."

"That's okay, Heidi. Your details have been very helpful," James tells her. "The next time he comes in, if you could just call the station and ask for DS Flynn."

She bobs her head enthusiastically. "Absolutely. I will most certainly do that. Are you sure you two don't want a coffee? On the house?"

Harry shakes his head for the both of them. "No thanks, Heidi, we've got to be heading back. See you soon."

As they leave the coffee shop Harry turns to James and says, "Tall ex-con with bright green eyes. I would say that narrows it down to almost all of them?"

James laughs. "Yep, pretty much. But hey, hopefully he'll be in there again soon."

When they get back to the station, they are greeted by a frantic Karen rushing at them. "Sergeant Flynn, Constable Ellis!"

James holds his hands up in surrender. "Calm down, Karen. What is it?"

"Whilst you were out, a letter came through," she says, nervously.

"What do you mean a letter? Who's it from?"

Karen twiddles her thumbs. "That's just it. We don't know. Our only clue is that it was signed with a sketch of a scythe."

Harry and James don't need to communicate with each other to know exactly who the letter is from.

James stares at Karen with a new sense of authority and concern. "Where is the letter? Bring it to my office immediately." He then begins marching off in the opposite direction.

"Wait!" Karen exclaims, hurrying after him. "Wait, that's not all. We got a letter through, but last night there was a call put in to 999. We have reason to believe it's the same person."

Karen is too frightened to speak their name, but Harry knows exactly who she is referring to.

The Grimm Reaper has finally made contact.

CHAPTER 55 - HARRY

Run, run, as fast as you can. You can't catch me I'm the gingerbread man

"Why now?" James asks, staring intensely at the creased piece of paper, decorated with magazine cut-outs forming words. "Why is he communicating with us now? After a decade and a half? What's changed?"

Harry shrugs. "I read somewhere that serial killers like being chased. They like the adrenaline rush. Maybe GR got bored with us not catching them and wanted to make things more interesting."

James scrunches his nose up, considering the idea. "Well, I suppose that would explain the sloppier execution of his last victims." He leans back, clasping his hands together. "Then again, I wouldn't really say this is much of a communication. I mean, it's more him taunting us than giving any clues whatsoever."

"Maybe this is just them getting started."

Karen pops her head around the door and sheepishly calls, "Detective Sergeant, um, the recording of the phone call has been sent to you now."

James thanks her and she scurries off back to her desk.

"999, what's your emergency?"

The line is silent for a few seconds.

"Hello?"

"I've killed people." A low, robotic voice whispers down the phone.

The panic in the 999 agent's voice is subtle, but obvious to Harry.

"Okay, can you please tell me where you are?"

"I've killed people," the voice repeats. *"And I'm going to do it again… and again…and again."*

"Can you please tell me who you've kil-"

"You pigs don't stand any chance of finding me. You're never going to find me."

The 999 agent is quick with her words now. Her calmness has thinned as the call has gone on. *"Can you please tell me who you are?"*

The voice laughs. *"I'm the incarnation of death. You can't stop death. Everybody's got to turn back into a pumpkin when their clock strikes midnight."*

"Please tell me where you are."

A song is then played into the phone. *"Ring-a-ring-a-roses, a pocket full of posies, atishoo, atishoo"* But the last part is cut off. Instead, the voice whispers *"you'll all fall down."*

The line goes flat.

James and Harry sit there, in silence.

Without uttering a word, James picks up the phone and smashes his fingers on the number pad.

"Why wasn't this brought to us first thing this morning?"

There is murmuring down the phone. James's face remains stiff.

"It's not good enough. Anything like this – even the slightest bit like this – comes to us immediately. Do you understand?" He then slams the phone back down.

"So, what's their excuse?" Harry asks timidly. He's not used to seeing James like this.

"The woman who took the call is new. Apparently she thought it was just some prank, so she didn't report it to her supervisor."

"I'll track the call and check out the location. You stay here and analyse every single letter on that piece of paper and every single word of that phone call."

"Are you sure?" Harry asks. "Are you sure you don't want me to come with you?"

James shakes his head. "No, it's better if we can deal with all the information as quickly as possible while it's still fresh."

Harry agrees and picks up the letter again. "So, what does all this mean?" Harry asks, all his training gone out the window.

"This means he want to play. He's taunting us, there's no doubt. But, is he warning us of an upcoming murder? Or is he just trying to drop hints of who he is, so he can keep up this charade of cat and mouse?"

"Is there a third option?" Harry pleads. "Because right now, I'm feeling more like the rodent."

CHAPTER 56 - AVERY

I've decided to surprise Him. I don't know what's got into me, I've never done something like this before. It gives me a thrill of excitement.

I finished work early today and I know he's going to be finished in thirty-three minutes.

I walk into the estate agents and I am greeted by the receptionist.

"Hi, welcome to McKenzie's Southhurst Estate Agent, can I help you?"

I wave her smile off. "Oh no, it's okay. I'm just waiting for someone," I assure her.

"Okay, if you want to take a seat in our waiting area, then."

I comply and head over to the leather sofas in the corner.

I've never been at his workplace before. It's a lot more aesthetically pleasing than I thought an estate agent's would be.

It has a very precise grey-purple colour scheme. The sofas are grey and are complemented by an array of violet cushions. It also has antique grey vases, filled with fresh lilac orchids. The walls are decorated with black and white photographs with one painting located in the centre of the far wall. The painting is of a ballerina in a violet leotard, with her hair tightly secured in a high bun. She is in the midst of doing the classical pirouette, from the way her body is soaring through the air, weightlessly carried upon a single toe. Although her body is elegant, her face tells a completely different story. She isn't looking up to the sky, but glancing down at her feet. The corners of her lips are ever so slightly turned down and her cheeks are drained of colour. It's as if she tries so hard to make her body beautiful, that she is unable to keep her true feelings from seeping through in her expression.

I check the time. 3:42pm. He'll be leaving in eighteen minutes.

I tap my foot impatiently, searching for something to turn my mind to until he is here. I spot a pile of magazines under the coffee table and so I grab the first one I see. Not that it makes much of a difference as they all appear to be the same issue.

As I flick through the magazine, I skim read the articles until I find one that interests me – even a little bit.

Freddie Mercury Tribute performing this Saturday at Southhurst Arena

There's something about the headline that sparks a déjà vu. I swear I've seen it before, I just can't remember where. I shake the feeling from my shoulders and settle on the article. I've always been a big fan of Freddie – he was my childhood crush. My interest piqued, I look for the date of the issue to see when the show is.

To my disappointment, the issue is from the beginning of March. I think I've definitely missed that tribute.

The other side of the page is full of local ads. Just a bunch of *second hand car for sale*, and *two bunnies looking for a good home*. Which is strange to have such different products on the same page, if you ask me.

There is only one ad that catches my eye.

In the top right-hand corner, there is an ad reading, *for sale: Rotary Lawnmower. Only used twice, great condition*. And below it is a picture of the lawnmower.

I place my finger over the ad and flick the page back over to the Freddie Mercury tribute. My finger lines up with the 'F' of Freddie. Or of Fairy tale.

I slap my hand over my open mouth, not wanting to believe what I have seen. I rack my brain for every possible excuse I can find, it must just be a coincidence. Yes, it's just a coincidence.

But as my reason loves to remind me, I've never believed in coincidences.

CHAPTER 57 - AVERY

I shake the spiders from my back as I pull away from the estate agent. I couldn't get out of there fast enough. I'm stopped briefly, when I see Him coming down the stairs. If it had been only a few minutes earlier, I would have been waiting there for Him. He looks so happy, so perfect. But I can't pretend I didn't see what I just did.

I am jolted back into the present by a road-rage driver slamming on his horn at me. I suppose it isn't completely unwarranted, since I am positioned right in the middle of the road.

I try and get it out of my head as I drive home, but I fail. I knew I'd fail. I've never been able to prohibit my imagination from running wild whenever I get new, unexpected information. I try and focus on curling up in a blanket, watching crappy TV and wasting my entire afternoon away. Yes, that will make me feel better.

My plans are squashed as soon as I turn the corner onto my street.

Only a few doors down from my house, there is a police car parked and a policeman speaking with one of my neighbours. Not just any policeman, though. He is one of the detectives working my case.

I swallow my anxiety and park my car out the front of my house, as I normally would. I then walk straight up to my door without giving my eyes over to their interaction for even a second. As I unlock the door, I can see him looking at me, though. He knows I'm home. Which means it surely won't be long until I have a very similar knock at my door.

It looks like this bastard is really pulling out all the stops. Mailing a letter to the police? And making a 999 call? From *my* street, no less. It really does make me wonder what they're up to.

I haven't been able to find what was said on the call yet, but I've managed to sneak a look at the letter. To be honest, it just confused me even more. What on earth are they planning? It's not like the letter is necessarily leading the police to me specifically, it's just taunting them. I suppose the phone call rings a little too close to home, but still the detective is speaking with all of my neighbours.

Perhaps they're just pushing the cops in my direction, running circles around me until I'm the only one that's left.

There's a knock at my door and I quickly slam my laptop closed – I don't think the detective would be best pleased by discovering my surveillance access.

I walk over to the door and stand still in front of it. Taking in a deep breath I calm myself. *Be cool, Avery. Be cool.* Then, with a big smile painted on my face I open the door.

"Hi," the detective says as soon as the door is ajar. "I am Detective Sergeant Flynn."

I look at him with a concerned expression. "Hello, detective. What can I help you with?"

"There was a phone call placed to 999 last night at eleven-fifty, that we believe is significant to an ongoing investigation. We traced the phone's location to this street and so I just wanted to ask you a few questions."

"Absolutely," I respond in my best Good Samaritan voice. "Would you like to come inside?"

He waves off my invitation. "That's okay, I only have a few questions. Firstly, I want to know if you made a phone call to emergency services, or if you may know who did?"

I shake my head slowly. "No, detective, I was upstairs and in bed at that time. My—" I stumble slightly, this is the first time I have had to speak about him to someone else, "My boyfriend stayed over last night. We were both in bed at eleven because we had to be up early for work."

Detective...*Flynn, was it?* He bobs his head and asks, "Is there any way your boyfriend could have placed the call?"

At the time of the phone call, I was on my way to Old Oak Street, but there's no way *he's* going to find that out. A horrible thought flashes across my vision – he was at my house. Alone. "No, not that I know of. I'm sorry I can't be more help," I quickly respond, erasing the thought from my mind.

"That's okay. Would you be able to listen to this recording and tell me if you recognise the voice?"

I lean my head across the threshold, so that I'm in a better position for listening. My enthusiasm to help isn't an act, now. I really am eager to find out if I recognise the voice. This will be the first time that I hear that bastard's voice. I bet it sounds ugly.

A muffled, robotic voice whispers, "I've killed people. I've killed people and I'm going to do it again and again and again. You pigs don't stand any chance of finding me. You're never going to find me."

The detective then pauses the recording.

He's waiting for my answer, but I am too puzzled by the phone call to even begin to process the voice.

Of course, the voice is computerised so that it is unrecognisable, so I suppose that part is kind of moot. But no one ever sounds the same through a computer. Perhaps I could figure out who it is...

"Ma'am." The detective calls me away from my daze. "Ma'am, do you recognise the voice?"

"Oh, sorry. No I don't."

He glances down, disappointed. "Okay, thank you for your time." He then reaches into his pocket and pulls out a small piece of card. "Here are my details. If you ever think of anything else, or have any more information, please call me." The intense look in his eyes makes me uneasy. I thought the presence of an officer was supposed to make you feel safe.

Well, I suppose that may go for people who he's protecting, not the people he's protecting against.

I wave goodbye to the detective and he grabs his beer-belly, waddling off down the street to the next house.

What the hell is this person up to? Apart from the phone tracking, neither the letter nor the call has led the police to me. Are they just going for the slow burn? Are they just trying to freak me out? Or maybe they're building me up, piece by piece, so that they can tap the top and I'll come tumbling down.

CHAPTER 58 - AVERY

"Hey, Todd. Long time no speak, how are you doing?" I ask down the phone, with a sweet and innocent tone, faking my curiosity and interest.

""Avery, hi. I definitely wasn't expecting to hear from you again." Todd sounds a little hesitant. "Were you hoping to, um, meet up again? Because, I've kind of got a fiancée now. It's Claire, actually,"

Dammit. That's one bribe off the table.

"Oh wow!" I exclaim. "That's so wonderful, congratulations. Gosh, the last time I saw you, you'd only been with Claire for a month or two."

"Yeah, I know. It was kind of a whirlwind thing. We met and four months later I popped the question. But um, yeah about the last time we met...I never told her about that and we're in a really great place, I just wouldn't want to ruin what we have, you know? I mean..."

"Listen, Todd, you don't have to worry," I reassure him. "I'm actually in a relationship now, myself."

His overly surprised reaction is just the slightest bit offensive. "Oh, wow, I never expected to hear you say that! Wow, good for you, finally settling down. Wow. Well, then if that's not the reason you're calling, what's up?"

I'm grinding my teeth, stopping myself from snapping at him. I have to play nice. "Yeah, well basically I was just needing to ask you a teensy little favour..."

He most certainly does not sound impressed. "What is it?"

"Well, I happen to remember that your job gives you access to street surveillance, right?"

"Right…"

"I'm in a bit of a pickle and I was wondering if there was any way I can get the footage from August 4th. Um, on Redmount Road?"

Don't make the connection, I pray with both fingers crossed. *Don't think about it, just say yes. Say yes, say yes.*

Todd sighs rather unenthusiastically. "Well, suffice to say I could lose my job over it, but I mean…" He pauses, weighing up his options. "Sure why not? But after this, we're even, okay?"

I jump up and down. "Absolutely, completely square. Thanks, Todd."

"That's okay." I hear him about to hang up but something stops him. "Hold on a minute, why do I recognise that road name?"

I smack my forehead. "I don't know, maybe you've been down it before?"

"No, that's not it." His voice trails off and I hear him tapping at his keyboard. He gasps. "Christ, Avery! That's the street where those women were murdered last week…on Friday 4th! What the hell have you got yourself into?"

I go on the defensive. "I know, I know it sounds bad, Todd but seriously it's not at all what I'm sure you're cooking up in your mind. Please, please don't think anything else about it."

"What I think about it is irrelevant, to be honest. This footage is part of an ongoing investigation – from a week ago! There is no way I can get my hands on that and give it to you without getting caught and then the police thinking I'm involved. I'm getting married, Avery! For God's sake, you can't ask me to do this."

I don't say anything for two minutes. He seems to have worked himself up quite a bit, I'd best let him calm back down.

When I hear his breathing return to a normal rate, I say, "I know, Todd. You're completely right, I can't ask that of you. I'm sorry I even did. Why don't you tell me a little bit more about you and Claire? Where are you guys getting married?"

He seems thrown off by my question. "Um, we're going to her family's cottage down in Cornwall. We want it to be a small ceremony – family and close friends only."

"Oh how lovely. Have you set a date?"

"Yes, mid-September."

"Oh, that's pretty soon isn't it?" I lean back in my chair and drum my fingers on the desk. "I can imagine she must be starting to get cold feet. All brides do as the wedding gets closer. It's funny how the human brain works like that, isn't it?" My voice is steady and calm. He knows to be wary. "How, even if she knows in her heart what she wants, all her mind needs is that one little thing to push her over the edge, and she'll back out completely. I mean, that can be something as small as finding out you snore. Let alone something as big as, oh I don't know, discovering her husband-to-be hasn't been completely honest? Or faithful."

"You wouldn't." Todd's tone is cold now. He's trying to sound menacing, but I can hear his tiny little heart fluttering.

I lean forward over the desk. Leaning into the phone call. "Oh, I think we both know I would."

"I can't do it, Avery!" I can hear him spitting through his teeth.

"You *can* do it, Todd. You're just choosing not to. It's completely up to you, sweetie. I've given you your options. So, if you want your perfect little wedding in Cornwall, I suggest you get it done."

The line goes flat.

I go into the kitchen and grab myself a beer. That phone call got my blood boiling a little bit. I hate having to be cruel to get people to reach their full potential. I really don't want to break up a relationship, but this is a life or death situation here, what am I meant to do?

I slump back into the sofa with my ready meal and beer, watching mindless television. I think this is the first time I've relaxed in months.

Half way through watching *The Big Bang Theory*, my ears are drawn away from Sheldon and towards my front porch. I mute the TV and shakily creep towards the window.

It's still light out, so it's not difficult for me to see someone – if there's anyone there. I scan the area that is visible from the window and I shake off my ridiculous paranoia, sitting back down.

Only five minutes later do I hear something else. I'm not even sure what it is I think I'm hearing. I just feel that there is something.

I sit upright and stretch my neck forward, refusing to go up to the window again and feel like an idiot when there is nothing there.

But this time I am not just being paranoid. This time there is definitely someone at my door.

I throw myself up and run to the door. There is half an envelope pushed through the letterbox. And a shadow behind it.

"Hey!" I shout and I rush to unlock all three bolts. I finally reach the main lock and it sticks. "God dammit!" I scream at the door. "Why won't you bloody move!"

Finally it gives in and I swing the door open, slamming a dent into my wall. Whoever it was is gone.

I step outside and scan the street. I see a figure all in black power-walking down the concrete.

Without even thinking, I pull my door shut and chase after them. They look behind under a black hat and as they see me gaining on them, they begin to run as well.

It's not my muscles moving my legs, but the adrenaline shooting all through my body. I can't see anything around me, all I see is them. All I see is that silhouette speeding away from me.

The blood is pumping in my ears so loudly that I can't hear my own voice shouting after them. I don't know how long I've been running. All I know is that figure. Time isn't real right now. It doesn't mean anything to me.

I don't see any of the cars beeping at me as I dive across the different roads.

My entire body is numb, but I can feel my mouth open wide, baring my teeth. I am sprinting at them like a madman. This is the first time I have felt inhuman.

They take a turn and we enter an area filled with trees. They haven't looked behind them once, they just keep going forward.

The light has begun to fade now and I am having to be more careful as I leap over the tree roots.

They can hear me huffing, now that I am only ten feet from them. I'm so close.

With every step I am gaining on them. I hear the nocturnal animals beginning to yawn themselves from slumber and as they watch me pass they cheer me on.

I'm only two feet from them now. I can smell them. I can almost taste them. Yet, my rage-filled eyes stop me from seeing them clearly. Instead, they are a blurred figure. A cartoon.

I reach my hand out, ready to grab at their knockoff trench coat. My fingertips are grazing it, I'm so close. I lunge for them.

My open mouth is filled with mud, wood and stones.

By the time I lift my head, they're gone.

CHAPTER 59 - AVERY

I feel like an idiot. I was so focused on catching them that I didn't even pay attention to the details. How tall they were, what their hair was like, how they ran, not even their goddamn gender.

My reason gave me a huge scolding on the pathetic, long walk home.

Regardless of my lack of observation, I'm kicking myself about not catching the bastard. I was so close. *So close.* And who put that stupid log there anyway?

I stand on the pavement, facing my front door. There is nothing inside me that wants to walk up those steps and go into that house. If I do that, I truly lose. I don't like losing.

I pat down my coat. "Are you kidding me?" I growl, finding my pockets empty. I ran out of my house so fast that I forgot a key.

I'm about to journey round to the back door and break my kitchen window, when something catches my attention.

I take a closer look at the door and there is something hanging out of it.

"Of course, the letter." I sigh. How could I have forgotten about that? That's the entire reason I did all that cardio.

The envelope is slightly torn and jammed into the letterbox only a quarter of the way. But it isn't alone.

Caught in the metal's grasp is something else. Something blue – it looks like a plastic sort of material. I wiggle it, and the letter, free from the door's prison.

It's a glove. A disposable glove.

I suppose that's one way to eliminate the issue of fingerprints – though, I do it in a little bit more style with Italian calf leather.

I'm not sure exactly what I can do with this to help me find them, but one thing I am sure of, is that they most certainly did *not* leave it in my door on purpose. That means they slipped up.

I shriek, my lungs not expecting the bang that would come from the window. *Inside* my house.

The butterflies try to escape my stomach and I'm not far behind them, as I approach the window slowly, trying to work out who the shadow is.

I sigh and growl to myself as they come to open the door.

"My goodness, Buttercup. You know, you really shouldn't be creeping around a house like that. I thought you were a burglar."

I stare at Julian's smug little face, completely unamused. "Shut up." I shove past him. "What the hell are you doing in here anyway? *Again?*"

He shakes his head at me. "Avery, I thought we had gained clarity on this one already. I haven't got a job, and I'm going to keep bugging you and bugging you until I help you meet your untimely downfall."

I stare at him. Expressionless and silent. My silence starts to make him a little fidgety and he widens his grin. I merely stick my nose up and say, "If you break in here again I'm going to report you to the police and file for a restraining order. You ex-cons can't be having any more dealings with the police, can you?"

His face drops. "You wouldn't dare. I've got too much on you. Stop being grumpy, little grumpy pants." His tone changes as if he's talking to a five-year-old and he begins to approach me. When my expression doesn't change in the slightest, he holds his hands up. "Okay, okay. I'll go, I'll leave you to your night of self-pity. See you soon, Buttercup." Julian brushes past me on his way to the door, planting a kiss on my cheek as he goes.

As soon as he's gone I abruptly rub off the ghost of his lips and rip open the envelope to see what kind words my stalker has for me today.

Don't worry, it won't be long until we meet. I know you've been racking your brain trying to figure out who I am. When I reveal myself you'll kick yourself for not knowing. But it won't be long. It won't be long.

It was too close tonight. She chased me. She chased me for miles. I was sure she was going to reach me – and then this would've all been over. I have to be more careful. I've had my fun playing games, I need to get serious. I left my glove. It got stuck in that stupid letterbox. That wouldn't give her anything to go on, though. You could buy those things anywhere. And even though my fingerprints will be on the glove, she isn't smart enough to do anything with it, anyway. And she doesn't have the resources. It will get her nowhere.

Right?

CHAPTER 60 - HARRY

The suffocating stench of death is impossible to truly get rid of, once it's seeped through into the very foundations of a house.

A body needs only be festering for a few hours and you can kiss your dreams of a lavender scented home goodbye.

This place has no hope, Harry thinks whilst walking around the newly-built three-storey house. *Four bodies in here? No way is that smell ever coming out.*

He and James are doing another sweep of the most recent GR scene, to see if perhaps they left any more clues. The phone call put into 999 was extremely cryptic and the two of them can't figure out what they mean. But they are sure their choice of words is important.

"I've checked upstairs," James bellows down. "I can't find anything up there."

"Okay, help me have a look down here."

The forensics team have done a good job at cleaning up the mess that was found here ten days ago, but Harry can still see the ghost of what was. He can still see the young woman elegantly lying across the sofa. He can still see the three other women, neatly placed next to each other with their arms crossed over their chests. He can still see the pools of dark, thick fluid that was forming around their heads. He remembers it almost like a halo, like a sign that they are in a better place, now.

"Harry, I think I've got something."

"Huh?" Harry seems surprised and rushes into the kitchen to find James crouched down in the corner. "What have you found?"

"I think it's a hair." James stretches his hand out behind him. "Do me a favour, will you give me your gloves, I haven't got mine."

Shrugging, Harry replies, "Sorry, mate. Martha keeps nicking mine to do the gardening."

James sighs, pulls his sleeves over his hands and picks up the hair. He squints to get a clearer view, but it does him no good.

Harry places a small magnifying glass in front of James's face, James smiles at him and puts it between him and the hair.

"It looks dark and coarse. That doesn't match any of the women." James stares at it a little longer. "And it's short."

"Well," Harry interjects, "it may just be my bad eyesight, but I can't see a root on there – that means it must have snapped off. So I suppose the length doesn't really matter much."

James agrees and hurls himself back up. "Come on, let's get this back to the station so it can be analysed."

"Are you sure?" Harry asks. "Are you sure we've checked this place thoroughly?"

"Yeah, we've gone through it five times over. We've got what we came for – something we can work with. Let's head back."

Although he seems slightly reluctant, Harry follows James to the front door, but changes course and goes back into the living room.

"Mate, what are you doing?" James moans while trailing after him.

"I just thought I saw…" His voice fades out and he pushes the sofa away from the door a few inches. "There." He points to the wall that is now revealed.

James bends down to inspect it.

There are etchings in the wall. Since the wall is painted cream, they are faint and difficult to make sense of, but once they study them for a few minutes, it becomes clear.

The drawing seems to tell a story. There is an outline of two pigs chasing a rabbit, but not far behind them is a cloaked figure holding a scythe. Below this is another story of the pigs lying on the ground with crosses for eyes – and the scythe is above them. The final sketch is of three bear heads.

"Now," James says, his eyes fixed on the drawings. "What the hell does he mean by this?"

CHAPTER 61 - HARRY

"So the pigs must represent us," James declares, staring at the photos of the drawings on the board. "The scythe is obviously GR. But what are the bear heads? And what message are they sending?"

Harry's mind flashes back to that night, seeing the outline of a bear's head etched into the wood. When he returns to the present he shrugs. "I don't know. If here we're chasing a rabbit and they're behind us, maybe they're trying to say we're chasing the wrong person?"

James nods slowly. "Yeah, okay, but that doesn't explain the dead pigs below." He rests his hands on his belly. "So clearly the pigs are killed by GR, but why? How is he implying he got the better of us? And then the bear heads seem to have absolutely no relevance to whatever story they're trying to tell. Something isn't adding up."

The two of them stare at the drawings in silence, both stroking their unshaven chins. Harry knows what the third sketch is referring to, but he doesn't want to say. It's too painful. It's too personal.

Of course, this entire case is personal for Harry, but he has been able to separate that event and GR's case as a whole so far, and he doesn't want to change that now. However, if James figures it out, Harry will have to look into it with him. There is no way he can help James come to that conclusion, he needs to avoid it at all costs.

"Got it!" James's exclamation breaks their silence. "Of course, how could I have not realised earlier!"

Harry stares at him, puzzled.

"The bear heads. At GR's first murder scene, the etching he left was a bear head. He's referring to his origin!" James's face is brightened by the light bulb that just formed over his head. He casts a wide grin at Harry.

Harry is sighing inside, but he smiles back at James with fake enthusiasm. "Oh yeah, I remember now from reading up on the cases. I can't believe I didn't think of that."

"You?" James laughs. "You just read up on the case, I investigated it! This whole age thing must be getting to me. I suppose I'm retiring at the right time, eh?"

Harry mimics his laugh and nudges him gently.

"So," Harry sighs. "We're looking into the first case, yeah? Was that the Pinocchio one?"

"Yes because what does a bear have to do with Pinocchio?" James remarks. "No, it was Goldilocks."

"Okay, I'll get the file," Harry says and begins walking out of the office.

"Wait," James calls after him. "Look, I know you said you had to be somewhere for lunch and I'm more familiar with the ins and outs of the case. Why don't you take your lunch break, I'll go over the case and fill you in on what I find?"

Harry is puzzled by his suggestion, but he doesn't object. James is right, he does have somewhere to be.

They're taking a bit of a risk, today. This is the first time they've been out in public before – well, properly anyway. Before they would find old, rundown cafés to meet in, or an abandoned park which is concealed by overgrown hedges.

Today they are meeting in the Cosy Coffee. It seems like a terrible idea, since Harry is a regular, but he is sure that there will be no one he knows in there at this time.

"Hey," he greets them and sits in the seat opposite. Harry is nervous today. "Um, did you want a refill?" he asks, spotting their mug is nearly empty.

They shake their head. It seems like there is something bugging them, but Harry isn't sure what.

"What's wrong, are you okay?" Harry asks, but his mind is distracted by a man sitting on the other side of the room, staring at the two of them.

They sigh. "I don't know, I'm just not feeling so good about this anymore."

"About what?" Harry queries, flicking his eyes back and forth from the ogling man.

"About us, this, whatever we're doing. All this sneaking around? It's making me feel so guilty. I'm not a bad person and being here with you is making me feel like a bad person."

Harry scoots to the edge of his seat and leans in closer. "Look, it won't be long until it doesn't have to be a secret anymore. It's just not the time, right now."

"Harry, you said that three months ago." There is a new grit in their voice now. "You said now isn't the time but it will be soon. How much longer are you going to spin me this bullshit?"

"I know I did. I know, but I mean it this time. Everything just needs to be a little more stable, and then we can tell the truth."

They sigh again. Harry's words don't make them feel any better, but they know that they have to trust him.

After Harry persuades them, they ease up and agree to the second coffee.

About half an hour later, Heidi trots up to their table and crouches down to Harry's level.

"Hi, Harry," she says.

Harry smiles back at her, but he can't keep his gaze on her, afraid she might take notice of the person opposite him.

"Sorry, I don't mean to disturb you," Heidi continues, and she then cups her hands over her mouth and leans in to Harry. "That man over there is the one I was talking to you and your detective friend about on Friday."

Harry subtly rolls his eyes to follow the direction of Heidi's brief finger point. It is the same man that has been staring at the two of them since Harry got here.

Harry studies him, but quickly retreats as the man begins to hold the stare.

The only distinct feature Harry can pick out is his bright green eyes – the same feature Heidi had mentioned. Harry recognises him, he knows he's an ex-con, but he can't remember what he went in for. He knows it was something big, but Harry didn't work the case – he just heard about it. It was years ago, now.

"Okay, that's great, thank you, Heidi," Harry says quietly and Heidi scurries back to her counter.

"So, you've got to be getting back," they tell Harry, having caught a look at the time.

"Oh, yes I do. When am I seeing you again?"

They shrug. "A few days? We can't be meeting late after you finish work much more because of," they pause, a streak of guilt shooting across their face, and take a breath, "because of Martha. So, maybe lunchtime is best again? It wasn't so bad today, was it? No one saw us."

Harry slowly nods. "Yes, I suppose. It just feels a little too risky. But, I agree. We aren't left with many alternatives. Lunch on Wednesday it is."

The two say goodbye and part ways.

"Give me some good news," Harry exclaims as he bursts into James's office. "Tell me we've got a lead."

James just stares at him. "That," Harry says while pointing at James's face, "Is definitely *not* the face I want from you right now. Oh," Harry quickly says, "I almost forgot to say, I was at the Cosy Coffee and Heidi pointed out the guy she was talking about. I can't remember who he is exactly, but he's definitely ex-con. We'll have to look into him, but I'm pretty sure he only just got out of prison, so he can't be our guy. But anyway, why don't you tell me what you've found?"

"I've found nothing," James growls. "We've got nothing. It doesn't make sense. I've been going through every detail of the first GR case, I can't find any holes."

"Okay, well now we've made the connection with the case and the drawings, why don't we go back to them? Like, here." Harry points at the bear heads. "Why are there three? I read that there were only two victims."

James nods. "Yeah, you're right there were, but they had a son."

Harry's jaw locks, but he continues to smile and nod.

"GR didn't find him. At the time, since we didn't know the pattern, we didn't think anything of it at all. Just one lucky kid. But maybe…"

Harry's heart starts to race. His mouth doesn't want to, but his brain forces it to form the words. "So, where's the kid now, then?"

James doesn't respond for a few seconds. Harry begins to get nervous, but then James lifts his arms and flaps them back down to his sides. "Who the hell knows? He bounced between foster homes for years, left school as soon as he could and that's all I know about him. It was fifteen years ago, you know? He kind of dropped off the radar."

Nodding slowly, Harry asks, "so maybe they want us to track down the kid."

James quickly shakes his head. "No, I don't think so. I took the kid's statement, he has nothing to do with this. Besides, having his parents killed practically in front of him? That's not the kind of thing you want to relive. No, I think there's something else they're trying to say."

Harry exhales, relieved by James's response. Harry can't look for himself. If James ever found out, it would jeopardise Harry's entire position and the investigation. Harry can't have that. He has to catch them.

CHAPTER 62 - AVERY

April 2010

"Who the fuck is she?" I screamed into Julian's face as soon as he opened the door. "Who the fuck is she?"

Julian raised his hands, protecting his face while I lashed out at him. "What are you on about? I don't know what you're talking about, Buttercup."

"Don't *Buttercup* me, you two-timing asshole!" I shoved him back against the door. "How long has this been going on, huh? How long have you been screwing her?"

I continued to throw my weight against him, until he began to push back. "Now, wait a flippin' minute, Avery!" he yelled, pinning my arms down to my sides and skidding me into the lounge. "Tell me what the hell is going on? What girl are you talking about?"

"Oh, don't put on the innocent act. You've been getting all secretive again, like you were when we first moved in together when I didn't know about your part-time job. I followed you and saw you with her last week!" I squinted my eyes at him with my teeth grinding. "So, I decided to pay her a little visit."

Julian's eyes widened and I heard his heart jump a little. "Avery, what did you do...?"

I shook off his worry. "Oh calm down, will you? I didn't do anything like *that*, you halfwit. The broken-hearted girlfriend? I'm the first person they'd look at. We just had a little chat. Let's just say she won't be answering your booty calls anymore."

He clenched his fists and growled, "Jesus, Avery, it was nothing, just some harmless flirting! Why do you have to be like this?"

"Me? What do you mean why am I like this? I'm not the one sleeping around. You should be grateful I didn't let my anger get the better of me and actually do some damage." I tensed my hands and my fingers were visibly shaking. I rush towards him and pull at his tangled tufts of hair. "The way I feel towards you right now, I would love nothing more to rip that smug little grin right off." After a few moments of seriously considering it, I loosened my grip and took a step back. "But, I can't do that either. So, I'll just have to settle for putting you in jail."

He shook his head and laughed. *Laughed.* The fire roaring in my eyes exploded at the sight.

"Oh, Buttercup, you're not going to do that." He seemed so sure of himself. It made my blood boil.

"Really? You don't think I would do it? Come on, Julian. I thought you knew me better than that."

He raised his hands. "I have no doubt that you are perfectly capable of doing that, but I also know how self-preserving you are. You wouldn't take me down if it meant you came with me."

Grinding my teeth, I spat, "What the hell are you talking about?"

He slowly began walking towards me. "That night? I may have been in complete shock, but I wasn't debilitated. No, I made sure to get the evidence I needed, a video I could hold over your head like you hold those documents over mine." Julian was now breathing his words onto my skin. I could feel his heat joining with mine. "You aren't going to do a single thing."

I wanted to throw him backwards, pick up the phone and put him away for good. But one of the things I liked about him? He wasn't one to bluff.

I could almost taste his lips. They were so close to mine. The devil on my shoulder was begging me to lean closer, but the angel was telling me to turn around and back away. Just because I couldn't turn him in didn't mean I had to stay with him. Julian pressed his body into mine and I could feel all of him. The angel suddenly fizzled out into nothing.

"And there's no need to worry about anyone else. No one could keep me as interested as you can." His words were just sounds now, I wasn't listening.

I hurled my arms around him, yanked his head towards mine and our lips finally touched.

CHAPTER 63 - AVERY

"Avery," my boss calls as I walk through the door after my lunch break. He approaches me. "Someone dropped a present off for you. I left it on your desk."

I frown at him. "Who was it?"

He shrugs. "It was just left by the door with a note saying 'I look forward to seeing you tonight'. I didn't see who it was. Hey, you didn't tell me it was your birthday."

"Didn't I? I must've forgot." I smile back at him while trying to subtly exit the conversation.

"Well, happy birthday anyway." He gives me a wide grin and then walks off in the other direction.

I skip over to my desk, excited to see what gift he left for me. I am meeting his friends tonight – I hope it's something to calm my nerves.

Ripping the champagne-coloured paper off the cardboard box, I make sure I'm not looking too enthusiastic over a birthday present at *my* age.

I lift the lid and as soon as the sun's rays reveal what's inside, I slam it shut again and my hands begin to shake. To my disappointment, it isn't from Him.

After scooping the box into my arms, I casually hurry out of the office and into the ladies' toilet. Once I am in a locked stall, I reopen the box.

There, in a bed of *Happy Birthday* confetti, is a knife. There doesn't seem to be anything too special about the knife – it's just a standard kitchen knife. However, the thing that scares me is that it is in a zip-lock plastic bag. With *Southhurst Police Department* in the top right-hand corner.

I rummage through the confetti and sure enough I find a letter at the very bottom.

Happy Birthday dear friend. I hope you enjoy my gift. I can't wait to see you later. I may be a little late to the celebration, but I'll be sure not to miss the cake.

CHAPTER 64 - AVERY

I stare at the sign for Old Bernie's and take in three deep breaths, willing myself to go in.

I've always been skilled at getting people to like me when I want them to. I don't usually get nervous. But tonight I am. Tonight the butterflies are zipping around, as if they're high. For some stupid reason, I care if his friends like me. I want them to like me.

After I have stood outside the pub for enough time that I feel like an idiot, I make my way inside.

"Happy birthday!" A chorus of voices greets me as I walk through the door. Shocked and overwhelmed by it all, the butterflies hold hand and dance circles in my belly. Not only do I see Him smiling back at me, but I see several other familiar faces too.

I can't wipe the grin from my face as I look around at everyone staring back at me.

I rush up to one of them. "Kelly!" She runs at me and I squeeze her tightly.

When we loosen our grip on one another, I exclaim, "Oh my God, I haven't seen you in forever, I thought you were in Australia?"

Kelly swings her tightly curled hair over her shoulder. "Yeah I was," she replies in a soft Aussie accent, "but I couldn't miss my bestie's birthday, could I?"

We squeal like two schoolgirls and embrace each other again. She whispers in my ear, "I know I'm a million miles away but you still have to keep me up to date. Like for example why am I only just meeting your new boy toy?"

I shush her, conscious that he is only two feet away.

She then mouths *tell me everything later.*

As I turn my attention to Him, he wraps one arm around my shoulder and pulls me in. I stretch up onto my tiptoes and kiss his cheek.

"Did you do this?"

He shrugs with a subtle smirk. "Well, I had to do *something* for your birthday, didn't I?"

"How did you find my friends?"

"I may have taken a sneak peek through your phone a couple months ago."

I shake my head. "If I wasn't really happy to see Kelly I would be so angry at you for going through my phone." I then kiss him again and wiggle out of his grip.

"Thank you so much for coming, this is amazing!" I go around the room and repeat this to everyone as I briefly put my arm around them before moving on to the next.

Most of them are friends from work, so as glad as I am to see them, I see them every day. I'm more excited to see Kelly.

"Here you go, Avery. On the house," Frank calls to me as he slides a pint down the bar. I've known Frank since we were little kids, he used to swim naked in my paddling pool. He took over the pub after his father passed a few years back.

"Cheers," I mouth to Frank, and I have now circled back to Him.

I see Him there with Kelly and his friends. A sudden wave hits me – I completely forgot to introduce myself to them. They must think I'm so rude.

"Hi." I greet the circle with an overly enthusiastic flick of my hand. "I'm so sorry I haven't introduced myself yet, this is all so overwhelming."

For a moment I'm afraid they're all going to stick their noses up at me, but they flash me a grin and wave off my apology.

He puts his arm back around me and gestures to the short man to my left, whose hair seems to be shy as it has crept to the back of his head. "This is Leslie. Don't comment on his hair or name, he's very self-conscious," he mutters into my ear, although he intentionally says it loud enough that Leslie overhears.

"Hey!" Leslie remarks, but the two of them laugh it off. He turns his attention to me. "It's a pleasure to meet the woman that's got my wingman so off his game."

I chuckle softly at his sideways smile.

"And this," he points to the tall, slim woman opposite me with a Rachel from *Friends* style bob, "This is Celine."

"It is so, so great to finally meet you," a New York voice squeaks out as she leaps up to me and squeezes me tightly. "We're going to be best friends! I know the best little places that we can go for lunch and there is this gorgeous little boutique down my street that really isn't as known as it should be. I just have to show it to you, you're going to love it!"

He pulls me back from her. "Easy, Celine, give her a chance to breathe."

"It's okay," I smile. "That sounds great, I would love to." I quickly glance at Kelly who, as I suspected, is holding back her laughter at Celine's bouncy personality. Celine is the kind of girl we used to sit on the benches at school and gossip about. Australia hasn't changed Kelly one bit.

"And finally…" He turns my attention to the final man in the circle, though I really don't need an introduction to him. "This is Grant. He's a detective, so I'd watch what you say around him."

Oh, I know he's a detective. I know exactly who he is. He's working Cinderella's case with the beer-belly. Thankfully, he is blissfully unaware of who I am.

"Now, now, don't worry about me." He raises his hands. "When the badge is off, I'm not a detective. Don't feel like you have to be touchy around me, honey. Ask your fella, here. He was involved in a knife fight a few months back and I turned a blind eye – but when I was put on the case, I had no choice but to take his sorry arse to jail. He was just lucky that Rugrat busted the drug deal wide open before our boy got charged!"

I stare up at Him with a smirk. "You were arrested? You've managed to keep that one quiet."

He shrugs and holds me closer. "You never asked…but anyway I had nothing to do with it, before you *do* ask, just the wrong place at the wrong time."

I nudge Him and turn back to the others. I quite like the fact he has been involved in some crime. Maybe we aren't as different after all.

"But anyway, let's move on from this introduction crap," Grant declares. "It's your birthday, right? Let's get you drunk!"

They all scream, "Cheers." And Grant tips the bottom of my beer up so that it travels down my throat faster.

This is the first time in months that my attention has been obscured – not by paranoia, but by good old-fashioned booze.

Thankfully, I'm not the only one who's going to have a headache tomorrow. As I glance around the pub, there are huddles of people slumped down in booths, resting on one another with their mouths hanging open and saliva creeping out.

Lovely, I think to myself.

Leslie can't seem to hold his beer – he passed out after the fourth round. Celine and Grant, however, are still standing and continue to pour drinks into me.

When they turn around for a second, I sneak off outside to get some fresh air.

"Hey," Kelly murmurs through her teeth as she lights up a cigarette. "Pretty crazy in there, huh?"

I stumble into her and grab her shoulder to prevent my knees from buckling. "Yeah, it is." She offers me a cigarette and I shake my head. "No thanks, hon. I quit years ago."

Kelly raises her eyebrows. "Gosh, we really haven't seen each other in a while, have we?" She takes another drag and blows the suffocating puff of smoke in my direction. "So, that's a pretty nice fish you've caught."

I laugh. "Yeah, I suppose you could say that."

"I didn't think he was really your type. You've always been more attracted to the Julians of the world."

"That's true." I shrug. "But I guess it's quite nice to have a bit of a change. It was worth it."

She stares at me intensely. "Do you love him?"

My eyes widen and my heart races at her abrupt question, but I take in a deep breath to calm it. "I think so." Kelly smiles in surprise. "Is that crazy? He's told me he loves me and I've wanted to say it back but I'm scared, you know?"

"Of course I do. I've known you forever – I know what you're like. You date the Julians because you don't have to worry about really deep feelings. They're always just a bit of fun and great sex. A guy like the one you've got in there…he's more serious. It scares you." She stamps out the fag end and turns her whole body to me. "You and me? We're two of a kind. I was exactly the same before I met Seb. And look at me now? I moved halfway across the bloody world to be with him. I think you've found your Seb."

She squeezes my shoulder and I lift my arms up, wrapping them around her. "It really is so good to see you, Kel," I muffle into her coat.

She pulls back from me, plants a quick kiss on my cheek and smiles, "it's great to see you too, *chica*. We aren't going to leave it so long next time, okay?"

I nod my head and we squeeze each other again before she makes her way back inside.

Leaning my head against the window, I observe the street, thinking about what she said. Thinking about Him. He has done so much for me. I mean, organising Kelly to come all the way from Australia? I can't even do that. He must really care about me.

My euphoria is cut short when the paranoia kicks back in.

On the other side of the street, there is someone staring at me. All dressed in black.

CHAPTER 65 - AVERY

I spring into a completely upright position and stare back at them, as if I am a deer stuck in headlights.

I can't see their face, but I can feel their eyes burning my skin. They lift their hand out of their coat pocket and slowly wave.

I want to run after them. I know who they are. But my legs are frozen – my reason is screaming at me to move them, but they won't obey.

I watch the figure turn, stroll down the street and round the corner. As if they know I can't move.

They have disappeared from my sight for a few minutes before my frozen body decides to thaw.

When it does, I clench my fists and scold myself. *What the hell am I doing?*

I then shoot down the street and follow their route around the corner. I don't see them, but I spot the tail of their coat flap in the wind as they turn another corner. I pursue them, being careful of my footing so that there is not a repeat of last time.

It's late, but there is still a sliver of light seeping through the night's blanket, so I am aware of where I am and where I'm going.

I see them again. I'm closer this time, but they're still round the next corner before I can reach them. I'll get them this time.

When I turned onto the new street, my body is pumping with adrenaline, ready to lunge at that stupid black trench coat.

But they aren't there.

I growl in frustration. Where could they have gone? How could they have disappeared so quickly? I was *right* behind them.

I sprint to the end of the street and survey the area – nothing. I sprint back to see if I have missed them – nothing.

My eyebrows tense and my jaw is locked. I don't understand, it doesn't make any sense.

And then I see it. I know why they led me here.

At the end of this street, opposite the road is a house standing on its own. A little white clapboard with worn away wooden shutters. Its thatched roof is no longer tightly enough bound that it is stable and will keep the rain from seeping through.

I can still smell the thick scent of scorched wood, radiating out of the clogged-up chimney. Dad always wanted to use coal, because it burns better, but Mum liked the homeliness of a wood fire. I can't say I understand her logic, exactly, but I have to agree that it was the cosiest to snuggle in front of in winter, in our ski clothes with a mug of hot chocolate. Dad made the best hot chocolate.

I haven't been back here in years – not since I moved back to Southhurst. It's uninhabitable – practically falling apart. I'm surprised the council haven't bulldozed it yet – that's what they usually do nowadays.

Once I've spent enough time staring at the broken down structure, I shake the nostalgia from my back and spin around, making my way back to the pub. I've been gone for thirty-two minutes. Hopefully everyone is drunk enough that they haven't noticed.

"Babe!" he bellows while he zigzags towards me with his arms open. I'm not certain if his arms are out to hug me or to give himself balance. "Where have you been? I've been looking for you," he slurs as he collapses onto me.

I may be feisty but I'm certainly not strong enough to take his weight – I drop him as my knees are about to give, but luckily he doesn't smash headfirst into the pavement. I help Him to find his balance and I reply, "I just went to get some fresh air. Don't worry." I peer through the window and see everyone but Kelly and Grant either lying on the sofa or on a stool.

"I think we should get you into bed, okay? You stay right here," I say whilst propping him up against the brick wall, "And I'll call us a taxi."

I don't wait for his response – he's pretty much unconscious.

Once I've called a taxi service, I pop back inside to say goodbye to those who are still standing.

"Hey, guys, I think we're going to call it a night," I announce.

Grant throws his arms into the air. "Oh, good riddance! Your fella gets way too handsy when he's had a few too many."

I giggle softly, "It was great to meet you, Grant." I turn my attention to Kelly and I nestle my face into her curls. "I love you, girl. I'll see you soon okay? You have to invite me to Australia sometime."

She laughs. "I don't think you'd be able to handle the outback."

I squeeze her one last time, wave goodbye to Frank and head back outside to tend to my passed-out boyfriend. The taxi really couldn't have arrived any sooner.

CHAPTER 66 - AVERY

Getting from the taxi to my front door is a challenge.

Not only am I having to drag Him up each step behind me, but I also have to pull Him straight when he swings off to one side. On the bright side, it's a great arm workout.

He hangs his arms over my shoulders as I struggle to shove the key into the lock. Why does it have to be so tiny?

Once I do, I immediately throw Him inside, crouch down and scoop up the letter at the foot of the door. He may be hammered, but I still can't let him see that.

As I am helping Him clamber onto the first step, I hear a rattling in the kitchen. He hears it too.

"Wha-i-at?"

"Oh it's nothing, just the wind. Come on, let's get you to bed."

He shrugs and continues his mighty task of conquering the stairs, not thinking twice about it.

Seven agonising minutes later, we reach the top and I throw the bedroom door open. He quickly flops onto the bed and instantly passes out.

I am kind enough to remove his shoes and shift his entire body onto the bed rather than just his torso, but my kindness stops there. He is going to have to sleep in his jacket tonight.

Quietly closing the door and tiptoeing back downstairs, I pull the envelope from inside my coat and rip it open.

Inside, there is a picture of Him. From tonight. Laughing and drinking with his friends. I can see the dirt of the pub's glass window on the photograph, showing it was taken from the street.

My heart gradually beats faster and faster as I take out the other contents of the envelope – a letter.

Have I found your Achilles' heel, I wonder?

The message is clear. He is now a target. I have to protect Him.

My heart stops when there is another rattling from the kitchen. I storm in and am rather unsurprised by my findings.

"Oh hey, Buttercup. I'm sorry, I was trying to be quiet – was I not quiet?" His fake sincerity only irritates me more.

I whisper a growl; "no you weren't being quiet and what the hell are you doing here? Did you not hear me last time?"

JJulian nods, taking a large chunk out of my scotch pancakes – of which I see he has already eaten four. "I did, and I considered it. But then I decided to call your bluff – I think you're all talk." He gulps down the food and waltzes towards me with those…eyes. "I thought we could maybe crack open the wine." Julian snakes his hands around my neck, closing the gap between us, and I feel his fingers interlock in loose strands of my hair. "Maybe bring out Twister, have a little bit of fun and," he pulls me into him so that our hips are pressed together, "I don't know, see where the night takes us…"

I don't move for a millisecond, letting my mind see exactly how that would play out, before I duck my head under his arms and back out of the kitchen. It was a millisecond too long.

"Why do you insist on being such a dick?"

He shrugs, following me into the lounge. "I can't help it, love. It's just who I am."

"Well," I begin while spinning around to face him, "I am going to bed so unless you would like me to physically remove you, please exit my house."

He tilts his head back and mouths a laugh. "As much as I would love to see that, I only came to give you a message."

I frown. "What message? From who?"

"You don't need to know who. Just watch your man. You don't know all there is to him, and someone else does."

Everything was starting to fall into place. It wouldn't be long now until it was time. I was just waiting on a few more things to play out before it could come to a head. But I could feel the end drawing near.

CHAPTER 67 - AVERY

"Fucking shoe," I moan to myself as the tip of my heel wedges itself in the un-kempt concrete of the walkway leading up to the station doors.

Once I yank my ankle free, I stare at the old, broken down building. This is it. I'm finally going to do it.

My legs are nervous and are whining for me not to go through the doors – that's probably why my heel got stuck. A final attempt at making me spin myself around, drive home and never come within a hundred metres of this place again.

I don't listen to them. I stomp my feet forward, forcing them to shut up.

My heartbeat increases as each step draws me closer to the dreaded truth.

It's warmer than I thought it would be. From its outer appearance, I assumed the term *central heating* would be completely foreign, but to my surprise my hair doesn't actually stand up on end as soon as I cross the threshold.

I stand in the doorway for a few seconds, scanning the small reception for someone who looks like they have some authority. I'm out of luck.

Although, I do catch sight of a fragile woman typing frantically behind a desk in the centre. I approach her.

"Hi," I say softly.

Still, she is startled by my presence. "Oh, hello. I'm sorry, give me one moment and I'll be with you." She continues tapping away at her keyboard. There is a frailty in her voice that makes me feel like if I breathe too heavy, she'll shatter. "There we go. Now," She turns her attention back to me. "What can I help you with?"

My breath breaks as the words form in my mind. It all seems too real now, it has only just hit me that I'm actually going to do it. "Um," I struggle to form words. "I was wondering who I need to speak to, to, um, file a harassment report?"

She offers me a warm smile. "Yes, absolutely. If you take a seat over there and I will go find an officer for you."

I walk over to the stiff, cheap plastic chairs she pointed at and hover over them. They are so uncomfortable, I can immediately feel the pins and needles planning their attack.

Thankfully, she is quick to reappear and with her is a tall, clean-shaven man. Through all my observation of this place, I have never seen *him* before, and he isn't the sort of face I'd forget. He has military cut, jet black hair, the bluest eyes I think I've ever seen, and a jawline that should be covered for safety.

He flashes me a smile. And white teeth. Very white teeth. "Hi there, I'm DC White. Karen has informed me that you would like me to file a harassment report? Is that right?"

I stumble to my feet and extend my hand which he shakes firmly. "Yes, that's right. And a restraining order would be great."

He bobs his head. "Absolutely, if you would like to come through to my office, I'll ask you a few questions and I'll see what we can do."

He then turns and heads down the corridor and I trail along behind him. He leads me down some stairs that are so narrow and steep that I have the rusty bannister in a deadlock, trying to distract myself from thinking about all the dirt and grime that is attaching itself to my skin as I do so.

We reach the bottom. *Thank God.* And he ushers me into the office to the left.

It's a simple office, it doesn't have much of a personality. The walls are painted white, although they are stained with a grey tinge from the dust that has gathered over the years. At the back of the office is a metal table with an old-fashioned computer in the corner, an array of unorganised documents and a standard, unpleasant-looking swivel chair behind it.

"So, can I please take your name, address and contact details," he asks me as he settles down into the squeaky chair.

I comply with his requests and answer all the boring procedural questions like when's my birthday, do I live alone, am I employed, if so what do I do?

Twenty-two minutes into the conversation we actually begin with the important questions.

"So, who is it that has been harassing you?"

I clear my throat. "Julian Tanner."

He scribbles down on his notepad. "Right, and what relation is he to you and why do you believe he has been harassing you?"

"He's my ex-boyfriend – we broke up in 2010. He's been breaking into my house and taunting me. It makes me very uncomfortable." I twiddle with my thumbs and glance down at my lap.

"Right," DC White looks up from his notepad. "You say you broke up in 2010. How long has he been breaking into your house? Does he cause you any bodily harm?"

I shake my head. "No, he just scares me and threatens me. He made first contact at the beginning of May – he's only just got out of prison."

"What sort of threats is he making?" His interest seems piqued by my mention of prison. "And what was he in prison for?"

"He has just said that something is coming for me, that he's going to take me down. Those sorts of things. He went to prison for terrorism through hacking government security."

"I see." He puts his hand to his chin. "Yes, I think I'm familiar with that case – he was supposed to go away for a minimum period of ten years, wasn't he?"

"Yes," I confirm, "but he got out early. I haven't stopped to ask him how, but I assume it was on good behaviour? I don't know much about the system – I'm sure you'll have a better idea than me."

He shuffles around in his seat. "So, how often has he been breaking in?"

I shrug and answer fraily, "it started with just once a month, then once a week and now it's every couple of days – sometimes even twice in a row." I glance down again and snuffle. "It's really starting to scare me."

He reaches forward and squeezes my arm gently. "It's okay, we'll make sure he doesn't come anywhere near you or your house. Okay?"

He takes pleasure in playing the role of my protector as he wipes away the tears from my cheeks. I throw my head up and look into his eyes. "Yes please. Thank you so much, officer." My eyes well up again and kicking it up a notch, I begin to cough frantically. "I'm so sorry," I croak, "Could I please have a glass of water?"

"Of course, of course," he returns and quickly stands up, exiting the room.

The communal kitchen is on the ground floor and down two corridors, so I have exactly four minutes until he reappears.

I swiftly scoot around the desk and switch his computer on. My fingers twitch as I hear the cogs in the computer slowly wake up to display the buffering symbol.

Come on, come on, I will it, although I haven't yet mastered the control of technology.

I finally hear the *welcome* jingle and the login screen appears. I tap on the keys and after a few failed attempts of passing through the protection, it gives up and gives me access. The stuff Julian taught me all those years ago is kind of like a master key – once you're logged on, nothing is off limits.

I search through the files until I find the one dedicated to me and I click on the file named *Sleeping Beauty – 4ᵗʰ August*.

After I've opened it up, the screen fills with reports, information and other files that are completely irrelevant to me. There's only one item on my agenda. I type into the search bar *CCTV*, hoping that I will get a late birthday present.

Nothing is found.

I type in *street footage*.

Nothing.

Street camera

Nothing.

Security camera

Nothing.

I'm so confused. How can I not find it? Surely they will have gained access to the footage by now. Why isn't it on here?

I don't have time to find out. I've been so focused on the screen that I forgot to keep an eye on the time – I hear White's footsteps echoing down the steps.

As I try to close the files, the screen freezes. I tap persistently on the mouse but nothing happens.

I growl in frustration and I see the bottom of his legs appearing.

I'm out of ideas and my mind has triggered panic mode. I do the only thing I can think of – pull the plug out.

"You okay?" I hear White call from behind me.

I'm still behind the desk and I have just stood back up from unplugging the computer. My heart is racing and my throat feels suffocated, as if my lungs refuse to inhale any oxygen.

Thinking on my feet, I wobble on my shoe and sway from side to side. "Yes, I'm fine," I say whilst regaining my balance. "I was just going to open a window, but I tripped over these wires." Looking down at the cable, I lightly weep, "I'm so sorry, I think I unplugged your computer. I hope I didn't lose any important files you were working on."

White hurries across the room, hands me the water and crouches down to place the plug back in the wall. "Oh no, don't worry about it. It wasn't even turned on."

I sigh in relief and down half the glass. Panic really does make you thirsty.

Clearing my throat, I glance over to him. "I really appreciate your time, thank you. Is there anything else…?"

"No, that's everything. You can be on your way." He comes closer to me and offers me another flash of his teeth. "Don't worry, we'll make sure he doesn't harm you or make you feel uneasy."

I smile back at him and thank him.

After following him back up to the reception and exiting the station, I sigh a *real* sigh of relief. "Thank fuck I'm out of there," I mutter to myself as I pull my phone from my pocket and dial his number.

After I got that photo of him on Monday, I haven't been able to think about Him without being put on edge. What if something happens to Him? It will be all my fault. As I have been pondering this thought, another thought has kept cropping up. One that I've never *ever* considered before. The thought that maybe he should know.

I know it sounds crazy, but maybe it will be for the best. I mean, he said himself that nothing I tell Him would change how he feels – maybe this won't either. It will be safer, if I do. Then I can tell Him the real reason behind the letters and he can watch out for himself as well. If I tell Him, maybe I can really let Him in. Maybe it will be the best thing I ever do. Maybe.

It's around his lunchtime now, so I thought maybe we could get something to eat.

I'm disappointed when the phone rings three times and then goes straight to voicemail. I call Him again, in case it was a mistake and the same thing happens.

He's probably in a meeting that ran over. Or a house viewing, I reason and head over to the Cosy Coffee to grab myself something – I only just realised I'm starving.

CHAPTER 68 - HARRY

They are better today – they are feeling less guilty about it all. Harry is relieved by this, he really didn't want to lose them now.

"Hey, Karen," Harry says as he walks through the station doors. "Have we had any more contact from GR?"

Karen glances down, biting her lip. "No, I don't think so. I'll keep an eye on it, though."

"Okay." Harry returns and heads to James's office.

Karen smiles as he goes past. Since that Christian Grey paid a visit, she has gradually grown in confidence. Harry has noticed that she is holding her head higher now, rather than always looking down. She has more of a brightness to her face, as before she always seemed dull and low. Although he didn't go far to help the investigation, at least he did some good for Karen.

"Hey." Harry grabs James's attention as he approaches his office. "I just went to the evidence locker. The knife is gone."

That certainly does get James's attention. "What knife?"

"The one from the Sleeping Beauty murder. I can't find it anywhere."

James sighs, biting the inside of his cheek. "How strange. I checked Monday morning when I put the hair we found in there and everything seemed to be accounted for. Let me go have a look."

Once he has left the room, Harry approaches the board and studies its content. Since the beginning of this week, they have been looking back over the Goldilocks case and trying to see how it links in. They haven't gotten very far with it, though. They've looked for holes in the investigation, key points ignored, statements lost over the years…but they've come up with nothing. Everything seems to be in perfect order. That's no surprise, though, since James was one of the main detectives working on the case.

As for the son? James still thinks he is somewhere far away, living his life as well as he can, trying to move on from the tragedy. That's how Harry wants it to stay.

A few minutes later, James returns with a stern look on his face. "I can't find it either. It can't have just disappeared."

Harry shrugs. "Well, we found some of the prints on the knife, didn't we? Maybe GR is trying to cover their tracks."

James nods, but he doesn't seem convinced. "Hmm, if that's the case it's a bit late now, isn't it? We've already put the prints from the knife onto the system. He's escaped us for so long, he must know the system well enough to know that." He joins Harry, staring at the board. "None of this is adding up. The Goldilocks case…the drawings…the letter and call… now the knife has gone missing? None of this is making sense."

"Maybe when we get the street CCTV we can get a clearer picture," Harry suggests.

James doesn't reply. Both of them remain silent, pondering the scattered information, trying and failing to make sense of it all.

Harry agrees — none of it is adding up. But Harry doesn't think they are done taunting them, yet. Harry knows there is more to come.

CHAPTER 69 - AVERY

July 2010

Julian was out for the day and I was stuck at home. Bored. And he'd left his laptop behind.

I tried to keep myself busy, doing the boring chores and catching up with work that I had been putting off. I knew that a good girlfriend shouldn't go through her boyfriend's private laptop. What would happen to the trust in the relationship if she did that?

But it had already been established that I wasn't the *ideal* girlfriend. And my nosiness really did get the better of me.

Since Julian had taught me the basics of all his computer skills, I was able to break through his security relatively easily.

I didn't really have a goal, there wasn't anything I was searching for – I was just trying to waste away my day. So, I went through his open internet tabs – which were disgusting, by the way. I went through his emails, just in case his little skank from before decided to go back on our pact. To her good fortune, she hadn't.

When I went through his files, I didn't understand what half of them even meant – they were all related to his part-time job. I tried my very best not to talk about that with him, since I really didn't care.

Although, there was one file that caught my attention. A video labelled *Avery – that night.*

There was only one thing I could think of that could be on that video. And if I had found it, he would have nothing to hold over me.

I opened the file and clicked *play*. The footage wasn't the best quality, so it took me a while to figure out exactly what it was showing. It was *not* what I was expecting at all.

It wasn't the night he followed me. It was us. In bed. As the video got going, I slammed the laptop closed and clasped my hands over my mouth.

He filmed us? That disgusting son of a bitch. What the hell did he think he was doing?

The adrenaline began to course through my veins and the red spots were emerging across my vision.

As my breath began to quicken, I pulled the laptop open again, deleted the video and copied all of the other files. The ones relating to his part-time job.

"That bastard thinks he can film me and get away with it," I growled to myself as I attach the files to an email. "Two-timing, lying bastard. I bet he doesn't even have a video of *that* night. Good, he has nothing on me."

Slamming on the keys, I typed in the Southhurst Police Department's email address and clicked *send*.

As soon as I did, my fingers were shaking uncontrollably with anger. He'd lied to me too many times now. I was done.

As the rage resurged, I grasped the laptop, raised it above my head with trembling arms and watched as it plummeted onto the ground.

He wouldn't be needing that where he was going.

CHAPTER 70 - AVERY

I haven't been able to get hold of Him all day, but I don't worry about it too much. I may have fallen into a relationship, but I refuse to become the overbearing girlfriend.

I get home at eleven minutes past five and I have a present waiting for me. When I was first receiving these letters, my heart would skip a beat every time I saw them. However, now they have become a normality for me. When they finally stop, I think I might miss them.

Hickory dickory dock
The mouse ran up the clock
The clock struck one
The mouse never came down
Hickory dickory dock
Remember?

I frown as I stare down at the piece of paper. I know that rhyme. I mean, of course I know it – every child who grew up in England knows that rhyme. But there's something about it that is eating away at my mind. It wasn't just a nursery rhyme. There was more to it.

"But what the hell is it?" I mutter to myself.

I shriek as my heart leaps from my chest at the bang on my window. I spin myself into its direction to find Julian with his hands slammed against the glass, pressing a document up against it. There is a fire alight in his eyes. One I haven't seen in a very long time. Not since I sent that email.

"What the fuck do you think you're doing you stupid bitch?" he spits at the window.

I don't reply and I don't come any closer. Squinting my eyes, I just about make out the words in bold writing at the top of the document reading *restraining order*.

Curling up his lips and baring his teeth, he bellows, "Is this some kind of a joke to you? You think this is funny? You really must be more stupid that I thought you were." As the time goes by and I am still frozen in place, I see the fire roar louder. "I've been out of jail for less than six months. You know that means if I have any run-ins with the police I'm reassessed and might have to fucking go back. Saying I'm stalking you? What the fuck do you think you're doing?"

After taking in all the oxygen my lungs will allow, I hold my head high and say in the most confident tone I can muster, "I did warn you. I told you if you came in again I would report you."

I think that my speaking will calm him down. It doesn't.

He sucks in air and his nostrils flare. "Oh you're going down, you little bitch. I'm done playing games, I'm taking you down. You see this face?" He presses his nose up to the glass and his breath fogs it up. His eyes are wide, he's panting like a beast. I fear the glass between us won't protect me. "This is the face of the man who puts you behind bars. And I'd watch out for your little boyfriend. I'll take pleasure in seeing him pay for your crimes as well."

Julian stares at me through the window for a few more seconds. I don't want to look at him, but I can't tear my eyes away from his. The look in his eye doesn't seem angry – it seems monstrous.

After banging both fists on the glass again, making me jump out of my skin, he slowly backs away from the window, not taking his twitching eyes off me until he is out of sight. Even though he is gone, I still feel him here.

I gasp for air. I only just realise that I was holding my breath.

I knew that was coming – I knew that was how he'd react. I was prepared. Still, it's made my hands shake uncontrollably, it takes all my strength to force them to stop. My legs won't remove.

Now I have to protect Him from two people. I've put Him in so much danger, I can't do it anymore. He deserves to know.

CHAPTER 71 - AVERY

Stop moving.

Stop. Moving.

My foot refuses to listen to my brain. It persists in tapping on the ground, creating the most irritating noise.

Oh great, none of my limbs are listening to me, I groan as my fingers drum the side of the mug, complementing the beat my shoes are providing.

Heidi keeps glancing at me with a worried expression painted onto her face. She can tell that I'm anxious about something. If it's that obvious to Heidi, he is going to notice the moment he walks through the door.

But when he does, my entire body freezes. My ribcage won't even move to allow room for my lungs to expand.

My lack of movement actually concerns Him more.

He rushes over to my corner table and rests his hand over mine. "Avery, what's wrong? Is everything okay?"

I stare at Him mindlessly for a few seconds. Well, at least he thinks it is mindlessly – I'm simply trying to get my ribcage to move.

"Yes," I finally blurt when the sweet oxygen molecules enter my alveoli again. "Yes, everything is fine, I just wanted to talk to you."

My reassurance doesn't exactly reassure Him, he is still staring at me, frowning with those gorgeous brown eyes.

"What did you want to talk about? You seemed quite serious on the phone."

I glance up at Him but I am unable to speak. It is now that I realise I'm scared.

I'm scared of losing Him. I'm scared he'll go back on his promise to always accept me whatever I tell him.

But he isn't perfect, right? I've accepted his flaws. I mean, he leaves the lid off the toothpaste – every single time. Who does that? It's so unhygienic. Sometimes when he laughs too hard, he snorts a little bit. When I first heard it I was so repulsed by it that I almost fled right there and then. But I got used to it, right? Actually, I've grown to quite like it. He's always wanting to know every detail of everything I'm doing and everything I'm feeling. That's really clingy, isn't it? But I've got used to that. They may not seem like flaws to Him, but they are to me. Surely it's the same thing. I know it will be difficult, but eventually he'll be able to accept my *flaw*. Because he loves me. He has to.

"Avery?" he calls to me and I realise I have been staring at him for a minute or two. He doesn't look concerned anymore, he looks slightly creeped out.

"Sorry," I croak and clear my throat. "I've just never done this before and I don't know how to."

He brings my hands up to his lips and kisses them. "Don't worry. You can tell me anything. You know that."

I take in a deep breath and nod. "Yeah, I know. It's just, this is different."

Removing my hands from his, I clasp them both around my coffee mug and rock back and forth on my chair. I didn't bother to practise what I would say last night – I just thought it would come naturally and if I practise I might get too nervous. I really regret that now.

I don't know what the best way to even approach it is. How to soften the blow and make it seem less awful to Him.

I open my mouth and as I do my heartbeat quickens, causing my voice to shake. The adrenaline begins pumping through my body and my hands rattle the mug.

Don't be stupid. My reason pops up again. She was trying to talk me out of it all of last night, but gave up this morning. This is the first time she's made a reappearance.

Come on, Avery. Think about this. You haven't thought about this.

That's where she is wrong. Over the past few days I've done nothing *but* think about it.

My mouth begins to form the words.

"I'm in love with you."

His face lights up with my words and he clasps my hands again as a beam spreads across his face and I am blinded by his teeth. I frown briefly, but I loosen my face, pretending I am as happy as he is.

That was *not* what I was expecting to come out. This conversation was supposed to go in an entirely different direction.

"Avery, you have no idea how long I've been waiting for you to say that." He pulls his chair closer to mine and cups my face. "I've felt like I've been feeling this way for so long and I never wanted to push you to find out if you felt the same, but it means so much to hear you say it."

Pulling me closer, he presses his lips against mine. I'm still confused about what *I* said. I feel like I'm lagging a mile behind in this conversation. But I kiss him back, I wouldn't want Him thinking there is anything still wrong.

"You know how much I love you, don't you?" he whispers into my ear. I'm warmed by his comforting breath.

I bob my head and he draws back.

After *that* just happened, we return to a normal conversation. While he is talking, all I can think about it how what I said is definitely not what I meant to say. I can't work out how it happened. I suppose my reason took over. She just couldn't let me do it.

"I've got to go. I've got to be at work in fifteen. I'll call you on my lunch break, okay?"

I lean in and kiss his cheek. "Okay."

He smiles at me, his expression so endearing. He always looks at me like I'm something special. Always. Without taking his eyes off mine, he squeezes my hands and stands up before heading for the exit.

Once he is out of sight, I slouch back in my chair, throw my hands over my face and sigh.

"Well that didn't go as planned..." I mutter to myself.

After I have downed the, now cold, remaining droplets of my latte I push my chair out and head off to work myself.

I am glancing down at the floor as I approach the door and my journey is interrupted by something knocking my shoulder back.

Bringing my head back up, I look behind me to see what, or who, it was.

I am greeted by a short, dark-haired woman. "Oh I am so sorry," she says to me. Her cheeks turn a bright rosy-red. "I'm never quite with it in the mornings until I get my coffee!"

"That's okay." I smile at her. "I'm the same." I then turn around, intending to continue my journey, but she taps my shoulder. Again.

"Wait."

I turn back around with a slightly less genuine smile on my face.

"I'm sorry, it's just…" Her voice trails off as she studies my face. "You look so familiar, have we met before?"

"I don't think so," I reply, slowly. "I just have one of those faces."

She chuckles lightly. "You most certainly don't. Look at you – you're stunning. You don't see many faces like yours around." She removes her hand from my shoulder. "No, it's probably just me. Like I said – me before my coffee is never a pretty sight."

Once again, I laugh softly – although my hostility peeks through – and turn back for the door, hoping she doesn't turn me around again.

To my delight, she doesn't and I make it out of the café.

Although, her face does linger in my mind, as I try to place it. She seemed familiar to me too.

CHAPTER 72 - HARRY

Outside the house of brick

The wolf is very quick

"I'll huff and I'll puff and I'll blow your house down"

"No, not by the hair of our chinny, chin, chin"

Say the three little pigs, as they tremble within

The wolf prowls to and fro

He howls a bit, for show

He huffs and he puffs as hard as he could

And the bricks hold firm and the house still stood

But the pigs still tremble – as they should

The pigs think they know all

But from their failure they'll fall

For the pigs neglect to look again

They assume the wolf is at its end

But little pigs, how wrong you are my friends

You build your house

You think it can't be unbound

But the foundations are weak

And while you sleep

The wolf creeps down the chimney

"What the hell is this?" James exclaims, his eyes fixed on the letter. "If they're trying to give us clues of some sort, can they not make it more obvious?"

Harry laughs. "That would make us redundant then, wouldn't it?"

Swivelling around on his chair, James sighs. "It doesn't make sense. It's just another thing we can add to the pile of *doesn't add up*." James glances up at Harry, unamused. "Why are you laughing at me? Stop it."

Harry holds his hands up. "I'm sorry, it's just quite a sight. To see you so stumped on something. I want to enjoy it while it lasts."

James doesn't seem entirely amused by him.

Perching on the edge of the desk, Harry leans over James's shoulder and studies the letter. "Okay, let's pick this apart. The pigs resemble us again – like in the drawings. The wolf must be GR, unless there is someone else we don't know about, of course. Then the house must be…the station? No…"

A light bulb appears above James's head. "Wait, say that again."

"The house is the station?"

James frowns. "No before that."

"Unless there's someone else we don't know about?"

Rising to his feet James exclaims, "Yes. That's it. What if there is someone we don't know about? We've been assuming this entire time that GR is a person – singular. What if there's two of them? What if there's always been two of them?" James's grin stretches from ear to ear. "Of course, that's why they directed us back to the first case. There aren't any loopholes in the investigation – the investigation was just carried out on the assumption that there was only one killer."

Harry stares at James, stroking his chin. He isn't convinced. "I don't know, that seems a pretty far stretch. I mean, I think it's a possibility, sure – but there's lots of things this letter could mean. The simple answer is the wolf represents GR. That way it's still aligned with the tale of the three little pigs. Besides—" Harry stands up and begins pacing. "If there are two of them, why would one of them be trying to hand the other one in? Why now? After fifteen years?"

James doesn't reply for a long time. He simply stares up at the ceiling and rests his hands on his belly. When he leans forward, he nods. "Yeah, you're probably right. I'm jumping to conclusions – I shouldn't do that. But it's still a possibility. Now, what does the house represent?"

CHAPTER 73 - HARRY

"Babe," Harry calls as he slams the door shut. He doesn't get a response. "Babe," he repeats.

"I'm out here," a tiny little voice replies. Harry follows the source and finds Martha lying on one of the deck chairs in the garden.

Harry sighs, "What are you doing out here?"

Removing her sunglasses, Martha shrugs. "It's summer – I wanted to enjoy the sun."

"But the sun has set. It set half an hour ago."

Martha throws herself up, growling as she does. Her tone holds a type of attitude that you would usually find in a teenager. "Yes, I know that, thank you, Harry. I just wanted to sit out here for a while. I didn't realise that was a problem." She marches back into the kitchen, nudging his shoulder as she passes.

"Oh Jesus," Harry mutters to himself through gritted teeth as he clenches his fists. His voice isn't in the conversation, it seems tired and uninterested. Like it's on autopilot. "No, of course it isn't a problem. I was just asking, I didn't mean to offend you."

As she slides her robe on, Martha shakes her head, held high in the air. "Oh, you didn't offend me. I'm not a sensitive little child, Harry."

Sighing, he says, "That's great, I'm glad we got that cleared up. Now, why don't you tell me how your day was?"

"Oh well, the normal. Work, work, blah, blah, work, work, blah." She pours herself a glass of wine and offers Harry one. He declines. "It was odd today though, actually. When I got my morning coffee I bumped into this woman by accident and I swear she looked so familiar. It has been eating away at me all day, I just can't place her. She was drop-dead gorgeous. Dark blue eyes, gorgeous long dark hair…"

Harry stares at her blankly. "Are you expecting me to tell you who she is?"

Downing the glass of wine, she lets out an exaggerated sigh. "I'm sorry, Harry. You asked me about my day – I told you about my day. You really can't decide what you want from me, can you?" She disregards him, waving her hand and walking into the lounge. "Honestly, I have had it up to here with your nonsense."

"Oh, and you can cook for yourself tonight," she calls.

A few seconds later, Harry's phone vibrates in his pocket. He pulls it out and it is not who he's expecting.

"James, hey," Harry greets as he smashes the green button. "What's up?"

"I figured it out." James's voice resembles that of an overenthusiastic seven-year-old.

"You figured what out?"

"I figured out what the poem means."

When he doesn't elaborate, Harry encourages him. "Okay…and?"

"So, the pigs are us, the wolf is GR and I've decided that the house is the case. As in the Goldilocks case. The entire poem is about GR blowing the case up, right?"

"Right…" Harry agrees hesitantly.

"And the last verse is about the pigs, us, thinking we built the house, the case, to be really strong, but it's not because the wolf, GR, can find a way in."

"Mate, where are you going with this?" Harry asks.

"The part of the house that is weak are the foundations. The foundations of the house…the foundations of the case. We have to strip the case right back to its foundations to find where we went wrong."

Harry can't help but laugh at James's tone. "And what would the foundations of the case be?"

"The victims!" James exclaims like it is the punchline to a joke he has built up.

"The victims?" Harry repeats, confused and having trouble following James's train of thought.

"Yes, the victims! The foundations of a house are what starts the building off. The thing that starts a case is the victims. Think about it, there couldn't be a case without victims."

After he has caught up with James's thought process, he nods. "Okay, I'm with you. That makes sense. So, we need to look into the victims. What do we need to know about them specifically?"

Harry hears James shrug. "I've spent my entire evening getting to this point – I'm all out of detective juice for today. Tomorrow we'll go over every single aspect of them, their lives and their deaths. Okay? Oh, one sec—" James muffles his end of the phone and Harry can hear him speaking with someone. He turns his attention back to Harry. "Mate, I've got to go – dinner's on the table."

"Oh no, please don't," Harry pleads. "I just got home and Martha is in an absolutely foul mood. You aren't going to leave me to deal with that, are you? Where's the friendship?"

James laughs. "Come on, Harry. You're a big boy, you can handle a testy wife."

Harry moans a little while longer, but James quickly gets bored and ends the conversation. Harry is left to ponder James's theory. The more he thinks about it, the more sense it starts to make.

Things were getting rocky for a second there. The detectives weren't taking my letters in the right direction. That could have really messed things up. They'd gotten back on track, though. My track. And it wasn't long until that train came to its final destination.

CHAPTER 74 - AVERY

It's 3:07pm. I haven't heard from Him all day. Literally all day. Not a *good morning* text. Not a *how's your day going* text. Not an *I miss you* text. Just radio silence.

I've messaged Him a few times to check in, as well. No reply. I've even called Him twice.

I've just come out of my last meeting of the day. It's safe to say it did not go well. I couldn't concentrate on selling points, when I haven't heard from Him all day. Especially after Julian's threat. I am fifty/fifty on whether the threat from the bastard after me is serious, since it seems like a pretty convenient tool to blackmail me with. But Julian is different. He doesn't throw words about without intention behind them. And now I haven't heard from Him all day.

As I am driving home, I lose count of the amount of horns that are beeping in my direction. I can't focus properly, let alone drive safely.

When I finally do make it home, I can do nothing but worry and watch the time tick by. One painful second at a time.

3:33pm

3:47pm

4:04pm

Still nothing.

I start to imagine the worst. Since Julian has been in prison, I don't know what he is capable of. How far he is willing to go.

None of this would have happened if I had just told Him, I complain to myself. If I had just built up the courage to come clean, he could've been on the lookout himself. He wouldn't be the sitting duck he is now.

I sit on the couch, staring blankly at the clock. The sound of its *tick* is like a high-pitched ringing in my ear. Every second that goes by is another second that I don't know where he is. What he's doing. Who he's with.

Julian can be charming. He's always been a lad's lad. He could've easily befriended Him. If I had warned Him about Julian, he would know not to fall into his trap. It's my fault. Whatever happens to Him is my fault.

I can't take this any longer. I have to do something to get my mind off Him. I hurl myself from the couch, slip on some running leggings and trainers, put my earphones in, and leave the house.

And I run. I run and run and run. I block out the world and focus on the music playing in my ears. The sound of my foot rebounding off the tarmac is almost hypnotic, it blocks out my thoughts and I think only about where I will next meet the road. If I stop I'll think about Him. If I stop I'll blame myself. If I stop I'll break down.

My music suddenly cuts off. I struggle to pull my phone from my pocket, as I continue at a steady pace, to find the cause.

It's a phone call.

It's a phone call from Him.

I grind myself to a halt.

"Hello? Hello?" I say frantically and out of breath.

"Avery, are you okay?" he replies. His voice is as calm and soft as ever.

I sigh and my knees buckle. "Oh my God, where the hell have you been all day?" My tone is now a mixture of relief and anger.

"I handed my phone in to Apple today to get it fixed. I told you that."

"What? No you didn't," I quickly reply. "I would've remembered that. You definitely didn't tell me." I sigh heavily, trying to regain my breath. "Jesus, I was so worried, I thought something had happened."

I hear Him chuckle softly. "Don't worry, I'm okay. I promise. I'm not going anywhere. Do you want me to come over tonight?"

A million thoughts fly through my mind as I contemplate his question. I'm not contemplating whether or not he should come round. I'm contemplating whether or not I should tell Him. "Yes," I say confidently, "See you at seven. Don't be late." I hang up the phone.

That *yes* isn't for Him, as much as it is for me. This is it. It's time.

CHAPTER 75 - AVERY

I check the time as I get back to my front door – 6:37pm. I was out for a long time.

When I open the door, I'm greeted by an envelope as I cross the threshold.

I kick off my trainers, snatch up the envelope and rip it open whilst heading towards the kitchen.

Once I have poured myself a glass of water and downed three-quarters of it, I turn my attention to the letter.

I'm a little disappointed in you, Avery. I thought you would've caught on by now. Come on, think. Didn't you always get straight A's in school?

How do they know I got straight A's? They must have really done their research. Unless...

My hand jolts, releasing the glass from my fingers as the bang on the door vibrates through the walls. He's early.

I shake the shards of glass from my feet and tiptoe over to the hallway.

He smiles at me. "Hey." His voice makes my knees almost buckle beneath me.

"Hi. You made me jump – come see what you did to my kitchen floor."

As he walks into the house, he leans down to kiss me. "Oh I'm sorry. Did you spill something? I'll help you clean it up." And he goes straight into the kitchen.

By the time I enter the kitchen, he is crouched down with a dustpan and brush, sweeping the shards up. I watch Him, admiring Him.

Is it weird that I kind of love the fact he knows where I keep my dustpan?

As I watch Him, my smile fades and my stomach drops. After this evening, this is all going to change. I don't want to lose this. I can't lose Him.

"Right," he says as he hoists himself back up once the danger of cutting my toe has been eliminated. "Now that's done. Where were we...?" His voice trails off as he approaches me, wrapping his arms around my waist, lifting my feet off the ground and trailing kisses up my neck.

I shut my eyes and give in to Him. I just want to enjoy the moment. At least for a little while.

But my eyes quickly fly back open and I push Him off me, marching into the lounge.

"No, no, no," I murmur. "We can't do any of that. We have to talk."

Taking a seat on the couch, I gesture for Him to join me. He does so hesitantly.

"What's wrong? What do we need to talk about? Is it bad? Is it me? Do you not want to be with me?" I see the worry start to surge up as his imagination begins to wander.

I take his hands and reassure Him. "No, no, it's not you. You've done nothing, you're perfect, we're perfect. I just have to tell you something. Frankly, I think afterwards it might be *you* who doesn't want to be with *me*."

He frowns. "Avery, that could never happen."

I stare into his eyes. *Oh I hope that's true.*

I take in a deep breath. And then another. And then another. With every breath I mean to speak, but I just can't. My voice won't allow it. I know how this is going to go. I don't want to do it. I feel the salty water surge up my throat and it is too late for me to swallow the tears down – they have already started trickling down my cheek.

He wipes them away, pulls me into him and kisses me gently. "Avery, please tell me." His voice is so soft, so comforting. "You know you can tell me anything. Don't be worried, it will be fine."

I believe Him, I do, but I can't stop the tears from streaming. It's uncontrollable. It's like my body knows what's about to happen, even though my mind won't admit it yet.

He pulls me in closer and I wrap my arms around Him, pressing my cheek against his warm chest. I close my eyes, savouring the moment. Making it stay with me forever. Just in case.

"Avery, please." I hear the concern and the worry in his voice. "Tell me what's making you so upset. I'm here for you."

"You don't understand," I muffle into his now dampened shirt. "You don't understand how difficult this is."

"It shouldn't be difficult. You can tell me anything."

"You don't understand," I repeat beneath a flood of tears.

He lifts my head up and our eyes meet. "Avery. You can tell me anything. Absolutely anything. Okay?"

I stare back at Him for what feels like an eternity, oh how I wish I could stay lost in his eyes forever. But I can't. Forever has to end.

Wiping the tears from my face and bringing myself back upright, I close my eyes and take in three deep breaths.

"I kill people."

CHAPTER 76 - AVERY

I count the seconds as my words flow through his brain.

One…He hears me.

Two…He understands what I've said.

Three…He thinks I'm joking.

Four…He considers the possibility that I'm not joking.

Five…He convinces himself that I must be joking. I have to be joking.

Six…He studies the expression on my face.

Seven…He realises that there is nothing funny about my expression.

Eight…He processes the idea that I am serious.

Nine…He now actually, truly understands what I've said.

Ten…His entire facial and bodily expressions change.

The warm, comforting eyes I looked into only a few minutes ago have now closed themselves off to me. His body, which used to be so welcoming and kind, is now stiff and tense. The loving way he looked at me a mere ten seconds ago, has been replaced with the eyes of someone looking at a monster. I'm the monster.

He opens his mouth but no sound comes out. His eyes widen and he ever so slightly moves back into the sofa – away from me.

"I…I…I don't understand," he stutters. His voice is no longer gentle, but harsh and hostile. "I don't understand. You…*kill* people. What do you mean you kill people? You can't kill people. That's impossible." A shakiness develops in his voice. "You kill people? How can you do that?"

The tears start to fall again. Seeing the way he is seeing at me. Seeing the way he is *thinking* about me. It makes me crumble.

"I don't know," I whimper. "I just do. I just always have."

His eyes widen more. "What do you mean, you always have? When did you start? How many people have you killed, Avery?"

I breathe in salt-water-filled air. "I first killed two people when I was sixteen," I mumble through tear-soaked hair. "Since then I've killed nineteen people."

His expression isn't changing with new information, now. It's as if his face is completely paralysed. He can't even process what I'm telling Him anymore.

"Nineteen people," he repeats, with a scarily calm tone. "You have killed nineteen people. Is..." His voice trails off and I see a new, awful thought come into his head. "Is that why you went out with me? Because you wanted to kill me?" The fear in his voice increases with every word. "Do you still want to kill me? Are you going to kill me?"

"What? No, no." I stretch out for his hand but he quickly takes it out of my reach. "No, it doesn't work like that, I wouldn't do that, I just, it's not..."

"Then how does it work, Avery? How do you choose your victims? Do you pick them out of a hat? Jesus, this is sick. How have you not been put in prison?"

"It's hard to explain!" I exclaim. "I follow people who fit the tale. And then if..." My voice fades out, I have no idea what I'm saying now. I have no idea what there is to say.

"What do you mean a *tale*?" he asks. But he answers the question himself. He gasps and edges further away from me. "You're the Grimm Reaper."

There is no tone of a question. I don't need to say anything. I *can't* say anything. Al I can do is wipe the tears as they continue to blur up my vision. In a way it's a blessing, I can't bear to see the horrified expression in his eyes.

"You're the Grimm Reaper," he repeats. "I don't understand, please, Avery, explain this to me. You have to explain this to me."

"I just enjoy killing people," I mumble with my head held low. I can't look into his eyes. "Everyone enjoys different things. Everyone has different hobbies. I can't explain it, I just do. So I do."

He shakes his head vigorously. "No. No, I don't accept that. You can't kill people for no reason. You're supposed to have a reason. You have to have a reason." He sighs. "Jesus, Avery, why did you even tell me this?"

"Because of what you said. You said you loved me. You said you would accept me no matter what." As I recall the memory, my voice turns high-pitched and it's nearly impossible to make out what I'm saying. "You said I could tell you anything."

He doesn't respond. He sits there, in silence, staring at the coffee table; he can't even look at me. Seconds go by…then minutes…then ten minutes…

I won't allow myself to break the silence. I don't even know what I can say. I have to let him process this. I have to let him deal with this.

"You're right," he finally says. "I did say that you could tell me anything."

Just for a moment, I feel the corners of my lips turn up. Just briefly. "There's more." I cough. "You know that I told you I gamble and that's why someone was threatening me?" I wait for his nod before continuing. "Well, I don't gamble. There's someone after me because they know who I am and they know what I do. They want to take me down."

"Well I can't really blame them," he murmurs under his breath.

This time mine are the eyes that widen. He sees this and his expression turns defensive.

"I'm sorry, Avery, but come on. You *kill* people. People are supposed to go to jail for that."

I gulp down further tears and tell Him the part I've been dreading the most. "The thing is," I begin, "The person after me has been watching my every move. They know that you're important to me, and now they're threatening you."

"Are you kidding me?" he replies with a tiny spark of fire in his eyes. "You *kill* people. Someone is trying to bring you to justice and now you've put me in danger? Jesus, did you even mean it when you said you loved me?"

"Yes, of course I did!" I wail immediately, my heart jumping at the accusation. "I'm sorry, I didn't know what to do." The tears start surging again. "I didn't know how to handle it. I didn't want to stop seeing you, but I didn't want to tell you. Not until you said you accepted me. Not until you said I could tell you anything."

He sighs, glancing down at the floor. "I did say that. And I'm sorry. I'm sorry because I am a man of my word and when I say you can tell me anything and it changes nothing, I stick to that." My spirits lift as he speaks and I think for just a second this could end well. "But I don't know if I can stand by my word this time. This is too much."

"No," I mumble. "No, please. We can get past this. Please, nothing has to change. I'm still the same person. I'm still the person you fell in love with. Please don't do this."

I reach out for Him but he pushes me away. "I'm sorry, Avery. It's not the same now. I can't see you in the same way. I have to take some time to think."

He stands up and heads into the hallway.

Giving me one last glance, he opens the door. I don't know the glimmer in his eye, I've never seen it before. I soak in his appearance, knowing full well this might be the last time I ever see Him. And before I know it, he's gone.

My entire body vibrates with the door as it slams shut. He slammed it shut.

My hands lie in my lap and collect the pools of water that fall from my face. I shriek and weep for hours, going over what happened and trying to convince myself that it didn't. That he still loves me. That we're fine. But we aren't.

He rejected me. He doesn't accept me for me. He's gone. I've lost Him.

CHAPTER 77 - HARRY

"Honestly, don't worry about it, mate – I've got it," James insists. "You go have lunch with Martha and I'll look over the case. Okay? It doesn't take two of us. I can just fill you in when you're back."

Harry sighs. "Are you sure?"

Nudging him, James replies, "Yeah of course. Your marriage is important. Besides, I'm the brains behind this anyway, right?" James says. As he laughs, his belly jiggles up and down a little.

"Okay, okay," Harry finally agrees. "I'll see you in a bit – I won't be long."

Harry arranged to have lunch with Martha because he thought maybe he should start making a bit more of an effort. He wants them to be in a relatively stable place – even if it's all going to come tumbling down.

Speaking of which, he hasn't heard from them since Friday. He's getting worried again, now. What if their guilt of ruining a marriage has got the better of them? Harry feels like lately all he does is try and persuade them not to feel guilty, but he doesn't think it's done much good.

"Hey." Harry greets Martha with a kiss on the cheek. "How has your morning been, babe?"

Martha shrugs. She seems somewhat nervous, as if this is an actual date rather than lunch with her husband. "Same old, really. Just boring office work. How about you?"

"Me too. We think we're slowly scratching away at this case – but it feels like there's still a long way to go."

There's a certain pretence in their tones, today. Both of them are being far too polite. Both of them are smiling as though they are meeting a business partner. Although they are staring right at each other, there is a concrete wall between them.

"Oh my goodness, well hello, you two!" Heidi exclaims as she bounces over. "I swear, I see you guys so often every week but never together! It truly is the craziest thing that you guys don't just run into each other when you're coming in here. My goodness, well it's so nice to see you two together, such a lovely couple." Heidi gasps. "Oh look at me rambling on. Would you believe I've almost got through half my life and I still haven't learnt when to shut my mouth? But anyway, what can I get you two?"

"I'll just have a BLT and a black coffee, please, Heidi," Harry says.

Immediately after, Martha smiles at her. "Can I get the cheese and ham toastie and another cup of the same? Thanks."

When she is gone, they turn back to each other and smile. They've known each other their entire lives, but today they have nothing to say. There's a coldness in the air between them. One that hasn't been there before.

After a few minutes of silence, Harry's vibrating phone saves him. He glances down at the caller ID.

"Sorry, babe," he says to Martha. "Do you mind if I get this? It's the station."

She shakes her head; Harry skids his chair back and heads for the toilet. When he is in a locked stall he picks up the call.

"Where have you been the last few days? I've been calling nonstop. I've been getting worried."

For a long moment, there is silence on the other end before Harry hears a faint sigh and the sound of footsteps. "I'm done. I can't do this anymore."

"What do you mean? After all this, you're going to walk away from me now? Come on, don't do this."

"No. I mean it this time. I can't do it, it's killing me. We're through. Don't contact me again."

The line goes flat.

"Dammit!" Harry exclaims as he punches the wall next to him.

He sits on the toilet seat for several minutes, trying to calm himself down before going back out to Martha. If he goes out in the state he's in now, she's sure to know that something is up.

When Harry has collected his scattered mind, he calms his boiling veins and heads back out to the table. The food has arrived by the time he does.

He breathes the cheesy goodness steaming off Martha's food. "Mm," he moans, "That smells amazing – I should have got that. Oh well, next time."

Martha smiles in response but there doesn't seem to be any sincerity behind her lips. She gulps down a large bite of bread, abruptly places the toastie back on its plate and sits with her back pressed against the chair, staring at him.

He frowns. "What?"

She sighs and then slowly says, "I want a divorce."

Harry chokes on the tomato he is trying to swallow. Once his airway is clear, he looks at her with wide eyes. "What?"

"I want a divorce!" she repeats. As her words spill out, the entire café flicks their attention towards them.

"Martha, you don't mean that. Sure we've been going through a rocky patch lately, but all marriages have—"

"We're not happy, James," she interrupts him.

He drops his sandwich and stares back at her. "You haven't called me that in twelve years."

"I know," Martha mumbles. "I haven't called you by your real name in twelve years."

"That's not my name—"

"Yes it is!" she exclaims. "This is our problem. Don't you see? You never worked through what happened. And I was part of that time, for you. I've come to realise that I am a constant reminder of what happened – and you've never worked through it. After all the therapy sessions, the medication, the illnesses…you pretended that you were fine but you weren't. You're still not. I have a feeling that I'm part of the reason."

"Martha…" Harry begins, although he has no idea where he's going with it.

"We had a good run," she continues. "Really, we did. But I think we're at different points in our lives now. The only way I can be what you need me to be is if I'm not with you. The only way you can become the little boy that I fell in love with again, is if we're apart. I've been thinking about this for a long time now. It's the right thing for the both of us."

Harry is speechless – he can't process what she is saying. It's crazy. He and Martha have been together their entire lives. They can't suddenly be apart.

"I've arranged to stay with my sister until we work out the details of it all and I can find a permanent place to live." After she has collected her coat from the back of the chair and swung her handbag over her shoulder, she reaches out and takes Harry's hand. "We'll still be in each other's lives. It just can't be in the same way." She then bends down, kisses his cheek and walks away. Leaving him there alone.

Harry sits there, motionless. He doesn't know how long for. He doesn't know what to think or to feel.

The thing that scares him the most about this, is that he doesn't care.

CHAPTER 78 - HARRY

"Hey, hey, hey," James greets Harry enthusiastically. "Ready for some good news? The CCTV from the Sleeping Beauty case is being sent over now. How great is that?"

Harry attempts a half-smile and James immediately catches on.

"What's wrong? Lunch didn't go well?"

Harry sighs and slumps down into James's chair, stroking Bertie. "She wants a divorce. She doesn't think we can be what the other needs."

"Oh, man, I'm sorry. That sucks. How are you feeling?"

Harry thinks about the question. He thinks about it deeply. But he can't come up with an answer. So, he changes the subject. "Fine, let's have a look at this footage, shall we?"

James is quick to catch on to the fact that Harry doesn't want to talk about it and he goes along with the subject change. "Absolutely, I was just downloading it onto my computer so it should be done now. Oh would you look at that," James says as he studies the screen. "It is! Let's catch this bastard, shall we?"

"Sounds good to me," Harry agrees and hits the *play* button.

They fast-forward through several of the cameras when they show nothing to help the case. They have to go through eleven cameras, so they know they're going to be there for a while. By the ninth, it gets rather hard to stay as focused as they were at camera one, so it isn't surprising when they miss something.

"Wait," Harry suddenly exclaims.

James is startled by his sudden outburst. "I'm getting old, don't give me a heart attack. What have you seen?"

"Just go back to camera nine."

"There wasn't anything on that camera, let's just keep going, we've only got a couple left."

"No," Harry says firmly. "I really think I saw something, can we just go back? It will take two seconds."

James reluctantly agrees and rewinds through camera nine. Harry's eyes are intently fixed on the screen.

"Stop!" he exclaims and James does as he says. He points to a vehicle displayed at the back left corner of the screen. Parked right outside Sleeping Beauty's house. "There, can you zoom in?"

Sighing, James insists, "I really don't think it's anything."

"Just do it."

James takes the image closer in until the vehicle fills the screen. Harry studies the pixelated image.

"James," Harry says with a reservation in his voice. "Is that..." He looks closer before taking himself back from the desk and from James. "James, that's your car."

As soon as Harry says this, James quickly closes down the screen and slowly turns to face Harry, with his mouth open but no sound coming out.

Harry jumps to accusations, the betrayal making his palms twitch. "Why the hell is your car outside the victims' house on the night they were murdered?"

James holds his hands up. "Look, Harry, I didn't want you to see it because it's really not a big deal. I knew how you'd react." James's voice is calm and gentle. "Please don't think anything of it, okay? Let's just go back to the footage and see if we can see this person."

Harry backs away. "Did you see it? Did you see what happened? You were there. I can't believe you were there."

With a more angry voice, James replies, "of course I didn't see it! I know that as a detective you shouldn't believe in coincidences but just this once I'm telling you that it is one. I didn't want to tell you because I thought it would jeopardise the investigation and by the time I'm cleared, we'd have lost our window of catching GR."

Shaking his head, Harry throws his hands over his open mouth and through them he murmurs, "I can't believe this. You've lied to me this entire time. I need to tell Chief." He announces and marches towards the door.

"Chief already knows," James calls. Harry turns back around. "Chief knows. See? I told you not to worry about it. I didn't see anything at all – if I had done, I would've said something. Please, you've got to trust me, okay?"

Harry ponders the idea for a few seconds, but eventually he nods his head reluctantly and walks back over to James.

James thinks Harry has accepted it. James thinks Harry believes him.

James is wrong

CHAPTER 79 - AVERY

It's been seven days. *Seven days*. He hasn't said anything to me. Nothing. Not a single word.

Granted, I haven't called or messaged Him either, but I feel like under these circumstances, he should be the one to contact me when he's ready.

He's really making me sweat, though. I know that our last conversation didn't go as well as I would have hoped, but I'm still holding on to that frayed strand of thread that he might come back to me.

I've been trying to focus on them. I've been trying to make sense of their recent letters. What do they mean? Are they giving me a clue? Or are they just taunting me?

For the fourth time this week, I throw on my trainers, get out the door and head to the woods. I need to get out of my head.

This afternoon, running does the exact opposite of what I want it to. Instead of forgetting about everything, all I can do is think about everything.

You can't kill people for no reason...you have to have a reason...

I shriek as I stumble over a tree root.

Hickory dickory dock...the mouse runs up the clock...

What do you mean, the tale...You're the Grimm Reaper...

I can feel the trees closing in on me. They're trying to trap me. I run faster, but I can't escape them. Everywhere I turn there are trees, there are bushes blocking my way. There's no way out.

The animals are joining in now, too. I can hear the squirrels scuttling all through the bushes and up the branches. They're cornering me.

The clock strikes one...

Did you even mean it when you said you loved me...

My heart is pounding so vigorously, I can feel my ribcage crack a little bit with every beat.

The mouse never comes down...

The mouse never comes down...

Something starts to come back to me. Images flashing across my eyes. I can't make it out.

Never comes down...

Never comes down...

Didn't you always get straight A's in school...

I can see something. It's blurry, but I can see it. What is it...?

The mouse never comes down...

Never comes down...

I grind to a halt, keel over and trying to regain my breath.

"Christ, of course!" I gasp through crushed lungs. I can't believe I didn't realise. "Stupid," I growl at myself.

Once the force of my heart is no longer a danger to my ribs, I spin back around and sprint home. The trees aren't closing in on me anymore, instead they are parting, guiding the way. It's as if every tree root shrivels up as I come past, so that they don't slow me down. I have to get back. I have to make sure.

I get home and slam the door shut behind me before dialling Todd's number.

I can feel him staring at his phone, watching it ring and contemplating whether to answer. He does.

Wise choice.

"Tell me you have some good news," I say as soon as I hear his breathing.

"I've got the video," he states flatly.

I crouch down with a grin on my face and jump back up. *Yes!* "Great, send it to me now."

"Okay," Todd replies hesitantly. "But, Avery, I only got you the camera that shows the front of the victims' house – I could only snag one since the others were given to the police and I thought that was the best one to give you. But this means we're square – even if you don't find what you're looking for. I don't want to hear from you again."

I laugh at his serious tone. "Sweetie, I would love nothing more than for us to never speak again. Have you sent it?"

I hear some clicks before he says, "yes. Goodbye, Avery."

After hanging up, I download the video. This is it.

I'm about to open up the file when there is a knock at my door. *Inconvenient…* I moan as I get up from my desk to answer it.

There is no one there – only a letter. The final letter.

I pick it up and head back over to the desk.

The video loads and I fast-forward through the footage until I see it. Until I see them. I squint my eyes, creeping closer to my screen. I can see their face. Finally.

"That little bastard."

Ripping the letter open, I feel the blood rush up to my face and its simmer turns to a boil.

Meet me at ten. You know where.

I give the letter a sideways grin and as I'm getting up, ready to face them once and for all, my phone buzzes. It's Him.

Avery, I'm sorry I haven't contacted you. I needed time to think things through. But I'm ready to meet, now. I need to meet. Please, come and see me. Right now. It's urgent. I really need to see you.

I stare down at the message. The butterflies I missed so much, finally woke up again. But I have to go and meet them, I have to finish this. Don't I? If not for me, then for Him. So that he's safe again.

But I want to see Him. What if this is my only chance to make things right?

I don't know who to listen to. My reason or my emotion.

This was it. Finally, I was going to confront her. I had been waiting for this moment for as long as I could remember. It was finally here.

CHAPTER 80 - AVERY

There it is. The rundown, little old cottage of my childhood memories. I haven't been here in years and now I've visited twice in one week. This will be the last time, though. The last time ever.

Everything is silent. The trees whipped by the breeze are pushing its force onto me, causing my hair to fly across my face, obscuring my vision. The wind doesn't speak to me, like it usually does. It isn't warning me to stay away, it isn't warning me to stay home. It just caresses my face with its icy hand and the fair hairs on my cheeks stand up, attracted to it like an iron nail to a magnet.

The house sulks. Its cracked lips and droopy eyes weep, hurt by its abandonment. It hasn't forgiven me for leaving it, for leaving it all alone. Its only company being the rodents that have invaded its rotting foundations.

I walk around its perimeter, trying to follow the stepping stone pathway. Although, it isn't easy, since the stones are disguised by the weeds and flowers that have overcome them.

As I reach the back, I see the wooden gate leading into the garden. Without it even crossing my mind, I lift the latch, kick the door up with my foot and hurl it open. I may not have been through this gate since I was a teenager, but my muscles still remember its quirks.

I'm startled by the sudden pressure I feel on my head. Then another jolt of pressure. I touch my hair and feeling its dampness, I cover it with my hands as the droplets begin to fall faster and heavier, hurrying to the back door on my tiptoes.

Yanking the handle upwards, I throw my shoulder into the door and I hear a crack as its frame gives and I stumble into the dust and the cobwebs.

Shaking myself off, I take a step forward and cringe as I hear the squelching of my soaked shoe.

I shriek and my entire body shivers as I suddenly catch sight of an eight-legged arachnoid creeping up my shoulder.

I fucking hate spiders.

I don't bother looking around the house for them – I know where they'll be.

A slideshow of memories shoots across my vision as I walk through the kitchen, through the dining room.

I stop and stare at the oak table. Amongst all the carnage I have walked through, this has managed to sustain itself. It doesn't look much different from the last time I sat at it.

"Ave, you've got to take a break at some point," Mum insisted. Come on, let's go shopping. My treat."

I firmly shook my head. "Nope, I still have three units of chemistry to study."

She sighed. "Okay, let me help you then." She picked up the revision sheet I had just written and began shooting questions at me. "What's the cathode?"

"It's the negative electrode used to separate compounds in electrolysis," I instantly replied, my mind on auto-pilot.

"What state does the compound have to be in to work? Why?"

"A liquid state because the ions have to be free to move."

"Last question…what happens when you apply the process to aluminium oxide?"

"Um…" I suddenly had a mental blank. "Aluminium goes to positive electrode and oxygen to the negative – then aluminium settles at the bottom?"

Mum scrunched up her face. "Sorry, Ave, aluminium goes to the negative and oxygen to the positive."

I threw my pen across the table. "Dammit."

Mum put her hand on my shoulder. "Don't worry, honey. You'll get it. Of course you'll get it."

The corners of my lips turn up slightly at the memory. As I stroll through the corridor, I run my fingertips along the dust-stained walls, feeling every ridge and uneven texture. My hand stops over a circular indent in the wall. That's where Dad hit the hockey ball into the wall. It was raining nonstop that day. I was seven, and hanging around indoors all day didn't sound like fun at all. So, Dad brought the outdoor games inside.

"Ready, Ave? Remember, eyes on the ball," he said as he lifted the hockey stick above his head, brought it down and the ball went flying. Right into the wall.

We both stared at the hockey ball shaped hole with contorted faces. He hurried towards me with a silly grin on his face, put his finger to his mouth and whispered, "Shhh, don't tell Mum."

Dad and I always had our little secrets. We'd always giggle at the dinner table at our silly inside jokes and at Mum getting frustrated that she wasn't 'in the loop'. Mum used to act annoyed, but I think she was only pretending – she secretly loved how close we used to be.

I enter the lounge and as I walk through it, I admire the soft leather couch and breathe in its addictive scent. I modelled my own living room on this room. The one thing my mother always had is good taste. Must be where I got it from.

When I hear a shuffling behind me, I quickly spin round.

There, lurking in the shadow of the doorway, is the person who has been lurking in my shadow all this time.

As they step forward, the sun's light that has sneaked past the moon illuminates their face. Their eyes reflect the light and their grimace glows.

"Hello, Avery."

THEM

"Hello," she replies in the same tone as me. My heart is pounding so hard as I study her. I can't believe we're finally here. The truth can finally come out.

I clear my throat, suddenly nervous of her presence. "So nice to see you again." She's finally here, in front of me. We're finally face to face.

She smiles back at me. "Likewise." Laughing slightly, she begins to approach me. I instinctively jump backwards. As soon as I do, I scold myself. I can't be afraid of her now. "Oh, sweetie, I still make you jump. After all this time – haven't you grown up at all?"

"You don't make me jump," I snap back a little too hastily. "You just disgust me. I don't want to be anywhere near you."

She clasps her hands to her chest. "Wow, that really hurts. I have to say, your letters gave me an entirely different impression." She stops in line with the couch and gives me a sideways glance. "Will you stop looking at me like that? It's creepy."

I immediately concede to her, but I have to force myself to stand back upright. I continue to stare. "I've thought about you every single night before I go to sleep. It's the only way I can sleep peacefully, now. By imagining you and imagining you behind bars." I glance down and smile. "I've thought about this moment every day. I planned out every detail. Although, I didn't plan for how amazing it would feel to see you here, in front of me. Doing as *I* want, since *I'm* the one with all the power. *I* am in control of *you*."

She doesn't argue, she knows I'm right. She simply smiles at me. Her expression seems affectionate – it confuses me. "Oh, sweetie, I'm proud of you. Really, I am. I couldn't have wanted anything more for my little brother."

AVERY

His eyes suddenly roar. "*Don't* call me that!" he exclaims. "You do not deserve the right to call me that."

His eyes glisten. It seems as though I've struck a nerve. "Oh come now, don't be like that," I reply in a calm, soft voice. "I know we've got our history, but it's time to rebuild those bridges. Don't you agree?"

Throwing his head back, he laughs. "Those bridges never even existed."

I shrug. "Okay, if that's what you want. It'll take time but I'll get over it. So," I spark up with a newfound intrigue, "why don't you tell me what you had cooked up for your big sis? I have to say, I definitely taught you well – you really had me going for a minute there. Cinderella's little quest for vengeance was your doing, I take it."

He doesn't even blink. "She was a lovely girl. It was truly sad what you did to her."

"Oh please," I interrupt. "You wanted me to kill her. You put her up to it, didn't you?"

"I may have convinced her that the only way to get closure was to bring you to justice, and I may have pointed her in the direction of where she might find you."

I snap my fingers. "I knew it. I knew she wasn't smart enough to find me all by her lonesome. So, I kill Cinderella and my DNA is at the crime scene. How was that going to get me into the interrogation room?"

"I'm not stupid. I do have some experience," he snaps, "I knew that wouldn't be enough to get you charged. Besides, I didn't just want you in jail, I wanted you to pay for all your crimes. I had no choice. I had to do it."

I tut, shaking my head. "Poor Sleeping Beauty. She wasn't even my next tale, she had a long, happy life to live before I put a tick next to her name. How could you do that? How could you be such a monster?"

"I'm not a monster!" he shouts with a fragile voice. "I had no choice. They had to die. It was the only way I could make sure you would definitely be brought to justice. So no one else would get hurt."

"Okay," I chuckle, "you keep telling yourself that, if it helps you sleep at night. But you're just lying to yourself. Admit it – you're just as bad as me. Worse, in fact. I don't pretend like I kill people because of some twisted sense of justice that I've made myself believe."

"Stop it," he warns me. I don't listen.

"But you have, haven't you? You've tried to make the act better. You've tried to make yourself better than me."

"Stop it!"

"But you're no better than me. How can you even look yourself in the mirror, knowing that you have become the same monster you think I am?"

"I'm not a monster!" He growls and lunges at me. The blade catches the moonlight and I quickly jerk out the way. He falls past me.

"Now, now. Let's not do that. If you kill me, where's that justice you've worked so hard for? All of this – those four women you killed – will all be for nothing."

I can hear his breath from across the room reaching the hairs on the back of my neck. My heartrate remains steady and I continue to treat this how I intended – like a business deal. My poor little brother has never been able to stand up to me. Just because he has a knife, doesn't mean he's going to be able to now.

"So let me guess," I begin again once I hear his breathing has calmed slightly. "You ensured they would find my DNA at the Cinderella and Sleeping Beauty crime scenes…then assumed they'd make the link when they discovered it matched…but then what? You still haven't explained how you were planning to get me on their persons of interest list." I spin round and gasp. "Oh wait, could you have been stupid enough to, I don't know, plant recording devices around this house, expecting me to admit it all to you when we met?" I ask as I reveal the devices I have zipped up in my pocket.

His eyes flare when he sees them. "How did you find them?"

"You seriously think this is my first rodeo? I'm not stupid. Oh, James...have you not seen every crime movie ever?"

His face goes stiff. "That is *not* my name."

"Ooh, my bad." I contort my face. "I forgot – you changed it, didn't you? Harry... Was that to honour Dad? How did it feel, by the way? Taking your *wife's* name instead of her taking *yours*?" I look down, trying to withhold my laughter. "That must have been very emasculating."

"You changed your name too!" he blurts before taking a deep breath. "Besides, I didn't care. I just wanted to be rid of all my connection to you. She understood."

"Of course she did," I agree. "She has been with you through it all, hasn't she? How is my sister-in-law, by the way? I saw her the other day, although I didn't recognise her – she really has changed. Is it rude of me to say she's changed in width?" I see his eyes widen and I hear his teeth grind. I hold my hands up in defence. "Well it's true...you know what they say, putting on weight usually means an unhappy marriage..."

"Don't you dare comment on my marriage."

"Okay, okay. Anyway, that's not the bit I'm interested in. No, I didn't remember Martha until this afternoon. Suddenly, it all clicked."

THEM

"I've been watching you for years, working on my case, trying to figure out who I am. Granted, I didn't realise it was you for a good few years, but when I did and I started getting these letters? You didn't even cross my mind. Props to you, you really are a great actor – you fooled me. And then I remembered…"

"James…" Mum warned me. I kept jumping out of bed and running into the closet. "Come on, honey. It's time for bed."

"I can't believe I have to share a room with my seven-year-old brother – I'm fourteen! It's just embarrassing."

"Ave, come on, can you be a little more accommodating? It's only until the renovations have been done, okay?"

Avery groaned and turned away from her, facing the wall. Mum turned back to me.

"Now, James, why don't you and I sing the song we learnt today?"

"Yes, yay! Okay…hickory dickory dock, the mouse runs up the clock…" I began, waiting for Mum to join in.

"The clock strikes one…"

"The mouse runs down!" I shrieked. "Hickory dickory dock."

Mum smiled at me, kissing my forehead and wishing me goodnight.

I snuggled up with my new teddy, closed my eyes and started falling asleep.

A few minutes later, I heard Avery roll over, lean towards me and whisper, "the mouse never comes down."

I watch her as she runs her fingers along the wooden column. "I can't believe this is still here," she remarks.

I don't need to see to know what she is referring to. As I see her trace the line she once carved, I feel the rage surging up my spine. "You killed them!" I burst. "You killed them and you were going to kill me! You planned it all out, it wasn't in the moment, it was all planned out. You went to a sleepover, you snuck back in in the middle of the night...Why? Why would you do that? What did they ever do but love you? What did *I* ever do to you?"

She shakes her head and sighs, "They didn't do anything to me, James. The thought was always floating around in the back of my mind and frankly, I just wanted to know what it would feel like. And you know what? It was amazing. As for you, you were more just to finish off the tale – I've never liked loose ends." She glances down. "But, I was inexperienced back then, I hadn't quite established what I did and didn't like – that's why I left you. I didn't think that Baby Bear needed to die as well. Well, I did sort of complete the tale, I suppose..."

I hold back tears as I remember. I don't look at her – I can't. I just go into my pocket and pull out the picture. The picture of Mum, Dad and Lucy. One tear manages to escape my blockade and trickles down my cheek. I am quick to wipe it away. She can't see me being weak.

She approaches me slightly to get a better view of the photo. "That really hurts, James, why would you cut me out? That's just really rude."

I sniffle and collect myself again. When I can muster the strength, I stare her straight in the eyes and smile. "You think you've got it all figured out, don't you? You think you're so goddamn smart. You didn't see this coming, though."

Once I finish talking, a silhouette appears in the doorway behind her.

AVERY

It takes me a few seconds to process what he is saying. What does he mean by this? See what coming? Why is he wearing such a smug little grin?

Then I feel the hairs on the back of my neck stand up as they detect the warm breath. I recognise that breath.

I don't want to turn around. I don't want to face it. I don't want it to be true. It can't be true.

"Avery."

My knees buckle as I hear his voice and I can't control the river flowing from my eyes. I stare at my feet. I fixate on them. I can't look anywhere else. I can't look at either of them.

I see James, though, in my peripheral vision. I see the grin smeared across his face. Seeing how much he enjoys this makes the tears fall harder.

His hands slide down my shoulders and gently grip my arms, helping me to my feet. As soon as my brittle legs will take my weight, I throw Him away from me.

"Don't touch me!" I scream through sobs.

Though my vision is completely blurred by the salt water filling my eyes, I can see the tears fall onto his face. "I'm sorry, Avery. I'm so sorry."

"How could you do this?" I whisper, since I can't will my voice to produce any significant sound.

"I'm so sorry...I didn't want to do this," he weeps, "I'm so sorry."

Through the ringing in my ears, I hear James sigh, "Well since you two are incapable of communicating properly, I'll just explain, shall I?" The joy in his voice rips right through me. "Your boyfriend here got into a little bit of trouble, didn't you?" James addresses Him, with a patronising expression and high-pitched tone before turning back to me. "He was arrested for being involved in a knife fight back in March. Now, usually, he wouldn't be looking at that bad of a punishment, but this knife fight happened to be involved in an ongoing drug investigation. Do you know what that means, Avery? That means as a detective I could have planted all the evidence on him. I could've put him in jail for the rest of his sorry little life."

"I had no choice." He sniffles. "I couldn't spend the rest of my life in prison. I didn't know I would get so…attached."

"Aw, poor soul. In case you haven't quite caught on yet, Avery, his meeting you wasn't a coincidence. He wasn't struck by your beauty and hypnotised by your magnificent eyes. He knew where you'd be. He knew what to say."

"What was the aim then?" I turn to James, merely trying to avoid his eyes. "You wanted me to fall in love and then get betrayed? So I would know how it felt?"

He laughs. "Oh no, that was just a bonus. No, every single time he's been with you he's been wearing a wire. His instructions were very simple; get close enough to you so that you trust him, then slowly coax out your secret."

I gawk at Him. "So you knew all along?"

"Oh no, don't get all hot-headed. I didn't tell him *what* secret to get from you, I just told him that you were key in an ongoing investigation. You really think he would've taken a second look at you if he knew your secret from the beginning?" He laughs. "That's quite something, I thought you were supposed to be smart. But anyway, you can never trust anyone, can you? You never trusted him enough to tell him – even when I made him a target."

My eyes quickly flicker onto his, confused. But in the millisecond that our eyes meet, I know what he did. He lied. He lied to protect me.

"You know—" I turn my attention back to James as he starts speaking again. "After years and years of therapy sessions and drugs and Martha telling me to get on with my life, I really wanted to. At first, I changed my name because I wanted to avoid the association with what happened. You moved away – by the time you came back everyone had forgotten about the Grimm Reaper's first victims. But I have always been here. I had to change my name. If I didn't, I would forever be the poor little boy who lost his parents and escaped death. I wanted to do some good for the world. I thought the only way for me to do that was by becoming a police officer. Martha and I had just got married, I was about to go to my first day on the job. My life was good. I was happy."

Since my tears have now calmed themselves down, I ask, my tone trembling more than I want it to, "So what changed?"

"I saw you," he replies. "I saw you across the coffee shop, sitting in the corner, tapping away at your computer. Even though I hadn't seen you in nine years, I instantly knew who you were. As soon as I looked at your face, all those therapy sessions never happened. I was that nine-year-old boy again, walking into this living room and finding his parents. Dead. All the rage came back. I realised that the only way to move on was to take you down."

I take a deep breath, collecting myself. "Well, you played a really good game. I'm very impressed. But it's time for this to end."

I pull out my phone, bring up the video and press *play*.

THEM

"Hey, Chief, I need to talk to you about something."

I recognise that voice – that's James.

"I've been going back through old GR cases since the one from September last year and I found something."

"Well," Chief said, "What is it? Why aren't you discussing this with Ellis?"

"That's just it. DC Ellis is actually James Foster. As in James Foster, the son that escaped from GR's first case."

"How on earth did that not go through our system when he joined the force?" Chief's voice was angry now.

"He changed his name a couple years before. I guess he just didn't disclose the name change. But it got me thinking…if he hid that from us, what else could he be hiding? When the Little Mermaid case happened, I slipped into the conversation what he was doing that night and he lied."

I hear James sigh.

"I can't really believe it. When he came into this department, I took him under my wing. I stuck up for him when the others were bashing him about. And he's been involved all this time? I was going to confront him about it-"

""No!" Chief abruptly interrupted. "No, absolutely not. If you're suspecting what I'm suspecting, then this could be the answer to a fifteen-year-old case. We have to let this play out. He cannot know that we are even the slightest bit aware of his real identity. I want you to follow him – everywhere he goes. Keep close to him and keep friendly with him. Find out who he talks to,

*if he's hiding anything and report back to me. This has to be a slow process.
We can't risk him finding out we're onto him."*

*"But," James protests, "Chief, he's my partner on the case. We're together
nearly every day, he'll see right through me."*

"Well then, you better invest in an acting class."

I stare at Avery's phone, completely speechless. James has been playing
me, this entire time. Was he ever really my friend?

"That was my reaction too." Avery interrupts my paralysis. "I stumbled upon this recently when I was going back over Little Mermaid's
case. I couldn't believe my luck. Honestly, it was as if the gods were in
my favour after all. So, when I heard that you wanted another sweep of
the Little Mermaid's crime scene, I saw my opportunity and when I paid
a visit to the police station last week, I snuck into your office and took
whatever I was able to find from your cubicle. Since they have a strand of
your hair at the Sleeping Beauty crime – oh and the beer-belly saw you
there – you've practically set yourself up. Oh, and I can't forget the knife.
The knife you gave to me for my birthday? You'll find that tucked neatly
under your front yard. Thank you for that, by the way. I apologise for not
sending a thank-you note – that was rude of me. Mum taught us better
than that."

Her voice trails off and my mind is suddenly taken back to the train,
when my car battery died. The homeless person on the same carriage as
me, or the person I *thought* was homeless. I study his face and realise. It
was him.

I can't speak. I can't. I don't know what there is to say. I shake my head
in disbelief and I have to manually close my mouth. This can't be happening. This can't be happening. After everything. I planned everything.

Once I have swallowed down my denial, I suck in a fragile breath and
with as steady a voice as I can muster, I say, "I'll tell them I've been set up.
Screw getting a confession off you, I'll just give your name to the police.
They'll see you're the victim's daughter and realise you are responsible."

She isn't fazed by my threat. She laughs. *Laughs.* Of all the times I
imagined this scenario, none of them went like this. "They know you've
lied to them about your entire identity. Flynn *saw* you at Sleeping Beauty's house. You really think they're going to believe you? The best chance
you've got is pleading insanity."

"Your heart is as black as the blood on your hands!" I scream at her, unable to fathom this level of rage.

Suddenly, the faint sound of sirens reaches my ears. They reach Avery's at the same time.

"Oh, look at that – they're on their way now," she says, unfazed by my beastly expression. "Don't worry, I'll give you a head start – after all, I am your big sis. Siblings have to look out for each other, don't they?"

The adrenaline floods into my veins. My breath quickens and my heart is punching, aiming for her but being stopped at my ribcage.

I can't hear anything now apart from the blood bursting through my ears. I can't see anything except red spots and the smug grimace on her face. My hands shake as my fingers curl into fists, my left gripping the knife.

She can't get away with this. She can't. She has to pay.

Suddenly my lungs burst out with a roar and I hurl myself onto her.

AVERY

He lunges at me. I'm not prepared for it and I don't get out the way in time. The weight of his body throws me off balance and a burst of pain explodes across the back of my head as it hits the hard surface.

As he falls onto me, the blade grazes my shoulder. I yelp as the skin parts and the blood seeps out. The knife slips out of his hand and he straddles me, clasping his hands over my throat.

"You did this!" he spits at me. "You made me like this! Why did you do it? Why kill our parents then stay playing the grieving little daughter until your chance came to abandon me?"

Gasping for air that repels my throat, I faintly turn up my lip corners and through chokes, reply, "it would…ave…been…" I shriek for a fraction more oxygen. "Suspicious if I…not stay."

He screams into my face. Tightening his hands around my throat, he presses his thumbs into my trachea and my throat tries to cough, but it can't. I gasp for air but my lungs refuse to expand. My arms flail at my sides, smacking into him but having little effect. Every atom in my body shrieks, screaming at me to keep them alive. But I can't. I have no control.

My back arches up, trying to escape the pain.

A few moments later, my body's screams mute and my vision blurs with my eyes rolling back into the abyss.

I leapt up from the uncomfortable chair that was giving me pins and needles as soon as I caught sight of Mum. The nurse was pushing the wheelchair she rested in in my direction.

"Mum!" I ran up to hug her but was abruptly halted by my father blocking my path. I frowned at him.

"Careful, Ave. Don't hurt the baby," he warned as he removed his hand from my shoulder.

My heart was now in my throat, I was terrified of the little ball wrapped up in a blanket on Mum's lap.

"Ave," Mum whispered fragilely, "meet your little brother. James."

I smiled down at my new sibling and gently stroked his rosy cheek. He was so tiny, so frail. So vulnerable.

My parents saw a beaming child, ecstatic at the new family's new arrival. Inside, I was raging.

Suddenly the pressure on my throat is gone and I gasp one last time. This time, my lungs fill up. I cough up the lack of air and choke on the oxygen entering my blood again.

Throwing myself up, I see Him with his foot flattening James's throat, the knife poised in his hand.

I stumble to my feet and while the oxygen is being pumped back into my brain, I throw my arms around Him, laying all my weight onto Him and lowering the hand with the knife in and taking it from Him.

"It's okay," I whisper and gently place my lips against his neck. "I'm fine." The sirens are near, now. "Let him go. He won't get far before they catch him, anyway."

His heavy breath gradually begins to calm. For a second, I see James's eyes wide as the pressure against his throat increases, but then he stomps his foot down beside James's head. James stares at me with wide eyes.

I crouch down to his level, smiling as I stare into his dilated eyes that are a reflection of my mother's. I then unbutton his shirt a few and yank the wire taped to his chest, before crushing the device beneath my shoe and saying, "run, run, as fast as you can, gingerbread man."

He wipes the tears from his face, throws himself up to his feet and without a second look, runs out of the house.

I turn to Him and he pulls me in. I give in to his warm embrace, treasuring it. I never thought I would be able to touch Him again.

"Avery, I'm so sorry. I'm so sorry. I didn't know what I was getting myself into. I didn't know what I was doing." He cups my face and lifts it up so that my eyes are fixed on his. "But you know what? I don't regret it for a moment. Because if I hadn't agreed, I wouldn't have met you. I don't care about your secret, I know we can work through it. I love you."

I swallow down the tears but some of them sneak through and trickle down my face. I lean up on my tiptoes, wrap my arms around him and kiss him. My tears fall down onto our lips and I hold Him there for as long as I can. I don't ever want to let go. But forever has to end.

Pulling away from Him, I see the joy in his face and I trail my fingers along his cheek and jawline, memorising its shape. I drop my hands down from his neck but stay on my tiptoes so that my head is level with his. I then put my lips to his ear and whisper, "hell hath no fury like a woman scorned."

The blade meets his stomach.

CHAPTER 81 - AVERY

His eyes go wide and I feel my hand become wet. I catch Him as he collapses and I lower Him to the ground.

I place my hand over the wound and I cradle Him, my tears melting into his face.

"Why?" he whispers as I stroke his cheek with my shaking hands.

I lean down and kiss his quivering lips. "You'll always be my Prince Charming."

I stay with Him, watching as he fades away. It doesn't take long – a few minutes maybe – but it feels like an eternity. An eternity I want to hold on to forever. But forever has to end. When he's gone, I close his eyelids and pull myself away from Him.

Dragging my knees up and wrapping my arms tightly around them, I rock back and forth and weep. I weep, staring at Him. I can't take my eyes away, as much as I want to, I just can't.

The only reason I know the police have entered the house is the light coming from their torches. I can't hear their cars. I don't hear their sirens. I don't hear their footsteps. I don't hear them talking to me.

All I hear is nothing. And all I see is Him.

CHAPTER 82 - AVERY

"Miss Blake? Miss Blake?" Detective Flynn calls me out of my daze and back into the hostile embrace of the interrogation room.

"Sorry, what was the question?" I ask, although my enthusiasm is lacking.

"It wasn't a question – I was going back over your statement and I wanted you to confirm the details."

I nod my head and he looks down at his notepad.

"So, you've been seeing this man for nearly five months. He took you to this abandoned house – why?"

I gulp down the memory. "Um, he said he discovered it a couple months back and thought it was a cool place. He's always been fascinated by morbid stuff like that. I never understood it. He wanted to show it to me."

"Right, okay. And then he tried to have sex with you and you refused. When you refused him, that's when he started to become aggressive."

I bob my head and answer shakily, "Yes, that's when he forced himself on me."

"Yes okay," Detective Flynn agrees and continues. "This is when things progressed and he threw himself on top of you and began strangling you. When he pulled out the knife you managed to throw him off. How did you have the strength to do that?"

Stroking my sore throat, I shrug. "I don't know. I suppose it's the adrenaline? I read once that we all have a warrior gene that instigates the fight or flight response. Some mothers have lifted entire cars up because their babies are trapped under it. I guess this kicked in and my response was fight."

"Okay. When you got him off you he came at you with the knife, you then grabbed his hand with the knife in and twisted it so that he dropped it. What made you pick up the knife?"

"I had a sudden realisation that it was me or him. I couldn't under-stand what had come over him – he's always been such a loving and caring man. I'd never seen this side of him before. I was so scared, I didn't know what else I could do. I certainly couldn't fight him – he'd easily beat me. I didn't see any other option." I stutter and quickly add, "I didn't think he'd die…I just wanted to injure him so I could get away."

"I understand. How long after you stabbed him, did you call 999?"

"Oh I don't know, time didn't really mean much in that moment. If I had to make a guess, I suppose about two minutes? Once I had processed what had happened, I got straight on the phone to you."

"Thank you, Avery. One finally question, can you please confirm that this is the identity of the man you have been seeing since the beginning of April?"

I lean across the table to get a better view of the sheet of paper. I stare at the man's face for a little longer than I should have. The butterflies gasp at the sight of him, but they quickly skulk back down to the pit of my stomach. "That's Him."

"I'm sorry to say this, Avery, but you are not the first woman to have suffered this violence. The day you met him, we believe he killed another woman in the alley near that coffee shop."

I gasp and throw my hands over my mouth. "Oh my goodness, I had no idea."

"I understand it can be a frightening thought, I'm sorry to have to tell you. We found his DNA on the victim's body and we have phone records from the both of them that suggest they were in a relationship after she split with her husband. We can only presume that the reason for him killing her was the same as what happened to you early this morning."

I glance down to avoid eye contact as the tears begin to form. He doesn't need to see them, though, to know they're there.

"Now, Miss Blake, I want to make something very clear to you." I look back to him. "This man was a dangerous member of society. He killed a woman before you, he was going to harm you and we don't know as of yet who else he may have harmed. I want to make sure you know that you have done a service, here. You have taken a murderer off the streets. Don't blame yourself, okay?"

I sniffle and mutter, "Okay. If it's okay with you I'd like to go home now."

Flynn nods as he stands up. "Absolutely. We will give you a police escort back to your home. First we need to quickly take your fingerprints and a swab sample so that we can eliminate you from the investigation when we go over the scene."

My heart stops. I try and hide my surprise but fail miserably.

"Is that going to be a problem?" he asks.

I smile and say, "no, of course not. I just don't understand why you need it?"

"It's just standard procedure. Even when we have a good idea of how a case plays out we still have to go through with the investigation."

I gulp down my nerves and nod. "Okay, that's fine." And I follow him to the room in which the prints and swab are taken.

Once they are, they are immediately inputted into the system and I catch the screen read *searching*.

"Don't worry," Flynn reassures me. "We just have to run it through the system to see if we already have your prints. So there isn't any confusion."

That most certainly does not make me feel any better. My entire plan is about to crumble.

When the bar reaches 100%, Flynn studies the screen and my breathing starts to quicken in anticipation. This is it. Everything I have built is about to come crashing down. Right onto my head.

Finally, he turns to me, smiling, and announces, "Okay, great. That's all done. Now let's get you home."

I'm completely puzzled by the results. I was prepared for disaster to strike. My prints should definitely be on there. I can't understand why they're not – or if the search missed them. But would that happen?

Regardless of the cause, I count my blessings. Everything could have been for nothing if they'd found a match.

He then leads me out of the interview room, down the hall and heading into the reception. As we go down the corridor, I jump as a mutt hurls himself at the glass door of Flynn's office.

"Oh, sorry about Bertie. He's a very loving dog – he doesn't like to see me go past him."

I offer him a half-smile. "That's okay, I love dogs." I peer into the window, wave my hand and mouth *hi*. Bertie stares at me and instead of jumping up at the glass with enthusiasm like he did when he saw Flynn, instead he curls up his gums, baring his teeth and growls at me.

"That's strange, Bertie usually loves everyone."

I shrug and encourage him to keep walking. I know why Bertie doesn't like me.

Once I get into the police car, I rest my head on the cold glass window, close my eyes and let the world fade away.

CHAPTER 83 - AVERY

"There you go, miss," the officer says to me as we pull up outside my house.

I don't want to get out of the car. I don't want to move. I don't have any energy.

"Miss?" the officer calls after I haven't responded to him.

Slowly turning my head, I give him a brief smile. "Thank you, officer. Have a good day." Although my tone doesn't project sincerity, he nods and says the same to me. I force my feet to step out of the car and my legs to stand up straight.

I don't want to breathe. My ribcage feels too heavy – my lungs aren't strong enough to expand underneath them. I drag my feet up the pathway leading to my front door, tripping over each step as I go. When I reach the top, I poise my key in front of the lock, but I don't have the strength to push it in.

For a while, I stand there, staring at the key loosely held in my frail hand. My brain tells my hand to move, but I can't feel anything past my elbow.

When I lift my head upright, I catch sight of the fuzzy purple monster smiling back at me. I don't want to go in there, with that. I immediately give up, drop the keys in the hanging basket and walk back down the steps.

I don't know where I'm going, I just want to walk. For some absurd reason, I think that if I do, perhaps I'll figure out how I'm feeling. What I'm feeling.

About fifteen minutes later, I find myself in familiar territory. I'm at the park. Our park. I curse my feet for taking me here – this is the last place I wanted to go. But at the same time, I feel comfortable here – like he's with me.

Taking a seat on the bench, I lean my head back and stare mindlessly up at the clouds.

I'm sure there are a million thoughts running through your head right now. Let me settle them for you.

After Cinderella faced me, it didn't take me long to know that I would need to find someone to take the fall for her untimely death. Even if they never linked me to the case, I couldn't live my life wondering *what if?* The case had to close.

As soon as it happened, my plan was to plant it on her husband. It seemed like the easiest, best option and it would be a quick, easy case for the police to close.

However, I had to have a contingency plan. What if the Prince had a strong alibi? What if I couldn't foil it? What if the police didn't think the evidence against him was strong enough?

When I went to the Cosy Coffee to clean myself up, I had all sorts of ideas coming in and out of my mind. Then he showed up. His timing could not have been more perfect. He was my plan B. If the Prince wasn't charged, I could make it seem like he was having an affair with her and he was going to do the same thing to me as he did to her. He wouldn't be around to defend himself. Fool-proof, right?

Wrong. I didn't account for the possibility of me getting attached. I knew I had to be in a relationship with Him to some extent, so that it was believable, but I didn't realise the effect it would have on me. I thought it would be the same attachment I had with Julian – purely physical.

I suppose the question you're all asking is; did I love Him?

Of course I did. The person most surprised by that answer is me. I didn't know I could feel like that. I didn't know I could be as close to someone as that. I so wanted plan A to work. I didn't want to have to do what I did to the one person I think I've ever truly loved. But I love me more.

    And this isn't a fairy tale.

CHAPTER 84 - AVERY

By the time I force myself to return home, the light is beginning to fade away as the sun gives up.

After struggling to open the door for quite some time, I am finally thrown into the hallway. As soon as I do, my shoe lands on something that isn't my wooden floor. I glance down.

Buttercups.

I walk cautiously into the lounge, expecting to see a familiar shadow at my desk – but I am disappointed. Suddenly my radio switches on.

Why do you build me up, Buttercup

Just to let me down, mess me around

Although he is not sitting behind my desk, I can see something lying on it. As I approach it, my vision becomes clear and I see that it is a USB with a tag attached reading *watch me.*

Sitting behind my desk, I open my computer and plug the device in. When I do, a video comes up onto my screen. The quality is poor and the lighting is dark – I can hardly see what it is of.

And then it becomes clear. My jaw drops. I lean forward and listen to my voice.

"I saw my opportunity and when I paid a visit to the police station last week, I snuck into your office…since they have a strand of your hair at the Sleeping Beauty crime – oh and James saw you there – you've practically set yourself up."

The sound crackles. Then another voice speaks.

"They'll see you're the victim's daughter and realise you are responsible."

I squint my eyes as the video suddenly jumps and my dear brother is no longer there. It is Him and me close together. I see myself lean forward and put my lips to his ear. I have to look away for the next part – I can't see it. I won't.

The video jumps again and once I am certain that the scene has changed, I glance back. The camera is on Julian's face.

"Hey, Buttercup. What did you think of my short movie? I'm thinking of entering it in this year's competition. You killing the boy? That was cold, Buttercup – even for you. Then again, I suppose it's for the best. He wasn't right for you, you need someone more like you. Someone more... twisted." His voice is raspy and the camera shakes with each footstep. "But I digress. I told you I would get something on you. A stupid little restraining order can't save you, now. You know," he swallows and glances away for a moment, "you reporting me? It really hurt. I understand why you turned me in, but I never thought you'd want a piece of paper keeping us apart. So, I continued paying visits to your house – when you weren't there of course. I watched hours and hours of CCTV from the station. I get why you enjoy that so much, it really is quite intriguing. But anyway, I'm drifting from my point. So, in one of those Chief-Detective conversations, the fat one doesn't believe your bro did it alone. He still believes there was someone else. And who better than his very own sister to tie it all in pretty little bow, hey?"

He stares directly into the lens. I can feel his eyes on me.

"Oh, now don't worry your pretty little head. You took seven years of my life – you really think I'm going to hand this in to the police and let that be that? Why would I have erased your prints from their system if I was going to do that? No, that's not enough. This video gives me what I've always wanted – control of you. You're going to wake up every single day thinking *is today the day that the police knock on my door?* Your heart will leap with joy whenever you see me – because it means I haven't turned you in yet. You'll wonder if I'm ever going to turn you in. If so, is it going to be tomorrow...next week...next year...in ten years? When you're on your death bed?"

He laughs into the camera and grinds to a halt underneath a streetlamp. Its light bleeds onto his head, making his menacing grin even more so, and his emerald eyes burn right through me. "Don't worry, Buttercup. I'm not going anywhere anytime soon. You and me are gonna get real cosy." Finally, Julian winks and blows a kiss at the camera before the screen goes black.

I suppose many of you think I deserve this. That this is my comeuppance. But you're basing that on the assumption that I'm insane. Do you not know that one person's craziness is another person's reality?

Besides, if you think this is so, you better be careful.

Insanity is contagious.

A NOTE FROM THE AUTHOR

I decided to write this novel because I love moral philosophy. I love that there is no right answer. That nothing is universal. In fact, there are some theories that are entirely opposite. Deontological Ethics believes it is the motive that makes an act right or wrong. Teleological Ethics believes it is the outcome. Then, we have Aristotelian Ethics, that suggests it is down to our intuition. That it is down to the individual. So, with moral theories being so different, how can we as people say what is categorically right or wrong? And furthermore, how can we judge the acts of others?

With this novel, I wanted to explore the different influences on people's perception of morality. More specifically; how different they can be. If there can be such different factors that affect our individual moral compasses and lead them to be so different in themselves - then no one is right. I wanted this novel and these characters to portray morality in a new light. As ever-changing and relative. As something we cannot judge another person by, since we don't all agree. I'm now going to talk a little bit about the influences I chose to portray in this story. And I want to give the quick disclaimer:

WARNING: SPOILERS ALERT

This next section will include discussion about plot points and twists, so please read it after you have finished the story.

SOCIETY

The majority of us are shaped by the society and culture we grow up in. We are shaped by our family, our religion, the law. Society will influence your behaviour, because whether consciously or not, we feel pressured to comply with social expectations. The rules that have been laid out for us. Popular culture (such as films and media) generally presents content that is within the bounds of existing moral codes instead of creating them. So unless our family has an entirely opposite view to the general population we live amongst, we are unlikely to form morals that differ from our society.

This brings us to Him. He is as universally relatable as possible. He is the control variable, the "normal". The one to base the other characters on, to see how far their morals stray from our own.

When Avery tells him about herself, you may ask yourself "could I accept someone who does such things? If I loved them?" Your immediate answer may be no - but use a real example. Your brother, your mother, your children. Could you absolutely, categorically declare that you would turn your back on them? There is no right answer. People who were friends or relatives of killers all had very different reactions - no two are the same. We can't know how our affection for someone might influence our perception of morality.

"COULD I ACCEPT SOMEONE WHO DOES SUCH THINGS? IF I LOVED THEM?"

REVENGE

The need for revenge - whether sought after or not - has baffled psychologists for years. This is mainly due to something known as the "Revenge Paradox" (Kevin Carlsmith, Daniel Gilbert, Timothy Wilson). This theory suggests that revenge gives an "altruistic punishment to keep society running smoothly", since it is the most common experience that if people choose to exact their revenge, they are not left with a sense of fulfilment - but rather a feeling of emptiness. So why do we seek it? Well, it is believed to be a product of evolution, triggering the seeking system in the brain once originated in the rage circuit.

So what can revenge make us do? It can make us irrational and obscure our perception of what we think is right and wrong. It makes us discard our moral compass, and instead be driven by this insatiable hunger to serve some kind of justice.

Although revenge can obscure your morality and make you irrational for a short period of time, it does not necessarily change who you are as a person and your core values. Some are overcome by the need for revenge, but when they have a chance to achieve it - they back out. Cinderella does this. When faced with the chance to kill Avery and get vengeance for her family, she is unable to go through with it. And having made this decision, she is relieved.

Cinderella doesn't go through with killing Avery in order to show all the stages of revenge from start to finish and how much it can change you, yet how you still stay the same underneath. Making the entire ordeal drastically worse if you were to follow through with your revenge. And allow your need for it to influence your perception of morality.

George Stephenson, of the Burgate House Murders, is one man who succumbed to the effects of the need for revenge. In 1986 he killed a family of four along with their nurse and the event that triggered this reaction - he was fired by them. This is only one of many cases which have the defendant acting due to a need for revenge.

HARRY ELLIS

All of us have experienced trauma at some point in our lives. All of us have events in our past that have affected us, perhaps even changed us. Some traumatic events can lead to post-traumatic stress disorder. PTSD is a crippling illness, causing anxiety, the inability to distinguish between past and present and an increased chance of developed an antisocial personality disorder (specifically sociopathy). If untreated, chronic PTSD can lead its victims deep into denial and although violence is not a symptom, it can be a consequence.

Tormented by the memory of having his parents killed in the next room as a child, Harry was given extensive therapy to help treat his PTSD. And although it had a positive effect initially, it led him to bury his hatred and rage deep within himself. He thought that he could have a positive influence on society - he could do good.

But when he sees Avery after so many years, the rage comes flooding back. He convinces himself that the only way he would ever get any peace, is if he gave her the justice the law wouldn't. This belief and mission led him to kill innocent people - as part of his scheme to take Avery down. He did the very thing he arrested other people for.

But Harry was sure that his reasons were different. His reasons were better. He had to kill them - to stop more from dying. Well, in the long run he hoped. Ultimately, because his desire for justice twisted his own morals, it made him believe that what Avery did was wrong - but what he did was necessary. His own issues prevented him from seeing the hypocrisy, from seeing the influence his past had had on his perception of morality.

"EVENTUALLY HIS CRITERIA FOR 'SCUM' EXPANDED TO ANYONE"

John Bunting is one of the most prolific serial killers of Australia. He was sexually abused as a child - but he never spoke about it. He never worked through it. As time went on, he turned his anger towards homosexuals and paedophiles, believing they were scum and did not deserve to live. Believing he was serving society by killing them. Eventually, everyone he didn't like was a homosexual or paedophile. Eventually his criteria for 'scum'; expanded to anyone.

NATURE

Let's talk about Avery Blake. When confronted with the topic of serial killers, most people will instinctively say "there must be something wrong with them. They must be crazy." Well, for some cases this is true. Although there is no agreed upon definition for insanity, the one used in court is that the person is unaware of the illegality of their actions. Avery Blake does not fit this profile.

Most people are so sure that there is some twisted reason that a serial killer is a serial killer. Like Harry, we can understand why he killed those people. Because he thought he had to. But Avery? She's more difficult to understand. How can someone kill without a reason? Without a purpose? Well,

why not? Just because it isn't something you don't do, doesn't mean it's not possible - and it doesn't mean they're crazy.

Everyone has their hobbies. Some people love horse-riding or parkour. Some people hate it. Some people love golf or snooker. Some people don't. So why can't killing be a hobby? Sure, it's not the norm, but it's possible and it does happen.

Now it doesn't mean that these people can't feel. Avery is not a psychopath - but she does have psychopathic tendencies. But guess what? Everyone does. It's actually an evolutionary advantage, since you are more able to be objective and decide what is the best way for you to survive. Plus, it's believed that most successful businessmen have strong psychopathic tendencies. Would you call businessmen crazy? Would you say businessmen are unable to feel, to love? Psychopaths do not have empathy. But this doesn't mean they don't feel. And if we all have psychopathic tendencies then is it not the normal?

"IN A STATE OF MIND THAT PREVENTS NORMAL PERCEPTION"

The dictionary definition of insanity is being "in a state of mind that prevents normal perception." If this is true, surely we are "insane" when we are hungry. When we are tired. When we're in love. So if we're all insane at some point, then is anyone really insane? If anything, when Avery kills she is in the soundest state of mind she can be in.

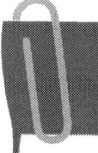

CASE FILES

I'M NOT EXPECTING ANYONE TO AGREE WITH KILLING FOR ANY REASON. NOR AM I CONDONING IT. BUT REALLY, WHO AM I TO JUDGE? MY MORALS ARE DIFFERENT FROM YOURS. AS ARE THE INFLUENCES ON MY PERCEPTION OF MORALITY. WE CAN'T UNDERSTAND EVERYTHING. BUT THAT DOESN'T MAKE WHAT WE DON'T UNDERSTAND WRONG. THERE IS NO GREATER OR LESSER INFLUENCE ON OUR PERCEPTION OF MORALITY.

MISCARRIAGES OF JUSTICE ORGANISATION
"Bringing hope to the innocent."

When you wake up in the morning. Get dressed. Put on your coat and shoes. Go to work. Do you expect to come home, to find the police in your living room? Because you fit a profile. Because no one can confirm that you went out for a run that one night. Because they want someone to blame.

It is a common misconception that wrongful convictions are a rare and infrequent occurrence, that have only happened in the well-documented cases such as the Birmingham Six, the Guildford Four, Stephen Downing and other well-known cases. Unfortunately, this is not the case - miscarriages of justice have simply faded from the political agenda. The system doesn't just sometimes get it wrong, it gets it wrong every day, of every week, of every month of every year.

Not only are these people's lives ruined whilst they are in prison for a crime they didn't commit, but they are also permanently tarnished if and when they are finally exonerated. This is because even though they have been cleared of the crime and are declared innocent, society still judges them and looks down on them - sure they are guilty of something.

Wrongful convictions can happen for any number of reasons - the most common being inaccurate eyewitness testimonies and also false expert and forensic evidence. The justice system seems to have its priorities set with seeking justice for the victim of a crime – however, the wrongfully convicted are victims too.

The Miscarriages of Justice Organisation (MOJO) is a unique human rights organisation dedicated to assisting innocent people who are in prison, and following their release. Their objective is to offer advice and support to people in prisons throughout the UK who are fighting to establish their innocence.

The organisation was founded in 2001 by Paddy Joe Hill, one of six innocent men wrongfully convicted in 1975 for the Birmingham pub bombings. The Birmingham Six's convictions were finally quashed, and they were rereleased in March 1991.

MOJO's work falls into two categories. Supporting those in prison fighting to clear their names, and supporting those who have had their convictions quashed, and are trying to put the pieces of their lives back together.

They currently support over 55 individuals, together with their family members, both in prison, and in their communities, and process over 100 new inquiries a year.

Miscarriages of justice are often overlooked in favour of giving closure to the victim of the crime. But this is not justice. This is why 50p of every copy of *Insane* sold is being donated to MOJO, to help bring hope to the innocent.

Find out more at www.miscarriagesofjustice.org

ACKNOWLEDGEMENTS

Firstly, I would like to thank you. Thank you for picking up this book, indulging me and the story. There is no point in producing a book if it isn't read, so thank you.

I would like to thank my mum. She has always gone after what she wants and has inspired me to do the same.

Thank you also to my dad. He has motivated me and made me determined to strive for more than I ever thought was possible. To always think big.

This book wouldn't be here without my sister – Becca – to whom the book is dedicated. She has always been there supporting everything I have done and cheering me on from the side-lines – figuratively and literally. Letting me ramble on for hours on end about my different storylines and plot ideas.

I am also very grateful to Rose Edmunds (Author of the Crazy Amy Series) for giving me such great advice about self-publishing this novel. The book world is definitely intimidating to jump right in head first, but Rose helped me get a handle on it all.

Finally, this is a bit of an odd one, I would like to thank my characters. I never realised you could build such a strong bond with a figment of your imagination. The characters of this book are like my children and when I finished writing it, I was sad they were gone.

ABOUT THE AUTHOR

Hollie Thubron is a singer, songwriter and author from the out-skirts of London and has been writing novels since she was a child. ~It has always been her dream to be a published author and that dream has been achieved, with Insane being her debut novel. She is fascinated by the psychology of serial killers as well as the debate about morality and so she is studying Philosophy at the University of Bristol.

Learn more at www.insanenovel.co.uk and connect with Hollie on social media - @holliethubron

If you have enjoyed Insane please review it on Amazon.

Made in the USA
Columbia, SC
15 March 2018